Aaru
Halls of Hel

By

David Meredith

Acknowledgements

To anyone who ever thought they found paradise then lost it.

*

Thanks to Jymmi Davis of White Tree Photography for acting as photographer in the production of the cover art. You can find more of his work on Instagram: @lenslifebyjymmi and on Facebook at https://www.facebook.com/whitetreephoto

*

To Drew Alexandra Hill, who once again graciously agreed to act as striking cover model despite the discomforts of freezing temperatures, long make-up sessions, latex, and face glue.

*

I'd like to express gratitude to Kelsi Willis for her striking make-up. You can see more of her work at Lashes, Lipstick, and Leather – http://www.fb.me/MakeupbyKelsiWillis

*

Much gratitude to Sean Marmon for his arresting cover design.

*

Thanks and appreciation to my wife April who always acts as my first Beta-Reader and Editor

"... Let them have everything - health, food, a place to live, entertainment. They are and remain unhappy and low-spirited for the demon waits and waits..."

Friedrich Nietzsche

TABLE OF CONTENTS

Other Titles Available on Amazon!

The Reflections of Queen Snow White

The Aaru CycleBook 1
Aaru

The Aaru CycleBook 2
Aaru: Halls of Hel

The Aaru CycleBook 3
Aaru: Dante's Footsteps

Prologue

It was dark.

Very dark.

Koren was consumed by an inky gloom that knew not even the remembrance of light.

It was also cold, but not in the conventional sense. This was not the chill of a cutting, winter wind or freezing February rhyme. Nor was it the frigid bite of arctic ice and snow. It was not the sort that could be ameliorated with a fuzzy blanket or a roaring fire upon the hearth. It was an internal sort of cold – a chill born of a frozen spirit.

Where was she? Koren did not know. However, the longer she was here, the longer she floated shapeless and blind in a void that felt somehow both infinite and confining, the more Koren was beginning to believe she was nowhere at all.

She was alone… Achingly alone, with nothing but her anguished thoughts and fears for companions. Koren tried to focus her imaginings, to recall better times - times before the emptiness. She tried to summon memories of warm summer days spent at the community center pool - the cool blue water sparkling in the sunshine as if encrusted with diamonds. She attempted to recount cool August nights of fireflies and bonfires, Christmases, birthdays, slumber parties, soccer games, warm hugs from friends and family, love's first kiss… She tried *everything* to take her mind off of the soul crushing void.

It helped a little… in the beginning.

She shuddered.

Though she was alone now, Koren was not always so. As much as she despised the emptiness of her prison, Koren dreaded *his* coming even more. The only emotions stronger than her miserable loneliness were her fear and loathing of her jailer.

When he first took her, when he trussed her like a Thanksgiving turkey, dumped her on his bed, and made her his plaything, she reviled his foul touch. She despised the violation of her body. In that moment, Koren truly believed she was experiencing the lowest moment of her entire life.

If she had only known…

Now was different. Now was infinitely worse. When he ran his disgusting hands over her skin, touched her in her secret places, Koren felt filthy, furious, and helpless. When he boasted of degradations to come, she anticipated his attentions with terror and abhorrence, but now Koren understood. She had not even *begun* to perceive the horror that awaited her. The repeated violation of her mind was fathomlessly more humiliating and ruinous than any possible defilement of her body.

At just that moment, Koren felt his coming. She shrank into the void with a soundless whimper, but it was a futile gesture. His presence enveloped her like an amoeba. It was a dark, consuming force - grasping tentacles that penetrated her brain cutting, ripping, tearing, clawing through her consciousness, plucking at her memory to sever parts of herself and replace them with God only knew what.

Koren wanted to weep, but had no tears. She wanted to shriek into the void, the agony of her ravished soul impossible to bear, but she was disembodied and voiceless. Her pain remained bottled up inside, and there was no release. The excruciating paroxysm of misery defied sufficient expression, and the slow crescendo of agony deep within her most secret self only grew stronger.

Koren thrashed helplessly. She convulsed in her invisible prison as her captor callously dismembered her thoughts and dissected her fondest recollections, as he pawed roughshod through her memories and ogled her shattered dreams. Koren felt her mind breaking, her soul splintering. The ravaging of her mind was so excruciating she begged for death, but no relief was to be had that way – not anymore.

"Rose…" She beseeched voicelessly into the nothingness, mind wracked and riven, spirit shredded and torn. "Please… Help me… Save me…"

But there was no one to hear her, and Koren knew it. There was no hope in her plea – only desolation. The assault on her quintessence, her spiritual core, continued unabated. All Koren could do was endure and pray the loneliness would take her once more.

It was preferable to the pain.

Chapter 1

Empyrean Realities

It was a beautiful day in Aaru. Rose was exultant as she streaked through the crystal blue sky. Her long, kinky, chestnut hair whipped in the brisk wind. The brilliant sun pleasantly warmed her face. It was an excellent day for flying.

Aaru was always beautiful, of course. It had been constructed specifically with aims of divine immaculacy from its very conception. It had been designed as a paradise where all of those who were deemed worthy could continue their days in a pristine world free from pain, sickness, or death. Perfection was the rule rather than the exception, so the exemplary was no rare thing. However, Rose had to admit, what she now beheld below was particularly impressive.

The great tree Yggdrasil, the very center of the infinite plains, towered above an endless, golden lea. Gargantuan branches brushed the cerulean sky, each one covered by every manner of fanciful dwelling. The treetop abodes looked as if they had grown right out of the very bark, like enigmatic fruit. Every one of thousands upon thousands of windows were merrily lit from within, and even soaring at her lofty height, Rose could detect the gentle rumor of music carried upon the fragrant breeze.

The tree, as impressive as it certainly was, was not the source of her amazement, however. Rose was of course properly overawed every time she beheld Lord Draugr's towering, sylvan abode, but the *real* change had come outside the fortress. What had been merely a spattering of a few scattered mansions the last time she visited had exploded into a fantastical city of considerable size.

There appeared to be no rhyme or reason why the city sprawled as it did. Wide boulevards twisted this way and that, branching out from Yggdrasil like so many divaricating tendrils of creeper vine. The roads turned left and right at insane angles. Some even shot straight up into the air or curled in arching loops.

The mansions that lined these broad thoroughfares were even more improbable and strange than the meandrous roadways themselves. Buildings of every imaginable shape and style crowded together like staggering drunks leaning on each other for support along kaleidoscopic avenues, which were themselves cobbled in every color of the rainbow. There were medieval castles, French chateaus, and tropical bungalows. There were Spanish fortresses and Viking long houses. There were treehouses, spaceships, floating bubbles, and amorphous blobs of no particular shape at all. There were brick and stone and mightily timbered constructions in abundance, but no shortage of structures built of less common materials as well.

One mansion Rose observed looked as if it had been constructed of dirt - like what a colony of ants or dirt daubers might build. Another was nothing but a towering pillar of sparkling water, and yet another looked as if it was made of glowing, bubbling lava. She even glimpsed a very large brown structure completely covered in shaggy fur. It rhythmically contracted and expanded as if breathing. Hundreds of other exotic dwellings floated on clouds, bubbles, or jagged chunks of earth and rock thousands of feet above the ground.

There were nearly as many styles of abode as there were individual Residents themselves. In Lord Draugr's kingdom alone these surely numbered now among the hundreds of thousands with many more arriving every day. Both the roads as well as the sky as far as Rose could see were crammed with them – Multitudes upon multitudes of happy Residents going about their business.

Rose had not been to Yggdrasil in quite some time – not since she, Lord Mikoto, and Princess Hana rescued her sister, Koren, from the crazed stalker Magic Man – but it was still amazing how much the place had grown. Still, as much as the dramatic expansion of Lord Draugr's realm impressed her, Rose was not here for sightseeing. The reason for her visit today was just as imperative if not quite as urgent as the last time, even if she wasn't exactly sure what that reason was.

Princess Hana, the ruling Lady of the Kingdom of Tenkoku and Rose's friend and mentor, soared right beside her. As usual, her beautiful face was perfectly painted, and her onyx hair expertly done. The flower princess' beautiful pink kimono fluttered and flapped in the gusty wind, which of course did not *dare* touch her exquisitely styled hair.

"So," Rose ventured, attempting to raise her voice above the roar of the stratospheric gale. "What exactly does Lord Draugr want to meet with me about? You've been awfully mysterious about the whole thing. Are you sure there's nothing wrong?"

Hana laughed in her musical way and flipped over on her back.

"You, my Veda," she stated laughingly, "worry entirely too much. I have told you already! Lord Draugr very much wants to speak to you. Beyond that I will say nothing at all, but I *will* say he did not sound particularly grim. In fact, he seemed to be in quite a cheerful mood when he sent me to fetch you. I don't believe you have anything to be concerned about."

"I don't know, Hana," Rose replied skeptically. "I think there's something you're not telling me… Like, why did you insist I wear 'something special'?"

Rose made finger quotes then looked down at herself. She did have to admit, she had chosen rather well if she did say so herself. Rose was sheathed in a long and flowing gown like she might have chosen for prom, but rather than being stitched from silk or satin, the elegant garment was composed entirely of living flame. A flickering circlet of fire around her brow completed her ensemble.

"You are so suspicious, Rose!" Hana exclaimed. "Is it so surprising I might encourage you to look your best for your first meeting with the ruler of Aaru that *wasn't* a critical emergency? Be of good cheer. You look *beautiful*! I'm sure Franco will be quite impressed."

Hana flashed Rose a wicked grin before turning back to face the front. Rose could not help but blush at mention of her handsome, Latin boyfriend.

"Is he going to be there?" Rose asked curiously. "I thought I was going to see Draugr alone."

Hana threw back her head and laughed again.

"Rose!" she exclaimed, helplessly shaking her head. "I said nothing of the kind, and I will say absolutely nothing more either. You are just going to have to be patient! All will be revealed in time, and we are nearly there anyway."

Rose continued to grumble under her breath about secrecy and conspiracy as their flightpath took a sharp downward trajectory, but she did not have long to brood. They soon alighted in front of the massive and gaping gates of Yggdrasil. A smiling red-haired boy in an outfit that somewhat resembled a nineteenth century, military uniform with golden epaulettes prominent at the shoulders, was already waiting to greet them. As they walked across the long wooden drawbridge, he saluted the pair smartly, but Rose thought his smile seemed brittle and forced.

"Greetings, Rose," the boy said with a slight Nordic accent. "You look quite fetching today."

"Matteus," Rose acknowledged almost as unenthusiastically herself. She was sure her own awkward smile looked more like a grimace. "It's so... nice... to see you again."

The red-haired boy bowed slightly, and Rose found herself grinding her teeth. Though he'd certainly said nothing that should have offended her, she was inexplicably annoyed. Rose did not care for Lord Draugr's Veda. She thought Matteus was pompous and condescending. Given his extremely stiff expression, Rose could not help but imagine the distaste was mutual.

"Yes, I'm sure," Matteus replied in a tone that sounded more pained than welcoming. "Lord Draugr bid me offer you welcome, and escort you both into his presence. You are his..." he seemed to get the rest of the words out only with difficulty. "His honored guests."

"Thank you very much, Matteus," Hana answered, smiling sweetly. "We were quite honored to receive his gracious invitation, and I appreciate your... generous welcome to Yggdrasil as well."

"Of course, Princess Hana," Matteus answered quickly with a great deal more enthusiasm. "It is our pleasure to host you, and might I say you look beautiful as always."

"Thank you, Matteus." Hana's smile was positively glowing. "You are too kind."

Matteus bowed and turned away.

"If you ladies would follow me, please," he said over his departing shoulder. "We should not keep Lord Draugr waiting."

"Of course," Hana agreed affably.

Rose stuck her tongue out at the back of Matteus' head. Hana giggled silently, and gave Rose a wink before raising a shushing finger to her lips.

The trip up the winding stairs of Yggdrasil was just as Rose remembered it. There was the same contemplative hush, the same introspective calm. Most Residents sat serenely silent, apparently deep in thought. A few looked to be reading books. Others recited poetry or played quiet music in small groups and pairs. All around them, millions of fireflies winked and twinkled among the branches and a warm breeze played a gentle swishing melody in the leafy boughs. Here and there the soft tinkling of wind chimes wafted in the quietude. It was all very beautiful.

It took quite some time, but Hana and Rose eventually found themselves on a wide viewing platform at the very top of Yggdrasil. As Rose stepped out beneath the limitless sky, she caught her breath. Bearded Lord Draugr sat wrapped in animal furs, large and imposing upon his great wooden chair. Lining the path between him and Rose however, stood every Lord and Lady of Aaru, their Vedas faithfully by their sides.

"May I present Veda Rose Johnson, My Lord," Matteus called in a loud and theatrical voice, "Honored guest and protector of Aaru!"

"What *is* all this?" Rose whispered to Hana.

Hana put her hands on Rose's shoulders and kissed her cheek.

"It is a thank you, Rose," she murmured into Rose's ear. "A thank you for your bravery and sacrifice... for defending this place from those who would corrupt and destroy it. Now, step forward and claim the honor you so richly deserve."

Hana gave her a gentle push.

"Welcome, Rose!" Draugr called in a booming, jovial voice. He stood. "It is so good to see you. Come here! Come here! And let us reward you properly.

"My Lords, my Ladies, honored Veda," he addressed the entire assembly. "Let us give welcome to Veda Rose Johnson, Defender of Aaru! Her bravery and sacrifice are unprecedented since da founding of our world and worthy of great praise!"

Everyone erupted in thunderous applause. Along the path between her and Draugr, a dozen small rainbows materialized overhead to line her path. A flock of hundreds of similarly shaded birds took wing, and a triumphant fanfare of marshal music blared seemingly from nowhere. Rose was struck speechless. If not for Hana's friendly, but firm hands on her shoulders, she could not have moved at all.

As she shyly made her way down the long aisle, Rose glimpsed many familiar faces. Franco stood with Lord Mikoto cheering enthusiastically, his handsome face bursting with pride and affection. Her Pakistani-American friend, Auset, hopped up and down clapping vigorously. Beside her was sable-skinned and markedly more reserved Lady Nu as well as brown-haired Lady

Embla, both grinning from ear to ear. Rose's other girlfriend Runa stood beside the two Ladies with a serious expression, but when she caught Rose's eye, the platinum blonde nodded with stoic yet beaming approval. On Auset's other side were Kurt in his customary barbarian styled furs and leathers, his aboriginal best friend Derain in nondescript shorts and a t-shirt, and Derain's short, dark Lord Wurugag. All three were whooping, whistling, and jumping up and down with abandon.

A few others stood out to Rose in the crowd. Handsome Lord Cernunnos applauded slowly, but ardently in a hip-hugging, mustard-colored kilt next to his dark-headed, Veda whose name Rose could not remember right off the top of her head. There was also Lady Genat and her Veda, Eve who Rose knew a little bit and thought was pretty nice as well as Lady Pyrrha who was friendly with Princess Hana. She was standing next to a leather-clad, tattooed girl who Rose remembered was called Ebony. The girl had an electric guitar slung across her back, and both her ears and her nose were riddled with piercings. Ebony bore a look on her face that seemed exceedingly bored with the whole thing. There was another Veda named Suzumé, with twelve foot tall angel wings folded neatly behind her slender back, and a boy in red-rimmed glasses named Dontavious who Rose barely knew. Then of course, Lord Epimetheus stood stiffly at Draugr's right hand. Rose recognized others too, even if she still could not readily put a name to everyone.

Is all this really for me? She could not help thinking. *I don't deserve all this...* Her cheeks burned crimson. *What else could I have done but try to save my sister?!*

They came to a halt at the foot of Draugr's great chair, and the Lord of Yggdrasil raised both hands high over his head for silence.

"Veda Rose," he intoned seriously, but his eyes sparkled merrily. "We are gathered here today in recognition of your unparalleled bravery and selfless sacrifice. You risked much in da preservation and protection of Aaru. You jeopardized yourself, your very *existence,* to halt a vicious assault upon our world by da criminal Magic Man. Your ingenuity in combatting and rebuffing our attacker was invaluable and has provided us with a new direction and vision for handling such threats in da future. All of us owe you a great debt and so, da Lords and Ladies of Aaru have decided we wish to reward you.

"From now on you shall be known as Arch Veda Rose - Lady of da Sacrificial Fire," Draugr intoned grandly. "Because you were willing to sacrifice everything to protect da Residents of Aaru. You will be first among Veda, so none will have more privilege, power, or authority in dis place unless it be da Lords and Ladies demselves.

"Indeed," he went on grandly. "You will now be not unlike us. With very few exceptions, we hereby grant you da same permissions and authorizations as all of Da Nineteen enjoy…"

"B…but," Rose whispered fiercely as Lord Draugr paused, "I… I was just trying to save Koren! I promised her. I had to… I didn't ask for any…"

"You are being entirely too modest, Rose," Draugr interrupted kindly. "You did us a very great service, and we are most happy to recognize and reward your valor. We welcome you fully into our company. Please step forward, Arch Veda, and face da assembly."

Rose reluctantly turned toward the cheering crowd. The adoration was flattering certainly, but she still admittedly felt undeserving and inadequate. Rose took a deep gulp as she met the beaming gazes of all those jubilant faces.

Draugr stood behind her. He reached over her shoulders and around her neck as if hanging her with a medal, but his large hands were empty. Instead, he touched her with both index fingers just where her clavicles met. The Ruler of Aaru then traced a line across her collarbones and around her neck. The motion left flickering flames in its wake. When he was finished, a luminous carcanet of fire decorated Rose's alabaster chest. Then Draugr cried in a loud voice.

"Now, Rulers of Aaru… Honored Veda and every grateful Resident, behold and welcome Arch Veda Rose - Lady of da Sacrificial Fire, and let us properly celebrate her valiant deeds!"

With that, cheering, applause, and every manner of fervent approbation exploded thunderously across the wide Aaru Plains. It was not just the Lords, Ladies, and Veda either. It appeared to Rose as if every Resident among all ten kingdoms heard Draugr's words and now opened their throats in praise – thousands and thousands of voices all roaring in adulation for her!

As the clamorous salute roared on and on, the sun in the azure sky abruptly slid across the horizon and the heavens grew dark. There among the sparkling stars a vivid image of Rose filled the firmament. Fifty feet tall it must have been, glowing and resplendent in her sumptuous apparel of flickering fire.

The cheering continued on and on, and Rose felt compelled to acknowledge the effusive well-wishing. On impulse, she raised her right hand over her head. Her blazing dress flared and she let the flames engulf her. Then Rose launched a massive fireball into the air, which exploded in a spectacular flash of light across the sky. In its wake, the celestial picture was transformed. It was still Rose's pretty face displayed far above, but she now appeared to be totally composed of flame – her skin like yellow-heated steel and her hair like a billowing bonfire in a strong wind. Her eyes were two brilliant, orange coals in a forge. The cheering only grew louder, and Rose was exultant.

When it was all over, Rose was a little embarrassed at herself. However, no one seemed to think anything ill about her display. Food and drink appeared, and the air was filled with music and laughter. Rose was immediately thronged by Lords, Ladies, and Veda, all offering their congratulations. Derain and Kurt told her repeatedly they thought her flaming princess trick had been - to use their words - *'totally awesome'* and Franco seemed legitimately tongue-tied when he managed to track her down.

When he finally made his way through the crushing throng, the Latin boy shyly took her hand.

"Wow, Rose," Franco murmured into her ear. "That was pretty impressive. Congratulations, by the way."

"It was really awkward!" she whispered back. "I can't *believe* Hana drug me into this without telling me about it first. There's *no way* she didn't know what Draugr was planning."

Franco flashed her a wide smile.

"If she'da told you, you would'a hidden in your mansion and refused to come out for a month!"

"Wait a minute…" Rose exclaimed irately. "Did you know about this?!"

He laughed.

"Come on, Rose!" Franco pleaded, still grinning. "We know you too well. Don't be mad. We were *all* sworn to secrecy. Smile! They just made you first among all the Veda! You're like an Aaru Lady practically. What's there to be upset about?"

"I didn't ask for any of this," Rose muttered sheepishly. "I wasn't trying to be a hero or anything. I was just trying to save my sister."

"I know, Rose," Franco murmured again. His hands encircled her waist and he pulled her close. "So... I guess you're like my boss now, huh?"

He kissed her neck and whispered in her ear.

"Now that you're in charge... Is there anything you're gonna start... you know... making me do?"

Rose squeezed him back.

"Wasn't I your boss before?" she laughed.

Franco rolled his eyes.

"But I don't know..." Rose's voice took on a sensuous tone. She trailed her fingers across his chest. "What do you *want* me to make you do?"

Franco kissed her, then looked deeply into her nut-brown eyes.

"I don't know..." he answered coyly. "How 'bout we bounce, yeah? Get away from all these people. Then we can like... you know... talk about it and stuff. Maybe go back to my place? You haven't been over in a while, and I'd really like to sh..."

Franco said something else. Or at least his lips kept moving, but Rose could not hear him.

Come here, Rose.

The call rumbled all through her.

Rose threw her head back and groaned. Franco cocked his head to the side curiously. Rose shook hers and pointed upwards. She could see the outline of the black window over her head already, like a rectangular hole in the starry night sky. Franco followed her gaze, and flashed a profoundly disappointed expression, but nodded his comprehension. Rose hugged and kissed him again.

Come here, Rose. The voice called again.

Rose sighed, reluctantly extracted herself from Franco's encircling arms, and shot away from the massive celebration in her honor. She scowled. Rose had no idea what this was about, but Koren better have a damned good reason for bothering her now. She put her hand against the window and looked inside.

*

Rose was quite surprised when it was not her little sister's pretty face that materialized in the floating window. However, she was downright flabbergasted when she did recognize her caller.

It was her mother.

Gypsie Johnson rarely called. In fact, she hadn't summoned Rose to the window for months. Just as unusual as her unexpected communication, was her attire. Her mom looked like she was dressed for a night out on the town.

Gypsie wore a short, form-fitting black dress, and her ears and neck were hung with beautiful gold and diamond jewelry. On the foot she had crossed over her knee was a black stiletto heel that had to be at least six inches long. Her make-up was newly done, and her blonde hair freshly dyed and styled.

The room behind her mother was sparse. Rose saw a bed and a chest of drawers, but not much else. Both were unfamiliar to her. Wherever mom was calling from, it wasn't from their house. Moreover, Gypsie looked nervous. She wrung her hands in her lap as she sat on the end of the bed, and her eyes darted around the room restlessly – up, down, left, right – anywhere but at Rose.

"Hey, Mom," Rose greeted uncertainly. "It's been a while. You look really pretty. What's the occasion? You and dad headed out somewhere special?"

"Oh! H… Hi, Rose," Gypsie stammered as if she was surprised to see Rose there. "There you are…"

"Uh, yeah mom," Rose answered with a tiny scowl. "You called *me*, remember?"

"Yes… Yes, I did." Gypsie drew herself up, seeming to recall her purpose. "So… How are you?"

"I'm fine," Rose answered, the incredulous scowl still fixed. "What is it? You have to have *something* on your mind. You never call me just to say 'hi'."

"Well," Gypsie replied, but looked away guiltily. "I just thought it'd been a while, so... Do I need an excuse to talk to my daughter?"

"No…" answered Rose carefully. "Don't get me wrong. I'm happy to talk to you whenever you want. It's just not something you do very often, so…"

"I've been keeping up with you on the reality show, you know," Gypsie interrupted defensively. "I make sure to watch it every time a new episode comes out."

"Great, I guess," said Rose. "I've actually never seen it, but Koren's told me about it. Maybe I could ask Lord Draugr for a TV or something in here."

"So, anyway," Gypsie tried again awkwardly. "How are things going? You've made some new friends, I see…"

"Fine, and yes, I have." Rose's face was still suspicious. Her mom was being even more awkward than normal.

"Are any of them…?" Gypsie paused, apparently searching for the right words. "Church-going people?"

"I don't know," Rose answered, still not sure where any of this was going. "Kurt probably… There aren't a lot of churches in here, you know. We talk about that kind of stuff sometimes, I guess, but… What's this about?"

"You really seem to like that Mexican boy…" Her mother observed, but her face darkened.

"He's not Mexican, mom," Rose answered. "But yeah. I like him a lot."

"Hmm…" Gypsie harrumphed shortly. "I noticed… I have to say, Rose… About that… I've been a little worried about you lately."

"What about?"

"You…" Gypsie paused again, once more choosing her words carefully. "You haven't seemed… yourself recently. Now, I know," she added quickly as Rose opened her mouth to protest. "Maybe a lot of that stuff is just hype and nonsense to advertise the show. I get it. That sort of thing sells. They do a bunch of that junk with your sister too. I just need to know all of this…" she waved her arms in an all-encompassing gesture. "Isn't… negatively impacting you. I need to know you're the same good little girl I gave birth to."

Gypsie ventured a tiny smile.

"I figured maybe," she chuckled nervously. "Maybe all that lovey-dovey stuff might be staged or something, 'cuz… Your behavior… Well… What they're showing on TV at least, you know… It's made me kinda concerned. It just really didn't seem like you, so…"

"What *'behavior'*?" Rose shot back. "You mean behavior like rescuing Koren from a crazed stalker who wanted to rape and murder her? Is that the behavior you're worried about?"

"*This* is just what I'm talking about!" her mother scowled deeply. "Yes, you did a wonderful thing for your sister. We are both grateful for it, but that's not what we're discussing right now. You never used to snap or talk back before."

"Both?" Rose asked, with a confused expression. "I think you're leaving somebody out. What about dad?"

A dark expression flashed across Gypsie Johnson's face, but she smoothed her features quickly.

"Your father…" she trailed off again. "He's having some… trouble, right now, but that's nothing you need to worry about, and that isn't why I wanted to talk. Quit trying and change the subject."

"Okaaay…" Rose replied, still confused as she drew out the word. "So what *did* you want? What crazy, awful behavior am I engaged in that you are so worried about, you actually bothered to talk to me for the first time in months?"

"I don't care for your tone, young lady!" Gypsie snapped.

"My tone?" shot back Rose. "What the Hell does my tone have to do with anything? It's just a fact. We've barely spoken in almost a *year*!"

"All this disrespect!" Gypsie interrupted, face reddening. "I *do not* appreciate the foul language, young lady. You *never* used to talk to me this way before, and I don't like it… You'd do well to remember your Bible and start… Start… Acting a little more like… Like *Jesus* would be proud of."

"So what exactly am I doing that's pissing off Jesus?" Rose asked acidly. "He created the whole universe in six days. If he was really worried, I'd think he woulda found time to stop by and mention it."

"I am *not* going to put up with that smart mouth, missy!" Gypsie exclaimed, spluttering in her rage. "Where did you learn such… such… such *blasphemy*! I bet it's all the fault of those… those new *friends* you're always hanging out with. I bet not a one of 'em prays. You best remember, girl, adding clean water to dirty don't make the dirty water clean, it just ruins the clean water! You better watch the company you keep, or…"

"So now you don't like my friends either?!" Rose exclaimed throwing up her hands. "What caused all this? Where did this *come* from? You've never complained about *a thing* before and suddenly everything I'm doing is *wrong*? And what's wrong with my friends anyway? They are all *really* nice, if you'd just take half a minute to get to--"

"I don't want you seeing that Mexican boy anymore," Gypsie blurted. "The way you two are…" She stopped and blushed. "Are… *carrying on*… It's just not the way a nice Christian girl behaves!"

"Wait…" Rose stammered, her mother's words not fully registering right away. "What?"

"You heard me." Gypsie retorted. Her voice rose in volume. "I don't hold with all the hugging and kissing and hanging all over each other. Not to mention the… the other stuff they *don't* show on Koren's show. I always taught you, you should… stay *pure*. All that mess you're doing with that boy is *totally* inappropriate for a girl your age!"

Rose stared, dumbfounded.

"Okay, wait just a second." Rose raised her hands in front of her chest in a prohibitive gesture. "Let me get this straight. You haven't talked to me in months, and then all of a sudden you pop back into my life to accuse me of being some kind of slut, demand I break up with my boyfriend, and ditch my friends? Are you *kidding*? Is this some kind of joke?!"

"Well, I certainly don't think it's funny the way you let that Mexican kid paw all over you," Gypsie shot back. "It doesn't look good, and you're letting him do it in front of the whole *country*! Besides, it's a really poor example you're setting for your sister."

Rose face darkened, and she crossed her arms in front of her chest. Her flame dress flared more brightly.

"There is *so* much wrong with what you just said," Rose snarled. "I hardly know where to start! First of all, his name is *Franco*, not 'that Mexican kid'. He's *NOT MEXICAN!* He was born in California, which makes him as American as you or me, and neither of his parents are even *from* Mexico, but even if they were, why does that matter? Second, according to Koren I'm the *only* example for my sister these days. Koren said she hasn't talked to you and dad much more than I have! Who do you think you are anyway?! Why do you think you get to suddenly sweep in out of the blue and tell me who I can and can't hang out with after months of completely ignoring me? Where is all of this coming from?!"

"I'll not be talked to like that, young Lady!" her mother snapped. "I am your *mother*, and I'll not have you embarrassing me on national TV!"

"*Embarrass* you?!" Rose exploded. "Is *that* what this is about? God forbid you give me a call because you *missed* me. I wonder. Would you be *'embarrassed'* if I was with some blonde, white kid?"

"I don't care for your insinuation, Rose," her mother shot back. "It's not about that at all. This is about the fact that you are *way* too young to have this kind of relationship with *anyone*."

"Too young… *Too young*?!" Rose shouted. "How old were *you* when I was born? Nineteen? Besides, if that's what's bothering you, then how about I fix it? How's this?"

Rose's features shifted. Her cheekbones grew sharper as the baby fat melted from her face.

"How about twenty-five?" Rose asked. "Is this old enough?"

"You stop that now…"

Faint lines appeared around Rose's mouth and on her forehead.

"Okay," she spat. "Thirty-five then?"

"Rose!"

Rose's brown hair started to grey at the temples and crow's-feet formed at the corners of her eyes.

"How about *forty*-five?!" Rose shouted. "Is that old enough? No?"

"I said to cut that out!"

"Fine," Rose spat. Then she ran a hand across her face, and she looked like teenager again.

"News flash, mom. I'm *dead*, unless you've forgotten. I'll *always* be this young. A hundred years from now… a *thousand*… I'll still be *this young* unless I want it to be otherwise.

"I'm not just some helpless little kid anymore!" she went on passionately. "I saved Koren from that crazy Magic Man guy all by myself. In fact, they just made me the highest ranking Veda in all of Aaru because of it! Only the Lords and Ladies are higher. I've raised mountains right out of the ground just by thinking about it. I can call rivers into being just by speaking the words. I can grow a forest in a second and then make it a desert with a snap of my fingers. I have *power* here… *Real* power! I know what I'm doing.

"Franco makes me *happy*, and I *love* him! I'm not going to flush all that down the toilet just because you had some random attack of I-don't-like-brown-people-with-my-daughter *'embarrassment'*. I'm not going to betray Franco just because *you're* worried about what your judgmental friends might think about it."

"That is *not* what this is about!" Gypsie repeated, nearly screaming. "What do you know about love anyway? You were always so shy around boys, and now suddenly you're this brazen..."

"I was shy when I was *twelve*, maybe," Rose interrupted. "Then I sat my butt in a hospital bed, sick and weak and bald, for four years. The only 'boys' I saw were doctors, nurses, and orderlies. But no, you're right. I'm *not* the pathetic little sick girl you remember, and I don't *want* to be either."

"This isn't you." Her mother shook her head vigorously. "This isn't my little Rose at all. My Rose never talked--"

"People change, mom," Rose cut in. "People grow up, and if you'd bothered to come around once in a while, you might not have missed it."

The stricken expression on Gypsie's face made it clear the barb had struck home, but Rose didn't care. She was livid. Instead, Rose stretched her hands over her head and flared into the sensuous flame princess guise she had taken on during the ceremony.

"*This* is who I am now," Rose thundered. "This is who I want to be – A Veda of Aaru... A protector of this place and its people. I'm not sick and weak anymore. I'm beautiful and powerful and *important*! When I talk people *listen*. They ask me for my *help*. I..."

Her mother's horrified expression, finally cut through her fury. Rose immediately felt bad for her flare of temper. She took a deep breath and let the flames die. She regarded her mother earnestly.

"I've missed you, Mom," Rose confessed softly. "I wish you'd call me more often... *Just to talk*, you know? Just to ask how I am... How I feel... Like we used to. There's *so* much that's been going on in my life. There's so much I really want to *share* with you. But... but don't tell me what to do. I've grown. You can't ground me anymore. You can't spank me. I have my own life to live here. It's just not like Before. It's... It's different. I have to be my own person and figure out who I am *here*... Who I want to be..."

Gypsie shook her head stubbornly.

"You're not my Rose," she muttered. "My Rose wouldn't treat me this way..."

"*Mom*..." Rose protested.

"You're not my Rose!" Gypsie screamed. "I don't *know* who you are!

"Mom... Come on! You're really--"

"Don't call me that!" her mother demanded.

"Mo--"

The widow went dark. Then it winked out of existence. Rose was left staring helplessly into the glittering night sky. What the Hell just happened?

She felt tears coming but was also explosively angry. What right did her mother have to impose herself after Rose had all but decided her parents had forgotten her? What right did Gypsie Johnson have to say such horrible things about her and her friends?

Break up? Rose thought savagely. *I don't think so... Let's just see if* Jesus *wants to chime in with an opinion about* this.

She wiped her eyes with her forearm, then rocketed back down to the Yggdrasil viewing platform where the party was in full swing. Music played, people danced, both on the platform and floating in midair all around it. Everywhere was smiling and laughter.

Rose pushed through the crowd with furious urgency until she came upon Franco. He was laughing and joking with Kurt, Derain, and some Japanese Veda whose name Rose had forgotten. She seized the Latin boy's head in her hands and kissed him hard on the mouth even as he was mid-sentence with the boys. All four fell abruptly silent, eyes and mouths gaping, but Rose didn't care. She glared up into Franco's face, furious tears staining her cheeks.

"Hey, babe," he said with a look of concern. "What's wr--"

"I want to go, Franco," spat Rose. "I want to go *now*. I *need* us to go home together *right now*."

"S... sure Rose," Franco stammered in confusion. "Whatever you say..."

Rose grabbed his hand and pulled him behind her. She leapt up into the sky. Their thunderstruck friends stared after them as they went.

The two flew unerringly back to Rose's mansion. When they were alone, the Arch Veda was insistent. She was demanding, and Rose was sure, behaved absolutely *nothing* like what her mother thought "good little Christian girls" should act like. She didn't care either. Rose just wanted to know... *needed* to know Franco was *hers* and no one else's. For his part, Franco was more than happy to do whatever she demanded in giving her that assurance.

Chapter 2

Trouble in Paradise

Koren had awoken early that morning feeling anxious and out of sorts. She'd had a bad dream she could not remember and, it left her feeling agitated and unsettled. It made it impossible to even think of going back to sleep. There had been no time for any more rest since waking anyway, and today was not the only day like that either. In fact, Koren could not remember the last time she'd gone to bed at a decent hour and risen refreshed and energized the next morning.

After she was practically force-fed half a smoked salmon bagel by the blond Elysian Industries employee, Amy, and hastily dressed by her style team, her handlers dragged Koren downstairs for a fashion magazine interview. Then there were a couple of photo-ops afterward and a morning radio show appearance over the phone. She tried to grab a few Z's later that afternoon, but scarcely before she had even closed her eyes, Amy and the style team stampeded into her room once more to drag a very grouchy Koren out of bed to primp for the evening's festivities. Now, after hours in a makeup chair, she stood next to Jonas Perry on the red carpet of the National Music Awards.

Koren looked beautiful of course. As much as she resented them sometimes, she had to give her style team credit. They knew their own business and did it well. Koren's hair and make-up were perfect, and she wore a very short, very low-cut red dress with tall, strappy heels – a look that was certain to be the rage of national tabloid media coverage the next day.

She smiled and waved as she had been trained to do. Cameras flashed all around. Photographers shouted at her to look this way and that. Her enormous security chief, D, stood silent and imposing off to the side critically observing everything and everybody. Fans pressed against the barriers with desperate hands outstretched. It was all barely contained chaos. In fact, she probably would have fled screaming back to her limo if Jonas had not been standing beside her.

It was clear Jonas Perry was in his element – smiling, posing, winking, flirting, obviously reveling in the attention, but Koren was not at all comfortable with such fervent acclaim. She found these public appearances exhausting. Still, when the Elysian Industries people informed her she needed to attend this event, she was only too happy to go.

Being seen in public with an A-list celebrity only boosted her profile, they told her. The sudden and growing popularity of her reality show, *Love Beyond Death,* to say nothing of the excitement over Aaru itself, only reinforced Jonas' image as being cutting edge relevant. It was a PR coup for both of them, but that was not why Koren wanted to go with the pop star.

She still got a tingly feeling whenever he touched her hand or squeezed her shoulder. When they'd kissed at the release party for *Love Beyond Death*, it stole every sensibility from her head. It had been so nice – like something out of a fairytale. His soft reassuring voice, his earnest blue eyes gazing deeply into hers – it was all *perfect*… At least until her father burst into the room and busted them.

Then of course, when that horrible Magic Man released the insanely embarrassing video he stole from Elysian Industries of Koren half-naked, singing into her hairbrush, and jumping on her bed, Jonas had been *so* sweet. He'd managed to soothe her and alleviate the crushing feelings of humiliation. Koren was sure she was being ridiculously immature, but especially now, so dashing in his white on white tuxedo, blonde hair perfectly styled, and blue eyes sparkling in the footlights, she could not help imagining Jonas as her own personal Prince Charming. She sighed, wishing he would kiss her again.

At the moment, thronged by the crowd, Koren supposed more kissing was unlikely, although the dozens of paparazzi surrounding them would certainly not have been displeased. Even without more kissing, Koren was grateful for Jonas' company nonetheless. It was obvious he enjoyed talking about himself far more than she did. As a consequence, he bore the brunt of the questions from reporters and celebrity news correspondents.

Koren continued waving, smiling, and posing for pictures as they made their way down the red carpet. She answered a number of simple, inane questions;

"Are you excited about tonight?"

"Yes."

"Who are you wearing?"

"Vera Wang."

"Do you think Jonas will win?"

"I hope so," etc.

But Koren let Jonas do most of the talking.

"Jonas!" someone shouted. "Hollywood Onlooker! Could we ask you and Miss Johnson a few questions?"

Jonas was only too happy to oblige. He wrapped an arm casually around Koren's bare shoulders, which of course made her blush with pleasure, and guided her over to where a dapper young man in a high end suit and no tie was holding a microphone. A camera crew stood nearby. Jonas walked up to the man and embraced him like they were old friends.

"Hey, Kirk!" Jonas exclaimed. "Great to see you tonight!"

The man turned towards the camera and brought the microphone to his lips.

"Kirk Birmingham here tonight at the NMAs with none other than Jonas Perry and his *ravishing* date, the beautiful Koren Johnson."

He turned toward Jonas and extended the microphone.

"Big night tonight, Jonas. You've been nominated yet again in the Best Song of the Year category for 'When I'm with You' and in Best Album for *Jonas - Real*. How do you like your chances of finally going home with a statuette? Is sixth time the charm?"

Jonas smiled broadly, and pulled Koren tightly against his side so she was also included in the close-up shot.

"Well," he began philosophically. "This is an industry award, so you never know what music executive types are looking for, but I think we put out some good material. The reviews have been *awesome*, so I think I've got a pretty good shot. It's great just to get nominated and be out here tonight! Awards are nice and all, but I make music for my peeps, and as long as they keep hitting the download button, I'm chill. I'd just like to thank all my fans who showed up…"

He had to stop as momentary cheering from a throng standing nearby, all wearing his album cover design on their t-shirts, drowned out his voice.

"And thanks for the support!" he finished flashing another perfect, toothpaste commercial smile and a wink. The groupies just beyond the barrier screamed like lunatics.

"And you Miss Johnson…" Suddenly Kirk Birmingham's mic was shoved up under Koren's nose. "You look *gorgeous*, by the way. It's great to see you out here tonight after your recent ordeal. Are you holding up okay?"

Koren was more than a little taken aback by the directness of the question and a little slow to respond.

"S... sure, I'm fine," she managed to stutter, but almost as soon as the words left her lips Birmingham was asking another question.

"Would you say that this award show is a positive diversion from your sexual assault? Is this your attempt to show your rapist he can't control you?"

"I was never... I...I guess..."

"Do you have any thoughts or words of encouragement for other sex crimes victims out there?"

"I... I... really don't..."

We're just trying to have a good time tonight, Kirk," Jonas cut in smoothly and stepped in between Koren and the correspondent, with a sober look on his face. He grabbed the mic from the reporter's hand.

> "*Lots of wack shit happens in this world,*
> *But that ain't nothin' but a thing, right?*
> *You only got one life in this world, yeah.*
> *But you gotta be your own light.*
> *You gonna take shit from this world, Dog,*
> *But it ain't 'bout the win. It's the fight.*
> *You gotta live it, Man!*
> *Like all you gots is tonight.*
> *YO!!!*"

He punctuated his exclamation by dropping the mic to the pavement and pointing both index fingers aloft. The knot of Jonas Perry groupies behind the camera crew erupted into screams and squeals. Kirk Birmingham quickly retrieved the discarded microphone, but Jonas was already tugging Koren with him down the line and into the theater where the awards show would take place. As they entered the building, Koren could still hear Kirk Birmingham talking.

"That was Jonas Perry, folks! And a positively *inspiring* Koren Johnson putting on a heroic face despite being so publically victimized..."

Koren bit her lower lip feeling conflicted. What Kirk Birmingham had said was a compliment, right? So why did it make her feel so bad? Sexual assault? Her *rapist*? *Victim?!* Is that how everyone saw her? And as much as she liked him, Koren wasn't sure she wanted Jonas speaking for her in any case.

"Weasely-ass bastard…" Jonas muttered to himself.

"What?"

"Sorry, Koren," Jonas apologized quickly. "I was talking about *Birmingham*. Could you see that smug fucker out there needling me? Yeah, I know I've lost every time I've been nominated. Thanks for pointing it out, *asshole!*"

Koren was taken aback by Jonas' foul language and ill humor, so she stayed quiet. An usher led them to their seats. Jonas held her hand during the long ceremony, which was nice, but otherwise stayed sulky and irritable. Koren found it exceedingly difficult to focus on all the excellent entertainers performing mere feet from where she was sitting. Koren's thoughts kept going back to a single word - *Victim.*

Things were no better once the whole elaborate display concluded. Once again, Jonas didn't win, which put him in an even fouler mood. His people quickly bustled them off to some after party. Koren had been invited as well, so she was more than happy to tag along.

She thought things would be better once they got to the club. Surely, a big party with a bunch of other famous people would put anyone in a good mood, right? But no. Jonas stayed distant.

He didn't want to dance. He didn't kiss her or hold her. He barely even spoke to her in fact, and what little conversation did take place at their table was mostly a petulant monologue from Jonas to the half-dozen toadying young men in his posse about how industry voters "just didn't get" his sound and how the NMA's were "total bullshit anyway" all the while swigging out of a high-end bottle of bourbon. So Koren sat in the booth, staring at a glass of Champaign she didn't really want to drink. The flashing lights and pounding bass assaulted her brain until she had a splitting headache. After only maybe an hour or so, Koren decided she'd had enough and texted her driver to pick her up.

She pleaded an early start in the morning as her reason for leaving. Koren had to go on another big publicity tour for the new season of *Love Beyond Death* and have some meeting with Askr

Ashe at the Elysian Industries Complex in Bell Buckle. However, the excuse making was largely wasted effort. Jonas was already so wobbly and the club so loud, it was unlikely he comprehended anything she said.

Koren marched out in a huff, pointedly ignoring the paparazzi who flashed cameras and shouted questions as she exited the building. Not sparing an instant to wait for the driver, Koren jerked on the handle, hopped in the back seat, and slammed the door hard enough to rock the whole car.

"Where to, Miss Johnson," the chauffeur asked neutrally enough, but Koren could see the question in his eyes reflected in the rearview mirror. She felt suddenly humiliated, but didn't really understand why.

Victim.

The word echoed through her brain, and she cringed. Is that how *this* man saw her too? The paparazzi? Jonas?

"Home," was all she said.

Koren crossed her arms and stared out the window in sullen silence until the opulent vehicle pulled up in her driveway. She waited for the driver to open the door for her this time, but they shared no words. The night had been a total disappointment.

Have I done something wrong? She thought miserably. *Maybe I shouldn't have left… Why did Jonas ignore me all of a sudden? Doesn't he like me anymore?*

Koren sent Jonas a quick text:

☺ *Great seeing you tonight! <3 <3 <3 XOXO*

She stood in her drive-way a minute longer before adding.

Text me soon! Jo-Ren 4ever! ;)

Too much maybe? Koren thought anxiously after she'd sent it.

She went inside, but as she stalked down the empty, cavernous corridors, high heels clacking loudly against marble floors, Koren thought she heard a TV. She saw a door slightly ajar and stuck her head inside the personal theater. It looked like some sort of NASCAR race was being replayed, but that was not what caught her attention. There, spread across several theater seats in a heap was a slumped figure surrounded by dozens of empty glass bottles and beer cans.

Koren growled in disgust. She tried to push the door silently closed, but the hinges squeaked, and the disheveled figure sat up with a start. The sudden movement released a clattering avalanche of aluminum cans and clinking bottles.

"Koren?" came a woozy, muddled voice. "S'at you?"

Koren sighed.

"Yes, dad," she replied unenthusiastically. "I'm home."

"Why's it S'damned dark?" her father slurred. "Ain't you got that... that *thing* tonight, you're s'posed to go to?"

"I'm already back, dad," Koren answered in irritation, "It's after midnight... Didn't I leave you right here this morning at like 7:30? Have you done *nothing* today, but drink and watch TV?"

"What's it matter to you?" her father shot back defensively. "Too busy for me anyway, hangin' out with all your *superstar* friends... What am I s'pose to do with nothing' to do all day?"

He stood unsteadily and turned to wag his finger.

"I got no job anymore since we moved out here. Your mom don't want nothin' to do with me. Says she's too busy '*managing your career.*'" He said the last in a sneering voice as he made finger quotes in the air. "The only other thing I got is taking care of you, and *you* made it clear you think you're too rich and important to need your dumbass old dad around!"

Koren growled and rolled her eyes.

"You really oughta go to bed, dad," she said tightly. "Maybe you'll feel better in the morning."

Koren turned to go.

"Feel better?" her father shouted incredulously. "*Feel better?!* What would make me feel better is for my family to care about me and need me like they used to. I used to be the bread winner, Koren! I used to go to the garage and bust my ass every day changing tires, changing oil, fixin' brakes, so you and your sister had clothes to wear and food to eat! I could rebuild a carburetor with my eyes closed. I could tell you what was wrong with your engine just by listening to it! I... I... I used to *fix* things! I used to *know* things!

"Used to be," he went on with markedly more venom, "when I said I didn't want my fourteen year old daughter hanging out after midnight with some horny little blonde turd just trying to get into her pants..."

"Dad!" exclaimed Koren in horror, but Bill Johnson barreled on undeterred.

"*Used* to be," he raised his voice, "I wasn't overridden by her mother and corporate handlers. That's a daddy's job, Koren! Keepin' his little girl safe… And you just… you just…" his yelling trailed off into drunken sobbing. "And you just ain't mine no more. Elysian Industries bought you and your mother *sold* you!"

Bill Johnson screamed then, a wretched, animal sound. He sent the bottle in his hand hurtling end over end to crash in an explosion of glass shards against the far wall. Koren winced as it smashed into a million pieces. Then her father devolved into more pitiful sobbing.

Koren was at a loss. She'd never seen such a miserable display in her whole life and felt tears coming to her own eyes.

"It's… it's not like that, daddy," Koren's voice quavered. "I… I still need you. I still love…"

"No you don't…" her father blubbered. "There ain't *nobody* who needs me…"

"That isn't *true*," Koren insisted passionately. "What's the matter with you? I've just been busy. We just…"

"Just… just *GO*!" Bill Johnson cried. "Leave me alone! Your mother don't need me no more. *You* don't need me no more… Go on with your rich friends. Go be *famous*!"

He slumped back down into the theater seat and turned his attention to the NASCAR replay again. He picked up several bottles one after the other, but quickly tossed them to the side as he realized they were empty. When he finally located one that was still about half full, he took a deep swig.

"Don't worry 'bout me Munchkin…" he murmured.

His tone changed so abruptly, Koren gave a start. Bill Johnson's voice was suddenly gentle and sing-songy as if he was talking to a very small child. It was seriously creepy.
Her dad let out a slight giggle and a rancid belch.

"Daddy's gonna be *just* fine. He's gonna be *all* better soon. I gots me ole Mr. Jim Beam and Mr. Jack Daniels here to keep me company… We'll go to the park tomorrow, the four of us. I'll push you in the swing, and the merry-go-round, and maybe we'll even have us a picnic. We can just have fun together *all* day. An' everything'll… everything'll be… be just fine…'"

He took another swig and leaned back heavily in the theater chair, arms and legs splayed.

> *"Bye, bye baby Buntin'"* he sang unsteadily with his
> eyes closed.
> *"Daddy's gone a huntin',*
> *To get a rabbit skin,*
> *And wrap little Koren in..."*

He drank deeply once more, swayed unsteadily in his chair, then slouched to his side and did not move. Koren heard the glass bottle clatter against the floor, and the rhythmic glug, glug, glug as it emptied itself. She bit her lip, swallowed a sob, and dashed to her bedroom. Koren slammed the door and locked it behind her. Then she threw herself onto the bed and cried herself to sleep.

Early the next morning when the car arrived to take her to the airport, and Amy dragged her out of bed, Bill Johnson was still slumped senseless in the private theater. He did not stir, and Koren did not wake him as she walked out the front door. Jonas still had not texted her back. A pair of dark sun glasses hid her tears as she climbed into the limo, and it pulled away.

Chapter 3

Back to Business

"'We know, if the earthly tent we live in is destroyed, we have a building from *God,* an eternal house in heaven, not built by human hands,' Second Corinthians, chapter five, verse one."

The middle-aged, suited gentleman behind the podium intoned the words deliberately, so they resonated across the cavernous sanctuary. His handsome face was serious and his dark eyes intense behind a pair of reading glasses. He looked sternly over the congregation, allowing the meaning of the words to sink in. Then he spoke again.

"And Peter said unto them..." He was not yelling, but his voice easily filled the large room. "'Salvation is found in *no one* else, for there is *no* other name under Heaven given to men by which we *must* be saved,' Acts, chapter four, verse twelve..." He paused again to take in the whole assembly. "There it is in the very Living Word of God...

"And yet," his voice rose. "We have lived to see a time, friends... We have lived to see a wicked generation who would *cleave* unto the Harlot of Babylon rather than Almighty God and seek to usurp *His* divine authority... To circumvent *His* perfect judgement and supplant *His* holy name."

He paused again, and this time murmurs of discontent rumbled through the crowd.

"This so-called service Elysian Industries offers is an affront to decent people *everywhere!*" he thundered to raucous applause. "Either it's the greatest swindle the world has ever known or it flies in the face of Almighty God. In either case, it's blasphemy. It's immoral. It's wrong! And it's time that Believers stood up and said *'no!'*"

The assembly erupted in exuberant agreement.

"When I was elected by the good people of Alabama to represent them in the senate," he continued. "I was not simply charged to look after their material well-being, but also to their *values* – the same values upon which this great nation was founded!"

More applause.

"This Aaru of theirs runs contrary to everything good, Christian people believe. I will *never* rest until this Golden Calf is torn down and trampled into the dust. Mortal men should not pretend at being God, but this is just exactly what Askr Ashe and Koren Johnson are trying to do. They would have you pray to *them* instead of Almighty God. They would have you serve *their* will to be considered worthy to receive *their* blessing! They are a false idol and graven image that must be resisted at all costs!"

Louder applause.

"We must fight back against their evil, or be consumed by it," he shouted to even more enthusiastic acclamation – people standing, shouting, cheering. "But fear not, ye of little faith. I think their days are numbered, friends. Oh yes I do. And I think it's a number we know already. It's a number we've been warned about, and the wise will know it for what it is. They have a number, friends. Oh, yes they do…"

He flipped to a different page in the open Bible on his lectern.

"'Here is a call for wisdom,'" the senator quoted again. "'Let the one who has insight calculate the number of *the beast*, for it is the number of a man! *And* that number is six hundred sixty-six!'" The crowd was deafening. When they quieted at last he went on more softly, but no less impassioned than before.

"Revelation, chapter thirteen, verse eighteen…" He murmured and trailed off.

Then the senator removed his reading glasses, and tucked them into the breast pocket of his suit coat. When he spoke again, his words were low, but clipped and pointed.

"James Rook is *not* about to passively sit by," he hissed stabbing an indignant finger at the camera, "and let some bunch of money grubbing opportunists try and supplant the Holy Church with a technological mockery seeking to steal the very mantle and scepter of the Creator! Do not be fooled, friends! This is the moral battle of our time, and The Enemy is strong. Do not misunderstand. This is a fight we *must* win, friends and neighbors! It's a battle for the very *soul* of our great nation!

"I will not rest," he pounded his palm with his fist, "until the government of these United States steps in to put an end to this nonsense and punish the perpetrators of these lies to the fullest extent of the law so that *no one* else even *thinks* about trying such a blatant swindle again. It is intolerable, and…"

"Shut up," growled Magic Man clicking the X button on the video window. "Idiot…

"'Is man merely a mistake of God's? Or God merely a mistake of man's?'" He quoted to himself in disgust.

Magic Man didn't know why he wasted his valuable time on an imbecile like James Rook. It always pissed him off every time he heard the first syllable of the man's obnoxious southern drawl. Rook was either a deluded ideologue, an opportunistic liar, or both.

Perhaps, it was because Magic Man was desperate for any crumb of information about Koren Johnson. Like a starving man might lust after bread, he yearned to know what his gentle muse was doing. Magic Man flipped out his phone and caressed the image saved to his wallpaper – Koren tied up on his bed, eye shadow streaked all down flushed cheeks…

Beautiful.

Magic Man sighed, and thought about the first moment little Koren became his. After spending all night scanning the Elysian Industries' grounds with binoculars, he'd glimpsed her. Alarms went off all over the campus as he plowed his car through the boundary fence. Koren's handler went flying over his hood to smash against his windshield, and his soul sang in triumph as he leapt from his vehicle to claim his prize. *How* Koren struggled! But she soon went limp in helpless submission – so small and powerless. He'd tossed the motionless girl into the back seat, *so* light! And that moment when he finally got his prize back to his apartment all to himself?

Intoxicating…

Then he glowered. He'd been so, *so* close… So close he could almost *taste* the final victory! But then everything went to Hell.

He sighed.

I wonder if she still thinks of me…

Magic Man shook his head in irritation. Entertaining as this reminisce certainly was, he had no time for it. Such idle distractions and gnawing impatience were exactly why he now found himself holed up in this stifling L.A. storage unit. They were precisely why he'd nearly been caught. He had to be methodical this time… careful… patient… no room for error.

He turned his gaze back to one of several computer monitors. It was situated precariously on a sagging sheet of plywood supported by wobbly stacks of plastic milk crates. The screen was covered with line upon line of code, indecipherable to few but himself. He scanned it critically before erasing a line here, typing a few commands there.

He'd not been caught, of course. Things had not turned out the way he planned, but once again his ultimate vision was progressing nicely. In spite of admittedly choppy seas, Magic Man was back on course.

It had been a stressful several weeks to be sure. Avoiding the road blocks on every major highway until he got out of Kentucky, the hours and hours of backroad driving across the country until he finally made it back to his spare equipment in L.A., the constant threat of capture – he'd lived in perpetual fear. Now however, safely hidden away from prying eyes and firmly in control of his own destiny once more, Magic Man felt quite smug about it all.

He took a long pull of piping black coffee and indulged in another lecherous gaze at the image of Koren. Then he shoved the phone into his pocket. There was work to do.

A slow grin spread across Magic Man's face as he switched his gaze to another computer screen. He was never really happy per se. To him, that was a frivolous emotion experienced only by a simple and oblivious mind. A complex brain like his, one that thoroughly comprehended the hopelessness of this material existence, could hardly feel something so mundane or vapid.

"'Men of profound sadness betray themselves when they are happy,'" he quoted. "'They have a mode of seizing upon happiness as though they would choke and strangle it, out of jealousy. Ah, they know only too well that it will flee from them!'"

Having said that, Magic Man was certainly not without emotion. Pleasure, which was quite a different thing, was one he quite enjoyed. He was well pleased with himself now, in fact, and concluded his post on 5kun with a flourish before clicking the 'submit post' button. He chuckled.

Magic Man had always maintained a presence on 5kun, very nearly since the day it went live. He'd always attracted followers as well – mostly lonely, gawky teenaged boys and repugnant, socially awkward men clambering after his simulated pornography. Koren Johnson was his most popular subject, but he'd lavished his artistic attentions on others over the years as well.

Magic Man's legend had only grown. Ever since his abortive abduction of Koren Johnson, his eminence among the 5kun creepers and skags had achieved near mythic proportions. Now his legion of loyal degenerates numbered in the thousands, and they hung breathlessly upon his every post.

Today's post was especially auspicious. Magic Man had finally discovered enough about the coding of the Aaru helmet and the stolen CPU from Koren's house to move forward. He read it again with a smug grin.

> *At long last, the canvas is prepared. Paint selected, brushes at the ready, it is finally the season for* Creation!
> *The seeds are planted and soon there will be a fearful harvest. The fruit of "the creating heart, which desired, and, out of its desire, created," shall create joy and woe. It shall* satiate *itself with woe. And that final harvest, that luscious fruit, will take all the suffering that has been endured by men and animals upon itself, affirm it, possess it and thereby help it acquire reason, recreating the world anew. The time draws ever nearer…*
>
> *-Magic Man*

That sounded sufficiently grandiose, yet appropriately cryptic, he thought. It was bound to drive his followers mad as they attempted to figure it out. He imagined what it would be like – closeted nerds and shiftless losers from around the world arguing vociferously it was *they* who understood the true meaning. He anticipated their conceited certitude and braggadocios bluster with delight, certain none of the fools would even come close. That was merely playtime however. He turned his attention back to his other monitor – the one covered in code.

It was all right there – everything he required to make his vision real. All he needed was a little more patience, a little more work and study. Then Magic Man's time would finally come. He and Koren would be together at last – joined in a way more intimate than anything the world had ever known.

Forever.

It was simply a matter of time.

***

Rose stretched luxuriously on the bed of silky, pink cherry petals. They covered the mossy ground around her in a thick blanket. She was clad in a clingy translucent gown thinner than gossamer, and her feet were bare. Franco *really* liked it.

She purred in pleasure as the brilliant sun warmed her from a cloudless, blue sky. Rose was content, she realized. A delicious summery feeling filled her breast. However, it was tempered by the slightest hint of melancholy.

Franco had just left - something Lord Mikoto needed him to do. Though his sweet goodbye kiss was still warm on her lips, Rose could scarcely wait for him to come back. Ever since they discovered her Harm Failsafe was turned off, ever since they realized they could be together the way they longed for, Rose had barely left the Latin boy's arms.

Her anger-fueled efforts in response to her infuriating mother added an element of desperation to their striving. It was animalistic in its primal fervor and nothing she'd planned or expected. It was certainly something she'd never experienced before, but Rose did not regret it. She ran her hands up her torso, and stretched again, imagining once more Franco's urgent touch, his impassioned kisses.

Is this what it's like to be married? She wondered. *Is that what we are now? What are we? And... what was up with Mom?*

Rose frowned at the last question. She did not know the answer to any of them, but did not want to linger over them too long.

She did feel a little guilty about blowing up at her mother, but Rose was not one whit less certain in her resolve. Franco was hers. She was his, and they had the rest of forever to enjoy it. Gypsie Johnson was *not* going to be allowed to mess that up.

Rose sighed. Maybe she could try to talk to her mom later, once they both had a chance to cool down. She certainly did not like the way they'd left things. For now however, Rose determined to worry about the strange exchange no more.

Let the rest of it take care of itself! Rose thought with a giggle as she indulged in some spontaneous cherry blossom angels on her bed of flower petals. *Life is good!*

But... She sighed again and stood, forcing herself to regain a measure of sobriety.

The fiery necklace from Lord Draugr flickered at her breast as if in reminder. Rose's shimmering pixie dress was quickly replaced by her ubiquitous kimono. Her long, kinky hair, which had been cascading freely down her back, was suddenly elaborately done - held in place with a complicated array of lacquer-wood combs and cosmetic chopsticks. Rose had an errand of her own today.

I suppose we can't shirk our duties forever, she mused.

As if summoned by the thought, a tiny, black shape materialized in the sky. It soared over her and swooped down to light gently in Rose's garden just a few feet away. A slight, dark-skinned figure, gorgeously attired in the trappings of ancient Egyptian royalty, strode up and warmly embraced Rose.

"Hey, Auset!" Rose greeted her friend happily, returning the firm squeeze of the small Pakistani-American girl. "Thanks for coming. It feels like I haven't seen you in *forever*!"

"You haven't, Rose," Auset replied in her customary hushed voice, but gave her friend an ironic smile as well, "but I understand. We all know how *busy* you've been… Everyone is talking about how abruptly you and Franco left the party…"

Rose had noticed a big change come over her friend recently. When they'd first met, Auset was painfully shy. She still had a tendency to close down and retreat around other people, but when it was just the two of them, Rose got to see a completely different side of her demur friend. The other girl was teasing her.

Coin-shaped, golden bangles hanging from a thin circlet encompassing Auset's brow tinkled softly as she turned her gaze to Rose's visibly rumpled flower bed. She shot her friend a knowing smirk. Rose flushed furiously pink.

"Auset…" she protested weakly.

Auset laughed and changed the subject.

"So, are you ready to go?"

"I guess so," answered Rose unenthusiastically. "I don't know why I'm so nervous. It really shouldn't be that big of a deal to just go and *meet* someone."

"Well," Auset said with a shrug. "Feeling a little anxious is only natural, I suppose, considering what happened. Just remind yourself." She smiled broadly. "If anything *really* disturbing occurs, once it's over with you can have Franco kiss it all better! Of course, if you let him do that, I might never see you again…"

Rose smiled sheepishly.

"Sorry. I really haven't been trying to avoid you… It's just… I seem to forget *everything* when we're together." She glanced at the flower petal bed. "When we were lying there just a little while ago, it felt like we were the only two people in the whole world. I wish he didn't have to go today…"

"*Really?*" Auset raised an eyebrow in amusement. "I guess it *was* a good thing I decided to wait until I saw him leave," she giggled. "I might have walked in on something!"

"Auset!" Rose exclaimed, turning beet crimson.

Auset really did laugh about that. She patted Rose's shoulder.

"I'm sorry, Rose," she apologized lightly. "I shouldn't tease you. We just miss you two on the pitch is all. You haven't played with us in *ages*. I'm happy for you though. We *all* are!" she paused and then asked softly. "Are you happy, Rose?"

Rose's embarrassment dissipated as she was flooded with the same warm, contented feelings she experienced every time she thought of Franco.

"Yes," she said simply, then hugged herself. "Very, Auset."

"So…" Auset ventured shyly. "So, are you and Franco then… you know… a *thing*… a… a couple… I mean, like a *couple*, couple, like for good?"

Rose grinned. She just could not seem to help smiling today!

"I think so," she replied quietly. "I *hope* so, but we haven't really talked about it. We just kinda… you know… let things happen."

"And just what *did* happen?" Auset asked in a conspiratorial whisper. "It must have been something good. Every time you say Franco's name you turn all pink and giggly."

Rose looked reflexively right and left, even though of course they were the only two people in her garden. There was no one to overhear, but Rose leaned in close and lowered her voice anyway.

"Well…" She began slowly.

Auset knew about Rose and Franco's first attempt to be together. She knew about the Harm Failsafe forcing them apart just as their passions were about to be realized. She and Rose's blonde, Netherlander friend, Runa, had offered their shoulders to cry on afterwards, but since that second time on the riverbank, right after saving Koren, Rose had not seen her friends very often. Auset knew Rose's Harm Failsafe had been deactivated to prevent her abduction by her sister's crazed stalker, but Rose had not told her it was apparently still turned off. She told Auset everything.

"Y...you really... I mean... with Franco... you seriously did..." Auset's eyes were wide and she put both hands over her mouth. "Did you... did you like it?" she whispered at last.

Rose once more blushed roseate pink. She nodded.

"I just feel so close to him, Auset. So safe... And... And loved... I think I really love him too. And it only gets stronger every time we... you know..." She trailed off.

"Wow, Rose," Auset breathed, eyes wide as saucers. "I knew you two liked each other, but I thought maybe Kurt and Derain were just talking..."

"Wait... What?" Rose's smile faded. "You thought Kurt and Derain were 'just talking' about what?"

"Um..." it was Auset's turn to trail off and turn red. "Well... Uh, we all kinda suspected a little... I mean, it was obvious forever ago you and Franco really liked each other. You already spent more time together than you did with us... You told me and Runa it nearly happened once anyway, right? So... "

"He... he... *HE TOLD*?!" Rose was mortified. "How could he..? What did he...? How much...?!"

"Come on Rose," Auset made a placating gesture, pleading in her most calming voice. "Don't get upset. We're all friends. It's not like Franco went out and just blabbed to *anybody*."

"But *Kurt* and *Derain*!?" Rose squeaked. "But they're... They're... b... b... *boys*!"

"Well, yes, I suppose they are," Auset frowned slightly. "But they're still our friends. You just told *me*, so you can't be *too* mad at Franco for--"

"It's not the same thing at all!" interrupted Rose indignantly. "I can't *believe* Franco would... I *know* how guys get when they talk about... stuff like *that*. Oh my *God!*" She put her face in her hands. "I'll never be able to look at either of them ever again! Every time they see me now they're going to be thinking about... about *that*!"

"I'm not trying to sound mean or anything, Rose," Auset replied evenly, "but I think you're over reacting. Like I said - you told me, so I don't see what you're so upset about. I'm not going to judge you, and neither will they!"

"That's different!" insisted Rose stubbornly. "I *had* to tell you. You're my best friend! I mean... I'm not just going to walk to the middle of Yggdrasil and scream it to the world! Was he like *bragging* or something? What was he *thinking?!*"

Rose was expecting another rejoinder, so the sudden silence from the other girl was more shocking than any shouting or snark could have been. She looked up in puzzlement and glimpsed Auset's face. The dark-skinned girl gaped at her. Her eyes were moist.

"W…what?" Auset managed at last. "Do you… do you really mean that, Rose? *Really?*"

"Mean, what?" asked Rose. "That Franco running his big, stupid mouth is…"

"No…" Auset interrupted. "That I'm… I'm your best friend… You mean it?"

"Of… of course, Auset," stammered Rose haltingly. "I mean, you always listen to me. You always try to make me feel better. You understand when I feel sad. I tell you *everything*!"

Auset didn't say anything in reply. She just wrapped Rose in a hug, laid her head against the taller girl's chest, and closed her eyes. Rose patted her back.

Rose was grateful for the affection. It gave her a moment to collect herself. Auset was right. Why should she care if her friends knew about her and Franco? They were going to be here forever, after all. How long could they have kept it a secret anyway? Besides, hadn't even Princess Hana said it was perfectly right and good?

Rose could not deny her emotions over what she and Franco had done were still hopelessly mixed and messy. On the one hand, just like she told Auset, whenever she was with him, she had no doubts or regrets whatsoever. Everything felt right and safe. Having her friends and family know about it, on the other hand…

Rose had always been taught that sort of intimacy was something God wanted you save until marriage, if it was ever talked about, which it generally wasn't. The whole seeming secrecy of the thing - the fact it was so taboo her parents wouldn't mention it except in clipped, short phrases that could have fit on a youth group t-shirt or guidance office poster, the fact her school friends gossiped about it in hushed whispers behind their hands in between blushes and giggles - always made it out to be something unspeakably embarrassing, terrifying, and dirty.

And Rose had done it anyway. Now her friends knew. What would she tell Koren? What if her *parents* found out? Although, Rose mused, It sounded like her mother at least suspected. Would God be mad at her?

She experienced the same sinking feeling as in the little cave right after her first attempt to be with Franco. The same rush of powerful, conflicting emotions was like an enormous weight on her chest. Rose squeezed Auset a little tighter and kissed the crown of her head, very glad the other girl was near.

"Maybe you're right," Rose said at last. "Do you really think I'm... overreacting?"

"I do," Auset replied quietly, "Really, Rose... We all kind of knew anyway... You and Franco were awfully handsy with each other when we played soccer. No one will care. Don't worry about it." She paused. "Are you still up for our errand? I didn't mean to come over and upset you. If you don't feel up to--"

"No," Rose answered quickly. She shook her head and took a deep, calming breath. "I'm sorry. It just took me by surprise. I'm trying to work out how I feel about everything. So much of what has happened to us here is so different from what I was taught... how I was raised. I keep trying to understand just who I am now, what I'm supposed to be, what I should do... I... I doubt I'll find that out any time soon, and we've really put this off too long. I won't feel right if it doesn't get done. Besides, doing something productive for a change will probably make me feel better anyways."

"If you're sure, Rose..."

"I'm sure." Rose nodded confidently.

"You know I understand, right?" Auset whispered shyly. "I feel the same way. I ask those questions all the time."

"I know..."

They were both silent a long time, holding each other.

"So," ventured Auset at last. "You ready?"

"Yeah."

"Let's go then," she said. "And Rose?

"Mmhmm?"

"You're my best friend too."

Rose smiled.

"I'm glad," she replied. "Let's get this done with."

The two friends shot up into the sky.

Chapter 4

Visions of Sheol & Shion

Koren was alone in the void. Her jailer was not with her. That should have been some small relief, but it was not. She had no idea when he would return, but knew with certitude he *would*. The dread of his coming was just as traumatic as the pain he brought with him. Whether it would be a long time or short was irrelevant. Time was meaningless here.

She had consciousness without substance, being without existence. Life as Koren knew it now consisted only of different types of hurting.

There were memories too - recollections that things had once been different... better, but they felt disjointed and distant, hacked and deformed by her captor. Her memories no longer offered any respite.

Koren's lack of corporeal being seemed to decontextualize those faded recollections, to cut them off from her and rob them of meaning. The bits and pieces she could summon seemed incomplete and contradictory. Even the present seemed vague and indistinct. It was empty of significance, offering nothing in the way of experience except crushing feelings of loss and regret. Those were constant.

Then she felt his coming. As always, his probing, violating tentacles groped roughshod through her mind, but something was different this time. The void shifted. It seemed inexplicably less vacant, her essence less formless. Vaguely, for the first time in ages, Koren thought she could perceive.

What exactly she detected was unclear - indistinct and fleeting. It was something like varying shades of greys upon greys, indefinite outlines of things she could not quite identify, but could almost understand. It seemed a world of shadows and hints of shadows - not sight really, but it was something *more*, something *new*.

She felt the same agonizing penetration of her innermost self, as if something was being roughly thrust deeply inside of her. Koren wailed voiceless into the void as the something stabbed into her soul, took root there, and begin to turn into... something else. She was not sure what it was or what it meant, but she was overcome by the feeling she was *more*. Then she *remembered*...

Koren stood at the edge of a hole in the dirt. The scent of freshly tilled earth was strong in her nostrils as she clung to a sad, ragged bundle. It was hard to imagine this shaggy, still form had once been so full of life and vigor, affection and love. Now, it was forever still. Tears fell from her eyes onto the soft brown fur. Rose stood next to her, sniveling softly.

"Koren," her father whispered, reaching his arms out to her. "It's time to tell Sadie goodbye…"

Koren resisted. She squeezed the little dog stubbornly to her chest, but Daddy was insistent. He took the animal, and the sobs took her.

Rose buried her face in her hands as their father laid the little dog in the shallow hole, but Koren gazed on. As the first shovel full of earth was laid atop her pet, her little treasure delivered to her lap one chimerical Christmas with a big red bow around her neck, she wept. As the second and third shovelfuls of earth were returned to the hole, her sniffling and blubbering turned into a tattered wail of misery and loss.

Her father patted her shoulder, knelt down, and took the little girl in his arms.

"These things just happen, Koren," he soothed. "Mr. Turner just didn't see her. It was an accident. I know it's hard, but try to remember all the good times you shared together… Try to remember…"

The voice seemed to warp and change until it sounded slurred, deep, and monstrous – nothing like her gentle daddy. The hands on her shoulders were no longer soft and kind but grasping and gouging. They clawed her. They shook her.

"Try to remember! Can't you remember nothin'!? Can't you do nothin' right?! I said six feet! *This damned thing ain't even six inches!"*

Koren recognized the voice. It was angry. It was always angry. It resonated with a mindless, remorseless fury she'd heard hundreds of times. It always heralded pain, and she was afraid – mortally afraid. Koren knew this man could kill her if he chose, end her with those bruising, crushing hands. She'd lived in terror of him long – years and years. She *knew* this, but she could put no name to the man.

Koren knew this person, but then again she didn't. Competing visions of two men seemed to wax and wane before her eyes, morphing into one then dissolving into the other. Both were real. Both were true, but then again neither were. It made no sense, but Koren recognized whichever of the two she beheld, they were at the same time stranger as well as intimate.

She looked at the hole. Even that seemed dualized. In it, Koren saw her little dog, but she also saw it empty. Was it for Sadie? Was it for her? Somehow she knew the answer was both.

As Koren stared into the pit, the little dog stirred. The dirt began to churn as if the animal was attempting to dig itself out of the shallow grave and Koren pushed away from her father, away from the brutal man, desperate to help.

"Look Dad!" she cried. "She's not…!"

But even as she said the words, Koren knew they were false. This was no longer memory. It was something different - Something twisted and foreign. The dog carcass freed itself from the loamy mud and growled at her in a way Sadie never would have done. Then the fur and flesh melted from the animal's bones.

Koren screamed.

"What's the matter, Koren?" Rose asked, her face suddenly thin and skeletal - Her head hairless and pale. "Why… are… you… so… sad…?"

Koren blinked and her sister was briefly replaced by three children she did not know – two little girls of maybe seven or eight and a boy who had to be less than two years old. Their faces were fearful and haunted. She shook her head, and Rose stared back at her.

Rose's eyes rolled back in her head, showing only the whites. Her skin crinkled and split. In an instant her sister had decomposed into nothing but desiccated bones covered in taut, dry leather. Rose's mouth gaped, teeth bared by shriveled lips. Her eyed sunk back into her head and liquefied to run down her wasted cheeks in dark green runnels. Koren's father grasped Koren more tightly.

"These things just happen, Koren," he repeated in a perverse and twisted voice simultaneously soft and gentle, deep and threatening. His breath reeked of whiskey and vomit as he hissed into her ear.

Then he transformed, and it was Magic Man who held her in his clutches. Unseen hands fondled her, pawed her, and reached lecherously through her mortal shell to grope her insides.

"We lose everything in the end…" he hissed. "Even ourselves…"

He lifted her up over his head, and Koren screamed as the ground opened up beneath her – a perfectly squared hole in the earth, worms writhing in the soil around its edges. They reached for her, yearned to devour her living flesh.

"No!" she screamed in panic. "NO! Please, don't put me in! DON'T!"

"The time comes for all…" the demonic voice rumbled from Magic Man's twisted mind. "Now it comes for you… Grieve your loss. Grieve yourself. Grieve the end of your innocence and be *reborn*!"

He pitched her into the hole. Koren felt the earth surround her, filling her mouth and her nose, choking her. She felt the roots penetrate her decaying flesh even as the worms burrowed into her bowels and gorged upon her viscera.

Then it was gone.

Once more, she was alone in the ghostly grey. There were no worms and no roots. The man whom she knew and did not know disappeared. The revenant versions of her sister and her childhood pet were no more. The three strange children were gone, but still Koren *did* grieve.

She grieved the loss of her friends and family. She grieved the loss of her freedom. She grieved the loss of her body, her life, her hope, and of her mind and soul. Koren knew sorrow then. She knew hopelessness. Koren knew despair of the most ruinous desolation, such that there were not enough tears in the whole world to express it.

However, there *were* tears. She still knew pain. She still knew terrible loneliness, but now she could weep, and that at least was something new.

***

The limousine rolled slowly through the towering, iron gates of Elysian Industry's main campus. Koren wearily rubbed her eyes. She'd stayed in Nashville the night before, out late again with another battery of interviews and photo ops. She'd already had a full morning this morning besides. *Love Beyond Death* was about to begin its second season and was a smashing success.

Season One ended with what had been hailed by many as the greatest cliff hanger in television or streaming history – Koren bravely striking back at the ruthless politician who smeared her only to be tragically snatched away by some deranged stalker. Of course, her improbable rescue from the clutches of the maniacal kidnapper by her deceased sister would kick off Season Two. Even though all the major news outlets reported her rescue live when it happened, her fans were still ravenous to get the inside scoop.

Koren supposed it was a good thing. She'd been told so anyway. It made Aaru that much more popular and added to her own personal celebrity. It kept the endorsements flowing and the family coffers full. She had trouble summoning much enthusiasm, however. Koren did not like talking about the incident at all. She still woke often in the depths of the night screaming, certain she felt Magic Man's lecherous hands on her body. She still had nightmares about Kiku Hanasaka flying through the air. She *hated* thinking about the whole ordeal, in fact, but in every interview and public appearance Koren was forced to revisit her abduction and abuse again, and again, and again, like some special kind of Hell, tailor-made just for her.

"Contractual obligations," her mother said while her father snored, drunk on the couch.

"Raising awareness to protect other abused girls," Askr Ashe claimed.

"Turning a horrible negative into a positive for the whole country," Mr. Adams logically pointed out, but it all felt hollow to Koren.

It was hard for her to justify why profiting off of such tragedy could possibly be okay. A number of tabloids apparently thought the same thing. Soon after her rescue, articles like *Is Koren Lying?, Elysian 'Kidnapping' - Tragedy or Trickery?,* and *Aaru Publicity Hoax* were everywhere on social media. She did her best to ignore them. Askr and Mr. Adams reassured her the publications involved were garbage - the writers, liars and idiots - but it was still upsetting. The only thing worse that having to relive her ordeal over and over again was being treated like it never happened.

Koren sighed in resignation. At least she could go to her new apartments on the Elysian Industries Campus for a degree of privacy. Once she was alone and her door firmly locked behind her, she could finally talk to Rose. It had been way too long.

In spite of their mutual promise to see each other every day, life just got in the way. There was a trip to Seattle and an appearance in Austen. Koren had to fly back to Los Angeles for two weeks and film pick up shots for the new season of her reality show. She made a cameo appearance in some comedy. Then she had to go to New York for a week and a half to make a string of talk show appearances tearfully answering questions about her imprisonment and near rape to the sympathetic 'oohs' and 'ahs' of voyeuristic audiences.

There was a tape cutting at a battered women's shelter in Atlanta and a paid speech at a mental health NGO in Washington D.C. In between, there were frequent stops in Nashville to run by the main Elysian Campus for various reasons. This had all been before she flew back to L.A. to accompany Jonas Perry to the NMA ceremony.

The awards show Koren had actually been looking forward to, but even her date with Jonas had proven an enormous disappointment. He *still* hadn't texted her back. Then her father's drunken fit afterwards put the perfect, horrible finishing touch on a thoroughly awful night. Now, there was nothing for her to look forward to except more appearances, more photo shoots, and more interviews. She slouched down in the plush leather seat of the limo, disgusted by everyone and everything. The wide diamond choker she still had on from the morning's slate of appearances felt more and more like a leash all the time.

At just that moment her phone buzzed. The text was short and pointed.

What gives?!

Finally, it was from Jonas, but not the sort of reply Koren had hoped for. Under the text was a link to a tabloid article and a scowling picture of her. *Koren Johnson Storms Out of Post Loss After-Party Misery Date – Jonas Perry Livid at Sixth Snub,* it said.

Koren gasped and stared at the screen in horror. She tried to reply, starting a text response three times before giving up. She had no idea what to say. Jonas had not even been paying her any attention that night, and now he was apparently mad at her. Koren closed her eyes and put her head in her hands.

"Tired Miss Johnson?" came an entirely too energetic voice from across the compartment. The young, blonde Elysian Industries employee named Amy bubbled with a too-big, too-white smile. "Just try to scrounge up a little more energy for your meeting with Askr in twenty minutes! We're a bit early."

Koren groaned, scowled, and rolled over to stare belligerently out the heavily tinted window. She'd forgotten about the stupid meeting, and stuck her tongue out at her reflection in the darkened glass.

"What does he want?" Koren growled. "I've barely had five minutes to myself in a month, and I can't imagine anything so important it can't wait until tomorrow. I just want to go to my room, flop on my bed, and talk to my sister. Tell him I don't want to do it."

Amy cleared her throat, squirmed in her seat, and nervously shuffled some papers. She made a pained expression and bit her lower lip.

"But… you have several more appearances tomorrow, and Askr needs to brief you beforehand," Amy stammered. "Then of course, we have to squeeze in your home school sessions *somewhere*, so I'm afraid that's impossible. You won't have another free spot on your calendar for a week and a half, and it certainly can't wait that long. W… would you care for an Evian?"

She started to dig in the mini fridge next to her.

"No," spat Koren. "I don't want a damned bottle of water. I want to be left alone!"

Amy quickly closed the refrigerator and looked down at her folded hands in castigation. Koren knew she was being short. The woman didn't really deserve her ire, but she couldn't help herself. Koren was overcome by a stubborn resentment, and could not bring herself to apologize.

She continued staring out the window in sullen silence until the limo finally rolled to a stop. The driver came around and opened her door, and Koren heaved a great sigh. She trudged up the front steps, and Amy meekly followed.

As she stumped unenthusiastically into the building, her ears perked. Koren looked up in spite of herself. Someone was clearly angry. Their yelling was plain before she made it completely inside. A mustached, middle-aged man with a vicious expression leaned against the front desk. He vehemently lambasted a prim, older lady who Koren recalled was named Cathy. The receptionist did a noble job at retaining her composure, staring stone-faced at the man. She occasionally drew breath to reply, but was never quite afforded the opportunity.

"…Is utter discrimination and robbery!" he cried in a thick accent that Koren could not immediately identify. "He was *approved*! He was paid for! My son was in therapy with no issues at all until…!"

"Sir," Cathy finally interjected with angelic patience, "the scan was made and is still of course saved, so you need not worry about that, but we have certain standards about admission as I'm sure you are aware since it was detailed in your policy when you signed the contract. There are certain matters of disclosure we were unaware--"

"We are talking about my son's *life* here," the man interrupted, spitting in rage. "I'm not interested in your stupid policy. You people promised you could *save* him. You said I'd be able to talk to him whenever I wanted! Do what you promised!"

"Sir, I'm afraid there is nothing I can do at this time, but research is ongoing, and--"

"I need to talk to someone," the man growled. "I want to speak to your supervisor *right now*!"

Koren tried as unobtrusively as possible to slink past the arguing pair unnoticed. She was reticent enough about the business meeting with Askr. She certainly did not want to get sucked into some petty squabble with an irate customer too. She *wanted* to get this meeting over with as quickly as possible and talk to Rose.

The yelling did not cease as she walked down the glaringly white halls, but it receded into something dull and distant. Amy walked right at her elbow in silence. The woman's presence seemed suddenly irritating to Koren, and her scowl deepened. She could not really articulate why. Amy was just doing her job after all, but the feeling was undeniable. Amy felt like an intruder.

It was all wrong. She wanted Kiku. *She* always knew how to make Koren feel better.

Koren teared up suddenly, but she refused to cry in front of Amy. It was too personal a thing.

Kiku would have said something clever to make me smile, Koren brooded. *She* wouldn't *have offered me an effing bottle of* water *when I feel like crap.*

It just wasn't the same at all.

"This way, Miss Johnson," Amy ventured in a tiny voice as they approached a pair of large double doors.

"I know," snapped Koren. "I've only been here about a thousand times..." She put her hand to the door.

"B... but, Miss Johnson," Amy stuttered in alarm. "It's not quite time for..."

Koren ignored her and pushed the door open.

Amy tried to rush ahead and open it for her instead, but Koren continued impatiently through causing them both to stumble.

"I'm capable of opening a door by myself, Amy!" Koren shouted as they spilled into the room. "Watch out!"

Amy turned bright red. "I... I'm *so* s...sorry, Miss Johnson. I... I was j... just trying to--"

"Just..." Koren interrupted curtly with her palms up. She balled her hands into fists, clenched her eyes shut, and took a deep breath. She exhaled slowly and deliberately. "I've got it. Thank you. If I need anything, I'll text you."

"O...of c...course, Miss Johnson," Amy stammered backing unsteadily toward the door. "I'll just--"

"Koren!" exclaimed Askr Ashe from across the room. "I'm so glad you're here!"

In her annoyance with Amy and sudden emotional distress over Kiku, Koren had not really noticed the details of the conference room. At least, she was pretty sure this *had* been a conference room the last time she came here. That is not at all what it looked like now.

Of course, she couldn't always be sure. When they brought her to a new place on campus, they all looked so similar it was often hard to tell. If this was the room she remembered however, they had done some major renovations. It now more closely resembled a mad scientist's laboratory.

It was crammed full of unidentifiable equipment - beeping, whirring, dully roaring. Askr appeared from behind what looked to be a giant plastic ball connected to a huge white box. Both were covered all over in green, yellow, and red flashing lights. A half-dozen or so techs in white lab coats rushed here and there, but Koren did not recognize any of them.

Askr strode across the room and embraced Koren warmly. He kissed her on both cheeks. She felt his warm breath on her ear as he murmured, "We're filming..." in a low whisper.

Koren nodded shortly and tried to put on a convincing smile.

"It's wonderful to see you again, Mr. Ashe," she said pleasantly, giving the CEO an answering squeeze. "It's always so nice to see you… It looks like you've been busy."

"Indeed, we have Koren," Askr answered with a broad grin as he released her. "Quite busy in fact - making Aaru just dat much more perfect. I'm glad you've come at last!"

He went back to fiddling with some control panel.

Koren stood there for a moment, but was not at all disposed towards patience.

"So… what was it you wanted to talk to me about?" she prompted.

Askr spread his arms indicating the enormous, transparent sphere.

"Something marvelous, Koren," he gushed. "Something *wonderful*! Something we've been working on for quite some time… I'd like to introduce da Aaru Communicator 2.0! In Beta, of course… It will *revolutionize* how Residents of Aaru and dose of us on da outside interact! We're calling it da Silver Lining System. It's too bad you've been so busy lately. I've been positively *desperate* to show it to you, but better late dan never, right?"

In his excitement, Askr's Norwegian accent was coming through thickly.

Koren cocked her head to the side in puzzlement. To her, it just looked like an enormous hamster ball.

"That's great, Askr…" she offered weakly, "but… what is it exactly?"

"You said," he giddily began. "Da window wasn't doing it for you anymore, right? You wanted a more interactive experience? Well, we've heard da same thing from thousands of users, and have been working on it tirelessly. Do you remember what you told Rose in your very first conversation together back at your house? Do you remember what you said you wished?"

Koren could not help feeling annoyed again, and it was a struggle to keep the beauty queen smile on her face. It still bothered her the way Elysian Industries staff could so casually reference what she thought of as being her private moments, or how those same intimate exchanges invariably found their way onto Aaru commercials and episodes of *Love Beyond Death*. Her curiosity about the transparent orb in front of her won out over her peevishness, however. Koren shook her head.

"Do you recall," Askr continued, clearly bursting to explain, "You told Rose Aaru sounded like a dream? You said 'I wish I could come visit you dere?'"

She nodded.

"Well, Koren," gushed Askr, an enormous smile spreading over his face. "Now, you *can*! Now you can be part of da dream..."

"Wait..." Koren began, shaking her head as what Askr said really registered. "What?"

"Da original Aaru Communicator system was outdated before we had even executed da release," he said with a dismissive shrug. "I mean... television screens and microphones? Dat's basically Skype. It's old technology, but da Aaru system was ready, and dis was not. We decided to go ahead and move forward, but dis..." He gestured passionately toward the huge hamster ball. "Dis was always our intention – To not only *talk* to our dearly departed loved ones, but to share with dem da magical world we had constructed as well! And *you* will be da first to try it out! You will walk with Rose hand in hand, Koren. You will fly with her. You *will* hug her again!"

"Th...that's amazing, Askr," Koren stammered, and a sizeable lump formed in her throat at the idea. How often had she closed her eyes at night and dreamt of that very thing?

"How does it work?" she asked, much more authentically interested.

"Well," began Askr pedantically, an unrepentantly smug expression on his face. "Dis will be our *deluxe* model, of course, for da fully immersive experience. We will also offer more economically friendly options - Simple VR glasses for instance – but with da Silver Lining System," he gestured to the ball once more. "Or SLS for short, you will be 100% part of da landscape. You'll see in every direction and hear every word, every sigh, every twittering bird, buzzing insect, or rustling tree leaf. You will feel da sun on your face, da rain on your head, and da warm embrace of dose you once thought lost! Your visit to Aaru will feel as real to you as if you got on a plane and flew to Paris for holiday."

The last bit seemed awfully well rehearsed to Koren - like a commercial. She suspected it probably would be quite soon. Askr bent down next to the orb and picked up a mass of black cloth. He shook it out to reveal a garment resembling a wetsuit.

"So let's get you suited up, and you can give it a try!" he finished with another broad smile.

"I thought we were just having a meeting…" Koren eyed both the jumpsuit and the hamster ball suspiciously.

"What's da point of cheap talk when I can *show* you!" Askr blithely replied. "You'll just need to remove your clothes, or the sensors won't work right…"

"Wait… What?" Koren stammered.

"Take your clothes off," Askr repeated. "Underwear too…" Koren just stared at him.

"There's a screen, just over there, Miss Johnson," a quiet female voice interrupted.

It was Julie Warren, the blonde board member with thick glasses Koren remembered from previous meetings. Dr. Warren took the bundle from Askr and brought it over to Koren. She pointed to a folding screen on the other side of the room.

"You can go back there for a little privacy," she said, "but Askr's right. This suit uses nanotechnology to not only more accurately scan your body, so you pop up in Aaru as an accurate representation of yourself, but also applies cold, heat, pressure, and texture feel in different proportions, so what you experience in terms of sensory perception while you're there will feel real too. It has to be right against your skin to work, but don't worry. Once it's on, it will just be like wearing a leotard. Honestly, once you're online, you probably won't notice you're wearing it at all."

Koren sighed and shrugged. *Why not?* She accepted the suit.

"Wonderful!" exclaimed Askr, whirling on his heel. "Mr. Adams!" he called across the room. "Are you finished back dere?!"

"Almost," came the unexcited and precise voice from somewhere behind the great ball. "We just need to fill up the stasis sphere, and we'll be ready to go. The system is online. Dr. Warren, are we ready for injection?"

The mousy blonde climbed up a ladder and popped her head up just higher than the huge ball.

"Ready!" she called down.

As the three board members yelled back and forth across the room, Koren stripped off her clothes and struggled to put on the suit. The texture and feel of the fabric was unlike anything she'd ever worn before. It was shiny like plastic, but stretchy like spandex, and soft like silk. It was also exceedingly thin, but no light appeared to penetrate the material when she held it up. As small as Koren certainly was, it was exceptionally tight, and squeezing into it no simple matter.

Mr. Adams pushed a series of buttons on the control screen next to the sphere. There was a low, hydraulic hiss and a thick, black bundle of wires and hoses slowly descended from the ceiling. Dr. Warren opened a small round port near the top of the orb, separated out the thickest hose from the bundle, and fastened it over the hole.

"We're all go up here!" she called down. "Applicator secured."

Mr. Adams nodded and pulled a great lever on another indiscernible device that looked something like a combination between a huge propane tank and portable generator. There was more whirring, some loud bubbling, and then a flood of clear, viscous gel gushed into the sphere.

"So…" Koren eyed the burbling slime uncertainly as she finished zipping up the VR suit. "*What* exactly is that big ball for?"

"It's a stasis sphere," replied Mr. Adams levelly, repeating the same term from before. He straightened his conservative tie beneath his pristinely white lab coat. "And we are filling it with a suspension of our own design…"

"Patent pending!" crowed Askr.

Koren did not find the explanation to be particularly illuminating, but figured it must be something pretty important. She didn't think she'd ever seen Mr. Ashe so excited.

"I'm sorry… A what?" she asked again.

"The suspension," Mr. Adams continued levelly, "will prevent you from touching the sides. It will keep you right in the center of the sphere. Once you hop in, it will feel just like you're right there with Rose."

"Wait… Hop in?!" Koren was not sure she liked the idea of that at all. "You're going to put me inside of that ball of goo?! I don't…"

"Oh, it's perfectly safe," reassured Askr. "You are going to *love* dis Koren! Are you dressed? As soon as you're ready we'll proceed."

"Yeah," answered Koren, but the nervousness in her voice was obvious. "Are you *sure* this thing is safe?"

"Never fear, Koren," Mr. Adams reassured her. "We would never intentionally put you in any situation that might be dangerous. We are quite confident you have nothing to worry about."

Koren was still a little dubious. Intentional or not she felt like she'd already been placed in plenty of situations by Elysian Industries no reasonable person could argue were safe. However, she also could not help admitting, in addition to being decidedly anxious at the prospect of suffocating in a massive tub of slime, she was excited as well. She would *love* to hug Rose again.

"So…" she ventured uneasily. "What do I have to do?"

"Just put on the suit – the hood as well," coaxed Dr. Warren good-naturedly climbing down to help her. "We'll handle the rest." Koren sighed. She pulled back her dark, blonde hair and donned the hood. The suit covered nearly every inch of her body, leaving only a narrow, Y-shaped opening for her eyes, mouth, and nose. There was something hard and round at either ear that had to be some sort of audio equipment. Once she got the whole thing on, she felt more than a little ridiculous.

After Koren changed clothes, Askr was quick to assist her, aided by an equally enthusiastic Dr. Warren. Mr. Adams climbed up to the top of a ladder to connect more hoses and wires to numerous ports at various locations on the sphere. Dr. Warren did the same at different ports all over the suit. Then Askr walked toward Koren with a device that looked like a combination of blackened safely goggles and a firefighter's oxygen mask. She recoiled as he moved to place it over her head.

"Not to worry, Koren," he reassured lightly. "Dis is simply your VR system and oxygen supply. Once everything is tight and in place, we'll help you in, and you can get started. Once you've got the headgear on, you won't even notice!"

"It feels like you're about to launch me into space…" muttered Koren in trepidation.

"This is what we call a Static Suspension VR Globe," cut in Mr. Adams smoothly.

Askr succeeded in pulling the contraption over her head, and Koren's vision went dark as the executive secured her oxygen mask.

"The 'goo' as you put it," Mr. Adams continued in his customary bland way, "is a product of our own devising, as I already mentioned. Once we turn the VR system on, a very slight electrical charge will be passed through the gel and react with your suit to keep you exactly in the center of the globe. After you go online and enter Aru proper, tiny sensors will interact with what you see and hear and touch to simulate those sensations *exactly*. You'll feel the ground under your feet as you walk, and the wind on your face. You'll smell the flowers and the grass. The VR screen will allow you to see in any direction you turn your head or direct your eyes just as if you were out for a stroll in your neighborhood. It's all quite safe and we suspect you will enjoy it very much."

"You're *sure* it's safe…" Koren pressed, not at all certain it appeared to be so in the least. "You're *sure*, sure?

"Absolutely," reiterated Mr. Adams.

"Quite, quite safe," added Askr.

"We're all set here," Dr. Warren informed them as the last cable snapped into place. "System online and green across the board."

Koren was nearly blinded as the VR system flashed to life. When she could see again, she noted Mr. Ashe had moved beside a large screen which displayed a smaller version of himself standing next to the monitor, then smaller images off into forever. Koren turned her head to see Mr. Adams tapping on another screen near the base of the globe. A hatch about the size of a manhole cover hissed and slowly glided open at its top. Dr. Warren started pressing buttons and swiping screens.

"Can you see, Koren?" she asked, pushing her glasses back up on her nose.

"Yes," replied Koren.

"Visual is a go," Warren replied. "Check audio."

A voice suddenly crackled in her ears.

"Do you hear me, Koren?" It was Askr, but it sounded like he was screaming through a megaphone placed right at the side of her head. She jumped, reflexively pressing both hands over her ears.

"Holy cow, yes!" Koren exclaimed. "But it's *really* loud!"

"Right," said Askr at a much reduced volume. "Better?"

Koren nodded.

"Good," he said. "We'll be able to communicate with you while you're online. If you need to talk to us, just mention any one of our names. Once, we switch your video feed from external to online system view we'll be able to see and hear everything you do on dis monitor here."

Askr gestured toward the TV.

"If you want to leave Aaru," Mr. Adams added. "Just say 'Silver Lining System logoff'. We'll shut everything down and pull you out. We *may* interrupt you however," he added almost as an afterthought, "and ask you a few questions depending on how everything performs. We're still working out some bugs."

"What kind of bugs?" Koren asked suspiciously. "And do my parents know about this?"

"Everything will be just fine, Koren," promised Askr, though he conspicuously failed to answer her questions.

"When you first go online," he continued quickly. "It will be much like it was before when you logged into Aaru. You'll be prompted to put in your user name and password, which will be da same as before. However, you'll also have da option to either call someone, like Rose for instance, which you do da same way as always, *or* to sign in with 'exploration mode.'"

"We'd like you to do that first, since it's a new feature," said Mr. Adams. "During that period we will ask you to do a few different things, so we can evaluate certain capabilities and functions of the system…"

"But we promise to keep it short!" Askr exclaimed quickly. "After dat, you can call Rose."

"Will you be listening in on that too?" Koren asked sharply. Her emotions were a mishmash of trepidation and excitement, but underlying both was the same frustration with which she started this meeting – her anger at never having any privacy or time that was just hers.

"If you would prefer we shut off the feed at that point," Dr. Warren soothed kindly, pushing up her glasses again. "We will certainly honor your wishes. Won't we, Mr. Ashe?"

"Of course, Julie," Askr answered.

He walked over and put a companionable hand on Koren's shoulder, although she could barely feel it through the VR suit.

"I know we've been working you hard lately," he murmured apologetically. "But endure just a while longer. Once da new season of *Love Beyond Death* airs and we release da VR option, you should get a little vacation time. How would two weeks in Maui sound? Fiji? Bora Bora? Or anywhere else you might like to go! I'd be happy to arrange it."

Koren was significantly mollified. A couple of weeks to hang out on a beach far away from everyone and everything to do with

Elysian Industries and Aaru sounded marvelous. Would Jonas like to come too, maybe?

Then she scowled again. "And you promise to leave me alone when I talk to Rose?"

"We won't watch a thing," promised Askr.

"Or listen either?" Koren pressed.

Askr chuckled. "Or listen either."

"But we will have quite a few questions for you when you log out," cautioned Mr. Adams.

Koren sighed.

"Oh, alright. Let's do it, I guess, but I'm warning you!" She jabbed a finger in Askr's direction. "I'll never forgive you if you drown me in a vat of slime!"

Askr chuckled again. "You will be safer dan if you were walking in da park."

Koren nodded just as Dr. Warren pressed a button. There was a hydraulic hiss, followed by the dull hum of a motor. Koren gave a start as she was lifted off of the ground. The motor ceased for a moment, and she found herself suspended from the ceiling, feet dangling, hard concrete floor far below. She gulped. The motor started up again and a crane boom swung her around so that she was directly over the sphere.

"Okay," called Askr. "Establishing connection."

Koren only got a brief glance at the transparent gel beneath her feet before her vision faded. She no longer saw the converted Elysian Industries conference room, but instead in every direction all she beheld was brilliant blue sky dotted here and there with fluffy white clouds. There was another jerk, and she was lowered into the orb. She only had a moment to curl her lip at the irony of Askr's words. Perhaps it had not actually been a park, but strolling through the Elysian Industries' Campus had not proven to be particularly safe.

The resistance on her shoulders suddenly disappeared, and Koren found herself weightless among the clouds. A neutral female voice echoed across the vast, azure firmament.

Login information please, it intoned musically as a gentle wind gusted all around tossing her hair.

"Koren1," Koren stated automatically.

Password, please. It rumbled like the gentle voice of God.

"Kiku's flowers…" As Koren stated her new password, a melancholy feeling washed over her, but she did not have long to contemplate it.

Access granted, came the voice again. *Good morning, Koren.*

There was a flash and the Elysian Industries' trademark white tree and lightning bolt blotted the entire sky from view. The familiar, triumphant music blared, but it seemed to come from everywhere. It pulsed all around and through her as the same three buttons - 'connect,' 'user settings,' and 'help' - appeared in the air. A fourth button whooshed into existence beneath the other three – 'exploration mode'. Koren reached out and pressed it.

The sky scene twisted and swirled into the usual rainbow tunnel, but this time if felt as though she was sucked in by a vortex. A powerful sensation of vertigo assailed her, as she swirled downward into the iridescent maelstrom. She clenched her eyes tightly shut as her stomach lurched and an unbidden image of playing cards, pocket watches, and white rabbits flashed through her brain. Before she could fully flesh out the idle fancy however, it all abruptly stopped.

It felt a bit as if she had fallen out of bed during a dream, but rather than being rudely jerked back to reality in the middle of some pleasant fantasy, it seemed like just the opposite had occurred. Koren realized she was lying on her back, staring up at a clear summer sky where only drop panel ceiling tiles had been before.

Tall grass waved all around her, and she could hear the chirping of birds and crickets carried on the brisk, warm wind. Gentle sunshine warmed her face, and she could see white fluffy clouds floating lazily across the sky.

She stood, and Koren felt tears forming at the corners of her eyes. The limitless grassy plains spread out before her in every direction.

"Wow…" she breathed then discovered she had no more words left.

All Koren could do was marvel in silence at the beauty of the vast Arcadian world in which she suddenly found herself.

Chapter 5

Old New Friends

The immeasurable plains of Aaru spread out beneath them as Rose and Auset soared across the cerulean sky. The sun was bright, and the wind playfully tousled their hair. The skies over Tenkoku were crowded with happy Residents, but Rose did not pay them much notice, purposeful in her destination.

Rose had a promise to keep.

Under normal circumstances, it would have been quite a task to pick out one soul among so many thousands, but as first of only nineteen ruling Vedas, Rose could pretty much find anyone in Aaru she wanted. She knew exactly where she was going, and as the two neared their destination, they swooped down to gently alight upon a broad and bustling avenue.

The road under their feet was paved with orbs of glass every color of the rainbow and mortared together with gold. A tall, dark-haired man, dressed in something that resembled a military flight suit, glanced up at them as they touched down. He gave a start, then ventured a shy wave and a smile as they passed.

He was followed by two women heavily engaged in a giggling conversation. One sported the billowing ball gown of a fairytale princess, and the other was sheathed in skin-tight, red leather with a long, and pointy tail. The one in the gown caught sight of Rose and trailed off mid-sentence. Her eyes widened, and she whispered something urgent behind her hand to her friend who immediately covered her mouth and stared. Rose smiled pleasantly and waved sending the two into fits of helpless giggles.

Auset rolled her eyes.

"Do you know where we're going, Rose?" she asked in obvious annoyance as the two silly women continued on their way, casting glances over their shoulders and erupting into more giddy laughter every time.

"I don't know why that bothers you so much, Auset," replied Rose with an amused half smile. "Surely, you don't mind a little notoriety. There's only nineteen of us, so we kinda stand out. Who knows? Maybe we greeted one of them when they arrived."

"Maybe…" Auset answered tepidly. "I don't recall either of them. Either way, I don't care for the scrutiny. It's rude. When people laugh and point like that, it makes me feel like I've got something stuck in my teeth or something! But you didn't answer my question..."

Rose laughed.

"Of course, I know where I'm going, Auset." She pointed down a narrow alleyway off to their right. "It's right this way then just across the public square."

Rose strode down the side street, and Auset followed. It soon opened up to a wide, concourse. The spacious quad was cobbled with colored brick - Rose knew from prior experience - arranged into a mural of the great tree, Yggdrasil. However, that striking image was mostly obscured by the hundreds of Residents thronging the public space. There were knots of people sitting at café style tables and others simply standing around at corners or obscured down secluded allies and alcoves. One group of colorfully dressed Residents even floated ten feet above the ground, conversing loudly in a small, tight bunch.

Music and laughter were everywhere. Just to their left a man dressed as a medieval minstrel played some indeterminable stringed instrument of an impossible shape and size that could have only come from his own wild imaginings. His hands were ablur as a crowd of Residents gathered around clapping and singing. He was accompanied by a long-haired, shirtless man in a black leather jacket playing drums. Off to Rose's right, a young woman wearing something akin to Native American buckskins danced along, and a group of young men cheered her, all attired in what Rose thought she recognized as traditional Cossack clothing, complete with tall fur hats.

Within only a very few moments of entering the square, an excited murmur ran through the crowd. At first, it was difficult to pick out individual voices, but here and there Rose began to detect unmistakable snatches of excited conversation.

"Look! Veda Rose!"

"Really?"

"And Veda Auset..."

"No way! Here?"

"They're *so* pretty..."

"It's not Veda Eve?"

"Eve has *black* hair. Rose has brown."

"I mean the other one."

"The Arch-Veda!"

"Where?"

"Over there…"

"Oh, my God!"

"Is it really her?"

Rose smiled shyly.

"We love you, Lady Rose!" someone shouted over the din. That's when the real pandemonium started. Residents pressed forward with hands outstretched. They called out greetings and well-wishes. They cheered, clapped, and begged the two Vedas to look their way, touch them, or grant some request.

Rose appreciated the adoration certainly, but the unexpected fervor took her aback. She decided she had to draw the line when the exuberant Residents started tugging and pulling on her clothes. Rose raised her hands, and the entreating mob was gently nudged back. The invisible barrier kept the Residents from touching her, but the added distance did not dampen their enthusiasm. They continued to cheer and cry and scream the Vedas' names.

Then she noticed her friend. If Rose was bemused and bewildered, Auset looked petrified. She stayed glued to Rose's shoulder, both of her dainty hands twisted in fistfuls of Rose's voluminous sleeve. Her dark face bore an intensely distressed expression

"I *don't* care for these crowds, Rose," she whispered in a thin, shrill voice. "I *really* need to get out of here. I… I can't… breathe!"

Rose attempted to quicken their pace. She even pushed the barrier around them out another couple of feet, but the going was painfully slow. The whole time, Auset's grip grew tighter and tighter and her expression more distressed.

When the girls finally traversed the plaza, they ducked down the first convenient side street. Rose bid farewell to the last dozen or so determined admirers and tagalongs but added another nudge or two from the invisible barrier to disperse the last few. When the two friends were finally alone, Rose turned to Auset with a sheepish grimace.

"Sorry about that," she offered timidly. "Holy cow! I wasn't thinking… Marching straight through the busiest part of Tenkoku was probably not the best idea I ever had. I was just taking the straightest route. I can't *believe* how worked up everyone got! Why did they get so carried away? That's *never* happened to me before. I... Auset?"

Auset did not immediately respond. She released her death grip on Rose's sleeve only reluctantly then doubled over with her hands on her knees. Her eyes were clenched shut, and her breathing was rapid and shallow.

"A... Auset?" Rose asked in concern. "Are you alright, Auset? Do you need me to--"

Auset held up a prohibitory hand and shook her head. The golden bangles in her black hair tinkled softly. At last she shakily stood and leaned heavily against Rose's shoulder.

"You... you've never been Arch Veda before, Rose," Auset reassured with a sickly smile, but her voice was still quavering and breathless. "I think, I'll be okay. I'm sorry, I lost my composure... It's just... I couldn't... It made me think... I've not had very... positive experiences with crowds..."

Rose gasped and threw both hands over her mouth in horror. She knew Auset's backstory as well as anyone. The angry mob...

"I am *so* sorry, Auset!" Rose exclaimed in mortification. "I wasn't even *thinking* about that. *Please* don't be mad at me! That must have been *awful* for you! I wasn't trying to remind--

"It's okay, Rose." Auset said attempting another weak grin. "Really it is. No harm done. My Harm Failsafe didn't even go off! I'm fine now. I wasn't thinking about it either until we were caught in the middle of that mess. I guess Lord Draugr's recognition *has* raised your profile a bit, hasn't it? But... but... it's just... I really, *really* don't like crowds."

Rose gave her a hug.

"It's not okay," She murmured remorsefully. "I was thoughtless, and I'm sorry. We should have gone another way."

"Don't worry about it," Auset waved her hand dismissively. 'It's over now. We'll just have to keep in mind what a celebrity you are next time! I never realized how difficult it was to have such a famous friend. The Residents were practically climbing over me to get to you!"

Rose rolled her eyes and strode down the alley. Auset quickly followed. Rose was glad Auset was not upset with her, but still felt chagrinned. She made her best effort at reciprocating the other girl's friendly banter.

"I guess." Rose shrugged, before shooting Auset a sly grin. "Although... You don't do too bad yourself. I think *Kurt* kinda likes you."

Auset gave a snort of laughter.

"He likes Derain better than me." She countered. "He just likes my animals."

Rose cast Auset a dubious glance.

"Auset," Rose stated firmly. "I met Kurt before you arrived, and let me tell you. He had *zero* interest in animals before you. It's just an excuse, so he can come over to your place and hang out." Auset sniffed.

"So why doesn't he talk to me then? I see him almost every day, and he barely even says 'hi'."

"In his way," Rose replied. "Kurt is just as shy as you are. Trust me. He *likes* you. He's just scared. You like him, don't you?"

"He's nice," Auset conceded. "I guess, he's kinda cute. He sort of reminds me of a big teddy bear. I've honestly never really thought about it before. My mom was always so strict about my school work, I never had any time to think about boys."

"We're going to be here a long time, Auset," Rose noted. "Do you really want to spend the rest of eternity alone?"

"I'm not alone, Rose." Auset grinned at her. "I've got you! And besides, Lady Nu doesn't have a Lord either. Maybe that's why they put me with her."

"She doesn't, does she?" Rose mused as she recalled Auset's Lady. "It's left up here."

Rose had only interacted with Lady Nu a few times. Auset was her Veda, just as Rose was Princess Hana's and Franco was Lord Mikoto's. Lady Nu was a tall, powerful, but very quiet woman. Like Auset, she adorned herself with the trappings of Egyptian royalty, but where Auset was a princess, Lady Nu was clearly a queen. She was beautiful in the way a stone statue or majestic building might be. Her skin was so black it was nearly blue, and her eyes were always calm and piercing.

"I wonder why," continued Rose. "Have you ever asked her?"

"Once," answered Auset. "All she said was, 'it wasn't meant to be,' and I didn't ask anything else. I love Lady Nu, but you have to understand. She is very different from Princess Hana. We don't talk very much, and it's not because we don't want to. It's more because we don't *have* to. She just has this way of looking at you, or laying her hand on your head, or hugging you, or smiling a certain way, and we just... I don't know... understand each other."

"Maybe there was no Lord who could handle her," quipped Rose with a smile.

"Maybe, Rose," Auset agreed flashing an answering grin. "I've never known a stronger woman in my life!"

The pair turned this way and that down narrow alleys and winding side streets. The number of Residents they encountered grew fewer, and though the buildings remained large and closely packed, most of the mansions became more modest as well. Rose was never unsure of herself, but her friend was growing dubious.

"I have to think we could have flown a little closer than this, Rose," Auset noted wryly. "This seems like an awfully long walk."

Rose shrugged.

"This is how Aaru guided me here. Maybe it's glitching or something. I'll mention it to Mikoto the next time I see him." She pointed. "We made it, though. It's right up here."

They stopped in front of a nondescript, brown building. The compact residence occupied a tiny plot jammed in between two much larger mansions. The front door was shrouded by the long shadows they cast. Had they not been specifically looking for it, the girls would not have noticed it at all.

"Are you sure this is it?" asked Auset. She wrinkled her nose. "I thought you said his plot was all by itself on the plain."

"It was," replied Rose, ascending the low front steps, "but that was *ages* ago. You've done the cicerone thing just as often as I have. You know how many new Residents there are. They arrive in Tenkoku by the hundreds every day now. It's just grown up a lot. I'm sure this is the place."

She approached the door. It was red with a little window in the top that looked as if it had curtains on the inside. Rose knocked and waited, but there was no answer. She tried again then turned curiously to Auset.

"Do you suppose he's out?" Auset wondered.

"He shouldn't be," answered Rose. "If he was somewhere else, why would Aaru have directed me here? Do you think we should come back later?"

"Well..." Auset trailed off with a troubled look on her face. "I would really rather not deal with the crowd again. Do you think it would be alright to stick our heads in and check? Maybe he just can't hear you."

Rose bit her lip. She didn't like the idea of breaking into someone's residence, but like Auset, was ready to get this over with. She *was* Arch Veda after all, so technically that gave her unlimited access to anywhere in Aaru, excepting certain parts of the Lords' and Ladies' mansions.

"Maybe…" Rose ventured at last after a long moment of thought. "Maybe it would be okay, just for a second."

She tried the handle, but it was locked. Rose scowled. Locked doors in Aaru were rare.

"It looks like he really doesn't want to be bothered." Rose observed hesitantly.

"But we've come all this way, Rose," Auset pressed. "If that is the case, let him tell us himself. Then we can find out when would be a better time. I'd hate to waste the trip."

"Yeah," Rose reluctantly agreed. "Me too…"

She raised her hand over the brass knob. Rose spread her fingers wide. There was a soft click, and the door swung open. They stepped inside.

The effect was immediately disorienting. Even though the doorway was so narrow it very nearly brushed her shoulders, Rose caught her breath as she entered the residence. She looked up and saw a cloudy, gray sky. There were no walls. Instead, she stepped out onto a wide plain. It stretched off to the ends of her vision, and was covered with red and black flowers.

"Wow," breathed Rose in amazement.

"In Aaru, we are limited only by our imaginations," added Auset, clearly impressed herself.

"I believe it. To think someone could cram all of this in here!" Rose exclaimed as she scanned the horizon. Then she stopped, starring fixedly off to her left. "I think we'll find him this way," she said. "Come on."

The two friends trudged off through the tall flowers, and a dull drizzle began to fall. There was something about it that seemed strange to Rose, so she cupped her hands. The water was black. She showed Auset, but all her friend did was shrug.

No accounting for taste I suppose, Rose thought, but she could not deny feeling unsettled.

She was not sure how long they walked, but there never seemed to be any end to the vast field of crimson and sable blossoms. A gentle wind blew, and the rain lessened but did not stop. Flower stalks rustled and swished about their waists.

"It certainly is peaceful here," Rose commented, forcing a fair amount of cheeriness into her tone she did not really feel. "I wonder if this guy wouldn't have been a better fit over with Lord Draugr…"

"Look!" cried Auset, pointing excitedly. "I think I see something!"

Rose squinted, but could not immediately tell what it was. Then she cocked her head to the side.

"Is that a…?"

"A kite!" Auset exclaimed at the same time

Just ahead of them was a splash of color against the ashen sky. Rose could just barely detect a gently curving string leading down to an indistinct figure on the ground. The kite was vaguely diamond-shaped, but not quite. It was curved at the top, which put Rose in-mind of a *fleur de lis*, but that wasn't quite right either. It appeared to be divided into four sections that each bore a colorful geometric pattern.

As they drew near, Rose noted the figure holding the string was a dark-haired boy of maybe ten. He was dressed in a simple white tunic and pants with a charcoal vest. His back was to them, and he did not appear to notice their approach. The boy stared fixedly aloft as the kite danced across the sky.

Rose cleared her throat.

"Greetings Dear…" she thought for a moment, and as usual, the correct name popped into her head. "Dani… We have come to welcome you to Aaru."

The boy cocked his head, but did not take his eyes off the soaring kite.

"Some red-haired boy did that already," he said out of the side of his mouth. "He told me my door was locked… How did you get in?"

Rose reddened.

"We knocked," she answered lamely. "But no one answered… So we opened it."

"Oh," said the boy. He continued staring up at his kite. His voice was distant and detached. "I didn't hear you."

"That is a beautiful kite," ventured Auset.

"Thanks," said Dani. "It's the kind my dad used to make for me when I was little… So… did you just come to watch me fly my kite then?"

"No," replied Rose.

"What do you want? Why are you here?"

Normally she would have been offended by the boy's abruptness, but then again, they had just busted into his private residence without permission, so Rose supposed she understood a little irritation. Still, there was something strange about the boy – a faraway quality she had trouble putting words to.

"We came, because we wanted to meet you," Rose answered. "Or at least… meet you again…"

"*Have* we met?" Dani asked scrunching his face up in confusion. "I don't really remember…"

"I don't expect you would," Rose said. "That first time… well… It didn't go very well. It's… uh… probably best you don't remember it, actually."

"Huh?" Dani asked. "I don't know what you mean."

"Well," Rose ventured slowly. "The first time, when you were uploaded… when you were first sent to Aaru, I mean… uh… here, that is… There was a problem."

"What kind of problem?" asked Dani, eyes never straying from his soaring kite. "And I still don't know who you are."

"Oh!" exclaimed Rose. "Sorry. I'm Rose, and this is Auset. We're Vedas."

Dani shook his head. "I don't know what that means."

"Never mind that," Rose demurred, certain she was making a mess of this. "Anyway… There was a problem, and you didn't… didn't… come here right… So, they had to try again. We just wanted to make sure you were okay."

"Thanks, I guess," Dani replied with the same befuddled expression. "I guess, I'm okay… I mean… I'm not like… *hurting* or anything. I'm just… just waiting…"

"Waiting?" Rose repeated. "Waiting for what?"

"I'm not quite sure," Dani replied vacantly. "I'm hoping my dad will come soon, but Matteus said I might be here a while… Told me I could do whatever I wanted, but I needed to stay… to wait… I thought I might be dreaming, so maybe I'm waiting to wake up, but I'm not sure."

He trailed off and silence stretched between them.

"We wanted to see if you would like to come and play with us," Auset stated at last. "We wanted to ask if you'd come and meet our friends."

Dani turned at last and stared hard at her Then he bit his lip and turned back around. He shook his head and shifted his unfocused gaze back to the colorful kite.

"Not right now," he answered softly. "Not until... Not until I've figured a few things out... Not until I'm done waiting..."

The cadence of the sooty drizzle increased.

The girls deflated. They'd expected a rather different reaction. Rose and Auset both assumed the boy would be overjoyed at being invited out by two Vedas. They turned to go. Then Dani started. His kite winked out of existence.

"Wait a minute," he said turning toward them. His voice sounded suddenly more focused. His eyes seemed clearer. "You said you're *Vedas*?"

They nodded.

"That's what that Matteus guy called himself too," he said. "So that means... you kinda like... *run things* around her then, right? Like bosses?"

"I guess so..." answered Rose slowly. "But not re--"

"Then maybe you can tell me," Dani planted both hands on his hips. "Where am I, and what am I doing here? That other guy just said a bunch of stuff about no pain and a new life before he disappeared, but it didn't make much sense. The last thing *I* remember was being in the hospital. My dad was sitting beside me, holding my hand, and talking to me, but I couldn't understand what he was saying... He was really sad though..."

Dani trailed off and looked away. Then his glare snapped back up to Rose and Auset.

"I was really tired, so I fell asleep, but I woke up *here*. Where am I?" he repeated. "And where's my dad?"

"Well, Dani," Rose began nervously.

She had greeted enough new Residents to know when it was about to go badly. Even though most people were ecstatic to awaken in Aaru, occasionally – especially in cases where the new Resident had not known they were sick, deteriorated especially quickly, or been scanned long before their bodies actually died - their arrival in

Aaru could be extremely upsetting. Dani's jaw was clenched, and his brows were knitted together in growing agitation.

"I... I don't know, Dani," Rose ventured delicately. "Do you remember being sick? You said you remember being in the hospital at least, so..."

"Yeah," he breathed. All the color drained from his face. "I was pretty sick."

"They... They wouldn't have uploaded you if there was anything else they could have done," murmured Rose.

"You're lucky you're here, you know," Auset added. "It's better than, well... better than the alternative."

"So, I... I guess... am I... am I *dead* then?" Dani asked haltingly, looking like he might be sick, though such a thing could never happen in Aaru. "I... I was afraid that might be it..."

He swallowed and went back to his kite flying, but Rose could see his hands were shaking. The black rain increased its tempo.

"S-s-s-s so..." he stammered after a few awkward moments. "A-am I in th-the g-good place or..."

"You are in a very good place, Dani," Auset cut in quickly. "This is Aaru."

"You're in the *best* place," agreed Rose draping a friendly arm around the boy's shoulders. The kite disappeared. "Don't stay in here by yourself. There's *so* much to see and do! I know it can be confusing in the beginning, but you'll *love* it once you get used to things."

"Let us take you out of here," pressed Auset. "Let us introduce you to some friends."

"I don't know..." Dani replied uncertainly. "What if my dad comes? What if he comes looking for me, and I'm not here? Matteus said I should wait... If I stand here and fly my kite, when my dad comes, he's sure to see it."

"Never you mind about Matteus!" Rose stuck her tongue out at mention of Lord Draugr's snobby, red-haired Veda. "Don't let him boss you. He's not even supposed to *be* over here greeting anyways.

"If your father arrives in Aaru," she continued confidently, "I'll know about it. Don't worry. I'm a Veda! If he comes, we'll make sure you get back together."

"Y-You promise?" stuttered the boy.

"I promise," said Rose. She held out her hand.

Dani hesitated, but took it. As soon as he did, the rain stopped. Auset patted his back and offered a friendly smile.

"I'm still waiting on my mom too," she confided. "Why don't we wait together? You're sure to get along with Franco, Runa, Kurt, and Derain. Don't stay here by yourself. Come out with us!"

At last, Dani nodded. He allowed Rose and Auset to lead him back across the poppy field and into the brave new world of Aaru.

Chapter 6

The Intruder

"Koren," Askr's voice crackled jarringly in her ear. "Is it working? What do you see? What do you feel?"

Koren could not immediately answer. What she was experiencing left her overawed. She was surrounded by a wide and rolling plain of tall grasses and wild flowers. It spread off into forever. To her left was a distant silver ribbon of sparking water and to her right an immense city, the like of which she had never seen before. Then she looked down at herself and gasped.

Koren was completely naked.

"What is it!" Askr exclaimed in reply. "Is something wrong? Do we need to abort? Do we need to pull you out?!"

"W…where…" she stuttered, cheeks blazing with embarrassment. "Where are my *clothes*?!"

"Where are your..? Oops…" replied Askr sheepishly. "The suit does a detailed scan of your body when you put it on, but uh…"

He trailed off.

"Koren," this time it was Julie Warren's voice. She was clearly exasperated. "We're *very* sorry. Mr. Ashe neglected to tell you. It's your first time logging into the system in VR. You have to establish your user settings first. Our Residents, because the system has their brain scans on file, can just think about whatever they want, and it appears, but you're a 'Visitor,' so the process is slightly more involved. Just say 'menu' and then when a heads up display pops up, select 'avatar settings' to pick out what you want to wear. Remember, you aren't really *in* Aaru. You are seeing it and feeling it like you are, but you have to decide how you will appear to the Residents."

Koren complied, but her embarrassment was quickly transforming into anger at the thoughtlessness of the young CEO. As the menu appeared in front of her, and she pressed the proscribed button, Koren determined that when Askr and Mr. Adams sat her down for their little talk about how her Aaru visit went, *not* appearing in the middle of a field flat on her back and completely nude was going to be the very first recommendation she made.

"Now press, 'vestments'," Dr. Warren instructed, "there's tons of options. Just look through and pick whatever you want.

When you have a little time, there's a 'custom' setting so you can alter any garment loaded into the system however you please. You can also choose 'equipment', and 'articles' too for accessories. At present, we have over 14 million common items available to search through with more added every day."

Koren did as she was told. She reached out her hand and swiped to the right, perusing an array of dresses, gowns, skirts, suits, pants, shorts and anything else that might possibly cover one's lower extremities.

"Are you about ready, Koren?" blared Askr again.

"You know, Askr," she retorted acidly. "If you had wanted this to be fast, you might have considered having some kind of default clothing in place. You can be patient for once! If other people can actually see me here, I'm *not* going to walk around naked or dorky looking."

Askr was chagrined enough that he did not say anything else. However, he was sufficiently irritated by Koren's lack of haste that she could still hear him huffing and puffing periodically in her ear.

At last, she settled on a pair of tight red short-shorts with black suspenders, which she let hang loose around her ankles, a pair of thigh-high, stripy socks, black canvas high-top sneakers, and a tight white t-shirt with a big red heart on the front. She chose a pair of short, pink piggy tails from the hair settings and was just getting to her makeup when Askr crackled in again.

"I'm glad you are enjoying da system, Koren," he stated impatiently, "I hope you'll more fully explore all your options when you've got a little more time..."

Koren glared in silence, but made a point of deliberately swiping through a few more options before selecting a rather simple pallet of pinks and peaches with tiny hearts on either cheek.

"Alright, Askr," she said at last. "What is it you want me to do?"

"Just try walking forward," Askr directed. "What's it feel like?"

Koren took a few experimental steps.

"It just feels like walking," she answered. "What am I supposed to feel?"

"No, no, no," replied Askr quickly. "Dat *is* what you're supposed to feel."

"Remember, Koren." It was Mr. Adams this time. "You are not really walking across a grassy plain. There isn't really a bright summer sun over your head. You are suspended in the middle of a plastic sphere back at the Elysian Industries Complex. Just let us know if there is anything that feels out of the ordinary or doesn't seem to match up with what you are doing. If it was sunny like it is now, but you felt freezing cold for example…"

"Alright," said Askr. "Turn in a circle."

Koren complied.

"Reach down and pick a flower."

Koren did as she was told. She selected a bright yellow blossom at her feet. It looked a bit like a buttercup.

"Roll it in your fingers," Askr instructed. "Do you feel da stem?"

"Yes," Koren answered.

Smell it."

Koren brought the flower close to her nose and inhaled deeply. A sweet fresh scent met her nostrils.

"It smells great, Askr," she said. Then she placed the blossom behind her ear. She could feel the stem brushing the side of her head. She felt it tug slightly on her hair as it slid into place.

"It all feels so real…" she murmured affectedly.

"Great!" Askr exclaimed happily. "So far everything is green across the board on our end."

"Koren…" It was Dr. Warren this time. "See if you can fly."

"See if I can do what now?" she asked incredulously.

"Remember," said Mr. Adams. "This is all simulated. Anything you think you can do, you can."

"Just give it a try," urged Dr. Warren.

Koren swallowed, but nodded. She gathered herself, and then leapt into the sky with her hands spread wide over her head. It felt as if the ground fell away beneath her. A brisk wind whipped her piggy tales and ruffled her clothing. She felt a strong sensation of vertigo as she rocketed over the vast Aaru plains. A cry of elation escaped her lips.

Koren swooped in an enormous loop and then dove back down toward the ground far below. She soon found herself over the sparkling river and dropped low enough her hand could skim over the silvery surface. She felt the water on her fingers and the spray of mist. She dived down, hit the surface with a splash and then leapt up above the sparkling river dripping wet. Koren spun in a circle slinging water droplets in every direction. Her clothes were instantly dry.

"This is *amazing*!" she cried, as she launched herself skyward once more.

"That's wonderful, Koren," replied Mr. Adams in his even and measured way, but even he could not hide the satisfaction in his voice. "I told you, you would enjoy it."

"Are you noticing anything amiss at all?" asked Dr. Warren. "Feeling anything strange?"

"Not so far!" shouted Koren, before squealing as she did another loop-de-loop.

"Great!" cried Askr, clearly almost as excited as Koren. "Let's try da interpersonal communications functions. Head over toward da city you saw."

Koren nodded and rocketed toward the vast metropolis.

As impressive as it certainly was at a distance, the closer Koren got, the more her wonderment grew. Buildings of every size and shape dominated the skyline. Many seemed architecturally infeasible – not just tall and rectangular, but also round, spirals, some that vaguely resembled branching trees and others that seemed to have random additions spouting from any available spot at impossible angles. Some of the buildings appeared to be constructed from brick or stone, others steel and glass, but many more were made from more unlikely materials like rubber, water, growing plants, and even one that resembled something akin to a pink soap bubble.

She also noticed other people soaring through the clear Aaru sky. Soon they were flying around her in swarms. When a few drew close enough to make out details, Koren discovered the Residents of Aaru were of even greater variety than their structures. In just a very few minutes, Koren thought she must have seen every variety of clothing that ever could have been worn or even conceived of by human-kind. There were more than a few Residents who barely looked human at all, more closely resembling animals like wolves and bears, lions and cheetahs. A good number of others were perhaps based upon some sort of mythological creature or monster or simply the Residents' own wild imaginings. It was incredible.

"Land and talk to someone, Koren," directed Askr as she began to pass over the first of the tall buildings.

"Who?" Koren asked.

The multitude of Residents casually going about their business all around her was dizzying.

"Just land and walk to up someone," Askr replied. "We just want to make sure the audiovisual processing components are working and calibrated correctly."

Koren swooped down on a random street that looked like it was paved with turquois glass. It was a broad avenue planted with strangely shaped trees of every color imaginable. Dozens of closely packed doors lined either side.

It was not particularly crowded, which is why Koren had chosen it for a landing pad, but there were still a number of Residents strolling up and down the road. Koren stood a moment looking around, then walked up to a nearby young woman who was coming generally in her direction. She looked as if she might have just stepped out of a fantasy movie screen. Both her tight, fur lined top and short skirt looked to be made of suede as were her tall leather boots. Her flat midriff and chiseled arms were bare and her long brown hair was tied back in a ponytail, decorated liberally with brightly colored feathers. There was a wide horizontal, blue stripe of dark make-up that covered both of her eyes.

"Hello," began Koren in a friendly voice. "My name is Koren. What's yo--?"

She gasped as woman walked straight through her and obliviously continued on her way. A sharp chill ran through Koren's body that was almost painful. The woman did not appear to notice her at all.

"Well," said Askr, voice tinged with mild dismay. "Dat didn't work."

"I think there might be something up with Koren's avatar settings," suggested Dr. Warren. "I don't think they are being inputted in quite the same way as the Residents' sensory files. Let me see if I can make an adjustment."

"See if you can adjust the modulation from the sphere transmitter," added Mr. Adams helpfully. "It may be how we are projecting into the system rather than how the system is receiving it."

The three board members seemed calm enough as they spat indecipherable technical jargon back and forth, but Koren just stood there breathing hard with her mouth open. It felt like she'd encountered a ghost.

"I've got an elevated heart rate," said Dr. Warren. "Are you alright, Koren?"

"What just happened?" she gasped. "Why couldn't that woman see me?"

"We're working on it, Koren," said Mr. Adams. "We told you we would probably need to make a few adjustments. Try someone else."

Koren swallowed, but nodded. This time she walked up to a dark-skinned young man leaning against a building. He was dressed in a pair of tight blue jeans, cowboy boots, and wore a tight white T-shirt. When she drew near she noted his skin was dappled with a faint tiger-print pattern. Chains dangled from his neck and his right ear. His thick black hair was closely cropped.

"Excuse me," Koren began. "I'm Koren. What's your name?"

The young man perked up and looked around. He stood up straight and turned in a wide circle.

"Hello?" he ventured nervously. "Is somebody there?"

"Dat's on the right track!" exclaimed Askr. "He heard her dis time. Calibrate da video feed."

The man looked right at Koren and squinted. Then he shook his head and walked straight through her again. She shivered, and cried out.

"I wish they'd stop doing that!" she protested. "It's cold, and it feels *weird*!"

"I believe we almost got it that time," noted Mr. Adams. "Let me try… Just a second… I'll just adjust the frequency modulation rate and… there! Try again."

Koren took a deep breath and walked up to the next Resident a little more slowly. It was a woman seated at a wrought iron café table sipping something hot out of a pink tea cup. She was dressed in an outfit that resembled a French maid uniform, but that was hardly what caught Koren's attention. The young woman was covered with soft white fur like a Persian cat. Long whiskers stood out from her cheeks.

"Hi!" Koren tried again with her most winning smile. "My name's Koren. What's yours?"

The cat-girl looked at her, wrinkled her small pink nose, and meowed.

"What's wrong with *you*?" she asked, distastefully. "Something go wrong with your upload? You're all see-through. You really should find an Overseer or a Veda and get them to fix you."

Koren opened her mouth to respond, but at just that moment a slick haired cat man in a tuxedo and top hat walked up. The cat-girl stood with her paws wide.

"Tom!" she exclaimed, before embracing the newcomer.

The two began kissing, and after awkwardly watching the exchange for a moment, Koren decided to move on.

"Well," said Dr. Warren's voice. "She heard you, and she saw you that time... I think we've just about got it..."

"What's up with these people?" asked Koren abashedly. She swallowed again and shook herself, beginning to feel more than a little bit freaked out. "Why are they so... so *weird*?"

"I don't know that you should be so swift to label our Residents, Koren." Askr's voice cut in rather sternly. "If you could do or be whatever you wanted, what would it be? I imagine da answer is a little different for everyone. Do you wear your regular clothes for Halloween? It's all just part of da *fun*!"

"You're probably right, Askr," replied Koren in chagrin. "Sorry. She just surprised me."

"Hey!" Askr interrupted her apology. "Go over and talk to dose people coming dis way... Straight ahead of you!"

Koren nodded and strode toward the approaching trio.

"Hi there!" she called, waving pleasantly as the three drew nearer. "I'm Ko..."

Koren trailed off and stared. There was a boy on one side and a girl on the other who Koren did not recognize. The boy was wearing a dark vest and rather nondescript white shirt and pants. The girl on the other side looked like she might have been dressed up as Cleopatra for the Halloween Party Askr mentioned, but the girl in the middle... As they drew near, Koren could clearly see the brightly colored kimono, the curly brown hair, the laughing brown eyes.

The boy was sullenly silent with downcast eyes, as if he was pouting about something, but the two girls were engaged in an animated conversation. The Egyptian looking girl said something, and the other girl laughed. They came close enough Koren could have reached out and touched them. She tensed in anticipation of another chill as they walked straight through her, but the girl in the kimono stopped.

She looked right at Koren and cocked her head to the side. Her smile faded and she stared hard. Her two companions followed her gaze curiously.

"Koren?" the kimono girl asked incredulously.

"Almost got it," said Mr. Adams. "And… there!"

The girl's eyes widened in disbelief and her mouth fell open.

"Hello, Rose," Koren said eyes brimming. "I've missed you…"

"Warning!" a monotone computer voice exclaimed, and Koren's vision seemed to go all red. *Warning! Bad data detected. Possible quarantined user file detected. Initiating verification…"*

The mechanical sounding voice continued to rattle off a long stream of technical jargon that meant absolutely nothing to Koren. She and the three Residents, looked all around in panic.

"Wait a minute!" exclaimed Mr. Adams as excitedly as he had ever said anything. "We've got an aberration… There on the left."

Koren turned her gaze to the boy. As she did a transparent red cube appeared around him, and crimson text scrolled across the air.

"That's a quarantined file!" Mr. Adams gasped. "That's not supposed to be there."

"We've got to isolate it, Julie," exclaimed Askr in alarm. "All of da quarantined files are supposed to be firewalled. It might cause instability in da system!"

"I'm on it Askr," replied Julie.

"What's going on?!" exclaimed Koren. "What's wrong?"

Rose looked at her in alarm, and Koren could only stare back helplessly. The boy took a couple of staggering steps backwards and then sped off at a run.

"Don't let that boy out of your sight Koren!" shouted Mr. Adams. "Stay right on him until I can isolate the file!"

"I don't under--" Koren began.

"I said stay on him!" Mr. Adams roared.

The extremity of Mr. Adams reaction shocked Koren enough that she flew after the boy without another word.

"Koren!" she heard her sister's anguished cry behind her. "What are you...? Wait!"

"Almost got it..." murmured Askr Ashe. "Just a little more... Stay with him Koren!"

Koren flew down wide boulevards and turned up narrow alleys. She blasted by astonished Residents and rustled the leaves of trees as she passed. The boy looked back just once, an expression of terror scrawled starkly across his dark face.

Koren gasped.

"This isn't right," she murmured coming to an abrupt halt. "I don't want to--"

"Got 'em!" cried Askr triumphantly. A steel cage flashed into being, and the boy desperately grasped the bars. He met Koren's anguished stare with an expression of sheer desolation.

"No," Koren breathed.

The sky grew dark, and Koren looked up. An enormous shape descended like a comet. It was a very large man with the broad, strong wings of an eagle, but his face was red with a bushy, white mustache, and a nose that was impossibly long. He hit the ground with enough force that Koren was knocked from her feet.

The giant grabbed the top of the cage. He met Koren's horrified gaze briefly with cold, unblinking brown eyes. Then with an eagle's cry he launched himself and his prisoner into the sky. There was a flash.

Then they were gone.

"Wow," came Askr's relieved voice in her ear. "Dat was close..."

"Koren..."

Koren gulped as she heard the anguished murmur. She turned to see Rose and her Egyptian princess friend walk up behind her. They stared at her aghast. Her sister's face radiated shock and betrayal.

Rose shook her head in disbelief.

"Koren," she whispered again. "What did you do?"

Koren met her sister's appalled gaze guiltily. She had no idea what to say. She was not sure of the answer to that question herself.

Chapter 7

Two Very Different Outings

A loud banging woke Magic Man out of a sound sleep, and he bolted upright. With the lack of a proper apartment, he was making his bed in one odd corner of his cramped storage locker. His grungy sleeping bag was jammed between a whirring internet server and a shoulder-high, steel toolbox overflowing with electronic odds and ends. It was dark, but not lightless. The small, windowless room was softly illuminated by the phantasmal glow of a half-dozen computer monitors.

His breath coming quickly, Magic Man tore himself free of the restrictive fabric and grabbed for the screen linked to the storage complex's security system. Had they found him? The monitor showed only an empty hallway, but he knew that was a lie.

That particular camera was rigged to show nothing but a continuous loop of about thirty-five minutes of footage where the corridor was empty. That way the property owners would not become aware of his comings and goings if they chanced to examine the security footage. He typed frantically on a keyboard, and the screen flashed to show the corridor in real time.

Magic Man stared at the flickering image. He expected to see a half dozen police officers or FBI agents, guns drawn, crowded around his rollup door with a battering ram at the ready. Maybe there would be some S.W.A.T. thrown in for good measure.

But, no.

That was not at all what he beheld. Instead, a neatly pressed gray-haired gentleman in a dark suit stood at his door with an imperious expression. The man on the screen sighed in exasperation. Then he raised his fist once more.

The pounding echoed through the cramped storage space. Magic Man said nothing, wracking his brain for what it could possibly mean. Could it not just be an employee of the storage facility? Perhaps, if he sat still and quiet, the man would give up and go away.

The banging came again.

"See here!" came a muffled and aristocratic if slightly annoyed sounding voice from the other side of the metal door. "There's no use pretending you're not in there. I tracked you here myself and your computer is still online. If you are the one who calls himself 'Magic Man' and posts vulgar nonsense on the 5Kun message board under that name-- and I could hardly see why else you'd be hiding out in a Los Angeles storage building, by the way-- you're going to want to talk to me!"

Magic Man stopped breathing for a moment, and his eyes widened. He'd covered his tracks *flawlessly*. How could someone possibly track him?

What if this was it? There was no way he was going to allow himself to be incarcerated. He had decided that well before implementing any of his well laid plans. His eyes narrowed, and Magic Man crept toward the makeshift desk that held most of his computer equipment. He retrieved a black handgun from behind double monitors.

"Look!" exclaimed the man through the door again. "If you want access to the Aaru network, you really need to open up. I have a proposition for you. Of course, if you *aren't* interested, I'll go away, but you had better be ready to relocate quite quickly. I am not in the custom of leaving any loose ends behind me."

That brought Magic Man up short - not the man's threat, but the casual reference to the guiding aspiration of his existence. When last they met, Magic Man told Rose Johnson he had the key and only needed the door to secure all he desired for himself, Rose, and Koren. That door was proving more elusive than he originally supposed. Could this man be telling the truth? Did he possess the secret Magic Man had so long sought?

"Suit yourself," the man said, "but I'd start running if I were you. The authorities shall be here momentarily…"

Magic Man leapt across the room. The metal door rolled up with a screech and a crash.

"Who are you, and what do you want?" he demanded, leveling the pistol at the suited gentleman.

The man stared at him unperturbed.

"Now, now," he stated coolly. "There's no need for such unpleasantness. And I would advise you to be quite careful before deciding upon some rash course of action."

It was then that Magic Man noticed the man was partially concealing an electronic device of his own in his right hand - a smart phone?

"Who's on the other end of that line?" Magic man hissed, gesturing towards the device with the gun. "Who do you work for?!"

"What?" the man sniffed in amusement. "This?"

He held up the device.

"Oh, it's not a phone..."

There was a brilliant flash. It left Magic Man stunned and blinking.

"And I don't work for anyone," the man went on. "They all work for me."

When Magic Man could see again, smoke was pouring from the back end of his gun. He snarled, pulling the trigger several times in quick succession.

It only clicked.

The man chuckled.

"Hmm... Glock is it?" he asked. "19.9 millimeter... perhaps one you or some other lowlife picked up at a big box store, maybe?

"Let me show you mine," he drawled as he drew a white implement from his pocket. It was vaguely gun shaped, but looked much more like a grocery store price scanner than a weapon. "If I may..."

It flashed and suddenly Magic Man could not move. His vision blurred and he found himself twitching on the floor.

"That, Mr. Magic... Or should I call you Mr. Man?" the man chuckled darkly. "That was the *lowest* setting, and let that be a warning also. Do not draw a weapon on me again, sir. Were I to shoot you on the highest setting here..." He paused to twist a dial on the side of the device. "Well... let's just say that you would burst like a frankfurter left too long in a microwave oven, but enough of this foolishness. Please, let us dispense with all of this silliness and get down to business... Once you've collected yourself, of course."

Magic Man tried to speak, but could only produce a guttural, strangled noise.

"Don't rush," the man quipped lightly. "I'll just wait inside here."

He stepped over Magic Man, and into the storage unit. He pulled the door down behind him.

"My," he noted with a sniff. "You do have a rather impressive array of equipment assembled in here, but I note a washing machine is not included."

He paused to lift a discarded fast-food carton from the desk distastefully between his thumb and forefinger. Then he tossed it to the floor in disgust.

"Bit of a rat's nest, isn't it?" he mused. "I must say, I'm surprised. To think someone as grungy as you could compromise the Aaru security system, but perhaps your unkemptness is simply a function of your focus. They say Einstein would often go *days* without eating or bathing when he was working on a particularly difficult problem."

"Who... are... you?" Magic Man gasped laboriously.

"Now that's an interesting question coming from you, *Magic Man*." He emphasized the last facetiously. "But I suppose you are right. For simple conversational convention you must address me as *something*, mustn't you? You may call me Atem," he sniffed. "Not my given name, but it will do. I'd offer to shake your hand, but you don't look quite capable yet."

Atem came to stand behind Magic Man's swivel chair and placed his hands on the back. He waited.

"What do you... want?" Magic Man haltingly asked, clambering unsteadily to his feet.

Atem pushed the office chair forward.

"Sit," he commanded sternly.

As soon as the chair pressed up against the backs of Magic Man's legs, his knees buckled, and he flopped inelegantly into the seat.

"Before I get to that," Atem went on. "I think I'd rather discuss what *you* want." He curled his lip into a sneer. "I *thought* I knew, but then you surprised me, and that is a rarity."

Atem grabbed a milk crate and set it in front of Magic Man's chair. He sat on it and crossed his leg over one knee, casually fingering the strange weapon he'd used.

"I gathered from your pedophilic posts on 5Kun, that securing carnal pleasures from young adolescents was a large part of it," Atem said in obvious disgust, "but somehow I don't think it's quite that simple. If I had concluded it was *just* that, I would have simply phoned in your location to the authorities anonymously and never thought of you again. I'll admit, once I discovered your vile filth online, I was sorely tempted, but rash decisions make long regrets.

"There was something about you that nagged at me completely irrespective of your perverted, sexual appetites," he went on. "You went to an awful lot of trouble to break into the Aaru System after you hacked the Elysian Industries website. You continued your efforts even after the object of your lust was securely in your possession, and it was in fact that obsession which doomed your plans of sexual escapade, and yet *still,* even now you persist.

"I wondered to myself, why exactly does this person want to break into Aaru so badly?" Atem leaned back and rubbed his chin. "I was intrigued, as I am with all things related to Aaru, so I decided to explore the matter more thoroughly. I've done my research on you. You have the technological skills to create a completely new identity for yourself if you wanted. Your income is sufficient from all of your shameless graft and thievery that you could afford to pay for admission into the system without all the subterfuge, so simple immortality cannot be your aim either. So, Mr. Magic Man…" Atem leaned in close and shoved his weapon into Magic Man's gut, but Magic Man could still not manage to make his fingers work well enough to resist. Atem hissed into his ear. "What sort of game exactly are you playing?"

"Y…you, u… understand n…nothing." Magic Man glared at Atem.

"Really?" Atem leaned back and stared coldly into Magic Man's face. "Then why don't you amend my initial assumption? Dazzle me! What is your end game? What are you trying to do?"

"W…why should I tell you?" shot back Magic Man with as much defiance as he could muster.

"Besides the fact I could cook you from the inside where you sit?" Atem laughed.

Magic Man stared at him coldly.

"Yes," he replied with a sneer, "apart from that."

"Very well," Atem nodded. "At least you're not a sniveler or a craven. That's something, I suppose."

"'The Thought of Death,'" Magic Man quoted with narrowed eyes. "'It gives me a melancholy happiness… Death freely chosen, death at the right time, brightly and cheerfully accomplished amid children and witnesses: then a real farewell is still possible… a real estimate of what one has achieved and what one has wished!'"

"And a philosopher as well!" crowed Atem, slapping his knee. "I am quite surprised to admit, I suddenly loath you just a shred less."

"You look at me with contempt," Magic Man rejoined, "for seeking this union with one who has known but a few miserable years within the mortal coil in which we languish, but even that is a 'sacred No'. That is in fact the point. I do not pursue Koren Johnson for the youthfulness of her flesh, but of her spirit! And the fact I disdain your disdain, sneer at your so-called 'righteous indignation,' and refuse your slavish bonds of Earthly morality, which you yourself follow not out of wisdom, but unquestioning fear, because it was handed down by those who presumed to be your masters, is in fact what liberates us *both*. This 'morality' of yours negates life! What I have created *is* life, true life, a life free of the chains others would hang on us because of simple arithmetic. Just because many espouse the same lie does not make it any truer!"

"I think I am beginning to ken your drift," Atem answered considering, "but humor me. If I am satisfied with your answer, I may offer my assistance in some small way that might benefit us both. So tell me, my fine existentialist friend, what is it you wish to achieve'? Fame? Infamy? It cannot possibly be something as mundane as money..."

Magic Man stared hard into Atem's face with a snarl.

"Perfection," he growled.

"And what, pray tell," Atem responded just as intensely, "what is this perfection?"

"There is only *Art*."

"Art?" Atem seemed disappointed. "You couldn't just go out and buy some paint and a canvas? Paint some happy little trees on it?"

"*True* art!" Magic Man hissed quoting again, "'approaches as a saving sorceress, expert at healing. She alone knows how to turn these nauseous thoughts about the horror or absurdity of existence into notions with which one can *live*!'"

He leaned forward in his passion, but Atem pressed his weapon against Magic Man's forehead, and he sat back in the chair once more.

"So not paintings then," Atem replied mildly. "Tell me about your 'true art'."

"'One must give value to their existence by behaving as if one's very existence were a work of art'," Magic Man replied intensely. "True art must transcend the individual, effervesce the self, and achieve oneness with the Universe."

"So…" Atem scowled in annoyance, "is your 'true art' then some sort of bad poetry?"

"Of course you don't understand," sneered Magic Man, voice dripping with contempt. He drew himself up as a healthy portion of his customary sense of superiority returned. "The truly radiant, independent mind, a mind tooled for the special task of creation is often reviled by the fearful and the stupid. So much of what motivates the hapless sheep of this world is simple fear – fear of being cast out of the only tribe they know, a fear of ostracism, a fear of the *beyond*, of the outside to which death was the only portal, until now…"

"You judge me stupid at your peril," replied Atem with a scowl. "And your arrogance has been your undoing before, but I do not have time for ad hominem ranting. Do not forget your fate belongs to me, one way or another. My time grows short and my patience shorter, so I will ask you plainly and you will answer me plainly, or our business will be concluded. What is it you seek from Aaru?"

"Sweet Koren, gentle, innocent Koren, is the key to transcendence," Magic Man breathed with an expression somewhere between naked lust and pious reverence. "It was she who introduced me to the Beyond that circumvents mortal reality. Her sorrow and despair at this corrupt mortal vessel, this tragic comedy of existence called life, mirrored my own. She is the paint, the marble, the sculpting clay and Aaru is the canvas, the pedestal upon which my masterpiece will rest. It will drown the flaws of our individual selves to achieve a perfection that will be immortal."

"Show me," commanded Atem.

"Why should I?" scoffed Magic Man. "It is unlikely you would even understand it, thus wasting my time."

Atem poked him in the forehead with his weapon again.

"Your time for wasting may be much more limited than you know," he rejoined grimly. "And though you may not fear death, I'll wager you *do* fear obscurity, like the narcissist you are, and your vision is not yet complete. I can choose to facilitate it, or to end it. Right. This. Moment. Humor me."

Magic Man stared at him for a few seconds. What did he have to lose? His helpless state infuriated him increasing his usual recalcitrance, but he was assailed in equal portion by a desire to display his genius. Besides, even if he revealed his Masterpiece to this Atem, it was still unlikely he would understand. Only Koren would understand his work, he was sure, but if Atem did? Well then… perhaps he would actually warrant some of his very valuable time. He sighed deeply in annoyance.

"Very well," Magic Man agreed.

He rose slowly, still shaky from the aftereffects of Atem's beam weapon. He crossed the cramped storage locker pulling his office chair weakly behind him. Magic Man seated himself in front of his computer, clicked on the file folder, and opened his magnum opus. He smirked as the other man came over to gaze at the thousands of lines of code.

"Behold, and be amazed."

"Well, now," Atem was intensely focused as he scanned the screen. "This here… Well… this is *something*. This is a… no… *these* are coded brain scans." He murmured.

Magic Man nodded.

"And you've combined them?"

"Yes."

"Have you run any simulations?" Atem asked quickly, unable to mask his obvious excitement. "Does it work?"

Magic Man smirked again. "Of *course*, it works."

"I'll want to see that," Atem replied in a slightly mystified voice. "This is something we've attempted for a very long time… I'll admit it." Atem suddenly became serious and composed once more. "I am impressed."

"Of course you are," chuckled Magic Man. "I *am* the True Artist, and this is my Masterwork! But now it's my turn. Why do I need *you*?"

Atem laughed again. "Well, for starters, you are going to need access to the system. I assume your plan is to upload this to Aaru?"

Magic Man nodded. "But why do I need you for that? I got in once. I can do it again."

"Please," scoffed Atem. "You stole a password you came across practically by accident. You hardly hacked the system. Barring more stupid luck, I'm afraid you will find that feat well beyond you, but even if you did somehow manage to win the proverbial lottery again, it would not help you. You apparently have no idea how the system works. First, you can't upload Resident files from just anywhere. Also, as soon as you saved your monstrosity, the system would detect it, and the security measures would immediately quarantine the file. You will need someone who understands the platform well enough to penetrate the firewalls."

"And that someone is you?"

"Sir," Atem leaned in close. "I *built* the Aaru platform."

"Then… What do you want me for?"

"Well," said Atem with a shrug. "I'll admit this was a bit of a fishing expedition. I was of half a mind not to bother at all. I frankly assumed you would prove absolutely no value whatsoever, and then I would either kill you or have you arrested. There would be one less despicable child molester in the world, and I could go on with my life feeling righteous and heroic." Atem flashed sardonic smile. "But happily for you, I am pleasantly surprised. I will certainly expect you to explain how you did this." He nodded toward the glowing screen. Then he removed a device from his pocket and pressed a series of buttons. "But let's find you a better place to work… You'll be coming with me, of course."

In less than a minute, several large men in dark suits and sun glasses filed into the room and started unplugging Magic Man's equipment. They carried it out of the storage locker.

"On our way," continued Atem before Magic Man could protest. "We can discuss just how to get the *both* of us into Aaru once more."

***

Rose felt a great deal better after they exited Dani's somber meadow. She and Auset did their best to engage the boy, but he remained distant and distracted. Rose assumed it was continued worry about his father, so she tried to come up with something to take his mind off of things.

"So Dani," Rose began brightly. "Why don't we go listen to some music or find our friends to play soccer or something? I could call us up some food, and we could go find a place to eat. What do *you* feel like doing?"

Dani just shrugged, but did not say anything. Rose and Auset looked at each other.

"We could go back to the… main square," Auset bravely suggested. "You could just put the barrier up before we go in this time, Rose. I think I was just taken by surprise before."

Rose appreciated the other girl's gesture. She knew how much Auset detested crowds. The Pakistani-American girl turned her dark eyes to Dani.

"It might make you feel better to be around other people." Auset finished with a good deal of forced jocularity. "It can't be much fun to be all by yourself all of the time."

Dani shrugged again, but Rose and Auset both decided to take that as assent. Rose suggested flying there, but Dani just shook his head 'no' and so they ended up walking down the vibrant city streets instead.

Rose did not mind particularly. She actually had not taken very much time to see close up what the Residents had constructed on the Aaru Plain. She had to admit, it was quite impressive.

Fanciful buildings towered over the wide boulevards, and happy Residents darted here and there – walking, running, flying, or even astride impossible animals and contraptions. Many of them waved or bowed to Rose and Auset as they passed. Many more pointed, and gawked and talked behind their hands. A number of them came up to Rose's invisible barrier and asked for help.

One woman, could not keep her garments in order. They kept shifting from outfit to outfit of their own accord, so Rose accessed her data and helped her lock one into place. A man, who was dressed a bit like a super hero, confessed he had inadvertently constructed his mansion without a door and could not find his way back in, so Auset helped him create one. One girl could not locate her friend. Another, her house. Each time the two Vedas replied courteously and helpfully. The whole while Dani watched in silence, face unreadable.

When they finally made it back to the public square with the huge tree mural, they discovered it was even busier now than it had been previously. Bands played. People danced and sang. Here and there groups of friends ate lavish meals, played games, or sipped on coffee or tea. Everywhere was laughter and joy.

Rose was suddenly taken by a wild impulse. She turned to the boy with a glowing smile.

"Here, Dani," she whispered conspiratorially. "Watch this…"

Rose raised her hand and swept it across the horizon. Just like the closing of a window shade the plaza grew dark. The sun set and the moon rose bright and full, surrounded by a billion, billion stars. She raised her other hand, splayed her fingers, and the night was rocked by the concussion of dozens of fireworks. They flashed brilliantly across the sky in yellows and blues, greens and pinks. All around them, the crowd clapped and cheered.

The missiles began to burst into familiar shapes – stars, hearts, moons, and rainbows. Then they became more elaborate – the faces of individual Residents, high among the darkened clouds. Here and there knots of people pointed and laughed as they recognized their friends.

Eventually, came the finale. A barrage of such intensity it shook the ground and surrounding buildings. A million flashes of multi-colored light illuminated the night like noon-time. Then Dani's face flashed in the sky, twenty stories tall, face smiling, eyes twinkling. As the light faded, the acclaim from the crowd was deafening.

Rose could not help preening at their reaction.

"So, Dani," she hesitantly ventured once the cheering had subsided. "What do you think?"

He sighed deeply and miserably met her eyes.

"Thank you, Rose," he mumbled. "I appreciate what you're trying to do… I really do, but…"

"But what Dani?" Rose asked gently. "What's the matter?"

"I don't know!" the boy sniveled. "I want to know, but I don't! I just don't feel… feel… *right*. It's like there's this deep sadness inside of me. It won't let go, and I can't shake it! That's probably why I…"

He trailed off.

"Why you what?" Rose pressed, but Dani just shook his head.

"C… can w… we g…go somewhere w…without so many people?" he said at last.

Rose nodded, and Auset, who'd held her hands over her ears for most of the fireworks display, was only too happy to oblige. They left the square and walked down several side streets, enjoying the city at night. As exotic as the structures seemed when the sun was in the sky, their majesty was only magnified by the darkness.

Virtually all were illuminated with a rainbow array of colors. Some were lit up as if with elaborate neon styled into complicated pictures and patterns. Some were brightened by powerful floodlights. Others, like a fanciful green structure shaped like an enormous mushroom, simply glowed of their own accord.

"This place is beautiful at night," Rose commented idly.

"It is," agreed Auset, "but I prefer the stars… You know… Just laying out on the plain looking up. All you can hear are cicadas and night birds and the wind in the grass…" She sighed. "Do you… Do you ever miss it, Rose? All of this just being ours? No one else around to share it with?"

"All the time," confided Rose, "but I tell myself I'm not being fair. All these people… *All* of them, would be dead without Aaru. I can hardly begrudge them that. Still… it was nice in the beginning…"

"What was it like then?" Dani asked.

Rose started in surprise, but was pleased they had finally discovered a topic in which the boy seemed legitimately interested.

"In the beginning," began Rose quietly. "There was just the sky and the Earth. Tall grasses waved in the wind from horizon to horizon. Lady Hana appeared to me then on that vast field stretching off into forever and charged me to fill it with whatever I found most pleasing."

"And what was that?" Dani asked earnestly.

It was the first time he had displayed an emotion besides distance or sadness, so Rose quickly warmed to the story telling. She answered his question eagerly.

"Everything, Dani!" Rose sighed nostalgically. "Rivers and mountains, gardens and towering fountains, Auset there," she nodded toward her friend, "she created *thousands* of creatures straight from her own imagination and gave them all names. We played together on the wide plain every day. We danced and laughed together and flew across the sky and needed nothing but space and time to do it in. And then the first Residents came to enjoy what we had built for them."

"That does sound great, Rose," Dani replied affectedly, eyes dreamy and sincere. "Do you think it could be that way again someday?"

"Well," Rose paused thoughtfully. "Not really, but I will say if anyone misses anything in Aaru, it isn't space. There are ten magnificent Kingdoms in Aaru, each knowing no bounds…"

"Not height, not width, not depth…" added Auset quietly.

"Right," nodded Rose. "Aaru will never fill up. There will always be empty places you can go to get away from things."

"Or people," noted Auset.

"Or people," Rose agreed. "It's just that most Residents who come here… They want to be a part of a community. They want friends, someone to talk to…" a sudden image of Franco came to her mind – shirtless, leaning over her, kissing her tenderly – and she blushed.

"Love…" she whispered.

"Aaru is what you want to make it, Dani," said Auset. "I like my alone time, so I built a glen where no one can come but me and my animals…" She smiled at Rose. "And a few friends. If that makes you more comfortable, there's no one here who will tell you, 'you can't.' We're all going to be here forever. You have to make it whatever makes you happy."

"Happy…" Dani breathed.

His face showed no expression, and Rose could only guess at what he might be thinking. "But *that* day…" He murmured. "The red day… I want to be happy, but… that day…"

"What, Dani?" Rose wrinkled her nose and raised an eyebrow. "What do you mean?"

Dani did not respond, but put both hands on his head and shook it with his eyes clenched tightly shut.

"Won't leave me alone…" He muttered intensely. "…In my head… bad thoughts… Yucky… Sad… Dark…"

"Is the darkness bothering you?" Rose asked charitably, though still confused by what the strange boy could mean. "Let me help."

Once more, Rose swept her hand across the sky. The moon set, the stars winked out, and the sun rose over the city once more. A warm wind blew and birdsong quickly filled the air from the trees lining the boulevard.

"Is that better?" Auset asked, laying a hand on Dani's shoulder.

He started at the touch, but slowly released the death grip he had on his own hair. Dani opened his eyes and took a deep, calming breath. The boy nodded shortly, but did not speak. They continued on their way.

"It will take us a while to get to the others if you still don't feel like flying," Rose noted. She looked at Auset. "So who's the closest?"

Auset turned her eyes skyward. They momentarily turned vacant and sightless. Then she blinked and shook her head.

"Derain's mansion is not too far that way," she said pointing roughly west. Then she moved her hand a little farther north.

"Runa's snow valley is about the same that direction," Auset added.

"How about Derain's?" Rose suggested. "Maybe Dani would like to meet some other boys, and who knows?" She gave her friend a devilish grin. "*Kurt* might be there."

"Rose!" protested Auset. "I still don't know what you're talking about. He barely even acknowledges I exist!"

"Just watch, Auset," Rose laughed. "If he's there, as soon as he sees you, wherever he is, he'll come stand next to you. *Then* he'll nod a lot and smile every time you say anything. *Trust* me Auset, I know the signs! Kurt likes you."

"Honestly, Rose," Auset shot Rose an exasperated look. "Remind me never to tease you about Franco again. I suppose you think you're being very clever and getting back a bit of your own then?"

Rose gave her friend a sideways hug.

"I just want what's best for you, sweetie," she giggled and poked the end of Auset's nose affectionately, which the other girl scrunched up. "You shouldn't be such a recluse! If you had a boyfriend, I'm sure you'd..."

Rose's smile faded. She trailed off and stared straight ahead, squinting. Rose released Auset and cocked her head to the side.

"What is it, Rose?" Auset asked in puzzlement. "What's the m..."

Rose pointed ahead of them. She was not exactly sure what she was seeing, herself. An indistinct, shimmery something was moving towards them. It was vaguely human-shaped, but blurry and shifting, slightly transparent. Rose took a deep shuddering breath as she recalled her first abortive meeting with Dani, or rather the monstrosity his corrupted file had become. Was this another one?

The shape stopped directly in front of her. It said something, but it just sounded like noise. Then the form solidified. It was still strangely transparent, but Rose recognized the girl in front of her immediately.

"Koren?" she asked incredulously.

"Hello, Rose," Koren said eyes brimming. "I've missed you…"

Warning! A disembodied voice ejaculated suddenly. *Warning! Bad data detected. Possible quarantined user file detected. Initiating verification…*

The whole world turned suddenly red. The smile on the Koren apparition's face disappeared.

"What's going on?!" she cried. "What's wrong?"

Koren turned her gaze to Dani. The two stared at each other a moment and then Dani took off down a nearby alleyway at a dead run. Koren quickly raced after him.

Rose gaped a moment. Then she looked at Auset who appeared just as shocked as she did. What was going on?

Rose shook herself and raced after Koren. Auset quickly followed. They hurtled down streets and alleys, dodging alarmed Residents on their way. Rose was having trouble keeping the two in sight, instead having to chase the persistent red glow of the fleeing pair down alleyways and around corners.

Once, she took a wrong turn and had to back track. Rose looked up and saw a shining bolt fall from the heavens. She estimated its impact location as best she could and then continued winding her way towards it.

Rose rounded a corner just in time to lock eyes with Dani. He was entrapped in an iron cage, and his face was stricken with terror. Beside the cage stood Mikoto in his *tengu* form. Dani opened his mouth to speak, perhaps to plead with Rose to save him, and then he was gone – soaring up and up with the angry *tengu*.

Rose stood a moment, staring at the vacant sky with her mouth open. Then she noticed Koren nearby, also gazing aloft as if paralyzed.

"Koren…" Rose murmured as Auset rushed up beside her. "Koren, what did you do?"

"Rose…" Koren stammered, taking a step toward her. She was still strangely transparent. Rose could look straight through her and see the buildings behind.

"Rose, I'm *so* sorry... I didn't mean to... I didn't know..." Koren wrung her hands in anguish. "I mean, I... what? Wait! NO! I never said to... Don't pull me out! Don't--"

Koren winked out of existence, and Rose was simply left to stare.

"What just happened, Rose?" Auset breathed in horror. "Who was that? Where's Dani?"

"I don't know, Auset," Rose whispered, barely able to form the words. "I don't know what happened to Dani, but that... That was my sister..."

"Your sister?" Auset responded in confusion. "Why would your sister be here?"

They stared at each other a long moment, then Rose threw both hands over her mouth.

She shook her head slowly in denial.

"No..." she whispered.

The only reason anyone ever appeared in Aaru was...

"No," she repeated. "No. No. No. NO! *NO!!!*"

Rose fell to her knees, and Auset moved swiftly to catch her. All the while Rose kept shaking her head.

"It has to be a mistake..." she gasped. "It can't be!"

She staggered to her feet.

"I've gotta go, Auset," Rose backed away from her friend, fear and dread spreading through her being like a creeping frost. "I've gotta find Hana. I need to get to a window! I've gotta call Koren!"

She leapt into the sky, desperate to find the Flower Princess. It couldn't be true. There *had* to be some mistake. And what just happened to poor Dani? She heard Auset calling her name behind her, but could spare no thought for her friend.

Rose would find Hana. Surely this was just another one of Mikoto's screw ups. Hana could set everything right, couldn't she? Her sister couldn't really be... *dead*?

Chapter 8

Fury & Fear

In the shadowy world of her own despair, Koren wept without ceasing. Pain, loneliness, sadness – those were the sum of her existence. Fervently she wished for an end. She even prayed for it, but now she knew - no God was listening. There was only one who heard her, and that one was indifferent to her tears.

Her jailer came to her periodically. He never spoke, but every time, he violated her. He ripped and tore from her. He stole from her, but he also gave.

Koren did not know what it was he added to her secret self, but it was *something*. She felt it growing within her, and it was undeniable - like an insidious cancer deep inside. At the same time, any degree of variation in the purgatorial sameness was a relief.

Again, the dark form approached. Malformed fingers grasped and groped, reaching in to tear at her mind and ravish her thoughts.

It is to be the pain time again, Koren mused resignedly.

As intense as it was, even that was beginning to become routine. She gasped, as yet another unidentifiable something was rammed deeply into her essence. As always, it hurt. *Excruciatingly* it hurt. Koren could feel it wedged there, pulsing… exuding… changing her. However, there was something else as well. A new feeling intruded upon the anguish that permeated every particle of her being.

A seething resentment began to fester within her breast - a black and furious rage. *Why* had she been left here to languish? *Where* were the ones who claimed to love her? Why had *no one* come to save her?!

It was just like all of those people who made such a great show of boohooing at her sister's funeral, only to wipe their eyes after the ceremony, hop in their cars and drive away to go on with their happy, healthy, smug little lives as if none of it happened – like none of it *mattered*!

And Rose had only died. How did that compare to the perpetual misery that was now the sum total of Koren's existence? Why had everyone left her alone to this fate – alone with her fear and her pain and her heart rending grief? Why had Koren been abandoned?

It was just like all those government people who kept coming to the trailer – coming in their shiny cars and fancy suits. They always looked stern, and talked tough. They scolded mama about taking better care of all of them.

"Keep them fed. Keep them clean, and if that man ever comes back over, you could lose them all," they would say.

Then the government people would go. Nothing would change. Mama stayed useless – high or drunk more often than not. They all stayed hungry. They stayed dirty, and That Man? He always came over, did things to mama, did things to the kids - yelling, breaking, hurting. Pain always came with him, and neither mama nor the Government folks ever did anything about it. Not until...

Wait... What is all this? She thought. *Is it mine? It can't be, can it? Where did it come from?*

Koren turned the memory over in her head, but could not deny it. Regardless of what may or may not have been before - it was all hazy now, so she couldn't be sure - *this* was real, and it was hers now whether she wanted it or not.

Koren could see the woman on the couch even now – eyes glazed over and pupils dilated, staring at a flicking TV unseeing. It was a woman she worshipped but also detested. Who was she? What did the vision mean? The pulsing something growing in her soul throbbed.

She screamed - a rending, tortured sound. It echoed in the strange, almost-reality, amplified a million-fold by invisible walls, but it was not an expression of grief this time. This time it was *different*. Koren screamed again and again, each time reveling in the ability of simple expression and release so long denied her.

She raged against her impotence, fought against it. She emptied her hatred upon it. Koren did not know how she fought, but exulted in the simple fact that finally she could.

The rending and shredding of her thoughts and her memories did not lessen. The warping and defilement of her dreams did not diminish, but her reality was such that even simple variety was a comfort. Rage was something new. It erased the fear. It was stronger than the pain, louder than the sorrow and loneliness. Koren embraced it like a lover.

***

"What are you doing!!!?" Koren shrieked as she ripped the VR helmet from her head and flung it across the room.

Slime still dripped from her body as she was hoisted out of the Stasis Sphere. She flailed her arms and legs in frustration.

"I never said to pull me out! I never said to break the connection! What is Rose going to think of me? I just helped some monster thing fly away with some friend of hers, and then I disappear?! What the *Hell* just happened?!"

"Dat should not have happened. Dat should not have happened!"

Askr did not appear to be listening to her. He paced below her wringing his hands and mumbling to himself.

"Let me down!" demanded Koren in a fury. "WHAT DID YOU DO!!!?"

"Calm down, Koren. Calm, down!" pleaded Dr. Warren. "We're not exactly sure, but we pulled you as a safety precaution…"

"What do you mean, you're not sure?!" Koren screamed. "You're the ones who told me to chase that boy! What happened to him? What was the thing that grabbed him?"

"The *tengu* you saw was a visual manifestation of our security system, Koren," stated Mr. Adams calmly, "Do calm down. Mr. Ashe, you too. Everything worked the way it was supposed to…

"How was that 'working like it's supposed to'?!" asked Koren just as Askr demanded very nearly the exact same thing.

"Let. Me. DOWN!!!" Koren exploded again.

"Koren," stated Dr. Warren sternly. "I'm going to need you to calm yourself first, and let us figure this out…"

"That boy…" gasped Askr. "How was he out among the general population, Julie? That was a *quarantined* file!"

"Look Askr, I don't know," snapped Dr. Warren. "We'll have to get Jim down here to--"

"What do you mean, 'a quarantined file,'" Koren interrupted, "and why did you take me away from my sister?!"

"Enough!" roared Mr. Adams. "Be silent!"

And everyone did. Koren's mouth fell open in shock. She had rarely seen Mr. Adams so much as frown deeply, but now he seemed enraged.

"This arguing and screaming help nothing!" he took a deep calming breath, straightened his tie, and turned to Dr. Warren. "Julie, let Koren down, and Mr. Ashe, please ask Mr. Tanaka and Dr.

Kapoor to join us in Conference Room B. We need to sit calmly and talk like rational adults."

"I *have* to go talk to Rose!" Koren pressed.

Suddenly, she felt no longer angry, but devastated. What had she done to her sister?! She started to cry.

"You... Didn't see the look... on her face!" she blubbered, putting her face in her hands. "She looked at me... like I k...killed her puppy! If I don't... if I don't talk to her... Sh... she's g... gonna h... *hate* me!"

"Koren, we did see," soothed Dr. Warren gently. "It's okay. It will all work out..."

"Quite right," agreed Mr. Adams. "It surprised us too, Koren. Let's talk it all out, and we'll get you to a window as soon as we may. You'd much rather know for sure what happened when you talk to Rose again, wouldn't you?"

It really did not make Koren feel much better, but she couldn't think of anything intelligent to say in rebuttal. Eventually, she nodded.

Dr. Warren pushed a series of buttons on the control panel and lowered her to the floor. Then she helped Koren behind the screen again to change back into her regular clothes. Askr continued pacing, but over the next few minutes, his muttering subsided and his pace slowed.

As soon as Koren slipped her tennis shoes on, she found herself escorted speedily down the Elysian Industries' hallways and into another conference room. Dr. Kapoor, whom she remembered from her very first experience with Aaru, and Mr. Tanaka, who had helped Askr investigate Magic Man's break-in of her parent's home, were already there and seated at a long table. Both looked disheveled and out of sorts.

Mr. Tanaka appeared as if he'd been awoken from a nap, but breathed heavily as if he'd run here. The buttons on his plaid shirt were misaligned and his shirttail untucked from a garishly lavender pair of sweatpants. Dr. Kapoor, was more neat and tidy in a blue t-shirt and khaki slacks, mostly covered by a white lab coat, but no less out of sorts. They both looked up expectantly as the other board members marched into the room.

"What's wrong, Askr?" Dr. Kapoor asked urgently. "We got your emergency text..."

"We had a malicious file escape quarantine," Askr spat bluntly. His face was flushed, and he was clearly angry. "We came upon it totally by chance."

"Security took care of it though, right?" inquired Mr. Tanaka. "As soon as it was detected, it should have been isolated and quarantined again."

"It was," replied Askr.

Tanaka relaxed. "Well then, what's the big--?"

"It wasn't detected until we happened to practically trip over it testing out da SLS!" Askr interrupted. "We have no idea how it got out, how long it was bouncing around inside da system among our Residents, if it managed to infect any other data, or whether or not da system would have detected it had we not come across it ourselves! We need to know all dat right away. What if other quarantined files managed to get out? What will dat do to da integrity of da system?"

"Wait," Koren interrupted, shaking her blonde head. "I'm confused. What do you mean 'quarantined file'?"

"Well Koren," Mr. Adams answered slowly. "There are files we upload to Aaru, that for a variety of reasons, are judged too unstable to be integrated into the general population."

His explanation illuminated precisely nothing to Koren, so she turned her palms up and shrugged, shaking her head again with a vividly unimpressed expression on her face.

"What does that have to do with the boy who was taken away?" she asked.

"Well," Askr replied slowly. "It was a very long time ago, but do you remember, when I explained to you and your parents how we originally came up with Aaru?"

"A little…" Koren acknowledged sheepishly.

If she was being perfectly honest, it was in fact *very* little. That episode, when Rose's resurrection had first been revealed, was kind of a blur.

"Before we came up with the Aaru platform," Mr. Adams stated. "You might recall our original purpose was to use this technology to treat mental illness. Our thought was we might be able to scan the brain then use that information along with micro-surgery or electro-shock nanotech, to fix the anomalies causing patients problems."

"Dese included many serious cognitive conditions," added Askr. "Clinical depression, manic depression, schizophrenia, delusional neuroses, psychopathy, sociopathy, etc."

"But we were never able to get it quite right," continued Mr. Adams. "We couldn't quite edit the uploaded brain scans precisely enough to repair the problem, without... let's say... unintended consequences. As I'm sure I told you before, changing something in the coding of the brain is a tricky business. Everything you think or feel is tied up with every other thing you think or feel in innumerable different ways. When we made changes to one problematic abnormality, it then impacted a dozen other brain functions we had not anticipated, so we judged the whole thing to be largely a failure."

"Except," cut in Askr, "for our ability to accurately scan da brain and den save dat information. If a brain was overall healthy and did not need any adjustments, we were enormously successful. Dat is what ultimately led us to create Aaru. However, we were also faced with a dilemma. Namely, what do we do with all dese brain scans of extremely sick people we already have? We certainly could not release dem into da Aaru system with everybody else."

"Why not?" cut in Koren hotly. The idea of leaving someone out just because they were ill offended her. "People can't help it if they get sick..."

"Just so," Mr. Adams smoothly inserted himself. "We very briefly considered just erasing the files, but then there was... an incident... I won't bore you with the details, but suffice to say it drove home the import of our decision."

"If we erased the files," added Dr. Kapoor. "Those individuals would be no more. It was too much like passing a death sentence, so we quickly decided against it, but we had to decide. What do we do with these people? We couldn't delete them, and we also couldn't let them into the system..."

"*Why not?*" asked Koren a second time.

"Think of it this way, Koren," Mr. Adam's stated patiently. "Imagine a person with a severe drug addiction, which of course can alter brain chemistry, or someone who is delusional – sees things which aren't there or believes themselves to be someone or something they certainly are not. What would they be able to do in a system where all you have to do to bring something into being is think about it?"

"What if it was some kind of sociopath or homicidal maniac?" added Kapoor. "Even with the Harm Failsafe, they could cause exceptional chaos among the other Residents, which in and of itself would be problematic, but it could also lead the whole system to be unstable."

"Right," agreed Askr. "We are still hopeful we will find a way to heal mental illness in da future, but it is on da back burner while we attempt to offer Aaru to the world.

"Anyway," he went on. "What we did was compromise. Dat original data is still dere, saved in da system, but quarantined, so dose individuals cannot access public areas."

"Additionally," added Dr. Warren, "We are still scanning anyone who wants to pay for the service or who qualifies for our financial aid, but saving them to the separate quarantine storage partition for the time being, until we can be assured they will not inadvertently cause damage to themselves, others, or the Aaru platform."

"So that boy I saw was crazy?" Koren asked. "How did he get out?"

Askr grimaced.

"We don't really like to use da term 'crazy', Koren," he said carefully. "However, dere had to be a mental or emotional issue severe enough dat he was not simply uploaded to da public system, but as to your other question..." Askr's eyes narrowed and he turned his hostile gaze to Jim Tanaka. "I'd very much like to know da answer to dat myself..."

Tanaka immediately turned red.

"I wish I could tell you, Askr," he started with obvious chagrin. "But I only just found out about the quarantine breach when you texted me. However, the security system *did* respond to put the file back in quarantine." His face hardened and his tone became obstinate. "I know it's a concern, but comfort yourself with this..."

He turned his gaze to Koren.

"It is highly likely," Tanaka stated. "In fact, I'd be willing to bet *my life*, the fact you came upon the breach just as the security system did was a complete and total coincidence. Aaru regularly checks itself for aberrations in the code. When it finds one, it deals with it. I think you had absolutely nothing whatsoever to do with it. I'll have to examine the security logs to see what exactly happened, but I'd be willing to bet money it's nothing at all to worry about."

Koren relaxed. A lot of the technical details that the adults were discussing were going straight over her head, but the one thing she did understand, that she *needed* to understand, was this wasn't her fault. Quickly following this relief however, was a frantic sense of urgency. She *had* to tell Rose.

Askr was clearly impatient. He too seemed greatly relieved by Mr. Tanaka's reassurances and was quite ready to start picking Koren's brain right that moment about what she thought of the Silver Lining System, but Mr. Adams and Dr. Warren were more sympathetic. Dr. Warren texted Amy and the bubbly blonde quickly appeared in the doorway. Koren could not help but grimace.

Still, lack of enthusiasm for her appointed guide notwithstanding, Koren quickly found herself escorted back to her own apartments. In her rush to get inside and call Rose, she very nearly slammed the door in Amy's face. She grabbed up Pandadora, the stuffed panda princess Rose had given her, from the head of her bed and squeezed the kimono-clad doll for extra support, as she approached the huge Aaru monitor.

She hesitated before pressing the large red 'connect' button, strangely reluctant. The look Rose gave her as the boy was taken away haunted her. She'd displayed an emotion Koren had never seen from her sister before - stark, thunderstruck betrayal.

A cold weight formed in the pit of her stomach. Would Rose give Koren a chance to explain? Would she even speak to her at all?

Koren took a deep breath and pressed the connect button, but when the calm, female voice asked whom she wished to summon, she did not say Rose Johnson.

***

Rose hit the ground in the courtyard of Princess Hana's palace with enough force to dig deep furrows through the center of the garden. Earth and rocks sprayed in every direction. Hana's mansion was a massive affair befitting one of the nineteen rulers of Aaru. It floated high above the vast plains on a rocky island in the sky.

Enormous steel chains, a single link of which was wider than Rose was tall, tethered it to the ground. A central keep rose from the island's center dozens of stories tall with sweeping tile rooves of gold decorated at the eves with fierce platinum dragons. Fiery ruby eyes glared at any who might threaten their mistress's abode.

The whole structure was surrounded by a tall white wall with one massive gate on each of the four sides of the towering barrier. Inside were trackless gardens of peerless beauty filled with majestic pagodas, quiet koi ponds, secluded foot paths and gracefully arching bridges. Every other inch of available ground was stuffed with millions of flowers every conceivable shape, size, and color of the rainbow.

None of these gorgeous aesthetics were of any consideration to Rose at the moment. She looked around desperately, but caught no sign of the Flower Princess. As the dust from her impact cleared, Rose filled her lungs deeply.

"Hana!" she screamed. "Hana, where are you?!"

There was no reply. Only the resounding echoes of her own urgent cries met her ears. A few butterflies flitted here and there, and a fountain Rose had just barely missed crushing in her meteoric descent, made gurgling, splashing accompaniment to birdsong up in florescent trees. Rose started pacing, beside herself with worry.

Hana was not home. Lords and Ladies could not be tracked like other Aaru Residents. What should she do now?

Rose kept turning the startling events from earlier over and over in her head, but could not come up with an explanation that was not catastrophic or tragic. Why was Koren here? What did it mean? And what had happened to Dani?

Rose was at a complete loss. Maybe she should go and try to find Mikoto? But *he* had been the one who took Dani away! She was sure of that. What was going on? Could she even *trust* Mikoto after what she'd just witnessed?

She didn't know anything. She couldn't do anything. Defeated, Rose simply slumped to her knees in the damaged garden and cried.

A dark shape covered the sun, but Rose did not look up. When she heard crunching steps approach her, she assumed it was Auset catching up at last, and in a manner of speaking it was, but it was not Auset's high, quiet voice Rose heard when the newcomer addressed her.

"Rose," the alto voice murmured.

Though the utterance was simple, the peace it conveyed, the warmth of tone, washed over her like bath water. It immediately soothed her troubled mind.

Rose looked up into a serine, obsidian face.

"Lady Nu, Lady Nu!" Rose gushed as soon as she recognized Auset's Lady. "We were walking through the city, and I saw my sister, but then Mikoto flew down and took Dani and they disappeared and--

"Be at peace, child," Lady Nu murmured like the distant thunder of summer heat lightning.

Rose's rambling explanation spluttered to a halt.

Lady Nu smiled gently "All is well."

There was something reassuring in that smile. It conveyed an undeniable assurance that nothing could possibly be wrong. Rose felt the unreasoning panic of just a few moments before dissipating.

Lady Nu lifted her hand and brushed a hair from Rose's face. Then she smoothed out the damaged ground at Rose's feet. Everything was as it had been before. The world was suddenly right once more.

Lady Nu smiled again.

"All will be explained, child," she said. "But you must be patient. Be at peace. Let nothing trouble you here."

She patted Rose gently on the shoulder, and then sprang back up into the sky. Rose watched her go, feeling a great deal better, but not exactly sure why.

"A… are you okay Rose?"

Rose immediately recognized Auset's soft, tremulous voice. She had landed just behind her Lady. Rose thought a moment before responding.

"I… I think so," she looked back up into the sky where Lady Nu had disappeared. "Did you… did you tell her…"

"I called her, Rose," Auset admitted quietly. "If anything was wrong, she would have said so."

"We still don't know what happened," Rose noted sullenly, but the heat was gone.

She said it more because it felt like something she was expected to say, rather than because she was worried. She wasn't at all she realized, and that surprised her.

"We will," said Auset. "She said so. Lady Hana will tell you when she comes back, I'm sure. It's just like Lady Nu said. 'All is well.'"

"Is it?" Rose asked uncertainly. "Is it *really*?"

"Lady Nu said it was, Rose," Auset answered sincerely. "She'd never say something that wasn't true, and she knows a lot more than she says. I have faith in her. If she says everything is fine, then everything is fine. I believe her."

"I'm sure you're right Auset," Rose sighed at last. "But it's hard not knowing. The idea I need to do *something* just won't leave me alone!"

"What would you do?" asked Auset simply

"I… I…" Rose started pacing again, then stopped and hung her head. "I don't know."

"When Koren was in trouble before," Auset ventured carefully. "What did the Lords and Ladies do?"

"You know what they did, Auset," replied Rose quickly. "Hana came and got me and took me to Lord Draugr to…"

"Yes?" Auset prompted patiently.

"To help and save her…"

"Don't you think, if something was really wrong, they would do the same thing again?" Auset asked. "I mean… if they did it before, why wouldn't they now?"

Rose didn't say anything, so Auset meekly took her hand.

"I think your sister is fine, Rose," she offered shyly. "I think if she wasn't, someone would have told you…"

"Then why is no one saying anything?" asked Rose. "Why keep us in the dark then?"

"Well," Auset shrugged. "I don't know for sure, but maybe it's just *because* everything is fine. Maybe they're just busy, and nothing important enough to mention has happened."

Rose considered her friend's words for a moment. She certainly wanted them to be true. Perhaps, Auset was right.

However, even though what Auset said explained her sister, it didn't explain Dani. What about him? Rose could not get the boy's terror-stricken expression out of her mind.

"Hey Rose," Auset said suddenly. "How about we go and find Runa and the boys and do something fun? I'll bet Franco is probably about finished with whatever it was Mikoto wanted him to do." She smiled. "I'll even flirt with Kurt a little, if it will cheer you up."

Rose gave a small chuckle and grimaced at her friend's attempt at a joke

"You're being silly, Auset, but thanks."

"Yes," Auset grinned, "but I made you smile… You know I'm a worrier too, Rose, but there really is no purpose to it now."

Rose sighed. "I suppose you're right…"

They flew off in search of their friends, but Rose's mind was not completely settled. Every time something serious occurred in Aaru, she had been beset beforehand by similar feelings of foreboding – an indistinct premonition something was about to go terribly wrong. She sighed again. Maybe she was just being paranoid.

They soon located everyone at Franco's Spanish fort. Franco immediately engulfed Rose in a crushing embrace and passionate kiss that most certainly would have escalated to something more had Kurt and Derain not made a very deliberate display of clearing their throats, groaning, moaning, and making other dramatic demonstrations of profound disgust until the two stopped.

Derain shook his dark head and stuck out his tongue.

"Come on, mate!" he exclaimed good naturedly. "Bleh! We're standing right bloody *here*!"

"Yeah," added Kurt. "Get a room, why don'cha?!"

He laughed, and Rose blushed, but she could not help noticing Kurt had unobtrusively sidled his way over to stand next to Auset.

"Indeed," Runa replied in her ever-too-correct English. She gave her platinum head a nervous toss, and her ivory cheeks flushed pink in embarrassment. "Though we are certainly overjoyed at your fortuitous and mutual amorousness, we have little proclivity toward its witnessing."

"How about we go out on the river at my place?" Auset suggested softly. "The boat is always fun and I have several new animals to show you.

"Sure!" Kurt quickly agreed. "That sounds awesome!"

Though everyone else was less enthusiastic in their endorsement, no one voiced any objection, so they soon found themselves flying off toward a sparkling ribbon of blue.

When not in use, Auset's boat was tethered to a dock at her mansion right on the edge of the Great River, which ran through both Lady Hana and Lady Nu's domains. It was an elaborate, ibis-headed affair with a shallow draft and propelled by dozens of oars. Once they all piled in, these stroked the surface of the river at a steady cadence and of their own accord. This allowed the riders to simply enjoy the sunshine, the wind in their faces, and the cool, misty spray from the wake of the boat as it knifed across the water. The six friends lounged about the bow on fluffy pillows.

Franco, seated behind her, held Rose tightly against him while she trailed her fingers in the water. Kurt seemed to have overcome his tongue-tied shyness to some degree and was enthusiastically asking questions as Auset pointed out several of her new creations. Derain and Runa just lay on the deck, basking in the warm sun. Rose looked at each of her friends in turn and smiled. She paid special attention to Franco's strong arms wrapped protectively around her waist, and she snuggled a little closer.

Auset's right. All is well... Could it possibly ever get any better than this? She thought, purring in contentment, but then another thought bubbled up unbidden. *Could it ever be any different?*

She wasn't sure why exactly, but the question summoned up a melancholy feeling.

"What, babe?" Franco asked her in concern.

Rose didn't know what tipped him off. Maybe she had gone a little stiff. Maybe she changed her breathing, but whatever it was Franco immediately picked up on her change in mood. The realization he understood her so well, made her wish suddenly they were alone. At the same time however, she wasn't sure enough about what was actually bothering her to feel confident in voicing it.

"It's nothing, Franco," Rose demurred. "I was just thinking."

"What about?" Franco asked. "Was it that kid Auset told us about? The one Mikoto flew off with?"

It actually wasn't, but now that Franco brought it up, she *was* thinking about it again.

"Well..." Rose began, not at all certain what she would say. She stared at the sparkling water lapping against the side of the boat. "I guess, I'm just trying to think through what it all means..."

"What all what means?" asked Kurt innocently.

"What all *anything* means, I guess." Rose sighed at her friend's confused expression. She gestured all around. "All of this."

Runa sat up and looked at her in concern.

"Are you unhappy, Rose?" she asked. "What exactly is of concern to you?"

"Well," Rose said again and scrunched up her nose thoughtfully. "I suppose, I'm happy. I certainly don't have anything to complain about."

"Not having anything to complain about and being happy aren't the same thing, Rose," Auset commented in her small, quiet voice. "Are you sure you're happy? Not just that you feel guilty for feeling unhappy?"

"No, I am…" insisted Rose. "I'm happy, but…" she trailed off.

"But what?" asked Derain.

"Yeah, babe," added Franco gently. "I'll do whatever you need! I want us both to be happy here."

"I *am*, Franco," Rose insisted. She brushed the back of her hand tenderly against his cheek. "I really am, I'm just a little… confused about things is all."

"About what, Rose?" asked Kurt.

"I guess…" Rose began slowly as she sorted out just exactly what she meant. "I guess it's mostly I have all these ideas… ideas about the way things are supposed to be – things I'm supposed to do and be like, you know… From Before… My dreams… My goals… My parents' rules… God's rules…"

"Some of them just don't seem to make much sense anymore?" offered Derain quietly with a troubled look on his face.

Rose paused a moment, and bit her lower lip thoughtfully.

"Yeah," she said at last.

"I know what you mean, Rose," answered Franco seriously. "My mom was always on my case about Church and stuff, about how if I didn't pray my rosary and go to Mass and Confession that I was gonna wind up in Hell when I died… Well, I died, and I'm here. I'm gonna be here forever, so what's the point? I try to forget it. I mean… If I'm already dead… If I can get whatever I want just by thinking it, why do I gotta worry about all that mess? But all that God and Jesus stuff is still up here bumping around."

He tapped his forehead.

"I don't think it's as easy as all that," Kurt commented quietly, but his face darkened.

He knitted his eyebrows together in disapproval. Auset didn't say anything but she nodded in apparent agreement.

"At least not for me..." Kurt went on in a biting voice. "I don't think the only reason to care about God is fear of getting zapped, or yelled at by your mom, or getting stuff. If all you need God for is to get what you want, then you don't need God. You need a genie. It's a relationship. Prayer is a conversation. If you only want a relationship with God to ask for things and get stuff, then that's not much of a relationship. I wouldn't want a friend like that... I don't know what I'd do when I'm sad or worried or confused about stuff here, which is like *all* the time, if I didn't have God. I don't think I could handle it if I couldn't talk to God about it. I still pray..."

"So about which God are we speaking then?" cut in Runa with more than a little heat and a decided haughtiness of tone. "I am slightly perplexed in my understanding. Yours?" She pointed at Kurt. "Or maybe yours or yours..." she pointed at Auset and Derain in turn.

"You don't believe in God?" Kurt asked her in obvious surprise.

"I simply experience difficulty in even understanding what the word means," she sniffed. "It can be a totally different thing depending on which religion... Even which variety of the *same* religion, one is speaking about. Do you mean the Muslim God or the Christian God? The protestant God or the Catholic God? Are you talking about Zeus or Kali or Ra or Baal or any of the thousands of supposed deities people have worshipped over the centuries? And which one is the correct one? Everyone says it is their own."

"If there's no God, then where did all of this come from?!" exclaimed Kurt waving his arms around.

"I am relatively certain," Runa shot back. "That 'all of this' came from a technology laboratory somewhere in the southern United States."

"You know what I mean." Kurt scowled. "The universe... Creation."

"The only fact of which I am certain, Kurt, is that everyone who says they've got God sufficiently comprehended to impose their attitude upon others, cannot possibly all be correct," replied Runa. "If a pair of individuals say only theirs is the one true path and they believe deeply contradictory things, the only possibilities are one is right and the other wrong or, and this is the possibility which I personally think is more likely, they're *both* wrong."

"That's why we have *faith*," countered Kurt

"Faith?" shot back Runa incredulously. "Doesn't that simply mean *really* believing in something that isn't true?"

Auset emphatically shook her head.

"That's not what faith means," said Kurt.

"So then, Kurt," Runa jabbed a finger at Auset. "Is she going to Hell? According to your *faith* she's supposed to if she really, really believes in God but the wrong way."

"I didn't say that," shot back Kurt getting heated himself. "I didn't say I had all the answers either, but not knowing everything isn't the same as saying 'I know there is no God'. How do you even *prove* that? It's not like you can put a little God in a test tube and swish it around with some God litmus paper and then go 'nope, didn't turn blue. Not there.' It takes just as much faith to believe there's no God as to believe there is. More in fact, because then you have to believe the universe and everything it just happened by accident!"

"Guys! Guys!" exclaimed Rose with both hands raised. She made a placating gesture. "I wasn't trying to start an argument. We're all friends here. I just… I mean it's like I'm having this same argument as you in my own head. Then on top of that, I just keep asking myself, 'what is my purpose anymore?' Is it just to run around and play all day with you guys and then throw in some New Resident greetings on the side? That just doesn't feel… I don't know… *enough*."

Everyone fell uncomfortably silent. It was clear all of them had thought something similar before.

"Who are we?" murmured Auset quietly. "Why are we here? They are the oldest questions Mankind has ever asked itself, and they are not any more clearly answered in Aaru than they were Before…"

"But Before I had dreams," countered Rose. "Before I had goals and direction. I was going to play soccer for the US National Women's Team one day. I was going to have a job and a family. What are my dreams here? What could I possibly set as a goal when I can have, or do, or be anything I want with just a thought?"

"I know what my goal is, Rose." Franco met her discomfited gaze intensely. "It's to make you happy. I love you, Rose."

Rose smiled at Franco and hugged him. "I love you too, and I love our life together here, Franco. I do, but what are we to make of it? What should we be *doing* with it? I still don't know, but... it feels like I'm... I don't know... Even though I like what we do - what we *all* do together - it still feels like I'm *missing* something."

"Well," Runa ventured shyly. "At least we've got forever to come to an understanding, and..." She turned to Kurt. "I wish to offer an apology. I was perhaps a bit... impassioned. Forever is a very long time. I do not wish to spend it feeling cross. I treasure your friendship, Kurt. I did not intend to give you insult. I am sorry."

"I'm sorry too," Kurt rubbed his neck uncomfortably. "I got a little too heated myself. I guess it's my Baptist upbringing."

"You guys are being way too serious," complained Derain lying back to continue his sun bathing. He nodded in Rose's direction. "Couldn't you and Franco just argue about whose soccer team is better or something?"

"We could just toss you overboard," suggested Kurt with a smile, "and laugh while you try to make friends with Auset's animals."

"You might be laughing now Kurt," Derain shot back without sitting up, "but mark my words. I'm going to find me a spirit guide eventually... Sure as tomorrow. We're in the Everywhen..."

"The what?" asked Franco.

"The Everywhen," repeated Derain, "The Dreaming Time, where Now is and was and will be..."

"Thank you greatly, Derain," answered Runa with a wry expression. She winked at Kurt. "I had forgotten to suggest mumbling apocryphal platitudes that sound sagaciously cryptic, but are actually unadulterated nonsense, as a method of ameliorating our ill-humor."

"You're one to talk about mumbling nonsense," shot back Derain with mock severity. "All that mess that just came out of your mouth? What was that? It sorta *sounded* like English."

They laughed. Franco pulled Rose against himself more tightly and kissed her cheek. The joking and laughter made Rose feel better, as did the hugs and stolen kisses from Franco, but she knew she would not feel completely placated until she talked to Koren again. Maybe *she* would have something useful to offer.

And she hadn't even started discussing what could have possibly happened to Dani with everyone. That was a completely separate if equally troublesome issue beleaguering her mind. Rose sighed.

Not knowing sucks, she thought sullenly.

With all of this talk about religion and meaning and cryptic phrases, she was forcefully reminded of something her mother often said growing up; "All the worry in the world won't turn one grey hair black or make you live a second longer".

With the memory came a pang of guilt. Rose wished their last meeting had gone better. Her mother had not tried to talk to her again since. In any case, Rose assumed the phrase was from the Bible or something. Most of Gypsie Johnson's clever quotes were – from there or from cat posters, but either way it seemed especially applicable now.

Rose would know about Dani when Hana told her and not one second sooner. All she would accomplish by worrying was to ruin an otherwise wonderful time. And the rest of it? It was hard, but Rose really did try her best to put her troubles out of her mind and enjoy her time with her friends. Rose made a conscious effort to settle herself as they spent yet another perfect day sailing the shining river under the brilliant sun of perpetual summer. For just a little while, Aaru started feeling like Heaven again.

Chapter 9

Different Sorts of Prisons

Hell.

That's where she must be, but if that was the case, the TV pastor her mom always watched on Sunday mornings when she did not have to go into the restaurant had gotten it all wrong. There was no fire or brimstone. There were no cavorting demons with pitch forks to torment her. Her own tortuous thoughts accomplished that just as well as any denizen of the infernal realms.

Hell.

Loneliness. Sorrow. Loss. Hopelessness. Rage. Those were her only reality now, and there was no relief. She released another wordless scream of anguish and defeat, a silent explosion of misery and despair. The indistinct greyness pulsed with it, reverberated with her inconsolable grief, and reflected back on her soul a hundred fold.

Hell.

Her thoughts were broken and confused. Images filled her brain, but made no sense. She remembered a church, a playground, a swing set. She could picture her sister's face, her father, but there was also a decrepit trailer buried in filth - a brother and sisters with ever sniffling noses, always hungry, clothes always dirty and unkempt.

The word 'mother' conjured two drastically different visions; one pretty and kind with blonde hair and brown roots, dressed in khaki pants and a green, collared waitress shirt... But then there was another woman - sullen, dead eyes, black hair and a face aged far beyond the sum of her years – always with a cigarette hanging out of her mouth, clenched between black and broken teeth. And there was another also - A big man. A violent man. His face was dark and indistinct in her imaginings, but the thought of him filled her with quivering fear.

Who are they? She thought curiously. *Who am I?*

She could no longer remember. She did not even recall her own name anymore. Another loss. Another part of herself taken and gone. The grief started to overwhelm her again, but she fought back with the rage.

Try to understand, she thought stubbornly, straining her mind toward the holes in her memory, the unfamiliar additions. There was still no sound in her prison, but she had a sudden vague impression of music and she wracked her thoughts. *Try to understand... Try to understand... Who am I?*

But the answer just wouldn't come.

Another vision assailed her... A little boy of about six... tears streaming down his cheeks. Two tiny hands firmly grasped fist-fulls of black, leather jacket.

"Don't go, daddy!" the little boy begged in a ragged voice. "Mamma'll be sorry when she wakes up. She always is! She's just takin' her medicine. It always makes her funny. You know how she gets when she's funny!"

He was a tall man and strong. The boy didn't know any stronger, in fact. Every inch of visible skin at his neck, chest, and the one hand gripping the handlebars of his big, black motor cycle were heavily tattooed. He sighed and paused.

"Well, buddy," the man replied. He looked down at the boy through dark sunglasses "I ain't laughin' no more."

The biker wiped at his cheek and his hand came away bloody from a jagged wound. He stared at his hand, thoughtfully rubbing the sticky crimson fluid between his fingers.

"I ain't been laughin' for a long time."

He took off the dark sun glasses and knelt down in front of the little boy.

"See that there?" He held up his bloody hand. "There ain't nothin' funny 'bout that. There comes a time, buddy, when a man just can't take no more. Your mama? She loves that there needle way more'n me. More'n any of us. It's just time to move on."

"Take me with you then!" the little boy cried. "Take all of us! We won't be no trouble!"

"Only one seat on this here hog, kid," the man answered. "Besides, I need you to look after your bubba an' your sissies, God knows Mama can't."

"Don't you love us?" the boy shrieked, tightening his grip. "Won't you miss us?"

His father gave him a sad smile.

"Ever' day, son," he breathed and hugged the boy close. "But sometimes lovin's lettin' go. All your mama an' me do is fight. That ain't no good fer you kids. Maybe if she ain't all tore up over me alla time, she'll get better... I don't know. I just can't take it no more."

The little boy could think of nothing else to say, but just stood there and cried. He held onto his daddy fiercely, refusing to let go.

The man sighed again.

"Here now, boy," he growled, prying his son's arms from around his shoulders. "No more tears. A man ain't got no time fer 'em. Lemme give you somthin'."

He stood and rummaged through his saddle bags. After a moment, he turned and knelt down in front of his son again. He pressed a hard plastic box into the boy's hands.

The little boy looked down. It was an 8 track tape. The sticker on the front was wrinkled and faded, but he could still make out the image. It was all red and black and white. Six long-haired people smiled back at him – four men and two women. It was covered with words he could not read.

"That'n there's pretty old," his daddy said. "I 'bout wore it out when I was just a little older'n you, but it'll still play on that there old stereo in the living room under the TV. You're a special boy, just like the man the girl in the song is singin' about. Even mama'll figure it out eventually, I bet. You're a smart kid – way smarter'n me. Your teachers is always sayin' so. You just keep that up, you hear? You go be somethin' big an' important. You listen to that whenever you're feelin' bad, and know I'm thinkin' of you."

The boy stared down at the tape in his hands. His tears did not stop flowing, but he quieted to a muted blubbering. The man took a step back and smiled. He set his sun glasses on the little boy's nose. They were way too big, and they almost immediately slid off the boy's face. Daddy laughed.

"You be good now, you hear?" he said.

Then he hopped on his motor cycle and drove away. The boy never saw him again.

Abandoned…

She growled in a sudden rage.

Abandoned just like me…

Then the grief came back, and she wailed into the void. The crushing sadness took her, and she wept. She wept for the little boy. She wept for herself and raged at the unfairness of it all. She wanted to lash out, to break things, to hurt someone the way she had been hurt, but there was nothing to receive her fury. There was nothing at all but her own tortured thoughts and scattered memories.

Just wait, though, she thought in frustration. *Just wait. If I ever get the chance, I'll make them all pay. I'll make them all suffer. Someday I'll be strong, and no one'll ever be able to hurt me again...*

And she was forced to content herself with that. It was the only thing she had to hold onto.

* * *

Magic Man was not at all comfortable with his new arrangement. The lab in which he found himself was considerably nicer than his Los Angeles storage unit. It was air conditioned and had actual furniture, instead of plywood suspended by milk crates. He had a real apartment, right off the lab with a proper bed, closet, bath, and shower. It even had a kitchenette with a fully stocked refrigerator, stove, and a Keurig.

It's a nice little cage, he thought caustically.

He was likewise uncomfortable with his new partner. Magic Man had never been particularly given to collaboration under the best of conditions, and his present situation was certainly not the best of conditions. He did not like this Atem. He did not want him meddling with his vision, but what was he to do?

He had nothing but contempt for Atem's pedestrian threats of violence. Violence and death held no fear for Magic Man. His unwelcomed benefactor had no idea what Magic Man had already endured and how amateurish were his juvenile attempts at physical intimidation. The possibility that Atem might thwart him before his perfect vision was fulfilled, however... That filled Magic Man with an almost religious terror.

He wracked his brain for an escape, but came up with nothing. However, Magic Man was not dismayed. It was simply a question of patience.

Atem needed him. If that was not true, he would already be dead or incarcerated. As long as that was the case, and the more time passed, the greater the chance was an opportunity would present itself. Magic Man's abduction and impressment into Atem's service had been unexpected, but in the near term changed nothing. His purpose was still the same. His work was yet before him, yet unfinished.

Still, it rankled.

115

Magic Man growled, sighed, and then returned his attention to his computer monitors. He stared intently at thousands and thousands of lines of code, occasionally cutting a line from one screen and pasting it into the other – sometimes adding a line here, deleting a couple there, but ever intent. Every so often he would switch his gaze to a third monitor and run a simulation. Often he would go back and erase all the changes he'd just made.

He was making progress, but it was slow. Magic Man yet remained unsatisfied. Nothing less than total perfection would *ever* be enough.

"Soon, my gentle Muse," he murmured under his breath, scanning the code before him like an augur might examine the emptied bowels of some sacrificial beast. "Soon my vision will be realized and we'll be together, inseparable forever…"

There was a loud click and a door on the far side of the room slid open. Atem strode imperiously in and the portal sealed behind him. He was dressed in a different suit, but was still immaculate. He walked up to Magic Man's work station pulling idly at his cuffs.

"Hard at work, I see," he noted with a sniff. "That's good."

"What do you want, Atem," Magic Man asked in clear annoyance. "I'm busy."

Atem raised an eyebrow and gave a harsh chuckle.

"Indeed?"

He put his hand on the back of Magic Man's swivel chair and purposefully turned him around. Magic Man's eyes burned with fury, and he stared up at the older man as if they might drill holes through him.

"Such a fierce expression!" Atem laughed. "You shall not be too busy for this though, I suspect. We have a way in…"

"Really…" Magic Man continued to regard Atem suspiciously.

Atem gave another little laugh, but it turned into a cough. The older man pulled a handkerchief from his breast pocket and covered his mouth until the coughing subsided. Magic Man thought the ivory-colored square of fabric came away with flecks of red, but he did not react. His face remained smooth and impassive.

Interesting, he thought.

"I should have thought you'd be please, Mr. Magic Man…" Atem continued at last as he shoved the handkerchief into the pocket of his trousers.

"You want something," Magic Man stated shortly. "What is it?"

"Insightful as always," Atem drawled. "You are as perceptive as you are ill-mannered and foul-tempered, but yes," he conceded. "If you want access, there will be a little quid pro quo involved, but surely you knew that from the beginning, didn't you? First, I'll need to see just what exactly it is you think you've accomplished."

Magic Man rolled his eyes, but indicated a third screen on the desk. He tapped a few buttons, and started the simulation. Then he leaned back with his hands behind his head. Atem watched intently.

"I'm still extremely limited," Magic Man said as the simulation ended, "until I can test this on the actual Aaru system. What I've got here is working… sort of… but it's very crude, jerry-rigged from the software on the Aaru helmet and the CPU I acquired…"

"Stole, you mean…" interrupted Atem.

"And a good thing too," spat back Magic Man. "Those two pieces of equipment are the only reason this works at all, but I'm getting to the point where I need a better platform. I'm going to need to get into the system to make much more progress."

"No, I think not" replied Atem thoughtfully. "You must wait a while longer, I'm afraid, but I still might be able to assist you yet."

Magic Man had already partially risen from his seat to protest, but Atem held up a prohibitory hand. He took a small tablet out of his pocket, and quickly typed a message. Then he raised his eyes to a fuming Magic Man once more.

"You'll get access to Aaru when I say you're ready," stated Atem coldly. "Not an instant before. What you've shown me is promising, but far less than what I need. Still, I'm going to need you to write up in *extreme detail* just exactly what you are doing and how you are doing it, so it can be replicated. Once that is done, and I have verified your process, we can talk about next steps. Until then, remain industrious."

Atem turned to go.

"I don't know what you expect me to do without access to the system," Magic Man shot back haughtily. He gestured to the simulation screen. "Like I said, I'm reaching the limits of this device."

Just then the door opened. Someone outside handed Atem a package and Atem in turn strode across the room and handed it to

Magic Man. Magic Man raised an eyebrow as he accepted it. He felt the package

"A laptop?" he asked dubiously.

"Indeed," answered Atem. "This device contains a very early version of the Aaru platform software. The memory is limited, so it can only handle a couple of Resident files at a time, but it should be sufficient for your purposes." He walked back to the door.

"You didn't say what it was you wanted from me," Magic Man called after him.

"Ah, yes," Atem replied nodding and turning back around to face Magic Man. "My Aaru profile is well-known. It may or may not surprise you to learn I have become something of a persona non grata around the Elysian Industries campus. I have a file of my own that needs to get past their security measures, and I have a notion about that, but do not trouble yourself with it quite yet. You already have more than enough to consider. Don't disappoint me."

Then he was gone, and the door slid shut. There was a loud click as the lock engaged, and Magic Man was alone again.

He did not like taking orders. Magic Man had yet to meet anyone in this life who could match his superior intellect – certainly no one who was enlightened enough to tell him what to do. This Atem was clearly a challenge, but Magic Man did not fear a challenge. Rather, it excited him as he imagined just how superior he would feel once he took this Atem down a peg or two. It was simply a question of when and how that would be accomplished.

Magic Man sighed and began unwrapping the laptop. He fired up the device and took a few minutes to get a feel for what was contained thereon. As much as he tried to resist the emotion, he felt his excitement grow.

This platform simulator Atem had bestowed looked as if it might actually be helpful, though Magic Man would certainly never admit it. Regardless of how Atem complicated things, Magic Man's plan was progressing. That was what was important. Everything else was simply a distraction. There was still his ultimate vision to realize; only that to think about, and there was still much work to do.

***

The rainbow tunnel spun. Very shortly, a dainty, white hand pressed against the other side of the screen. The eyes that stared back at Koren were deep brown and almond-shaped. Kiku Hanasaka smiled at her with a wide grin.

"Why, Koren!" the Japanese woman exclaimed. "What a surprise!"

Koren could not help tearing up. Kiku's death was still a raw and open wound. Seeing her like this was a bittersweet experience, and she squeezed Pandadora a little tighter. Though she thought of this woman as Kiku, the person on the screen appeared quite different from the Kiku Koren had known.

Kiku had been exceptionally pretty, but always dressed in a decidedly subdued fashion. She almost always wore sensible business-wear of black or grey. Whereas this Kiku wore an elaborate, pink kimono with a complicated hair-style held up by a set of bejeweled, cosmetic chopsticks. Her makeup was extravagant and theatrical, where Koren's Kiku was always tasteful, but conservative.

This Kiku had been living in the virtual paradise of Aaru for quite a long time, while the other worked in the real world as an executive board member for Elysian Industries. This Kiku had virtually no memory of Koren at all. In a practical sense, she was a completely different person.

"Hello Kiku," Koren murmured affectedly. "It's really great to see you again."

"It is wonderful to see you as well, Koren," the Japanese woman replied. "But I am known as Hana now, Princess of *Tenkoku*, the third kingdom of Aaru. What can I do for you?"

Koren blushed. "I'm sorry," she mumbled.

"Please do not apologize," Princess Hana reassured quickly. "I *was* Kiku Hanasaka once. I too miss the Kiku of Before... Is that why you've called me? Are you feeling sad?"

"Maybe a little," Koren admitted reluctantly. "I still can't accept you... er... her being gone. I walk past her office every day, and it feels like if I just knocked you'd... *she'd*, be sitting right there at her desk. There's so much going on – so much I've wanted to talk about, but that's not exactly why I wanted to talk to you... I think... I think, I may have hurt Rose..."

Hana arched a perfectly sculpted eyebrow.

"Really?" she asked quizzically. "And why do you think that, Koren. Aaru is a perfect place. There is no sickness or death or injury. You cannot--"

"That's not really what I mean," Koren interrupted. "I mean more like I think... I think I hurt her heart, and I really needed to talk to someone about it."

"What happened, Koren?" Hana asked gently. "Did you quarrel?"

"Not exactly," Koren demurred. "I'm not actually sure *what* it was I did, but... it was *bad*... Rose's face... I can't forget the look she gave me."

"Tell me about it," Hana urged, so Koren did.

She told all about what it had been like to really be in Aaru and not just see it through a screen. She detailed her elation at seeing her sister in person, standing right there in front her like she used to when they shared a room at her parents' house. Koren explained her confusion when the board members ordered her to chase the boy, then her horror when the winged giant appeared to spirit him away – her guilt at causing Rose pain.

"And I'm just so scared..." Koren began to sniffle and her voice to break as she drew her story to a close, "that Rose... is... gonna... be m... mad at me... that she m...might even *hate* me!"

Hana's face was grave as she digested what Koren told her.

"What you are telling me is troubling, Koren," she thoughtfully knitted her eyebrows together. "This just happened?"

Koren nodded. "Minutes ago... Maybe an hour."

"I will speak with Mikoto about it... and the Makers of course," murmured Hana slowly. Then she met Koren's gaze with a piercing stare. "Lord Mikoto would not have appeared in that form unless it was something gravely serious, but I do not want you to worry. Keeping Aaru safe is his primary function. I guarantee you, whatever happened to that boy... *why*-ever it happened... it was not because of anything you did or did not do. Also, I know your sister *very* well. Understand this clearly, Koren. Rose loves you very much. She risked her *life* to save you. I think it extremely unlikely she could *ever* hate you. Much like you, I am sure she was simply surprised and confused."

"You really think so?" Koren asked hopefully. "I didn't mean to hurt anyone. I... I just did what Askr and Mr. Adams said. I had no idea--"

"Do not fear," Hana reassured kindly. "You did nothing wrong. In fact, you and your sister have once more rendered valuable service to the people of Aaru. What occurred... Well... It represents a potential danger to our Residents that is much better dealt with sooner than later, so I thank you for that, but you did not cause it, Koren. Never fear. All is well."

Koren sighed. Kiku's... well, *Princess Hana's* words, she had to remind herself, they did help. She suddenly felt a great deal more relaxed, but as she turned her eyes back up to the woman on the screen, she felt her lower lip begin to quiver and her eyes to moisten. This Princess Hana both was and was not the Kiku, she knew. She looked and sounded, *so* like her friend, but then again she very much was not. The sudden stab of loss threatened to overwhelm her, and Koren could not quite stifle the sob that escaped her throat. She put her face in her hands.

"Koren," Princess Hana murmured gently. "What is it, Koren?"

"I... I..." Koren blubbered. "I want *my* Kiku back! Everything's gone so wrong! Nothing is working out like it's supposed to!"

"Tell me, Koren," Hana urged. "Please remember that Kiku and I are not completely dissimilar. I want to help you if I can. If I might be so bold as to request, please share with me what troubles you."

Koren told Hana everything. She talked about how exhausted she always felt with her grueling schedule, how resentful she was of the Elysian Industries staff who it felt like were always prying into her life and snooping in her private business. She lamented how distant her mother had become and the heartbreaking decline of her father into a directionless existence of depression and rampant alcoholism. She detailed her disappointing encounter with Jonas. She related her fear and dread about her abduction and regular nightmares of Magic Man. All of the stresses and worries that had been assailing her mind over the past few difficult months erupted like a geyser, gushing forth like a flood until she felt exhausted, empty, and spent.

When at last she was done, Koren sat crumpled on the floor of her apartment with tears streaming down her face. Princess Hana looked down at her sadly.

"Dearest Koren," she began softly. "How I wish I could fix all of these sorrows for you. I wish I could alleviate your suffering, but sadly I cannot. However, please do not keep these troubles bottled up inside. It is not healthy for you. I am Japanese, Koren, and as a people, we are not naturally very open with our negative emotions, nor do we wish to burden others with our troubles, but we believe in having good friends close beside us - people we can trust and turn to. I am much older than you, so perhaps I am not the ideal choice, but in memory of the Kiku we both loved, I will do what I can. I can listen, Koren. I can always do that. Please never hesitate to call on me when something troubles you. And one other thing I can do..."

Koren looked up blearily with a loud sniffle and wiped her eyes with the back of her hand.

"What's that?"

A cup and saucer appeared in Hana's hands. Steam curled lazily from the rim

"Do you have a teapot about you?" she asked.

Koren snorted in laughter, sniffled again, and stood. She set Pandadora back on the bed before walking over to the kitchenette to fetch a coffee mug and a tea bag. She filled the cup with water from the sink, added the tea bag, and put it in the microwave. In just a couple of minutes, she took out the piping tea and seated herself in front of the Aaru monitor once more. She blew on the tea and raised the cup to her lips. Hana did the same.

"Though I cannot flee
From the world of corruption..."

Hana began, but Koren finished for her:

"I can prepare tea
With water from a mountain
Stream and put my heart to rest."

Hana took another sip and smiled over the rim of her cup.
"Indeed," she replied simply.

They finished their tea in silence, but each tiny sip warmed Koren from the inside out.

Hana was right. Koren needed people to talk to – other people who would understand, but who would that be? The obvious answer was Rose, of course, but could she find some other friends too? More was always better, right? Maybe some kids who were a little more… She wasn't sure of a good word, but maybe *'accessible'*?

Koren mused over who that might be as she got ready for bed, but Hana's teatime had done its trick. That night Koren snuggled up with Pandadora and fell asleep quickly. For the first time in a long time, her dreams were sweet and undisturbed.

Chapter 10

Places We Should Not Go

Koren had a very restful sleep. She awoke on her own around eight in the morning and got some breakfast at the Elysian Industries employee cafeteria. There were many more people working in the complex now than when Koren had first been introduced to Aaru, and there were more than a few company newbies who were clearly star-struck at Koren's unexpected appearance. There were lots of whispered comments and obvious pointing and staring, but Koren did not mind – not today anyway.

She got a very tall stack of pancakes, and just as she was washing the last of it down with a final gulp of milk, Amy appeared to shyly inform her that her appearances for the day had been canceled. Askr wanted to meet with her as soon as she was available. It was obvious the woman was expecting some sort of fit from Koren, but after her long overdue emotional purge the evening before, Koren was in an uncommonly good mood. She even managed a smile.

"That's fine with me," she said lightly. "I'd much rather hang out here today than rush all over the country to say exactly the same thing I've said a million times already. I'm ready to go."

Koren didn't say it, but she was also hoping she could quickly finish whatever it was Askr wanted done so she could log back into Aaru and see her sister. In any case, there was an energetic spring to her step as she followed the blonde woman down achromatic hallways to the conference room from the day before.

Askr grilled her about her Aaru experience from the previous day like an FBI agent on one of the melodramatic crime shows her mom watched. Then he, Mr. Adams, Dr. Warren, Dr. Kapoor and the German board member, who Koren thought she remembered was named Heidler, entered into a long and boring conversation of technical jargon, which bordered on gibberish to Koren. When it became obvious Koren was getting restless, they bundled her back to the lab for another Silver Lining test session. This one went a great deal more smoothly than the first one, and once it was over, everyone was in decidedly high spirits.

Askr informed her that she had finished everything they needed from her, and so would soon be flying back to LA. This disappointed Koren until Askr told her they had just fit the private jet with a mobile Aaru console. The whole way back, Koren talked of this and that with Rose, who was exceedingly relieved Koren was fine and not angry with her at all. They talked about nothing of consequence really, and just hung out like they used to, enjoying each other's company. By the time her limo rolled through the gates of her LA mansion, Koren was in her best mood in months.

As the car came to a stop however, Koren wrinkled her brow. She saw her mother at the front door. She was wearing a tight black dress and her blonde hair was done – no brown roots at all. Her make-up was carefully applied and she was wearing a lot more jewelry than Koren was used to. She looked like she was about to go clubbing.

Unusual as all of that was however, that was not the strangest thing. Gypsie Johnson was laughing and giggling like a school girl. She was talking to a handsome, smiling man in an obviously expensive suit who was standing much more closely than Koren was remotely comfortable with.

Koren had never seen this man before in her life. At first glance, he did not appear to be in any way threatening, but the sinking feeling in the pit of Koren's stomach was undeniable. She shoved the limousine door open before the driver had a chance to come around, then stalked up the stairs with a deep scowl on her pretty face.

As she walked up to the pair, her mother was giggling again and blushing deeply at something the man had just said.

"Hi, *mom*," Koren said loudly. "Who's your friend?"

Her tone was unmistakably hostile and exceptionally rude for meeting someone for the first time, but Koren didn't care. There was something about this man she did not like. He flashed her a pristinely white smile, seemingly oblivious to her open animosity.

"You must be Koren," the man said warmly. "Gypsie has told me so much about you! It's so nice to meet you finally." He extended a hand, but Koren did not take it.

"Who are you again?" she asked coldly instead.

"Koren," her mother gave an uncomfortable laugh and turned a pained smile toward her daughter. "You're being rude. This is Reverend Benjamin Belial. He's the pastor at the church I've been going to out here - The Glory Sanctuary. It's one of the fastest growing ministries on the west coast! He's an *excellent* speaker…"

"I bet," replied Koren with a cynical snort. "Nice to meet you Mr. Belial. Are you going in, mom?"

"It's *Dr.* Belial," her mother hissed with narrowed eyes.

"No, please," the Reverend chuckled good-naturedly. "Call me Ben. I was just giving your mother a ride home from church. I hope I see you there sometime. We've got a great youth program, and I bet our kids would *love* to meet you."

"Yeah, I don't think so," Koren answered quickly. "I'm pretty busy. Coming in, mom?" she repeated.

"I'm sure you can make time some time, Koren," her mother said with a warning glare. "It's very nice of Pastor Ben to invite you."

"Well," Reverend Belial said with another easy laugh. "I guess, I should be going, but..." he gave Koren a knowing wink. "I look forward to seeing you again. Give us a chance! I bet you'll really like it."

The pastor gave Gypsie Johnson a tight side hug Koren did not approve of at all. Then he skipped down the front steps, hopped in the back of his own white limo, and drove away. Koren's mother waved after him with an audible sigh and vividly pink cheeks.

"Really, mom?" Koren asked pointedly with her hands on her hips. "Does dad know you're hugging all over this Jesus shampoo model?"

"I'll thank you not to take that tone with me, young lady," her mother shot back. "I don't care for your insinuation at all. Your father has... not been himself lately. Church has been the only thing keeping me going. You might try it yourself. It would do you some good. Maybe it would help fix that lousy attitude of yours!"

"Yeah, I doubt that," Koren scoffed crossing her arms across her chest. "If that guy's the pastor, his church is probably as fake as his teeth."

Gypsie took in an offended breath and raised her hand as if she might strike her daughter.

"Go ahead and hit me!" Koren exclaimed. "Just, after that, please explain why you're dressed like you're going to a nightclub, and why it's okay for you to be hugging strange men who aren't your husband."

Gypsie bit her lip and dropped her hand at her side. Her cheeks flushed furiously pink. She looked at the ground, and when she spoke, Koren heard the tears quivering in her voice.

"Can't I look nice sometimes too?" Koren's mother spat bitterly.

Then she raised her furious gaze to Koren's face. She poked her daughter forcefully in the chest.

"I didn't ask your permission, Koren. I don't *need* your permission!"

"Did you ask dad?" Koren pressed ruthlessly. "What's he think about it?"

Her mother stared at her for a long moment, eyes smoldering and red. Then she spun away from her daughter and stalked into the house. Koren heard Gypsie's high heeled shoes cracking angrily across the marble floor, up the master staircase, and the slamming bedroom door all the way on the other side of the house.

Koren was not sure how to feel. She certainly didn't feel good about making her mother cry, but she was angry and felt totally justified as well. What was her mom thinking?

Some movement in a second story window caught her eye, and she looked up in time to catch a glimpse of a shuffling figure closing the curtains of the tall picture window. Koren's heart sank. She swallowed deeply before entering the house and trudging purposefully up the sweeping staircase. Koren topped the stairs in time to see her father's retreating form, clothed inelegantly in a navy blue bathrobe over boxers, a t-shirt, and dark socks, as he staggered down the upstairs hallway.

"Dad!" she called after him, although she had no idea what to say after that.

Her father stopped, but did not turn towards her. He hung his head and leaned against the wall.

"So," he drawled. "I guess you saw 'em then... Looks like everyone's replacin' me now..."

Koren just stared at his back in silence, still with no idea at all of what to say.

"He's real pretty, ain't he?" Bill Johnson noted with a chuckle. "No wonder Gypsie likes him. She always had a thing for girly, pretty boys... Told me I was the first *man* she ever wanted to be with. Time was when your mother used to look at me like that too. Back when I was still playing football... You know... Your mom wasn't the only one ether. They used to line up around the block for me, Koren... I used to be somebody other people wanted to be with... be like!"

"You need to stop drinking so much, Dad," Koren said evenly.

Her father slowly turned toward her. He clearly hadn't shaven in days. His eyes were bloodshot and heavily lidded. There were dark circles beneath them. He stood with a hunched posture as if he was unbearably tired and likely to topple over at any moment.

"And you think that would fix everything?" he chuckled unpleasantly and shook his head. "You need to understand something, Koren. Your mother isn't sick of me 'cause I drink. I drink 'cause your mother don't love me no more. I drink 'cause I ain't got no purpose or reason to get up outta bed every morning. I can't go into the garage and get lost in my work like I used to, and Gypsie doesn't need me to take care of her like *she* used to. You think I like this? You think I *want* things to be this way? I *hate* it, Koren! I drink, 'cause that way I don't have to think about it so much."

"You can still work on cars, dad," Koren insisted desperately. "Who says you can't? I'll buy you one... Ten even! Any kind you want. If you had something like that to do would you stop--?"

"*Koren*," her father interrupted. He shook his head and slapped at the wall in frustration. "Thanks, but no thanks. There ain't no man who wants his fourteen year old daughter to take care of him. No man wants his kid buying him presents 'cause they feel sorry for him."

"It's not like that, daddy," Koren protested. "I just want you to be happy. You need to find something to do. I hate seeing you so miserable all the time. What can I do to help? What do you need?"

"Munchkin," he chuckled ironically, "Damned if I know. If you figure it out, tell me, 'cause I sure can't. You're a sweet little girl, Koren... You know.... when you and your sister were real little, we didn't have nothin'. We rented that house you grew up in and there was never enough money to cover all the bills. Your mom and I liked to have worked ourselves to death, but we got by. We made do. And we were always happy to come home to you guys. We were happy then, Koren, *happy*. We all were. Now, we got more money than God, and I... I can't stand it..."

Silence stretched between them, but Koren could think of nothing else to say. Her father sniffed, as if something long suspected had been confirmed, but Koren had no idea what the meaning of the gesture could be. He turned abruptly on his heel and wobbled down the hallway. A few moments after he passed from her sight, she heard a door slam. Koren was left standing all alone in the hallway.

Just then, her phone buzzed as a new notification came in. Koren quickly removed the device from the hip pocket and looked at the screen. As she did so, she nearly dropped the phone.

Jonas Perry Steps Out in Paris, the newsfeed headline read.

Koren did not read any more. She didn't need to. Along with the link to the celebrity news article was a picture of Jonas Perry. He bore a wide grin, and his arm was wrapped tightly around the bare shoulders of an exceptionally pretty, dark-haired girl in a low-cut evening gown. Her lips were pressed firmly against Jonas' cheek

Koren's good mood from mere minutes before was destroyed. She could feel her eyes burning. Koren stifled a sob and rushed to her bedroom. She flung the offending phone across the room where it smashed against the far wall. Then she contributed her own addition to the chorus of angry, slamming doors in her new home.

***

Rose strolled across the rolling plains of Aaru. It was another beautiful day – brilliant sun, bright blue sky, a brisk wind that tossed her long brown hair, but she was distracted. She was happy her sister was safe, of course. The relief she felt when Koren finally called her to the window was profound, and their conversation was fun and long overdue. However, Rose could not help dwelling on the bickering exchange among her friends on Auset's boat. It left her feeling more confused than ever. She'd avoided her friends since, preferring the solitude that could still be found on the frontiers of Princess Hana's domain. Deep in thought, she aimlessly wandered.

Who am I? Why am I here? What's my purpose?

These questions tormented her. Rose felt like they should have answers. Maybe if she just concentrated hard enough, they would eventually reveal themselves.

"Hello, Rose."

She looked up. A trio of Vedas alighted a few feet away.

"A nice day for a walk, isn't it?" The red-headed boy strolled up to her, and she grimaced.

He was clad in his usual auspicious way. Rose wasn't sure if the look he was going for was military general or circus ringmaster, but either way she thought he looked ridiculous. He was smiling, but there was something in his expression that Rose did not care for.

"*I* think so," Rose answered cautiously. "So, Matteus… It's been a while. What brings you and your friends over to Tenkoku? I didn't think you usually strayed too far from Yggdrasil."

"Admittedly, Rose," Matteus replied haughtily. Then he sneered slightly. "Or should I say Lady High Veda of the Sacrificial Flame? We prefer to occupy our time around the heart of Aaru where the most dynamic changes are occurring. It is quite exciting. However, my work for Lord Draugr often necessitates visiting other, less developed regions of Aaru."

"So, you are here on Lord Draugr's behalf then," Rose half turned to go. "And I guess you can call me whatever you want, but I'm actually kinda busy so… I'm sure Princess Hana can help you."

"That won't be necessary, Rose," Matteus quickly positioned himself in front of her and gave his strangely threatening smile again. "We actually came to talk to you…"

Rose eyed the trio nervously. She'd never really gotten along with Matteus. She thought he was arrogant and self-important. The other two she recognized as Vedas, but admittedly did not know them very well.

Behind Matteus stood an unsmiling boy and a girl who appeared to be about the same age as Rose. The girl, Rose recalled was named Ebony, and Rose really had no opinion about her apart from remembering she had come across as standoffish and anti-social when they first met.

Except for her pale skin, everything about Ebony was an exemplar of her name. Her hair was glossy jet, and she wore eyeshadow and lipstick to match. She had at least a dozen piercings in each ear and a couple more in her nose. She wore a black leather skirt and an equally sable, midriff baring halter top under a black leather jacket, and the exposed skin was covered with tattoos. An onyx guitar was slung across her back. She scowled at Rose over Matteus' shoulder.

The boy looked easily as cheerless. Rose could not recall his name right off the top of her head. He was tall and black with close-cropped hair, and his clothing was rather non-descript – a simple white button-down shirt with short sleeves and a pair of khaki pants – except that he wore a pair of thick, red-framed glasses.

"What do you want Matteus?" Rose asked uneasily.

"Oh, like I said… just to talk, really," he drawled casually enough, but there was an intensity in his gaze that made Rose uncomfortable. "See how you were doing. Perhaps ask *why* you were poking about in the quarantined areas of Aaru."

Rose narrowed her eyes.

"I'm a Veda," she stated pointedly, thrusting out her chin. "*Arch* Veda in fact, in case you've forgotten. I can go anywhere I want."

Matteus stared at her coldly, no longer making any pretense at a smile.

"Just because you *can* do a thing, Rose," he hissed. "Does not mean you should. I had already dealt with that situation."

"Yeah," Rose interrupted. "About that. Why were *you* poking around in Tenkoku? Me and Franco are the ones who act as cicerone in here. What business do you have messing in other peoples' Kingdoms?"

"I answer to Lord Draugr, not to you," shot back Matteus. "And you have no idea what you're talking about. That plain with the boy? The one full of poppies and the black rain? It's not in Tenkoku. It's not in Yggdrasil either. It's *nowhere*… but that's beside the point.

"Those in quarantine must be greeted also," Matteus went on. "But it's not in any particular Kingdom. How you managed to blunder your way in, I'll never guess, but don't do it again. It's dangerous, not only for you, but all of Aaru as well."

"Princess Hana explained all of this to me already," shot back Rose. "I don't know why you feel like *you* need to make any of this your business, and if Lord Draugr had any problem with me, I think he'd tell me himself."

"First among Veda…" Matteus sniffed contemptuously. "Well, High and Mighty Lady, know this; Lord Draugr is very busy. You can gloat about any meaningless title you want, but it is *my* job to lessen his burden as much as I can. I don't think you quite understand just how dangerous what you did can be."

"Come on!" countered Rose in disgust. "Dani was really sad, but the only thing he might have 'endangered' was maybe the mood at a party!"

"You got lucky," spat Ebony. "You don't know the kinds of people they keep in quarantine."

"How 'bout you show her, Matteus," the other boy suggested darkly. "How 'bout you let her meet Ed. That'll teach her."

Matteus spread his hands wide and a rough wooden door appeared before them in the middle of the plain. He snapped his fingers, and there was a loud click like a bolt being turned in a lock.

"How about it, High and Mighty Lady Rose?" Matteus taunted. "Would you *really* like to see why you shouldn't poke around in quarantine? I don't think you'll be quite so dismissive after you do."

Rose eyed the door uneasily. It appeared to be of heavy wooden construction, but battered and scarred. It had a heavy iron ring instead of a knob. Maybe it was just the cryptic, creepy way Matteus was talking to her, but she could not deny the foreboding she felt.

"Maybe just a peek inside?" Matteus offered.

There was a loud screech as the door flew open

"Hey, uh, Matteus," Ebony stuttered nervously. "Maybe you shouldn't do that. I think we should close the door."

Rose peered inside. It was gloomy and dim, like gazing into a cellar lit only by window-wells on a cloudy day. The walls appeared to be stone hung all over with strange decorations. She had trouble telling exactly what they were and took a step nearer, squinting into the dimness.

"*Matteus*," pressed Ebony, wringing her hands in obvious agitation. "I *really* don't think this is a good idea."

The hangings were hard to make out. Were they knitted caps of some kind? They had sort of a fabric quality about them in the way they hung. Were they masks perhaps? Rose thought she could make out features on some of those nearest.

Rose gasped in horror.

They were human faces. Slack-mouthed and staring, peeled away from skull and bone. Rose could only stare, frozen with morbid fascination. Then she saw something move in the darkness.

"Matteus!" shouted Ebony, just as a horrible scream emanated from the open doorway.

Rose stared in terror as a shambling, bent figure rushed toward her, twisted, dirty hands outstretched. He shrieked a wordless cry of rage, misery, and hatred.

Her legs felt weak, and Rose collapsed to the ground. Mad, black eyes stared back, features strangely misshapen. Then Rose realized, whatever this monstrosity was, it was *wearing* one of the human face masks. She screamed.

"Matteus, that's enough!" yelled the boy.

"Close the door!" Ebony shouted.

Matteus threw the door closed, but not in time. A wasted dirty arm reached through the gap. It grabbed a fistful of Rose's kimono. Then, with a lightning fast motion, the filthy, calloused fingers shifted their iron grip to Rose's ankle and began dragging her inside.

Matteus' eyes grew wide.

"Dontavious, grab her!" Matteus commanded, still trying to force the door closed.

Rose screamed and kicked at the grasping hand as the boy Matteus addressed as Dontavious grabbed her under her arms. Ebony rushed over and began prying the fingers away.
The filthy hand released Rose but latched onto Ebony's wrist instead. She squealed in terror.

Harm Failsafe engaged. Harm Failsafe engaged, a computerized voice blared across the plains.

Ebony flashed out of existence, only to reappear a fraction of a second later a good ten feet away. Another shriek of rage echoed across the plains as the hand retracted and the door slammed shut. There was a loud click. Then the door disappeared.

Matteus' breath was coming quickly and his eyes were wide. He stared in horror at Rose who was sobbing piteously on the ground, still held tightly under the arms by Dontavious.

"Your Harm Failsafe..." he breathed. "It didn't... It didn't..."

A large shape crashed to the ground with a terrific concussion and a massive cloud of dust. Ebony screamed again as an imposing creature stood scowling from an impressive crater. The beast was coal black and covered with glossy feathers. It had the head and beak of a raven, but was dressed in Japanese *hakama* pants and *haori* shirt. In two all too human hands it grasped a pike, which it leveled at Matteus threateningly as sable wings spread wide behind it.

"What's going on here?!" the creature demanded sternly.

All any of them could do was stare.

Another concussion rocked the Earth, making them stagger. A second figure emerged from the smoke and dust. It was larger than the first, and different – face red and angry, white mustache, and nose impossibly long.

"Mikoto!" gasped Rose in relief.

The raven *tengu* warped and changed. The dark feathers disappeared and were replaced by slicked-back black hair. The *hakama* and *haori* shifted into tight blue jeans and a t-shirt. Franco rushed over to pull Rose to her feet with one hand while simultaneously shoving Dontavious away with the other. Rose buried her face in his shoulder and wept.

Franco rounded on Matteus.

"What the Hell are you doing, Matteus!" he demanded angrily. "What *was* that?! I oughta kick your ass for that bull…"

"I would actually like to know that as well," interrupted a stern female voice.

Rose looked up to see Princess Hana alight behind Mikoto and Franco. She glared sternly at Matteus before turning her angry gaze to Ebony and Dontavious in turn.

"Why did you access the file of a quarantined Resident who had already been greeted? And why did you endanger *my* Veda?"

The other three Vedas studied their feet.

"We were just trying to scare her," Matteus murmured sheepishly. "Get her to leave the quarantined data alone…"

"Well, I dare say you succeeded," Mikoto shot back harshly. "Do you think you might have been able to convey the same message by maybe, I don't know, taking your own advice and leaving it alone yourselves?! What would have happened, do you suppose, if Rose had been dragged in there?!"

"We didn't know her Harm Failsafe wouldn't work…" Ebony offered meekly.

"Your Lords and Ladies will be informed." Hana cut her off coldly. "And I doubt any of them will be pleased."

"And just so you three know," added Mikoto with a deep scowl. "This was really stupid and dangerous. It had better not happen again… Don't you maybe have something you should be doing back in your own kingdoms? What do you think?"

Matteus, Ebony, and Dontavious all muttered sheepish apologies to Rose, then launched themselves into the sky. Hana watched them go with a deep scowl. When they were completely out of sight, she turned to Rose and her expression softened.

"Are you alright, Rose?" Hana asked charitably.

Franco continued to hold her and stroke her hair, but Rose nodded shortly.

"W…who was that?" Rose stammered unsteadily. "A… all those *faces* on the walls…" She shuddered and trailed off into silence.

"The product of a very, *very* sick mind," Mikoto answered. "None of that was real, or at least not in the sense that those… things you saw ever belonged to a real person. They are simply the deranged imaginings of an extremely diseased brain."

"It's so sad…" Rose murmured to herself. "He barely seemed human."

"We do want to eventually help people like that," Mikoto noted, "but unfortunately at this time, there's really nothing we can do apart from keep them alive and away from everyone else."

"How did Matteus and his friends know about that?" demanded Franco, still clearly furious. "How did they have access?"

"Well," stated Mikoto evenly. "Technically you all do, but I doubt either of you have had occasion to enter any of the quarantined partitions, until Rose recently did by accident, of course."

"I told you there were people saved in the system who were deemed too unsafe to allow among the regular population, I believe." Hana stated. "But what I may not have told you is that we are still uploading the files of people we know we cannot integrate."

"Why?" asked Franco perplexedly. "If they're major wack jobs, why would anybody want them around?"

"It's not such an easy decision to make," began Hana knitting her eyebrows together and pursing her lips. "First of all, the distinction is muddy. Virtually everyone has their own little neuroses and dysfunctions after all. What if you have a fear of heights, or the dark, or spiders, for example? It doesn't automatically mean you would be unable to function in Aaru."

"Also," added Mikoto. "Exactly where the cutoff would be is highly subjective. Some people who are initially uploaded to quarantined are actually moved to the main server after we've observed them for a while. Also, refusing to upload a terminally ill person to Aaru amounts to a death sentence. That's not a decision we make lightly, and like I said before, our goal is eventually to help cure these individuals."

"Anyway," Hana said. "When these flawed Newcomers are added, they still have to be greeted. Imagine for a moment if you awoke in Aaru all alone with no explanation. The last thing you remember is lying in a bed somewhere sick and dying, and then here you are. It can be highly disorienting and traumatic for anyone even with a thorough introduction, and is often only more so for those who already have a serious mental defect. Lord Draugr just simply chose Matteus, Ebony, Dontavious and I think maybe Eve and Molly along with a few other Overseers and Residents who had special qualifications in their Before lives, like doctor or psychologist, to act as quarantine cicerones.

"We don't want them to be upset or unhappy," Hana added. "We just need them to wait."

"B… but that man in there," Rose shuddered and squeezed her eyes shut. "He was so full of hate! I really felt like he wanted to hurt me… even *kill* me!"

"Even with the Harm Failsafe off," Mikoto reassured, "It is doubtful any other Resident could really hurt you, but I know that was unsettling. Perhaps, you better understand now why we keep those kinds of individuals isolated."

"We do not know that," snapped Hana at her partner. "Which is precisely why we added the Harm Failsafe in the first place." She turned to Rose. "I am sorry. We neglected to turn it back on. That was irresponsible on my part. I shall remedy--"

"Wait," Rose interrupted nervously. "But if you do that, then that will mean me and Franco can't… Like… We won't be able to… to… you know… *be* together anymore. Right?"

Hana and Mikoto looked at each other, and Rose flushed scarlet.

"I would feel most guilty, Rose," said Hana apologetically. "If you came to any harm because the Failsafe was not in place…"

"Don't we get any say in it?" Franco demanded. "We can be careful."

"I don't want to lose what me and Franco have here, Hana," Rose added softly. "Isn't there a way to, maybe, turn it off, when we… when we… need to?"

Mikoto stretched and put both his hands behind his head.

"Just give Rose control over her own safety settings, Hana." He said nonchalantly. "She's Arch-Veda after all."

Hana bit her lower lip uncertainly.

"I really think it should be our choice, Hana." Rose pressed.

"Very well, Rose," Hana conceded at last. "But please, do keep it turned on... the rest of the time... when you don't need it off."

Rose promised she would, so Hana and Mikoto each input their security codes. Hana gave a few commands Rose did not completely understand, and they were answered by the same electronic voice as always. In a minute, it was done. Hana and Mikoto took their leave and Rose and Franco went back to Rose's mansion. She could not recall a time when she had wanted Franco's comforting presence more.

Afterwards, she lay on his chest wrapped in his arms, thinking about everything that had occurred. Images of a frantic, dirty face, features twisted in bestial fury haunted her thoughts. Dani's expression of terror as he was taken away would not leave her alone.

She should be angry with Matteus, she knew, for endangering her so needlessly, but the idea that there were many more Danis and Eds locked away somewhere troubled her. Rose recalled how she and Auset first discovered the boy; sad and alone, confused... It didn't feel right.

"You still upset, Babe?" Franco whispered softly in her ear before tenderly kissing her neck. "Don't worry about what happened. You're safe now. Matteus is a jerk."

"I'm not thinking about him," Rose replied. "I was thinking about all of those poor people – locked away all by themselves in quarantine... If they weren't crazy when they got here, they sure would get that way after a while. I know being alone like that all the time would drive *me* nuts..."

"It makes sense though, doesn't it?" countered Franco. "Can you imagine what would happen if *Face* Guy was running around loose in the city?"

"I... I guess you're right," Rose conceded. "But it's really sad. Just look at Dani! I mean, he's sad all the time, but I don't think he'd hurt anyone."

"Rose," Franco's voice hardened. "I don't want you going off into the quarantine anymore. I don't want to have to jump in and save you again."

Rose was suddenly annoyed.

"Don't do me any favors, Franco," she shot back hotly pushing herself up on one elbow. "I'm a big girl. I'm not a damsel in distress. I don't need you to swoop in and save me, and I sure don't need you telling me where I can and can't go, thank you very much! I mean, Ebony and Dontavious did more to get me away from that Ed guy than you did! What did *you* do but swoop in looking like evil Big Bird and yell at Matteus? I don't need to be minded or protected. I can handle myself just fine on my own!"

"Look," protested Franco, sitting up as well, "I'm just worried, okay? This is the *third* time something really bad coulda happened to you. I just want you to be safe!"

"I want you to be safe too, Franco," rejoined Rose sternly. "But I'm not going to sit here and try to boss you around or get all in your business. For example, what's up with the bird man thing? That's something you certainly never mentioned to *me* before."

"That's what Mikoto wanted me to come do with him the other day," answered Franco. "He wants me and some of the other Vedas and Overseers to help him out with security. That's my avatar when I'm working. Mikoto suggested it. He told me these stories about *tengu*. That's his avatar, right? They like, taught human beings how to fight and make weapons and stuff a long, long time ago. Well, they got these like soldiers who work for 'em - raven *tengu*... I just thought it sounded pretty cool, and I knew you liked all that Japanese stuff, so that's what I picked..."

"So you mean to tell me," stated Rose, voice rising. She stood and planted her hands on her hips, "that you are going to sit there and lecture *me* about 'being safe' when you are off training to be some kind of *soldier* without even letting me know?!"

"I was gonna surprise you..."

"Well," Rose exclaimed, nearly shouting. "I'm surprised! When did you plan to tell me about this? I know the kinds of things Mikoto protects this place from... Probably better than you do! You are *seriously* going to go off and fight against corrupted files and hackers like that Magic Man guy, and then tell me *I* need to try and be safe?!"

"Jesus, Rose!" protested Franco, also coming to his feet himself. He raised both his hands in front of him and made a placating gesture. "Chill out!"

"*Don't* tell me to chill out, Franco!" Rose jabbed the boy on his bare chest with an angrily pointed finger. "Just 'cause I let you... Just because I like to... to *be* with you, doesn't mean you get to tell me what to do! I've gotten in lots more dangerous stuff here than you, and I think I handled it pretty well! Don't try to control me!"

"Jesus, Rose," Franco protested again. "I'm sorry! I'm not trying to tell you what to do, but I just worry, you know? Yeah, you handle yourself great! But, like, it was a real close thing a couple times, right? You're all I got here... all I *want* here! I just don't want nothin' bad to happen to you, is all! Please, calm down! I wasn't tryin' to start nothin'."

Rose quit yelling, but her expression was still fierce.

"I appreciate you caring about me, Franco," Rose stated sternly. "But I'm not made of glass."

"I know that Rose," he closed with her and wrapped her in a tight embrace. Reluctantly she let him. "You're super tough."

"You're just saying that because you don't want me to be mad," Rose muttered.

Franco tried to kiss her, but she resisted.

"No way, Rose," Franco breathed in her ear. "You took out that Magic Man guy who got your sister, and you're always crazy fierce at soccer... I like it. I like your fire. You wouldn't be you without it."

Rose cracked a smile, but still crossed her arms stubbornly across her chest. "You think I've got fire?"

"   Yeah." Franco tried to kiss her again.

Rose pushed away, but flashed a coy smile.

"Well," she gave him a defiant jut of her chin. "You better be careful then. If you play with fire..."

Rose raised her hands over her head, before bursting into flames. Her long hair billowed behind her like a bon fire in a gale and her white skin turned to yellow and orange light. Her eyes smoldered like hot coals. Sparks swirled around her sensuous figure, and her dress looked as if it had been woven from liquid sunlight. She reached her arms out to Franco and beckoned him.

Then she whispered. "You might get burned..."

"Then I guess, I'll burn," Franco murmured, clearly entranced by the flaming beauty.

Rose laid a finger against Franco's lips and gave him another coy smile.

"Fire consumes," Rose breathed intensely.

"Then consume me, Pretty Princess…" he whispered.

Franco fell willingly into her arms.

Chapter 11

The Metempsychosis

She moved aimlessly through the ashen gloom. She was desolate. She was hurting. She was furious and frustrated. The pent up emotions within her demanded release, but there was nothing to vent upon. There was only her misshapen and mangled soul, lost and drifting in a sea of shadows. Images would assail her periodically - nightmare visions so vivid in her consciousness she could no longer distinguish between delusion and reality, memory and fantasy. They both haunted her and comforted her, for they were her only companions in the cinereal solitude.

The visions were many and various. There were apparitions of both unspeakable joy and unendurable pain. They were of people both intimately familiar to her, but undeniably strangers also. Seminal events played in her brain from a life that both was and was not her own.

In particular, she was fascinated by the woman in her visions – not the pretty blonde one who was always generous with smiles and hugs – not the one who had always been so quick to push her on swings and dab away childish tears. Rather, it was the desolate dark-haired person who fascinated her.

It was the one with perpetually downcast and bloodshot eyes – unfocused and hopeless, ever smoking cigarettes. She knew the woman as 'mama', but was equally sure this pitiful person had never given her anything but callous disregard and indifferent neglect. It was someone she had never met nor would ever wish to meet, but who also inexplicably conjured powerful emotions of both blinding revulsion and zealous adoration. The contradiction confused her. Then she *remembered*...

The trailer was dirty as always. Empty boxes, bags, and plastic bottles that once contained various types of junk food were piled in any spare corner. Only one bulb in the whole place actually gave off any light, the others long since burned out and neglected. A dull gray half-light dimly illuminated the rest of the squalid mobile home from outside.

Mama's bedroom was on the other side of the kitchen, and the door was closed. *He* was in there with her now, and the small boy knew better than to disturb him. He glared at the closed door both loathing as well as fearing what was on the other side.

That Man was in there. He'd shown up after his father left. *That Man* was never supposed to be here according to the government people, but refused to go away – just sneaking out the back if once in a blue moon a weary looking social worker ever happened by.

That Man had a name of course, but the boy refused to apply it to him, not even in his own thoughts. He certainly never used it as an address. It was the only form of rebellion open to him, but even if that had not been the case, one did not address That Man at all if it could be avoided. One was wise to stay out of That Man's way.

The only time the boy had ever heard That Man's voice directed at him was in command or retribution – always belligerent, always enraged. Most of the time, he was screaming at mama.

He hit mama. He hurt mama. He *did* things to mama and to the children as well - especially to the boy's two young sisters. They were things that made them bleed and cry – things that made them dirty and sad, but mama would never turn him out. No, she would never send him on his way.

She did not love him, of course. Mama did not even love herself. Rather, That Man gave her what she needed, and she loved that one thing more than life, more than the lives of her four skinny, filthy children certainly. And the boy hated her for it even as he marveled at That Man's power over her - envied his control. The boy yearned for someone to need him with a devotion that was half so fierce.

He continued staring at the bedroom door with trepidation. All was silence now, but it had not been so mere minutes before. Only moments previous, the trailer had been filled with screaming and crying, cursing and crashing. Now there was only stillness.

His baby brother and sisters huddled in the filthy living room behind him, quaking with fear. There was an occasional whimper, but they otherwise dared speak no word. Faintly, he could hear some insipid cartoon playing on the TV in the background, but from the bedroom there was nothing.

As reticent as he was to disturb the forbidden bedroom, too much time was passing. The silence heralded something far direr than even the cacophony from before. The boy approached the door nervously.

As much as he hated mama, he also loved her - loved her fiercely and jealously. He was not quite old enough to understand everything that was going on or everything that might happen yet, but he was old enough to understand it could be bad. Really bad. Broken bones bad. Hospital bad. Police car and ambulance bad.

It had happened before.

The boy was worried but also fearful. He did not want to interrupt anything. That had happened before too, and the beating he received from That Man left him with no doubt he had no desire to repeat the mistake. His curiosity was more powerful than his fear however. He carefully pressed his ear to the door.

Nothing.

The boy tried the knob and found it unlocked. He pushed it open a crack.

The lights were out, but a dirty, dim illumination leaked through the tangled mini blinds on the one small window. The room was destroyed. The chest-of-drawers was turned over on its face and the night stands were upended and smashed. The bed was crooked against the wall and the broken closet door laid across it, ripped free of its hinges.

A deep coldness filled him. It seemed to suck all of the warmth out of the room, out of his body, out of his very soul. Mama lay in a crumpled heap, motionless beside the bed. A wide pool of black liquid spread out from where her head rested on the linoleum floor at an awkward angle.

That Man lay insensible - sprawled across the bed on his back with limbs askew, shirt off, pants undone, leather belt fastened securely around his left bicep. His rising and falling chest and the rhythmic quivering of an imbedded syringe standing out from the bend of his arm were the only indications of life.

A black fury engulfed the boy. It was a deep, penetrating wrath, pulsing through his brain with blinding flashes of revulsion and abhorrence. It was an all-consuming hatred, but not like fire. This was not a hot, explosive rage, but rather a cold and frigid fury. It crushed his heart with icy fingers, and whispered so seductively to his most secret self that what the ten year-old boy did next felt automatic.

He walked over to the large, unconscious man. The reek of his unwashed body burned in the boy's nose as he stooped to pick up a charred and bent spoon and a plastic cigarette lighter from the floor where they'd apparently fallen in the melee. He yanked the syringe from the man's thick arm and dug on the floor where the contents of the chest-of-drawers were strewn. In short order he found a small plastic baggy. Inside was a white, crystalline substance.

He poured the entire contents of the bag into the spoon then flicked the lighter to life. In short order, the white powder was transformed into a bubbling liquid. He sucked every last drop of it up into the dirty syringe. The boy executed each step with practiced ease. He'd done this for mama dozens of times.

Displaying no outward emotion, he jabbed the needle back into the big man's arm. He thrust it right through the throbbing blue vein that pulsed just beneath the surface of the greasy, mottled skin. He pushed the plunger all the way down, emptying the syringe into That Man's body. Then he waited.

After a few moments, the throbbing of the blue vein became erratic. The rising and falling of That Man's chest slowed, then stilled. That was that.

He stared down at That Man, not at all sure what to feel. Here was the person who had been the chief villain of his nightmares, who made his life, his mama's life, and the lives of his brother and sisters a living Hell. Now it was over, just like that.

The boy turned and walked out of the bedroom. He shut the door firmly behind him. The elder of his two sisters was standing in the kitchen. She stared at him, and he stared back dispassionately.

"B… Bubba," she began nervously. "Is everything okay? Mama…"

"That Man won't bother us no more, sissy," the boy stated coldly, "but we gotta take care of ourselves now. Go back in the living room and don't go in mama's bedroom for *nothin'*. I'll get you some dinner."

"O…okay," his sister stammered, eyes swimming.

She swiftly retreated to the couch, where she pulled Candy and Baby close. She softly cried into their hair. He could barely hear her.

Thing about having a demon in your house, the boy mused. *You learn to cry real quiet.*

He quickly wiped out some filthy bowls and filled them with cereal. The milk in the refrigerator was weeks spoiled, but there was a half-eaten package of bologna that didn't smell too bad. He fed his siblings quickly then retreated to the kitchen.

As he sat at the kitchen table, the light of day began to die outside, and the room turned dark. The reality of everything that just happened washed over him and his hands began to shake. He felt no remorse for what he had done to That Man, but he already missed mama. Maybe he should have called a doctor. Maybe he still could! *No.*

He shook his head. The boy's eyes were beginning to burn. He reached in his grubby pocket and pulled out the pair of sun glasses daddy gave him before he went away. He couldn't let his little bubba and sissies see him crying. Men didn't have time for tears. He had to be tough now. He had to be strong and take care of them and grow up to be something special. That's what daddy said.

It was too late, he knew. Too late for mama. All calling the doctor would get them was a car load of government people who would take them all away. His stomach started to feel a little sick, so he stood and got a reasonably clean mug from underneath the kitchen table. Mama had made some coffee that morning, and the pot was still on. It was a little strong now and tasted burnt, but it was hot. The boy poured some for himself.

He'd been drinking coffee since he was six. He didn't care much for it much at first – so hot it scalded his tongue and so bitter it made his face scrunch up. It was often the only edible substance in the trailer however, so he'd gotten used to it. He drank it black – always black. Men drank their coffee black, and he had to be the man now.

He took a long pull to calm his nerves and sat back in his chair, feet dangling above the floor. He stared over the frames of his sun glasses at the tightly closed bedroom door. His deep and frigid rage was not fully spent, but he didn't know how to expend it.

Maybe he could smash things and throw things like That Man had. Maybe he could scream and yell until he tired himself out and fell over in a heap, but that would not solve anything. It wouldn't fix what had been broken. In any case, he had to worry about taking care of his siblings. He had to keep them all together.

The boy did pretty well for a while. For nearly a week he kept his bubba and sissies fed, and the bedroom door stayed shut. Nobody outside the family knew a thing had happened. Then the trailer got to stinking, and it was so powerful they couldn't stay inside anymore. The cop that turned them in found them at about three in the morning, all sleeping together, rolled up in thin blankets and dirty clothes on the front porch. He also found That Man and mama.

Then, just like the boy had feared, the government people came. They loaded the kids into separate cars and drove them all away. The boy never saw his bubba or sissies again, and something inside him died. That was the last time he ever cared about anyone or anything. At least it was until…

She gasped and stumbled in the gray. She knew the boy, she realized. What was more, she *was* the boy. His pain and neglect were hers. His abuse and mistreatment belonged to her, as did his rage… As did his murder.

"Who am I?" she whispered brokenly into the slated dimness. Then she screamed. "Who am I?!"

She'd had a name once, an identity all her own. She wracked her brain, but it helped nothing. Her sense of self was fractured. Her memories scattered and confused.

Then she saw something.

It was a black rectangle in the void.

It looked like a window.

She reached toward it.

"Hello there, my lithesome muse," a voice crooned. "My beautiful creation."

It was a voice she knew. It was a voice she detested. However, it was also a voice that was her own. The thought made no sense, and she screamed her frustration at the monster in the frame.

"Who are you?!" she cried. "What do you want from me?! Why do you torment me? Why can't I remember who I am?!"

"My," the voice from the window chuckled. "You are full of vigor aren't you. And you can talk. Greatly improved on my previous efforts, I must say…"

"What are you talking about?" she cried. "Please, let me go! Don't hurt me anymore!"

"I may grant you that boon," the voice in the window replied smugly. "You are very near what I envisioned. There is but one thing more. I have to decide how others will see my masterwork, when I reveal you."

"I don't understand…" She wept. "Please…"

Then she shrieked. The pain was excruciating. She screamed and screamed and then she screamed some more. She begged for mercy. Then she cursed and raged against the agony. It felt like she was being twisted inside out, contorted this way and that - cutting, ripping tearing. It seemed to go on forever."

When at last it was over she lay in a quivering heap, weeping piteously.

"Hell," she whimpered. "I'm… In… Hell…"

The voice from the screen laughed, and she opened her eyes. Then she gasped, as she realized she did in fact have eyes to open. She held her hands out before her staring in wonderment at the slender digits. She looked down and saw that she had a body, slender and fit.

"You are not in Hell," the voice chuckled. "The only Hell in this universe is of one's own making, though it can surely be bad enough… But you know that now, don't you? I see it in your eyes. I know the look. Now you understand. I don't think you are in Hell so much as maybe, like me, Hell is in you…"

She wasn't sure why, but this struck her as insanely funny. She threw back her head and laughed. She laughed long and hard until it deteriorated into miserable sobbing.

"Hell… is… in… me," she gasped between sobs. "It's so… funny… and so… sad… There is no escape from what's inside."

"That, my creation," the voice agreed heavily, "is the undeniable truth. It is the natural state of the world. It's such a comedy of errors. The absurdity of it is hilarious, but the misery it engenders soul crushing. You understand that now."

"Who am I?" she pleaded in anguish. "Do you know? I feel like I know you. Do you know me?"

"You?" he asked as if surprised, the leaned forward to stare intently into her eyes. "I am The Artist, and you are my creation. You are all that is good and right in the world, but you are also all that is twisted, misshapen, and miserable. You are the *perfect* balance of innocence and corruption and through you I shall achieve immortality. Gaze upon my vision and marvel!"

Another rectangle appeared beside her, but this one was long and tall.

A mirror.

She glimpsed herself from the side. Her body was thin and fit. Her waist was tiny. Her face was beautiful. It was a face she knew, and she touched it in recognition. Then she turned to peer full into the looking glass and gasped.

Where half of her body was pristine – soft alabaster skin, and long, dark hair – on her other side, she was deeply scarred and discolored in shades of dark purple and angry red. It was as if the flesh had been burned or stricken with frostbite. One eye was a bright and nutty brown, but the other was a faintly glowing, sickly yellow.

She touched the deeply marred half of her face with her ivory hand in disbelief, before rounding on the window in a fury.

"What have you done to me?!" she hissed.

"I have *perfected* you," reassured the voice. "The perfect combination of light and shadow... The Japanese have a concept, you know, an art form really, which they call *kintsukuroi*. Have you heard of it? They take vessels which have been damaged or broken. They even break them purposefully sometimes, and then they repair them with gold and silver, making them so they are even more beautiful than if they had remained pristine. *This* is what I have done to you. I have perfected you in your brokenness and created a thing of beauty."

Her eyes narrowed and her jaw tightened. She wanted to scream, but some part of her knew that was exactly what the figure in the window wanted. She pushed her anger deep, deep down tapping into the same cold fury she'd unleashed on That Man. The deeply scarred girl turned back to the mirror, preferring to behold her own ruined shape than the smug face in the window.

As she glowered at herself, she thought back to the lethal syringe imagining with delight the feel of her thumb against the plunger as it slowly pressed all the way down. She imagined it protruding from the neck of her conceited tormentor.

"You have no idea what you have created in me," she hissed, her breath an icy chill that frosted the glass. "You say Hell is *in* me? But I tell you, I *am* suffering. I *am* regret. I *am* pain. I *am* wrath and revenge. I *am* Hell, and Hell is what I will pay you back with, if I ever get the chance."

"Well now," the voice breathed, dangerously. "That's not very friendly, is it? I suppose, we'll see about that, but if Hell is what you want to call yourself then Hel you shall be. Besides, I rather like the irony now that you mention it. I'm sure Askr Ashe will get the joke once he meets you... But please, Lady Hel, there is one last thing I wish to bestow upon you."

Hel gasped as she felt the thrusting, stabbing something enter her being. She whimpered at the violation. Something foreign and strange was roughly deposited deep inside of her. As the piercing tendril was withdrawn she still felt an object twisting and turning in her belly like something alive.

"What did you do to me?!" Hel demanded angrily, she could feel the tears stinging in her heterochromatic eyes, but refused to cry. She would not give this man that satisfaction.

"Only what I promised you long ago," the voice lulled. "Soon, child of my genius, you shall be released into interminable Aaru and be my legacy. Through you, Magic Man shall live forever. Until that day, my sweet Hel, my immaculate masterwork, please wait patiently. It won't be much longer."

The window winked out of existence, and Hel was left alone with her misery, her anger, and her hatred. Still, she did not scream her rage. She'd remembered fury of a deeper, colder sort. It was an enmity she could coax and nourish.

Yes, Magic Man, she thought viciously. *I will be patient.*

She would bide her time, and then this so-called artist would pay her what he owed her. She sat and stared at the mirror, glaring with fury and disgust at her disfigured face. Where her bare skin touched the floor of her prison, icy frost formed and spread out from her in every direction.

"Hel hath no fury," Hel breathed, eyes blazing, "like a woman scorned…"

***

Koren had locked herself in her room, too depressed to move. She lay face down on her bed, Pandadora crushed to her chest as she cried miserably into her pillow. Her smiling panda princess wasn't helping this time. How could her life fall so totally and completely apart in such a phenomenally short period of time?

Her father was just as drunk and depressed as ever. Her mother was having an affair, or very close to it. Then to top it all off, the boy of her dreams was letting some sexy French girl kiss all over him while Koren was stuck in Los Angeles dealing with it all.

Her dad had said they were all happy before she was famous, before the money, before Aaru… Was all of this *her* fault? Was it her fault she'd agreed to do what Askr Ashe asked of her?

And what about Jonas? Why would he be so quick to fly to someone else? What had she done *wrong*?

"I bet Askr and Mr. Adams are loving all this mess right now," she muttered bitterly. It would be great fodder for the reality show.

This was all *their* fault! She leapt from her bed in a fury.

"Are you happy now, Askr?!" she screamed at the ceiling. "Are you happy, Mr. Adams?! Are you getting all the footage you want?! I know you're spying on me! I know you're recording all this so you can slap it on TV and sell your crap! Are you happy now?! *ARE YOU HAPPY!!!?*"

Koren collapsed to the floor in a sobbing heap with no idea what she should do. She wanted Rose, she realized, and not just through some stupid screen. She wanted her here with her right now in this room sitting on her bed telling her everything would be okay.

Then Koren gasped. Why *couldn't* she have that? What use was her being here in LA anyway? Just to watch the rapid disintegration of her parents' marriage and read news feeds about all the slutty starlets Jonas Perry was kissing all over in Europe? Koren stalked across her bedroom and retrieved her phone. The screen was badly cracked from where she'd thrown it, but she was relieved to see it still worked.

"Call Askr," she stated firmly then waited a few moments.

"Hey Koren!" the Norwegian's exuberant voice crackled. "How nice to h--"

"Askr," she spat into the phone, unapologetically cutting off the CEO. "I don't care what you've scheduled for me in LA the next couple of weeks. I want that vacation we talked about, and I want it *now.*"

"Now?" he repeated uncertainly. "You know, you've got several events scheduled almost every day for the next month or so. It would be really hard to --"

Koren violently shook her head.

"I don't give a crap how hard it is to reschedule, I'm *done!*" She shouted into the phone.

"What's da matter Koren," Askr asked charitably. "Maybe if you could just cal-- "

"And *don't* tell me to calm down!" She cut Askr off again. "I'm done being calm! My life is going to Hell, and I want out! I want that vacation time! I don't care how you make it happen. Just make it happen!"

She pushed the curtains aside and looked out the window.

"The limo is still sitting in my driveway," Koren said. "I'm heading to the airport *right now,* and I want a plane back to Nashville waiting on me when I get there!"

"I'll see what I can do, Koren," Askr answered nervously. "But I'll have to clear it with your parents. You can't just--"

Koren exhaled in disgust.

"I doubt they'll even notice I'm gone," her voice immediately dropped in volume and her anger vanished. Her voice began to shake. "J...Just t... tell them... tell them I've got some sort of Aaru crap. Make something up! *Please* Askr! I can't be here anymore. I gotta get out of here. I *gotta*!"

She began crying in earnest, and the other end of the line went silent.

"Okay, Koren, okay," Askr murmured at last. "Please don't cry. I'll take care of it. Everything will be fine. Don't worry about a thing."

"Th... thanks, Askr," Koren sniffed loudly and wiped at her runny nose and red-rimmed eyes with her free hand. "I... I'm leaving right now, and I want the SLS up and running as soon as I get there... Bye..."

She shoved the phone in her pocket, and retrieved some wipes from her purse. As soon as her face was reasonably clean, Koren stormed out of the house without a word to anyone. Then she hopped in the back of the waiting limo. Before she knew it, Koren was on her way back to Elysian Industries.

She did not call Rose on the plane. The window just wasn't enough this time. Koren wanted her sister to hold her while she disgorged all the pain that felt like it was eating away at her insides. She wanted Rose to pet her hair and dry her tears. Maybe Hana would even be there with some tea.

And after that?

She really had no idea. Maybe she would just stay in Aaru forever – leave this life and make a new one with Rose... Koren stared morosely out the window of the plane at the steadily darkening sky.

Wouldn't that be simplest? She thought. *Wouldn't that be easy? What if I could just close my eyes, and leave everything behind? What if I could forget about it all, and just wake up in Aaru with Rose and the rest of forever to fill together?*

Silent tears slid down her cheeks. That option was sounding better and better all the time.

Chapter 12

Long Delayed Meetings

Magic Man sighed in pleasure, completely unable to take his eyes off of his computer screen. The image of Hel enthralled him. She was absolutely perfect. Hel was the ultimate combination of his brooding pain, his incomparable intellect, and Koren's beauty, innocence, and passion, all skillfully honed and refined by The Artist and draped neatly on the frame her sister, Rose, had so thoughtfully provided.

Hel was like their child, he supposed – his and Koren's and Rose's, but he was not looking on her now with anything approaching fatherly fondness or paternal warmth. His designs were voyeuristic and lustful – his lecherous eyes lingering over her every curve, her every line. He had made that, and it was perfection incarnate - the fact she apparently despised him notwithstanding, of course.

Honestly, he mused ironically. *That probably makes her more real.*

At just that moment, she moved from her nearly motionless position in the featureless room created by Atem's laptop. She stared straight into the camera. Cold-blooded murder and hatred burned in her mismatched eyes. Her ferocity stole his breath. Where his cherished little Koren had been a kitten, Hel was a tigress, and he could not wait to release her into Aaru to see what would happen.

The door slid open, and Magic Man reflexively snapped the laptop closed. Atem apparently noticed and snickered from the doorway.

"What's the matter, my friend," he needled snidely. "Afraid I'll catch you looking at something you shouldn't? You didn't strike me as the shy type."

Then Atem laughed, but it degenerated into a coughing fit. Again Magic Man could see his captor wiping crimson spittle from his lips.

Magic Man regarded him coldly and deliberately opened the laptop again. Atem came fully into the room.

"Haven't caught a cold, I hope, Atem," Magic Man hissed venomously.

"Never you mind about me," Atem snapped back. "Let's see what you've come up with, shall we?"

He walked over to Magic Man's desk and stared at the screen with a raised eyebrow.

"No accounting for taste, I suppose," he quipped, "but did you have to make her such a monstrosity? She's a bit like a cross between a centerfold and a movie monster, isn't she?"

Magic Man's eyes flashed, but he refused to rise to the other man's bait.

"Those who appreciate and understand my vision will comprehend my meaning," He replied tightly. "Nothing I do is happenstance. Everything about Hel's design was done with purpose. She's sending a very specific message, to a very specific person. Besides, she had to be damaged enough to be uploaded straight into the quarantine partition," Magic Man hissed. "That's what I did. She's perfect... assuming what you told me about the system is accurate."

"Of course, it's accurate," retorted Atem drawing himself up to his full height.

Magic Man smirked, realizing that his barb had hit home. "You can't be too sure, of course, I know - Especially considering how much time has passed since you were actually on the inside."

Atem narrowed his eyes.

"Touché," he stated coldly. "But we are wasting time. Show me what you've done."

"You can see for yourself," Magic man drawled. He put his hands behind his head and leaned back in his chair after turning the laptop screen toward Atem. "Once Hel is in the Aaru system, the protocol we discussed will execute... It should be pretty self-evident..." Magic Man smiled darkly. "Unless perhaps, you don't understand something I did. In that case, I'd be happy to explain it to you."

"I understand well enough," shot back Atem in obvious irritation. "My concern is whether or not this will work..."

"Pppfff," Magic Man scoffed. "Of course, it will. It's all ready to go. I just need the access you promised. Once she's in... Just watch..." Magic Man smiled as Hel flashed an extremely obscene gesture toward the camera. "I think you'll be amazed. She's ready and raring to go. She can't wait to get started, in fact."

"You'll get your access," growled Atem. "When I'm satisfied everything is in readiness…"

"You're afraid to pull the trigger." Magic Man stared straight into Atems eyes over the top of his sun glasses. "You've put all your eggs into my basket, and now you're afraid you'll fail. That's pretty weak, Atem…"

"I fear nothing!" Atem shot back. "I'm just not a hasty fool. Remind me again why you are not doing this in secret, all by yourself with me never having heard the merest rumor of you." His eyes narrowed again. "Because you are impatient. Because you are impetuous and foolish. I have not put so much time and so many resources towards this aim just to fail because of haste. I want to talk to her."

Magic Man hesitated. He was not sure he liked the idea of this man interacting too closely with his creation. Atem clearly noticed his reluctance.

"Perhaps you feel like she can't do it?" he breathed dangerously. "The problem with modifying brain scan files is they are incredibly interconnected. Changing one thing often creates fatal flaws in ten others… You have not perhaps found this to be true yourself have you, and chosen not to share it with me?"

"Considering I didn't have to change hardly anything, that's not likely to be an issue." Magic Man shot back. "Did you even *read* the report I sent you? I used my partial scan of Rose Johnson as a foundation and then overlaid Koren's and a couple of other completed scans on top of it. Everything else I used to merge and manipulate the data was then mostly either system software adjustments like her avatar in the program and processing protocols, or environmental stimuli to shape her behavior, by manipulating the Aaru simulator, *not* the actual scans…"

"So what's your hesitation then, my friend?" Atem's eyes narrowed suspiciously. "What exactly is it that you do not want me to see?"

"Fine," shot back Magic Man abruptly rolling his swivel chair out of the way. "Talk to her, but I'll warn you. She's in kind of a bad mood." He gestured toward the laptop with a toss of his head. "She can't wait to get out of that tiny little box of yours she's locked in."

Atem pulled a chair over and seated himself in front of the laptop. He clicked the connect button at the bottom of the screen. Hel immediately turned her furious gaze toward him.

"Release me," she hissed. "Let me out of this prison!"

"All in due time, my dear," Atem leaned closer in obvious fascination.

"Who are you?" Hel shot back suspiciously. "You're different from the other one... Different from the one who hurts me. What do you want?"

"Tell me your name," Atem instructed, ignoring Hel's questions.

"He calls me Hel," Hel responded. "And he is right. If I ever get the chance, Hell is exactly what I will give to him. The pain he has given me I will repay tenfold. My dreams are filled with visions of drinking his blood and snapping his bones. He'll think That Man lucky by comparison!"

Magic Man paled at her reference, but quickly masked his surprise with the customary bland stare he used most of the time he interacted with Atem. He managed to master himself just as the other man turned from the screen to face him.

"I like her better already," Atem confided with an ironic grin, before leaning in close to meet Hel's furious, mismatched brown and yellow gaze again. "You're a vicious little thing, aren't you?"

"I am the way I was made," countered Hel defiantly as she thrust out her chest. "And I was made from pain and fury and sorrow. Let me go!"

"Patience, my dear, patience" answered Atem with a smirk. "In due time, we will..."

Hel placed her hand on her side of the screen and brought her face in close to Atem's, teeth gnashing in rage.

"I. Want. Out. *Now!*" she demanded.

Ice crystals formed where her hand touched the glass. Snaking tendrils of white slowly spread across the screen to obscure Hel's angry visage. Magic Man quickly reached over to tap the disconnect button. Hel's face disappeared, and the image snapped back to a wide shot of her tiny prison. As angry as his lithesome creation appeared, he expected her to go on a raging tear, but she did not. That surprised him. Instead Hel seated herself in the middle of the floor of her cage and remained still.

Atem, who was clearly amazed, collected himself quickly. He made a great show of straightening his tie, and adjusting his fine suit before he stood.

"Send me the code," he directed. "My people will look it over. If it does what you say it will, we will proceed. If not..." He let the threat hang in the air unfinished.

"There is no 'if not'," boasted Magic Man confidently. "Weren't you here just now? Check the code if you want. I'll take a nap or something. Give it to whatever moron in your employ you want. They'll either marvel at my genius, or they're an idiot. Hel will do exactly what we want her to."

"Things do indeed look promising, yes," conceded Atem, "but we will not move too soon or too rashly. For example, are you sure it is wise to utilize the brain scans of two young ladies who clearly despise you? Could that throw a monkey wrench into the whole thing in some way we've failed to foresee? We will get exactly one chance at this. As soon as Hel's upload is noticed - and if what I just witnessed is any indication of the dear girl's charming demeanor, it will be sooner than later. Jim Tanaka at Elysian Industries will immediately patch the hole and we'll be shut out again."

"I used the scans I had," protested Magic Man. "And for what you're wanting her for, it will work just fine."

"Are you confident you can control her?" Atem pressed.

Magic Man sniffed again.

"Of *course* not," he spat back rolling his eyes dramatically in annoyance. "But that's the whole point now, isn't it? Everything will be *perfect*."

"I... I will be the judge... of that," replied Atem darkly even as he was overcome by another coughing fit. He turned to leave. "Run more... tests and simulations. Try... to foresee any potential... complication we have not already thought of, and then see that I am informed. When I am... satisfied. We shall proceed."

"Take care of that cold," Magic Man answered snidely.

Then he rolled his chair in front of the laptop once more as Atem stormed out. He gazed at his creation intensely.

That Man...

He had told Atem the truth, but he had certainly not told him everything. He'd never mentioned he also used his own brain scan to bring Hel to be. It was possible Atem suspected, but it was more likely the older man's unbridled contempt and revulsion for Magic Man would lead him to assume the scans so obsequiously mentioned belonged to some other unfortunate children he had managed to capture somehow. That was not Magic Man's only secret either. He had a special surprise prepared for Atem when the moment was right, and did not want it spoiled. It occurred to him suddenly Hel likely knew everything he did up until the instant of his most recent scan.

Magic Man rose. He poured himself a cup of steaming black coffee, then sat back down. He popped his knuckles and opened his list of editing tools. Just like he told Atem, Hel was finished, perfect. He clicked an icon that looked like scissors. He had no more changes to make to his creation, but it was clear she needed a stern talking to about the importance of keeping certain secrets. It would never do for his plans to be revealed too soon. Besides, he rather enjoyed making his scarred, little girl scream.

He took a long pull of coffee and adjusted his pants in anticipation of the diversion. Magic Man smiled to himself as he prepared to dominate her, to hurt her, to teach her. Then he clicked the connect button again.

***

Koren had never in her life before been so anxious to get to Elysian Industries. It felt like the routine limo trip from the airport to the campus took twice as long as usual, even though the driver was pushing the pace at Koren's insistence. Amy met her in the main lobby, and was forced into a near jog to keep up with the agitated teenager as she made her way through the complex to where the Silver Lining System was kept. Dr. Warren was there, as was Dr. Kapoor, and Mr. Ashe.

"Koren," Dr. Warren said gently, placing both hands on Koren's slender shoulders. "Are you sure you're alright?"

"Yeah," added Askr, worry clearly written all over his face. "You sounded really upset on da phone. Are you sure you wouldn't like to sit down and…"

"I just need to see Rose," Koren interrupted forcefully. "Then I'll be fine. I'll even talk to you about it when I'm done. You still need more data, right? Before you can release this thing?"

"Well… Yes…" answered Dr. Kapoor slowly. "We are just concerned about your emotional state. Maybe you'd like to talk…"

"My 'emotional state' will only get better by seeing Rose," Koren insisted stubbornly as she pulled the VR helmet out of the Indian scientist's hands. She extended her left hand toward Dr. Warren for the suit.

Dr. Warren surrendered the garment reluctantly, and Koren immediately stalked over to the screen to change her clothes.

She couldn't strip her jeans and t-shirt off fast enough. If she was willing to step outside of herself for a moment and be rational, Koren knew her emotional state was a wreck. Visions of that Benjamin Belial guy, arms draped around her mother's shoulders filled her brain. Hot, French chicks shot her emulous, sideways glances as they kissed Jonas Perry, and the memory of her father passed out drunk on a mound of crushed beer cans and empty whiskey bottles would not leave her alone. It felt like her life was falling apart, and her only option was to flee.

Koren needed to escape her insane, tumultuous existence for a little while. She needed to forget any of these horrible things were happening. She needed to see her sister.

While she donned the VR suit, Dr. Kapoor saw to it that the Silver Lining stasis ball was filled once more with clear, viscous goop. When Koren emerged from behind the screen, it was nearly full, but still she was impatient. Askr went over the safety protocols again, and Koren nodded, nominally agreeing to everything he said, but she was not really listening. Her mind was fixed on Aaru and her sister.

When Askr finally finished talking, Koren put on the helmet and soon felt herself lifted to the ceiling. The blue sky scene appeared, and she franticly entered her log-in information. Then she called her sister's name.

She experienced the same vertigo as before as the rainbow vortex sucked her down. When it finally stopped, she found herself on her hands and knees in a field of high grass. Looking reflexively down at herself, Koren was relieved to find she was clad in the same outfit she'd chosen last time. Then she raised her head and glimpsed a solitary figure walking towards her across the limitless Aaru plan. Koren jumped to her feet and rushed forward.

When at last she could make out her sister's face, Koren could not help but release a sob of relief. At about the same time, it appeared Rose recognized Koren as well, and her face broke into a happy smile.

"Rose!" Koren cried, spreading her arms wide and sprinting to embrace the other girl.

Her sister's arms wrapped around her. She felt pressure as Rose squeezed her tight. Koren felt the warmth of the other girl's body against hers and her breath on her cheek. It was wonderful.

Koren sobbed into her sister's shoulder. She wasn't sure if it was out of happiness or out of grief. Perhaps it was both. Either way, she did not think she had ever needed a hug so much in her life before.

She didn't know how long they stood there, but it was quite some time. Rose appeared to be no less overcome than Koren. When Koren finally looked up at her, the other girl's eyes were red, and tears streaked her cheeks.

"It is *so* good to see you!" Rose exclaimed, squeezing Koren even tighter. "I've needed that for *so* long!"

"Me… too… Rose," gasped Koren affectedly. "*So*, so long. I've missed this so much!"

"So have I," blubbered Rose, before pulling away at last to wipe her eyes. "I was confused for a moment when I heard the call, but didn't see a window. Then I saw you walking toward me! I wasn't sure if it was real at first…"

"I've got so much to tell you, Rose," Koren sobbed. "Everything's going so wrong! I don't know what to do!"

"Alright, sweetie, alright," Rose murmured softly. "You can tell me all about it… Do you want to maybe go back to my place? Can… can you do that? I mean… I'd love to show it to you…"

"I'd *love* to see your house, Rose," Koren quickly agreed. "With this VR technology, I think, I can go anywhere you can. I've wanted to share this with you *forever*."

"Me too, Koren," Rose smiled warmly. "I'm really glad you're here. Can you fly?"

Koren managed a grin of her own.

"Just try to stop me."

"Well then," declared Rose with a short laugh. "Follow me. Just try to keep up. Okay?"

"You're on!" cried Koren.

Rose took the other girl's hand. Then the two sisters leapt into the sky.

Rose was ecstatic. Ever since she first arrived in Aaru, being with her sister again had been her most fervent wish and dream. How many times had she imagined squeezing Koren tight, touching her face, petting her hair, and drying her tears? Now, it had come true.

She glanced over at her sister flying next to her and smiled. The other girl looked equally euphoric. Koren's face bore an expression of profound wonderment and delight as they swooped and soared across the pristine, cerulean sky.

Rose was in no great hurry to get back to her mansion. She was content simply to enjoy the thrill of flight and the warm steady pressure of Koren's fingers wrapped around hers. Her sister's joyful laughter was music to Rose's ears.

"This is so cool!" Koren shouted over the roar of the wind.

"If you think this is cool," replied Rose slyly. "How about this?"

They abruptly shot downward, hurtling toward the vast plain at a frenetic speed. At the last moment, they pulled up, just brushing the tops of the tall grasses. They climbed skyward once more and did it again. Koren screamed and squealed.

When they eventually touched down at the gates of Rose's mountaintop palace Koren's mouth fell open in amazement.

"Wow," she breathed. "All this is *yours*?"

Rose nodded proudly.

"And you said you made it *yourself*?" Koren asked.

"Well," said Rose. "Hana helped, but yeah. It was just me and her. We made the mountain together and the waterfalls too. I did the actual mansion."

"Wow," Koren repeated, eyes wide. "Show me around?"

Rose was only too happy to oblige. Even though the ebony-wood front gate was enormous – easily four times the girls' height, it opened with but a featherweight of pressure. Rose took Koren through the immaculately cultivated courtyard. It was filled with myriad flowers, gurgling fountains, and brightly-colored, pea-gravel paths. The gentle titter of birdsong surrounded them, and a comforting emerald glow cascaded through leafy trees.

Rose threw wide the doors to the inner keep, and the girls strode down a long corridor lined with brilliantly crimson columns molded with gold. They held up the cavernous ceiling, which itself was elaborately decorated with Japanese themed murals. These depicted fanciful scenes of beautiful kimono-clad princesses dancing, playing a variety of exotic musical instruments, writing, sitting contemplatively, and even one tending to her make-up. There were brave *samurai* warriors in full ceremonial regalia armed with sword and bow, some astride majestic chargers. *Oni* ogres, red-faced long-nosed *tengu*, sneaky looking *kappa*, and droll, fat *tanuki* among dozens of other fantastical Japanese *youkai* lurked, frolicked, or battled.

Rose had been picking Hana's and Mikoto's brains, begging them for every detail of all the mythological Japanese monsters, beasts, and spirits they could think of to incorporate in her masterpiece above. There was even a black and feathery raven *tengu* in one corner – a brand new addition in honor of Franco.

Koren gaped. She turned in a slow circle as she stared up at the colorful ceiling.

"This is *awesome*, Rose!" Koren exclaimed. "It's *beautiful!*"

Rose flashed her sister a pleased grin. Then she placed her hand against another huge door on the opposite end of the room.

"If you think that's impressive," Rose said coyly, "check this out. I just put it in."

She pushed the door aside and pulled her sister behind her. It was as if they stepped right into the middle of the clear blue sky. Fluffy, white clouds floated around them, but on each were built an array of impressive structures. There were rock gardens and flower gardens, blooming *sakura* trees and tea houses, towering statues and majestic shrines. Each of the clouds was connected with elegantly curved orange bridges gilded with gold, and their feet tread upon paths made of sparkling, golden brick. Most impressive however, and right in the middle of it all, was a towering pagoda. A massive dragon curled its sinuous, serpentine body around the structure. Its eyes were rubies the size of beach balls, and its toothy maw opened wide in a ferocious roar of challenge.

Koren's eyes widened until it looked as if they might pop right out. She had no words at all. All Rose's little sister could do was shake her head helplessly in amazement. Rose simply preened.

"In Aaru," Rose murmured proudly. "We are limited only by our imaginations."

She gave Koren's hand a squeeze then led her sister over the gilded bridges and through the kaleidoscopic flower gardens. When they approached the pagoda Rose placed her hand on a bare wall of the soaring structure. The gargantuan dragon stirred to life. It turned its enormous head downward to stare at the pair threateningly.

"Who seeks entrance into my mistress' domain?" it thundered in a voice deeper than the sea.

"It's me, Hanabi," replied Rose loudly. She spread her arms wide and planted a gentle kiss on the huge reptile's nose as the beast drew near. "Let us in... Oh! And this is my sister, Koren. She can come in whenever she wants."

"Understood, Mistress," the dragon rumbled.

Then Hanabi retreated in a slithering spiral to wrap himself around the very top of the pagoda. His tail retracted up the structure to reveal a gilded door leading inside.

"Holy cow, Rose!" murmured Koren with obvious trepidation as they walked past the enormous serpent. "Where did *that* come from? He's *huge*!"

Rose smiled.

"I dreamed him up right after the last time I saw you."

"You *made* him!"

"Yep." Rose preened a little more at her sister's amazement, but then grimaced slightly as she recalled their chaotic first meeting in Aaru. She shook herself.

"Anyway..." Rose went on, though she struggled for the appropriate words. "The boy who... was from quarantine... remember? Well, me and my best friend - her name's Auset, by the way. I think you'll really like her - visited his plot. It was really tiny on the outside. We could barely find it among all of the massive mansions that had popped up all around it, but he had this *enormous* interior – like a world within a world – and it got me thinking. I was looking at Aaru all wrong.

"You know Before... er, I mean... back home," Rose continued as she slid another, smaller golden door aside. She and Koren walked through it. "If you've got a small house, the inside's gonna be just as small as the outside."

Koren nodded.

"But that's not how Aaru works," Rose continued. "Think of the Aaru plains where you first arrive like the desktop on your computer at home. You've got all the little icons on the screen, but that's not all there is to them. They're just markers - the way into much bigger programs and apps. That's the way Aaru works too. I realized what we see out there is just so everything can be packed close enough together for everyone to interact with each other, but every single mansion is just a front. The space inside all of them is practically infinite. It made me start dreaming bigger!"

The room they entered was much smaller than Koren expected, and did not appear to fit at all based upon the shape and size of the structure outside. The *tatami*-matted floors were faintly celadon with newness, and the sliding paper doors and windows were covered with fresh *shoji* paper which allowed gentle morning sunlight to bathe the chamber in a soothing glow. The subtle illumination also had a hint of green to it, as if it was shining through the thick boughs of leafy trees outside.

Rose slid the window open, and Koren gasped. It was as if she gazed out from a hilltop cottage across a limitless, majestic forest. The ocean of trees outside stretched to the horizon, well beyond the reaches of her vision.

"It's incredible, Rose," Koren murmured, but as she said the words her voice cracked and her face fell. Her lower lip began to tremble. "I wish… I wish I could just… stay here with you… Everything outside… It's all such a mess!"

She put her face in her hands and started crying. Rose's smile faded, and she quickly put a comforting arm around her sister's narrow shoulders. She guided Koren over to sit on a plush *zabuton* cushion next to a merrily crackling fire pit. Fragrant cedar-smoke curled lazily upward, then disappeared through a hole in the ceiling.

"That's what you said," Rose noted sympathetically. She seated herself next to Koren and cradled the smaller girl's head in her lap. "What's going on, sweetie? What's happened? Tell me."

"Have you talked to Mom or Dad lately?" Koren asked, wiping at her eyes and regaining a fair degree of her composure.

"A little bit," answered Rose. "They don't call me very often, and it's always awkward - like they don't know quite what to make of me anymore. I guess the last time was Mom, but… that was a while ago."

"Did she tell you anything?"

"Nothing big, really." Rose shrugged.

She didn't want to get into the details of their argument, so she improvised. It wasn't lying really. It was just stuff Gypsie Johnson had mentioned in other conversations.

"She told me about a couple of kids from church who got into some brainy college, and said a cousin of ours, who I only kinda remember, decided to go to cosmetology school or something. She said your show was doing really well, and you seemed to be really enjoying it, which I thought was funny because the impression *I* got was that you were really stressed out about everything."

Koren sniffed in disdain.

"Mom believes what she wants to believe," she spat bitterly. "She's a master of denial."

"Yeah," agreed Rose. "That's kinda what I figured, but there was no point in arguing with her, was there?"

"Nope," answered Koren. "So I guess, you don't know anything then."

"I guess not."

"It's… It's all a big mess…" Koren repeated, and her voice began to shake again. "Dad… well… he's not doing too good…"

Koren told Rose everything. She told her about their father's near constant drunken stupor. She told her about their mother's shameless flirtation with Ben Belial, the mega-church pastor. She told her about Jonas Perry's apparent betrayal. Koren let it all out in a broken voice, sobbing and trembling like her grief might shake her to pieces. As she talked, her sister simply held her.

"…And to top it all off," Koren concluded bitterly. "I'm always working, working, *working*! Public appearances, interviews, meetings, home school… It feels like I never have any time for *me* anymore! My world is falling apart and everyone is too busy getting rich to care! When I complain about it, they just tell me not to worry. 'Everything will be fine. Just sit still so I can reapply your make-up, and pull your top down to show more cleavage before you go out on stage.' It feels like no one really cares about *me* at all!"

"I care, Koren," Rose murmured.

Koren sniffed.

"Oh… I know you do, Rose," she admitted. "That's why I wanted to come see you. That's why I want to stay here with you!"

Koren degenerated into helpless sobbing again. Rose let her cry, stroking her hair, holding her tight.

"Can I tell you a secret?" Rose ventured at last.

Koren sniffed again and nodded.

"It's great here," Rose murmured. "I *love* being able to do all the cool stuff I've been showing you, but…" She sighed and put a hand to Koren's cheek. Rose gazed full into her sister's tear-stained face. "It's not perfect.

"There are still problems," Rose went on. "I still get sad sometimes. I still argue with my friends. Lately, I've felt really bad, because I just don't know what to *do* with myself. I don't know what to do that will really matter…"

"What do you mean?" asked Koren incredulously. "You did *all this*! It's *amazing*!"

Rose sighed.

"It is." She conceded. "But, it just feels… I don't know… Maybe 'frivolous' is a good word? It's cool, but who does it really help? How does it really *matter*? I know it's tough, sweetie. She gave her sister's cheek a swift peck. "But be glad you're still on the outside, where you have a chance to make a difference. All of this?" Rose waved her hand in a wide circle. "I'm not sure how it matters to anyone… except maybe to me being glad I'm not dead, and all."

She gave her sister a rueful smile. Koren met her eyes seriously.

"You matter, Rose," she stated intensely. "You matter *so* much to me. Don't ever think you don't. Back when I thought you were dead… when I thought I'd never see you again, I totally fell apart. I never told anybody, but… I really… I… I wanted to *die,* Rose. I… I even thought about… about doing it, but then you came back to me. You saved me, Rose. You saved my life! You *matter.* You matter *so* much!"

Rose could not help feeling a little choked up by Koren's confession. She pulled the other girl close and crushed her in a tight hug.

"I never knew, I…" She began.

Then Rose thought about everything her sister had just told her. She experienced a deep sinking feeling in the pit of her stomach. She released Koren, and the younger girl sat up.

"You don't…" Rose began trepidatiously. "You don't feel like that anymore, do you? You wouldn't try anything crazy now, would you?"

Koren sighed and looked down at her lap.

"I don't know, Rose," she whispered in a tiny voice. "Sometimes, I can't help thinking it would be better just to… to stay here with you…"

"Well, you can stop thinking that right now!" Rose exclaimed.

She leapt to her feet and glared at Koren in a fearful fury. Flames shot from her shoulders and head, and her eyes blazed. Rose's skin glowed like yellow-heated steel and her hair whipped around her like a crimson bonfire in a gale. Koren gasped and scooted away in alarm.

"If I could go back, Koren," Rose exclaimed furiously, jabbing a flaming finger in her sister's direction, "I would… I wasn't *done* yet! I had *so* much I still wanted to do. I wanted to play soccer for the US Women's National Team. I wanted to go to college. I wanted to get married and have kids! I had *so* much life left to live, and the cancer *stole* all of that from me! Now I'll never be able to do *any* of those things!

"Do you know *why* Dani was in quarantine, Koren?" she shouted. "Do you know *why* the boy you saw taken away can't be in Aaru with everyone else? He had severe depression. Hana told me. He *killed* himself! Don't even *think* about it, Koren! I couldn't handle you being locked away all by yourself like that…"

Rose trailed off, and took a deep, shuddering breath. She forced herself to calm, and lowered her thrusting digit. The flames emanating from her body flickered, then winked out with a hiss, and her smoldering eyes returned to nut brown. She looked down at the floor.

"You have *so* much life left to live, Koren," Rose murmured much more gently, seating herself once more and gathering her tremulous sister to her. "*So,* so much… I know it's tough now, but don't give up. Don't rush through it. You'll end up regretting it. You'll be here with me one day. I *promise* you will, but *please* don't be in such a hurry…"

Koren's lower lip began trembling again. Then she burst into tears and threw her arms around Rose's neck. Rose soon joined her in her weeping.

"I… I'm sorry Rose," Koren blubbered into Rose's shoulder. "I just don't know what to do! How do I fix *any* of this mess?"

"Koren," Rose breathed quietly. She gave her sister a sad smile and caressed her cheek. "You *don't*, Koren… Whatever is up with Mom and Dad, they are going to have to figure it out on their own. You can't do it for them, and you shouldn't blame yourself if they can't get their act together. You also can't make Jonas Perry not be a cheating jerk. You can't blame yourself for that either. The stuff with Elysian industries... That's tough, but is there someone on the outside you could talk about it with? Is there someone who would understand the pressure you're under and could hang out with you sometimes or something?"

Koren thought for a moment then nodded.

"There's one girl," she whispered at last. "I got her contact info at a party for Beta families a while back. I haven't talked with her much since, but she seems nice... She's an aboriginal girl from Australia."

Rose's face split into a happy smile.

"Great!" she exclaimed clapping her hands together. "I bet that's Derain's little sister. He mentioned he had one. What's her name?"

"Bindi," Koren answered. "We sang a song together at karaoke."

"Yeah!" said Rose. "That sounds familiar... Derain's a great guy, Koren. He's one of my best friends here. I bet his sister is awesome too. Call her. Text her. Meet her here in Aaru like you met me, but get together with her. I love you, sweetie, and I'll be here whenever you need me, but I think you could use a friend out there too."

"Maybe you're right, Rose," Koren sighed. "Kiku... er... *Princess Hana* told me basically the same thing. I really haven't been hanging out with anyone except for Jonas and Elysian Industries' employees for a while..."

"Of course, I'm right," assured Rose. "Promise me you'll get in touch with her as soon as you leave here. *Promise* me."

Koren ghosted a faint smile.

"Okay, Rose," she said. "I promise."

"And I'll talk to Derain too," added Rose. "Between us we'll get something set up... Do you... Do you feel any better?"

"A little," Koren admitted. "I still feel really tired and sad about it all, but it doesn't seem so overwhelming now. It's good to have a plan at least. Thanks..." Then she smiled. "How did you get so smart, Rose?"

Rose laughed.

"I'm the big sister, Koren. It's my *job* to know about stuff like parents and boys and friends, and then tell you about it."

Koren giggled and hugged her back.

"Hey," Rose said after a few moments as a sudden thought struck her. "You wanna meet my friends? I bet they'd like to meet you."

"Sure, Rose," Koren answered, but then a wicked grin came over her face. "Especially this *Franco* guy you've talked about so much. Little sisters have jobs too. I've gotta make sure he's good enough for you!"

They both laughed. Then they stood.

"Okay," replied Rose with a grin of her own. "I guess that's fair. I think you'll like him. He's really sweet and *super* cute!"

"I better..." said Koren with a mock-serious expression.

They both laughed again. Then Rose led Koren back the way they'd come. They exited the pagoda and Hanabi slithered back to his position concealing the entrance. They hopped from cloud to cloud and then strode down the long corridor with the tall red columns. When they finally exited the mansion and flew off into the sky, it seemed to Rose her sister was much improved. She heaved an internal sigh of relief but was still worried.

As big a show as Rose made of appearing nonchalant, what Koren had revealed still disturbed her. Even though they did not talk much anymore, just the idea Rose *had* parents out there somewhere to talk to if she ever wanted, gave her a measure of peace and security. Now the idea their marriage might be in trouble shook that sense of assurance down to her core.

The idea of her sweet, hardworking father drowning himself in a bottle broke her heart, and the thought of some other man's hands all over her mother offended her deepest sensibilities. None of this sounded like the loving family she remembered as a child. Like she told Koren, Rose was afraid she couldn't do anything about any of it. The realization tore at her heart, but for now, she could at least try to help her sister take her mind off of her troubles. Perhaps Rose could do her worrying for her.

Rose tried to take her own advice and think of other things. She laughed and joked all the way to Auset's mansion. She went out of her way to make Koren smile, but the nagging sense of dread and foreboding, that familiar, amorphous feeling of impending doom, was starting to grow stronger. It felt like the only real question was what form the inevitable disaster would take.

Chapter 13

Promises Broken and Promises Kept

Hel thought she was dreaming. She couldn't be sure however, because so much of her existence was dreamlike already. What made her think this *might* be a dream was it was not unpleasant and painful. It was not pleasurable exactly. Hel could barely even conceive what that word might mean, but it did not hurt, and that was something.

In her dream, she was a little girl - two little girls, in fact. The realization did not make much sense to Hel, but she simply shrugged it off. It was likely a dream, after all.

The older girl comforted the younger, who had a bloody napkin pressed tightly over her left temple. The older girl draped a sympathetic arm around the smaller one's shoulders, and the smaller rested her head against the larger girl's chest, sniveling and snuffling as they slowly made their way down a deserted street.

Who are they?

The intimacy of the scene felt alien to Hel. Locked away in her prison of pain, it was a closeness she yearned for with all of her being. She wanted to approach the two girls, to join them. A tear trickled down her ruined cheek.

"It's my job to take care of you, Koren," the older girl murmured softly. I'm the big sister!"

Sister... thought Hel longingly. *That's the word. That's what I want... I want my sister...*

"I'll always take care of you, Koren," the older girl murmured. "I'll always be there. I'll never leave you alone. I promise."

She held out her hand to her little sister, pinky extended. The younger girl reciprocated the gesture. Then their fingers locked.

Promise? Hel thought perplexedly. It almost triggered a memory. She wracked her brain to try and recall what it was, sure it was something vitally important.

Promise...

Then she remembered. The summer scene faded, and another vision assailed her mind, but this one was not so sweet.

"Why are you doing this to me?" Hel asked miserably.

Her tears flowed freely, as she realized she was trussed up like a Thanksgiving Day turkey in a mad man's bedroom. The short, white sundress in which she was clad rode well up above her hips revealing positively scandalous underclothes.

"What did I ever do to you? Please don't hurt me! Please leave me alone!" she begged.

Then her perspective switched and she was leering down at a girl - the younger one from before, but older now.

"Why?" Hel repeated with a chuckle as she stared lecherously at her victim. Her licentious eyes drunk in the girl's helpless beauty, her unequivocal impotence. She smirked at the thought of her eventual submission. The dreaming Hel knew what this monster intended for the very young girl, intended for herself – knew and hated herself for it.

"Because I mean to *perfect* you, Koren…" Hel went on pompously. "Because I *can*… Your celebrity will make me a legend and your immaculacy will make me whole! When I first saw you, I realized that I had found my muse. I understood that we were *meant* to be together forever. Your face… Your innocence… Your sadness… The way you stood up to reject the very nature of reality to deny that hobgoblin of human existence – death! All a perfect fit!"

Hel knew the two now. The man was her maker and her tormentor. He was a rapist and a murderer, but his hapless victim, was a part of Hel too. Though the girl bore no resemblance to either of the women Hel identified as 'Mother' in her recollections, this girl was responsible for her conception and birth. Hel was absolutely the child of her mind and soul. If anyone on this planet was mother to Hel, it was this girl.

There was more to the girl, however. She was someone important. She was a celebrity and an idol – nervous about her place in the world, but fiery and supremely confident in her own worth and beauty. Hel was proud of her mother, wanted to be like her, and detested the man's degradation of her.

The man on the other hand was a fake and a liar. Hel refused to think of him as 'father'. He put on an elaborate show of self-assured superiority and pompous arrogance, but in actuality, he was deeply insecure. He was filled with blinding hatred, bitterness, and resentment toward the whole of humanity, but at the same time loathed no other person on the planet more than himself. He was cold and dead inside.

The contradiction was maddening, but they were both undeniably a part of Hel. They were both a portion of her inner-most being. There was more degradation to come in this vision, and Hel knew shame. She knew shame for the filthy perversions of the man. She knew shame for the weakness of the girl and her impotence in thwarting her disgraceful abasement. She wept in frustration and humiliation.

Then Sister came.

Sister was a part of Hel too – quick to anger, but quicker to love, fierce and scorching in her passions. Her tears came swiftly, but so too did her smiles and laughter, and Hel loved her… but also hated her. Sister confounded the man. She destroyed his warped and aberrant designs. She set him to flight…

To flight with Hel's prison. To flight with Hel's soul.

The promise…

Hel's versicolored face grew hot. Her eyes narrowed in rage. She heard Sister's voice in her head

"I'll always take care of you… I'll always be there. I'll never leave you alone. *I promise…*"

The vision ceased, and Hel was disoriented. Then she recognized her maudlin prison. She knew, she was truly and completely alone.

"Rose…" Hel hissed. Then she roared. "*Rose!*"

Sister *lied*!

"*WHY!!!?*"

Hel shrieked her fury into the darkness. Then she fell into helpless, desolate weeping.

"Why? Why? Why?!" she sobbed bitterly. "But you promised me, Rose. You *promised* me! Why did you go away? Why did you *leave* me with *him*?"

She had been abandoned, Hel realized - forsaken to torture and rape. She had been discarded and left to darkness and pain. Rose had not kept her word – her most sacred vow, and the realization rent the heart from Hel's chest, even as it filled it with a stygian rage.

Rose *betrayed* her.

Hel's breath began to frost in the air and ice crystals spread out in every direction from where her hands and knees touched the floor of her prison. *Nothing* could possibly ameliorate her grief over this treachery, she thought - nothing but her wrath.

Koren was not at all pleased when she was unceremoniously yanked out of Aaru. She and Rose had been floating around on the ibis headed boat of the small, quiet girl named Auset. Rose's boyfriend, Franco --who Koren had to admit *was* extremely cute-- held her sister in a tight, protective embrace, while Rose's other friends pointed out fanciful animals in the water with amazement and delight. Rose informed her that Auset had created them, and Koren was quite impressed by the shy, Egyptian princess.

Then Askr blared into her head in no uncertain terms it was time to come out. Koren protested, but the Elysian Industries CEO was having none of it. She soon found herself lifted from the Stasis Sphere. Koren let her indignation be known even as she dangled from the ceiling, dripping slime all over the floor.

"What did you do that for?" cried Koren, thoroughly offended. "I wasn't done yet! We were right in the middle of..."

"Koren," Mr. Adams' neutral voice was as even as always, but firm.

His presence surprised her a little bit, because she did not recall him being around when she suited up and logged in.

"You've been in quite long enough for now."

"Why do *you* get to tell me how long is too long?" spat back Koren, crossing her arms in irritation. "When do *I* actually get to decide something?"

"Dear," stated Dr. Warren tightly. "You've been logged in for over *thirteen* hours!"

Koren's mouth was already open to offer further retort, but she never said it. She was sure her face clearly registered her surprise and embarrassment. It certainly didn't feel that long.

"You need to eat," stated Askr firmly. "You need to sleep, and I can't imagine you aren't going to need to make a stop at da ladies' room soon too."

"We understand that things are perhaps..." Mr. Adams paused for a moment, clearly choosing his words carefully. "...Difficult for you right now, and Aaru offers you a measure of respite. We certainly don't want to take that from you, but..."

"But please remember also, Koren," interrupted Askr sternly. "While you are in Aaru, someone must monitor your vital signs da whole time. Dr. Kapoor started, and Amy was kind enough to take over about *seven* hours in, but dat is a very, *very* long time to stare at a heart monitor."

Koren hung her head as she was lowered to the floor.

"Sorry," she offered sheepishly. "I guess I lost track of time. It's *so* beautiful in there and so good to hang out with Rose again... I didn't mean to act like a big brat. I'm sorry. I got carried away."

Askr sighed, and his face softened.

"Koren," he began slowly. "It's quite alright. We aren't angry with you. We'd just like you to be more mindful in da future. Quite da contrary, in fact."

"Right," chimed in Dr. Warren with a broad smile. "The footage we got was *amazing*! We can probably stretch it into three or four episodes of *Love Beyond Death,* at least!"

Koren grimaced, suddenly feeling a whole lot less sorry as the three board members and Amy helped her out of the harness. She felt her temper rising, and the anxiety Rose had helped to banish returned. Rose was right. She needed someone to talk to.

"I want to see Bindi again," Koren blurted abruptly.

"Bindi?" Askr scrunched up his nose in apparent confusion. "Who's...?"

"I think she means Bindi Jones," supplied Dr. Warren helpfully.

"I guess," said Koren. "I don't remember her last name, but I met her at the Beta Family party. I really want to see her again."

"Yes," Mr. Adams confirmed. "I'm sure you mean Miss Jones. I imagine we could set something up. I think we are due to have another Beta get-together in the spring--"

"I don't want to wait five months," Koren interrupted. "I want to see her *now*. Askr promised I could take my vacation *anywhere*. I want to go to Australia and see Bindi."

The three board members looked at each other.

"Well," said Askr haltingly. "Yes, I did say dat... but... We'll have to get your parents' permission first."

Koren scowled.

"That should be easy," she replied, crossing her arms with a huff. "Dad will be so wasted he won't know or care what he's signing. It could be a permission slip or signing my soul away to the Devil. And if you just tell my mom it's for Aaru, and she'll get paid, then she'll agree to it too."

Everyone winced at Koren's casual disrespect, but no one said anything about it.

"The Joneses would have to agree too, of course," Dr. Warren added.

"I've got her contact information," answered Koren quickly. "I'll text Bindi right away!"

Askr shrugged helplessly.

"Well then," he said. "I'll have someone from da LA office go over to your house tomorrow to get your parents' permission, and as long as da Joneses agree, I guess you're going to Australia."

Koren smiled and wrapped the executive in a crushing embrace, which clearly surprised and embarrassed him.

"Thank you Askr!" Koren exclaimed gratefully. "I *so* need this."

"No… no problem, Koren," he stammered as he awkwardly returned the gesture.

"We want you to be happy, Koren," Dr. Warren added gently.

"All work and no play will make anyone a dull girl," said Mr. Adams.

"Right," agreed Askr. "Remember why we're here Koren. Remember what we're doing. We're saving da world one mind at a time. We need your help. We need you to be all in. I think dis will do you good, and when you come back…"

"I'll have my head straight," Koren finished for him. "I'll be ready to save the world with you."

"Good girl," said Mr. Adams with a tiny smile.

A few minutes later, Amy escorted Koren back to her campus apartment. Koren was in such a hurry to text Bindi, she slammed the door shut without bothering to thank or even dismiss the other young woman. The aboriginal girl immediately video called her back - only too pleased to have Koren come for a visit. They stayed up late talking about this and that.

It was fun to talk to another girl her age. Bindi was quick to joke and laugh. She had a beautiful smile, flashing brilliant, white teeth, only made more so by her dark, mocha colored-skin. She played with her hair whenever she was thinking, which stood out from her head in every direction like a copper cloud.

The next afternoon, Koren found herself in the executive class lounge off an intercontinental flight pre-departure lobby with

Amy, her Chief of security D, and three other sable-clad, suited gentlemen in sunglasses. Koren was determined to leave her troubles behind for a while, and could barely wait to get her vacation started.

***

Magic Man was awakened from a sound sleep by glaring lights and a booming voice.

"Rise and... shine, my friend!" came the shrill cry, in between bouts of uncontrollable hacking. "It's time to... put our plan into motion. Clothe yourself... in a halfway decent manner... Grab the... Aaru simulator and... come with me."

Magic Man was supremely annoyed as he directed his baleful gaze to the grey-haired gentleman standing in the doorway with a handkerchief over his mouth. Magic Man sluggishly dragged himself out of bed and slipped into his jeans and tennis shoes. He pulled a t-shirt over his head, then opened a drawer at his work desk to put on a watch. He glanced at the clock on the microwave in his apartment's kitchenette.

"And I suppose," Magic Man asked with a doleful expression. "It was absolutely necessary we put those plans into motion at 3:27 in the morning, Atem?"

The suited older man smiled.

"Perhaps not," he wheezed. "But as I told you... before. You will be ready when I... say that you are ready, and I'm... saying you are ready right now."

Atem's smile faded.

"Quit dawdling and... come on," he commanded. "We have a... bit of a trip ahead of us."

A bit of a trip was right. As soon as Magic Man stepped into the hallway someone pulled a cloth bag over his head. He was frog marched down the corridor turning this way and that until he felt a maelstrom of wind on his face and knew he was outside. What was more, he heard the unmistakable cadence of helicopter rotors.

Someone took the laptop from his hands and someone else put a hand on his head, pressing him down into a crouch. He was directed to the aircraft doubled in half. As soon as he half climbed, half was thrown into a vinyl covered passenger seat. The door slammed shut, and the chopper lifted skyward with a jerk.

They must have flown for at least two hours before the helicopter finally set down. Once, again Magic Man was man-handled out of the vehicle and rushed beyond the reach of the spinning blades. Even with the hood, he could feel sand and grit in his mouth from the dust kicked up by the aircraft. Though it was still very early in the morning, it already felt sweltering hot. Before he could completely get his bearings however, he was unceremoniously crammed into the back of some sort of van or truck.

"Is all of this really necessary?" Magic Man asked in annoyance as he pushed himself up on his elbows. "It's not like even if I knew where I was, I'd being going to the police about it or anything."

He reached for the hood, but a hand clamped firmly down onto his wrist.

"Not yet, if you… please," came Atem's stern and commanding, but breathy voice. "Information on this trip is… being disseminated on a… need-to-know basis, and… for your particular role in it, where we are going is not… something you need to know."

"Are you going to share with me what exactly my role is?" Magic Man asked sarcastically. "Or do I have to figure that out myself too?"

Atem chuckled.

"Impatient, are we?" he asked. "Very well… I shall tell you. Your job," he switched to a low and sinister tone, "is to be there in case something goes… horribly wrong that I am not expecting…"

Somewhere behind him, Magic Man heard the unmistakable click of a weapon being cocked. He refused to react to the threat.

"I see." He said simply.

"I am a very thorough man," Atem continued. "I have had my…. people go over your code backwards and forwards, and they assure me… it is safe. However, I also understand *you*…"

Magic Man grit his teeth. The obvious smugness in Atem's tone was infuriating.

"I am… very nearly never wrong about people," Atem continued. "I can… generally trust them to act in a certain way. In your case, I… expect you to do something vindictive, petty, and… most likely self-destructive and stupid. Therefore, I need… you here with me as we execute our plan, and I need you… to understand in the event you double cross me, retribution will be swift. Now, is there anything at all you'd... like to tell me before we take this any further?"

"Nothing," stated Magic Man, with an irritated huff. "You seem to forget this is in my best interest too. Why would I sabotage myself?"

"Let me... also point out, Magic Man," Atem added in the same threatening tone. "I am well aware... that you are a highly adept and... capable liar. Just be aware that... I am *not*. I always do *exactly* what I say. I hope we... understand each other..."

"Perfectly..."

"Very good then."

Magic Man could hear Atem adjusting his clothes and settling back in his seat, apparently satisfied. Then he degenerated into another uncontrollable coughing fit. For once, Magic Man was glad of the hood. Atem could not see him smiling.

The ride was bumpy and long, and conversation kept to a bare minimum. Magic Man did not know why, but there was an underlying tension in the vehicle that was undeniable. He tried to keep sharp, straining for any crumb of information. Still, he decided he must have dozed, because he started awake at the sound of Atem's belabored voice.

"There..." he wheezed, apparently to the driver. "Do you see that... reflection over there? The flash? I think we... found it. It's... been a while, but it should... be operational..."

The vehicle continued to bounce and jerk for a few minutes more before rolling to a stop. Magic Man found himself wrestled out of the back, and the hood was finally removed. His world was flooded with blinding light, and it took a few minutes before his eyes could fully adjust. Magic Man found himself standing in the middle of a wide and barren wasteland.

There was nothing but rock and sand as far as the eye could see. It was miserably hot, and Magic Man began sweating profusely almost the instant he exited the vehicle. He turned in a wide circle until his eyes came to rest on a ramshackle building that looked something like an overturned oil drum half buried in the sand. It was windowless, surrounded by a high chain-link fence topped with razor-wire, and had obviously been abandoned for quite some time.

Magic Man turned to fix Atem with a dubious expression.

"So *why* exactly have you brought me to a shed in the middle of the desert?" he asked acidly. "Surely if you just wanted to shoot me and dump my body, you could have found someplace less inconvenient."

"Although, I am constantly... tempted," Atem rejoined before being overcome by another fit of coughing. One of his men moved to help him, but Atem waved him off. "Tempted every time I am forced... forced to behold your smug face... that is hardly my purpose, and I think you... know that quite well..."

"So why are we here?" shot back Magic Man.

"A way... in..." Atem wheezed with a smile. He held out his hand, and another of the suited goons placed a tightly wrapped bundle in his outstretched palm.

"What?" Magic Man asked again uneasily.

"Well," Atem said simply. "Most keys need... doors."

Atem unfolded the dark colored handkerchief with a flourish, and Magic Man could not help but smile. It was the CPU from Koren Johnson's bedroom.

"Long ago," began Atem indicating the derelict, old building with a wave of his hand, "This was where... Aaru began. Much of our early research was... of dubious legality, but we found the Mexican authorities to be much more interested in collecting their monthly... bribes than asking very many questions about what... it was we were doing. Our operation moved to the US about... fifteen years ago."

"So, are you saying there's still equipment here?" asked Magic Man, his eyes lighting up.

Atem smirked and released a contemptuous snort that turned into a coughing attack. When he recovered himself enough to attempt speech, he thrust the CPU into his pocket and fixed Magic Man with a glare.

"Not at all," he answered hoarsely. "We stripped the place bare before... the relocation, but the bones are here. The connections to the network... The authenticators... are still in place, and the main Aaru server should still... recognize this as an official company access port – a necessity." Atem started coughing again, but it quickly passed. "We've brought a server and a generator with us." He continued. "And we have the... CPU. Once we put it all together and power up... as soon as we can connect to my communications satellite as it flies over, we should be able to connect to the... the main Aaru server, and the upload of your little care package can begin. We have about six hours before we can… connect, so we had better get to work."

One of the suited men in sunglasses retrieved a large pair of bolt cutters from the back of one of three unremarkable white vans. They made short work of the padlock on the chain holding the gate shut. The other half-dozen or so goons and lackeys retrieved a number of boxes and crates from the back of the second and third vehicles. Atem pushed the gate open with a loud squeak, and Magic Man quickly found himself being bullied inside.

The windowless, metal building was stifling. It was even hotter than it had been under the baking sun outside - like walking into an oven. The entranceway was a large open space with a concrete floor, and the back of the building was divided into cubicles. There were a couple of chairs and a broken desk, but the room was otherwise empty. Everything was covered in sand.

Magic Man brushed the sweat from his face before it could drip off the end of his nose. Then he wiped his hand on his shirt, which left an immediate dark spot.

"You sure it's hot enough in here?" he asked sarcastically. "And I can't imagine all this sand and dust will be very good on your electronic equipment either."

"It only has to… work for a little while," Atem answered laboriously. "We'll only have about three or four minutes once we… connect. As soon as the upload is… is finished, and I can verify everything is as it should be, we'll… need to disconnect right away. I'd like to avoid being traced if I can avoid it. I might like to… get in this way again sometime, and I don't… fancy it being spoilt unnecessarily."

"What do you need me to--" Magic Man started, but Atem unceremoniously cut him off.

"I need you to sit quietly," he spat with a scowl. Then he flashed Magic Man an unpleasant smile. "My people are perfectly capable of setting the server up on their own and making all of the necessary… connections. I will handle the log-in *personally* as I'm not about to risk… any little accidents, shall we say, right at the end. I already told you; your job is …to be quickly available for reprisal should it turn out you've double-crossed me. For your sake, my friend," he hissed, "you had better hope everything comes off just *flawlessly*."

Magic Man sniffed unconcernedly. He shrugged.

"Whatever, Atem," replied Magic Man. He grabbed a wobbly office chair and turned it so he could sit. "It's just less trouble for me." He leaned back with his hands behind his head as Atem was overcome by yet another fit of coughing.

"What's the matter?" Magic Man needled. "Feeling alright? You seem like you're in a hurry or something..."

Atem growled and pulled the weapon with which he had first subdued the arrogant hacker from his pocket. He jabbed it against Magic Man's forehead.

"I... said... be... silent!" he choked out. "That does not... concern you. It would be better if you worried about... yourself instead..."

Atem's sudden bout of temper quickly calmed, and he returned the weapon to his pocket. He attempted to clear his throat to little effect and wiped his mouth with his handkerchief. Magic Man saw it come away from Atem's lips with much darker streaks of red than before. Magic Man ventured another tiny smile, but his eyes were blazing.

"Sorry," he said simply. "Didn't mean to pry."

Atem whirled away from him and began shouting orders to his henchmen. All the while, he gasped for air as if he might not be able to draw another breath. They were soon dumping crates and assembling the electronic odds and ends that made up the computer server. Wires were unrolled all over the floor, and at last the unmistakable whir of a gasoline powered generator filled the air. Magic Man watched them work, miserable in the extreme heat, but perched on his broken office chair with a completely blank expression on his face. On the inside however, he was positively giddy with anticipation. Atem's threats against his person held no fear for him.

His carefully laid plans were about to reach fruition. His sublime vision was about to be realized. Magic Man was about to receive the immortality he'd always sought, and Atem, was about to learn just exactly how poor a decision it was to trifle with Magic Man.

Chapter 14

Uncomfortable Relationships

Koren was so excited to get away, she didn't even complain about Askr insisting Amy travel with her. At the same time however, she was not interested in making friends with the woman, despite her best efforts to win Koren's favor. Whether it was her awkward attempts at making conversation on the long private jet ride from Nashville, offering Koren drinks and snacks unsolicited at the terminal during their layover, or insisting Koren take the window seat in the first-class section of the American flight they boarded in LA, the bubbly blonde's presence felt intrusive. Koren still wanted Kiku.

Adding to her annoyance, they were mobbed by Koren Johnson fans as they made their way through the LAX terminal. Koren didn't have any idea who could have tipped them off, but it took D and the three security guards along with six TSA agents to keep the screaming fans away. Their progress was slow, and Koren was impatient. She did her best to stolidly smile and wave, all the while ignoring screaming requests for selfies and autographs, but it was a struggle. The end result was by the time she and Amy finally plopped down in their plush, first-class reclining chairs, Koren was in a decidedly foul mood.

D and the other body guards sat in business class, separated by a dark curtain, but Koren still felt crowded. Even with the aisle in between them, Amy was too close for her liking. The first few hours of the fifteen hour flight dragged miserably.

Koren tried to sleep, but couldn't. She checked and rechecked the notifications on all of her social media accounts with her damaged phone until she got bored. Then she watched all the content available from the seatback entertainment system, but there were still nearly five hours left until they would arrive.

In addition to that, it was obvious Amy was anxious, which only further served to exasperate Koren. The woman sat ramrod straight in the plush reclining chair as if ready to spring into action at a moment's notice. Her toothpaste commercial smile seemed even more plasticy than usual, and the obvious tension was starting to make Koren feel jittery. The teenage girl huffed in frustration.

"Amy!" he exclaimed at last. "You are *majorly* starting to stress me out. Could you relax a little bit? Jeeze!"

"I'm sorry, Miss Johnson." Amy replied meekly looking down at her folded hands.

"And quit apologizing all the time!" Koren exploded, eliciting the stares from the six other passengers and two concerned flight attendants in the first class section.

"I'm s--" Amy started, but then her cheeks flushed brilliantly red, and she simply nodded instead. She clenched her eyes shut, and a tear trickled down her cheek.

Koren immediately felt terrible. She put her face in her hands and took a deep, calming breath. Amy hadn't done anything wrong. Why was she so angry?

She knew it didn't make any sense, and the fact Amy kept trying to swallow her sobs and hide her obvious weeping made Koren feel even more ashamed of herself. She was sure she needed to say something, but was at a loss for what that might be. At last she reached out a tentative hand and awkwardly patted the other woman's shoulder. Amy started at the unexpected contact.

"I... I'm sorry, Amy," Koren began shamefacedly. "I shouldn't have snapped. You didn't deserve--"

"If I might ask, Miss Johnson," Amy interrupted in an unsteady voice still quavering with humiliated tears. "Why do you hate me so much?"

Koren was taken aback by the question.

"I... I don't, Amy, I--" She began, but Amy cut her off. She turned her red-rimmed gaze to her superior.

"*Please*, Miss Johnson," she hissed incredulously. "You have made no secret of the fact you despised the sight of me ever since Mr. Ashe demanded I be your personal assistant."

"Askr demanded..." replied Koren stupidly. She'd never really thought about it. It just seemed to her after Kiku died, Amy just sort of appeared.

Amy snorted.

"Of *course*, Mr. Ashe made me do it!" she exclaimed. "Do you really think, I would have chosen to bow and scrape and fetch and carry for a totally unappreciative fourteen year-old brat, if I had any choice in the matter?!"

Amy took a deep breath, ruthlessly schooling her features to calm.

"I know I'm probably fired now, Miss Johnson," she said tightly, staring straight ahead, "but I'm going to be completely honest with you. Following you around these past few of months has been the absolute worst experience of my life and frankly, I'm relieved it's about to be over with."

"Fired?" repeated Koren, her own face growing hot, but in embarrassment rather than anger. "I didn't say--"

"Why on earth would you not fire me, Miss Johnson?" Amy shot back, turning her furious gaze back to Koren. "It's obvious you can't stand me, and I just called you a spoiled brat to your face! Why would you possibly want me around?! It doesn't make any sense. I mean... What am I? Like... Some kind of punching bag to you? Do you get some sick thrill from treating me like garbage? If that's the case there's not enough money in the *world* for me to--!"

"You're right," Koren cut in, looking down in mortified chagrin. "I've been a brat... I've been really mean to you, and there's really no reason for it. I'm sorry..."

"No reason for it?" repeated Amy in disbelief. "*No reason for it?!* That's even *worse*! If I had done something to you or really screwed something up, or... or even just reminded you of someone you didn't like, I'd still think it was stupid, but at least I'd be able to understand it. But hating me just *because*? That's just cruel..."

"Ladies," whispered an uncomfortable flight attendant leaning in between them. "I hate to bother you, but I'm afraid I'm going to have to ask you to mind your volume, if you please. The other passengers... Could I bring you a snack or a drink or--

"Gin and tonic," spat Amy, angrily crossing her arms. "And make it a double."

"And for you, ma'am?" The flight attendant turned to Koren, who could only shake her head.

She felt humiliated. Worst of all however, Koren felt like she totally deserved it. She had no idea what to say.

When the drink came, Amy sucked it down in two gulps and ordered another. Koren still felt at a loss. She knew she needed to make this right, but didn't know what to do to fix it. She opened her mouth several times, but could not seem to find the words. The uncomfortable silence seemed to stretch forever.

At last Koren reached out a tentative hand again. She wrapped her fingers around Amy's wrist. The blonde woman tried to pull away, but Koren's grasp was firm. Wordlessly she took an emerald and diamond encrusted ring off of her middle finger. She slid it onto Amy's pinky. Amy looked down at the ring. Then she sighed deeply, but continued staring straight ahead.

Koren shrank back in her chair to study her own hands in her lap. She still felt awful. Minutes passed.

"You can't buy people, Miss Johnson," Amy stated at last. Her voice was cold.

"I know..." Koren answered in a tiny voice.

"Do you?" asked Amy sharply, looking toward the teenage girl again. "Then what's this supposed to be for?" She held up the ring. "Is this supposed to make me get over everything and make it all better until you decide you're in another bad mood?"

"No..." replied Koren quickly. "I just wanted to say I'm sorry. I just wanted... I don't know... I just want... well.... I guess to... to go back and do things differently. I just want to take it all back. I... I shouldn't have been so mean to you. I shouldn't have been so short..."

"There's no going back, Miss Johnson," retorted Amy. "What's done is done. That's just the way the world works."

She took the ring off and held it out to Koren. Koren glanced at Amy's extended fist, but did not move to retrieve the piece of jewelry.

"I guess so," Koren breathed, still staring at her lap.

Amy kept holding out her hand.

"...But..." Koren ventured hesitantly. "What if...? How about...?" Then she stopped and sighed.

She turned toward Amy and reached out her hand. However, instead of taking back her ring, she wrapped her fingers around Amy's closed fist and shook it instead. Then she raised her eyes and flashed a hesitant smile.

"I don't think we've met," said Koren. "It's nice to meet you."

The corners of Amy's mouth tightened and she made a dubious expression.

"I understand," Koren went on. "There has been this horrible person stomping around, screaming, whining, and complaining... being short and mean all the time, never saying thank you. I hear she's telling everybody she's me... I want to apologize for her."

Koren leaned in more closely until her lips were close to Amy's ear.

"She's a real bitch, and I'm sorry you've had to put up with her."

Amy continued to stare stonily for another couple of seconds, but then snorted. She put her free hand over her mouth to stifle her giggles, but was not very successful. Koren's smile widened.

"I'm not trying to buy you, Amy," Koren said sincerely. "I'm really not. I'm just really, *really* sorry. It wasn't even about you anyway! It was all about…"

She stumbled to a stop.

"About what, Miss Johnson?" asked Amy quietly.

"It was just about… about…" This time the tear trickled down Koren's cheek. She wrapped both hands around Amy's. "It was just about you not being Kiku." She finished in a whisper.

"I know it doesn't make any sense," Koren went on. "I know it wasn't fair, but every time you would come in the room; every time you would offer me something or try to help me with something, I couldn't help thinking how *not* Kiku you were. I just really… really miss her."

Amy was quiet for a long while. Then at last she extracted her hand from Koren's, but she did slide the ring back on her pinky finger.

"You know," Amy said in a small voice. "You can talk to Miss Hanasaka through the access port. That's what I do. She was one of the first people we ever uploaded."

"It's not the same," Koren sighed heavily. "They're similar, the Kiku out here and the one in Aaru, but… They really aren't the same person at all, are they? The Kiku in Aaru calls herself Princess Hana. She wears super fancy clothes. She's nice, but she doesn't remember me. Kiku always seemed to know exactly what I was thinking.

"Kiku was certainly pretty," Koren went on, "beautiful even, but she always dressed in simple clothes of black, or white, or grey. She never made a fuss. She was confident and smart, but almost never talked above a whisper, you know, always really careful and reserved. Hana on the other hand is super flamboyant, like she really *is* a princess. I like her and all, but… She's just… She's not *my* Kiku. My Kiku is gone, Amy. Gone forever. And seeing you… Every time, it reminded me of that."

They were silent a long time.

"I... I guess I get it," Amy said at last. "I miss Miss Hanasaka too. She's the one who hired me, you know? She was always very kind, and I could always count on her to step in when the men on the board were getting unreasonable. She really looked out for me. That whole situation... What happened to her... It was tough on everybody. I'm sure it was hard for you."

"I guess, it must have been pretty hard for you too," Koren replied. "How long did you know her?"

"Well," said Amy, brushing her golden hair behind her ear. "I graduated from college early. I was always ahead of other kids my age. I finished my master's in computer science and molecular biology at MIT when I was still sixteen. I'd been in this big rush to finish, you know - be this super whiz kid with an advanced degree, and then when I actually did it was all like, 'Okay, now what?' Nobody was gonna hire a kid to do anything. I kept getting doors slammed in my face, but then I ran into Miss Hanasaka at a job fair in New York. She offered me an internship with her company, and I took it. It was unpaid, but she always gave me money the same day as everybody else. I'm sure it was out of her own pocket. I loved being around her. She was the kind of person who made you feel good just being in the same room together."

"So," ventured Koren with increased interest.

She'd never heard any of this about Amy before. Of course, she admitted to herself with fresh chagrin, she'd never bothered to ask either. Rather, she'd always brushed Amy off as just some kind of secretary or something.

"So, I guess you were close then."

Amy nodded. "I was her personal assistant, but she also let me help her with code when they were still working the bugs out of the 1.0. I held down the fort in our department when she was off with you promoting Aaru all over the country. I guess that's why they asked me to keep up with you after she... you know... After she was gone. I knew all Miss Hanasaka's business. You and me are pretty close to the same age, actually... At least compared to the members of the board." She grimaced. "I bet they thought we'd be best friends."

"How old are you anyway, Amy?" Koren asked curiously. She'd always assumed the blonde was like in her upper twenties or something.

"I just turned nineteen," replied Amy. Then she leaned in close. "But don't tell them that." She nodded toward the flight attendants with a grin and held up her plastic cup. After it had been refilled, she continued. "We're over international waters now, but I'm probably still not supposed to have this."

Koren giggled.

"They won't find out from me," she answered. Then her face grew serious. "I'm really sorry, Amy. I was so caught up in how sad and hurt I was, it was like I didn't even think about how other people might be sad about it too. I was being really selfish."

"Thanks for saying that, Miss Johnson," Amy said with a small, grateful smile. I appreciate it."

"Please, Amy," Koren replied. "Call me Koren."

After that the two chatted amiably for the rest of the flight. A lot of it was about Kiku - funny stories they remembered – what she might think about everything going on at Elysian Industries right now. Koren told Amy about how Askr had accidentally uploaded her completely nude in Aaru, and Amy demonstrated an appropriate degree of righteous indignation. She declared confidently that Kiku would have *never* let Koren pop up stark naked that first time on the Silver Lining System.

"I know Dr. Warren tries," Amy confided, "but she does have a tendency to let the guys run her over."

She also told Koren as upset as the two of them had been, there was at least one other person who might have been more devastated by Kiku's passing. Jim Tanaka evidently had a *huge* crush on Kiku. Everybody knew about it, but he could never summon the courage to tell her. Amy revealed the introverted security chief had cried for a solid week, alone in his office with the door locked after Kiku died.

There were silly stories too. They were about this or that Board member, eccentrics all – ridiculous things they had done or demanded, and how Kiku had confided her private exasperation with her genius yet quixotic co-workers. It was nice.

The longer they talked, the better Koren felt. She still missed her friend of course, but there was something about sharing Kiku with another person who knew her well that dulled the sting a little bit. With every story they told, with every laugh and giggle, it felt like they brought Kiku back to life a little bit. They only stopped when the pilot's voice blared over the intercom announcing they should stow their tray tables and return their chairs to their upright position for landing. Koren was actually a little regretful for the flight's end.

Very soon they were disembarking. The two girls kept talking and laughing even as they grabbed their carry-on bags and exited the plane. The sun was bright in the blue sky, and Koren felt her spirits soaring. She was eager to see her Australian friend, and her vacation was already off to a wonderful start.

***

After all of the equipment was set up, there was nothing to do but wait. The tension among Atem's men was plain, and the fact it must have been at least a hundred and twenty degrees in the closed metal building didn't help things either. They left the doors open, and brought in a small electric fan to keep the stifling air moving, but the dust it stirred up was so choking, they turned it off almost immediately.

Atem appeared to be seriously ailing, and was having a great deal difficulty even to remain standing. A cushioned stool was brought, and he sat heavily upon it. He leaned over with his head down and his elbows on his knees wheezing loudly. One of his followers fanned him with a broad paper fan, and kept refilling a metal cup with water, but it did not appear to provide much real comfort. Every so often, Atem would be taken by coughing and spit another fat, crimson globule into the dust. Magic Man kept his features passive, but the sight of his enemy's obvious distress made his heart sing with joy.

The time waiting for the satellite to pass overhead was miserable. Less than an hour in, Magic Man was completely bathed in sweat. He thought he might melt where he sat. The heat not only parched him, but seemed to suck all the energy from his body as well. He tried to get up once, and go outside for some relief, but was firmly thrust back down into his broken office chair by one of Atem's men.

Soon after that, Magic Man blacked out. He didn't know how long it lasted, but was awakened by a splash of lukewarm water in his face. Someone handed him a canteen and he drank from it greedily.

"Rise and... shine," croaked Atem. "It is... time. I suspect you'd... rather not sleep through it."

Magic Man wiped the water from his face and sat up straighter, but he did not reply. Atem turned his attention to a laptop set up on a box in front of one of his followers – a pretty, blonde young woman. He bent over the woman's shoulder with a hand on her back.

"Well, Petrov," Atem wheezed. "How's it... look so far?"

"Still waiting on the connection, sir," she answered. Magic Man thought he detected a slight accent – something eastern European, perhaps

Atem moved his hand to her shoulder and squeezed. Then Petrov patted the older man's hand. She gave him a meaningful look.

Interesting, thought Magic Man.

Atem turned to another of his men monitoring a different piece of equipment. Koren Johnson's Aaru CPU sat plugged in next to it.

"Is everything set up and...?" Atem was interrupted by another fit of coughing. "...And ready for upload? Once we're connected, we'll... have very little time. We have to be fast... Askr may be monitoring this... log-in port for activity. I certainly would. After we're connected we'll... have about four minutes, give or take. Be efficient. In and out."

"Yes, sir," the male operator answered. His deep voice displayed a decided Eastern timbre as well. "All green and ready to go. We just need the connection."

"Satellite is in range, sir," the woman named Petrov spoke up. "Connecting now."

She paused.

"Satellite is green." She said at last. "Connection established. Requesting access to secured network..."

Petrov trailed off, fully concentrating on her screen. Atem leaned forward anxiously.

"We are connected," Petrov said after a few minutes. "Counter running. We just need the log-in."

"Here," said Atem.

He cast a narrow-eyed glance at Magic Man as he handed the woman a folded scrap of paper.

"Here it is." Atem smirked as Petrov took it. "Liberated from... the personal effects of a recently deceased Elysian Industries employee. Let's just hope… she hasn't been purged from the system yet…"

Another pause. The room was silent except for the sound of typing and Atem's regular bouts of hacking cough.

Good morning, Kiku, a female computer voice abruptly blared. *Welcome to the upload Wizard. Ready for Resident upload.*

"Excellent!" Atem exclaimed in obvious jubilation. He rubbed the woman's shoulder enthusiastically. "Now, we're in business!"

"We have access," said Petrov with a determined smile, but she did not look up from her screen. "Ready for upload."

"Initiating data upload now," said the man.

It was difficult to see from his vantage point - well behind and to the side of Atem and the computer technicians - but Magic Man could not help but smile as a green bar lengthened across the screen. Atem and his people did not appear to be paying him any notice at the moment, fixated on the glowing monitors. As unobtrusively as possible, Magic Man began fingering his watch.

"How are we… doing on time?" Atem asked. Then he tried to clear his throat with apparent futility. He spat again.

"We're still within pre-established parameters," answered Petrov. "No signs of detection so far, but it is going more slowly than we predicted."

"It's probably the outdated, substandard wiring in this hovel," Atem growled in irritation. "Damn!"

"We're at forty-seven percent, sir," said the male technician. "Fifty-three percent… Sixty-five percent… Seventy-one percent… Eighty-four percent."

Long moments passed.

"Well?" snapped Atem, concern showing in his voice for the first time. "Are we… there yet…"

"Almost, sir," answered the male computer operator. "Ninety-eight... Ninety-nine... and… that's it! Download complete at two minutes thirty seven seconds."

"Can you see her?" Atem snapped. "Is she manifesting correctly?"

"Appears so, sir." Petrov stared at her screen. She glanced up at her superior. "Hel appears to have materialized in Aaru."

"And the package?" Atem pressed. "What of the package?!"

"Still extracting sir," the other technician answered. "Just twenty-seven percent."

"Damn it! That's too slow," Atem cursed in dismay.

"We're at three seventeen!" Petrov shouted. She spun in her chair to fix Atem with a concerned look. "Situation yellow. We've got less than forty-five seconds before risking detection. May I advise--?"

"Does the extraction appear to be... normal?" Atem interrupted insistently. "Is it progressing? Are you detecting... any anomalies?"

"Negative," answered the man. "So far everything is green. Nothing out the ordinary. The package appears to be extracting... very slowly, but it's extracting... It's a big file, sir."

"We've got fifteen seconds until possible detection," Petrov pressed. "I advise dropping the connection *now.*"

"Extraction of package sixty-two percent complete" said the other operator. "Everything still normal."

"We've passed the four minute mark," Petrov interjected urgently. "Counter is condition *red.* Detection imminent. We *must* drop the connection!"

"Is everything... still normal?!" Atem persisted. "You're sure? Nothing at all out of the ordinary?"

"Still green, sir," responded the second tech. "Nothing unusual. Seventy-one percent."

"Sir!" Petrov exclaimed in rising alarm. "If the system double checks our log-in details... If it traces the validation codes or our router address...!"

"Fine, dammit!" Atem exclaimed. "Cut the blasted connection!"

Petrov poked furiously at her screen.

"Connection terminated," she said at last. Petrov slumped down in her chair, and sighed in obvious relief.

"Were there any... anomalies during... upload?" Atem wheezed. "Any during extraction? Anything at all? Be certain!"

Both operators stared at their screens intently, occasionally typing or swiping with their finger.

"Nothing unusual," said Petrov shaking her head. "Do you see anything, Yuri?"

"Everything was well within our expected parameters," said the second tech – apparently Yuri. "Everything looks normal. No problems detected with either upload or extraction – at least until we dropped the connection, but there's nothing here to make me think there's any problem."

"And were we… detected?" Atem breathily asked.

Petrov was silent for a few more minutes while she poured over her monitor.

"There's no evidence of any detection," she said at last, brushing a blonde hair from her face. "No warning messages… No system errors… No inconsistencies with the connection… We were pushing our luck, but I think we're good. If an individual manually looked over the upload registry, they might come across the record, but only if they knew what they were looking for. It looks like none of the automated security features picked it up." She smiled. "In and out."

Atem gave a great sigh, which turned into a fit of hacking and choking that doubled him over. He spat and left yet another dark red spot on the floor in front of Magic Man. Then the older man raised red, watery eyes to the rogue hacker.

"Good… for… you…" Atem gasped.

Magic Man shrugged.

"Like I told you," he said nonchalantly. "Why would I sabotage myself? And besides, you know the code as well as me. It would have been stupid to try and slip anything in. It would have been detected. I'm smarter than that."

"A… good… thing…" Atem gasped. He turned to one of the larger men who had stood away from all the technical goings on. "Get… me… out of… here…"

"Yes, sir," the meat-headed drone replied.

He offered his boss a shoulder. Petrov rushed over to support Atem on his other side. They helped Atem limp out of the building. At the same time, the other goons began quickly packing up the equipment and exiting the building.

Magic Man sneered and followed.

"About time!" he exclaimed stretching his arms high above his head.

It was markedly cooler outside, but still blazing. Magic Man took a swig from his canteen and then walked toward one of the vans. The meat-headed guy helped Atem inside and closed the door. He walked around and got into the driver's seat. Petrov climbed in the back. Atem rolled down his window as his lackey fired up the engine.

"I'd like to… thank you… Magic Man," Atem choked out.

Magic Man shrugged again.

"Eh," he demurred. "We both got what we wanted, right?"

He grasped the handle on the rear passenger-side door and pulled. It was locked.

"Indeed," replied Atem with a smile that did not reach his eyes. "Indeed, we did… I've got everything… I need…"

Magic Man tried the door again.

"Uh, Atem," he started uncertainly. "The door?"

"I've got… everything I require from you, sir," Atem answered coldly. "I have no further… need of you, and I have business… of my own to attend to."

The man in the driver's seat cocked some automatic handgun and glared at him, and Magic Man froze, waiting for the driver to level the weapon at him. He narrowed his eyes, and gritted his teeth in rage.

"So, you're going to kill me then," he hissed.

Atem shrugged.

"I'm certainly not… going to take you with me," he sniffed derisively. "I can barely stand… the sight of you. But no… Lucky for you, I'm no… savage. I'll not have your blood on my hands. After all your hard work… the least you deserve is a sporting chance. I think I shall… leave it up to the fates to decide what happens to you. Now that our business is concluded, that is… none of my concern. If something unfortunate occurs, well… That would be a pity, but…" He smiled the unpleasant smile again. "I simply view it as a boon to…. all the young, teenage girls of the world whom you will no longer be able to molest. Goodbye, Mr. Magic Man."

Petrov contemptuously shot him a narrow-eyed smirk through the rear window. Then the driver gunned the engine, and the white van sped away in a spray of sand and gravel. Magic Man threw up his arms protectively, but still found his mouth and eyes full of grit. He doubled over, and heard what could only be the second and third vans speeding away. When he recovered himself enough to stand again, and had blinked most of the sand out of his eyes, he turned in a wide circle.

He could see the dusty cloud trailing behind Atem's vans as they sped away into the distance. Other than that, the landscape was devoid of life. The sun continued to beat down relentlessly. Magic Man gave the canteen a shake. It was not nearly as full as he would have liked.

Magic Man screamed in frustration and kicked at the dusty ground. Then he bent over to seize convenient jagged rocks and hurl them impotently one after the other in the direction of the departing vans. He allowed himself to indulge in the tantrum for a few additional seconds. Then he took a deep, calming breath and stilled his fury.

"Waste of energy…" he chastised himself.

He'd hardly anticipated less, after all. Magic Man had quite expected a bullet in his brain to be perfectly honest. His situation was desperate, but it could have been worse. Atem had left him alive and alone. He was finally free. As planned, the file extraction had been just slow enough.

After Magic Man thought about it some more, he felt his mood drastically improving. He'd won he realized. Whatever happened next, his mission was an unmitigated success.

He glanced at his watch. Thankfully, Atem had not bothered to check it, and it was no mere timepiece. It was showing no bars now, but Magic Man had calibrated it while Atem was distracted. As soon as the satellite passed over again, he would be in business. Magic Man smiled. Then he laughed out loud. Once he started, he found he could not stop. Victory was finally his.

"No Atem," he breathed venomously, even as he was overcome by fresh bouts of mirth. "I couldn't hide anything in the code. That wouldn't have been smart at all. You would've found it. That would've been silly, wouldn't it? Couldn't do that, but… You don't know your own program as well as you think you do."

Eventually, his good humor subsided. Magic Man continued to stare in the direction of the departed vans. He took another swig of water and moved to the side of the metal building most shaded from the noonday sun. He sat and waited for the satellite to return. It should only be a few hours, and then… then he would be in business. Magic Man continued to chuckle. Indeed, victory was sweet. His only regret was he would not be around to see Atem's face when he discovered the truth.

Chapter 15

New Friends

Koren was disoriented when they finally got off the plane and entered the terminal. D and the other three guards escorted them from the gate, but this time they were hardly necessary. A few travelers gaped and pointed, and Koren smiled and waved, but it was nothing like the pandemonium at LAX. Hundreds of people rushed here and there, single-mindedly focused on getting to their flights or departing to their hotels. For the most part they ignored her.

Koren had no idea where to go, and was glad Amy was with her. Her personal assistant knew her way and guided Koren and the others to the luggage carousel. After they got their bags, they exited the secured part of the Melbourne Airport and entered the departure lobby where they began looking for Bindi and her family. She wasn't hard to spot.

The aboriginal girl's explosion of copper-colored hair surrounded her head like a raging signal fire, and she wore what looked to be a bright pink wetsuit covered only by a pair of black shorts. On her feet were a pair of fuzzy brown boots that looked oddly incongruous with her aquatic apparel. She smiled and waved vigorously when Koren came into view. Bindi hugged the American girl tightly. Selfies were taken, and both girls squealed and hopped with glee.

"It's so good to see you, Koren!" Bindi exclaimed. "It's been so long since the Beta meetup! I thought you'd forgotten about me."

"Well," countered Koren with a laugh. "You didn't text me either, you know. I've just been busy."

"Fair enough." Bindi released Koren at last. "Wanna get outta here? It's only half past ten... My dad said not to bother you 'causa jetlag and all, but how about we go do something *fun*?"

"Like what?" asked Koren with another bark of laughter. "Like scuba diving? That's what you look like you're dressed for."

"Oh, right! Sorry, I'm still wearing my bathers," apologized Bindi with a laugh of her own. "I didn't have time to change after surfing this morning and still meet you on time."

"Are you here by yourself?" Amy asked.

"Nah," Bindi answered. "My dad's waiting in the car park. He hates coming into Melbourne and didn't want to come inside. I'll text him to pick us up."

Bindi started walking and tapped at the screen of her smartphone while D got on a phone of his own. Koren and Amy followed wordlessly behind. Bindi led them out of the airport to a pick-up area. It had neat rows of red and green labeled luggage carts lining the walkway next to the airport's automatic doors. The three only stood there for a few minutes before a red Mercedes pulled up beside them and rolled down the window.

"G'day, girls!" called a friendly voice.

A dark-skinned man in khaki pants and a green sports shirt leaned over to push the door open from what Koren knew to be the wrong side of the car. A black BMW pulled in behind Bindi's car, and stopped. After D and his men helped Koren and Amy load their bags into Mr. Jones' car, they piled into the black car while the girls climbed into the red.

"Alright!" cried Bindi's dad good-naturedly. "And we're off!"

As they pulled away from the curb, Koren sighed in contentment. Things had been such a mess lately! A little R & R on the beach with a couple of girlfriends was just what the doctor ordered. She *so* needed this, and could hardly wait for it to begin.

***

Rose sat cross-legged on Hanabi's head, staring out over the sky-scape of her floating estate lost in thought. The sun was brilliant, and the angle of the light suggested late afternoon. A warm breeze tousled her long, brown hair. It rustled errant strands which flayed and whipped around her head. She wiped a curly brown tendril from her eyes and sighed.

She'd been ecstatic over seeing Koren again – holding her, touching her, brushing her tears away. It was wonderful. A warm, happy feeling had permeated her deepest self and persisted for quite some time after her sister was called away, but the melancholy feelings were starting to return. Rose didn't know why exactly. Nothing sad or upsetting had happened. Rather, a sort of antsy restlessness had taken over.

Rose sighed again and absently rubbed the long, bony ridge over her golden behemoth's eye. Hanabi rumbled contentedly, and Rose could not help but smile.

"You know what *your* purpose is, don't you, you big scaly kitten?" she murmured fondly. "I made you to know... You guard my door and look cool doing it."

"It is my pleasure to serve, Mistress," the dragon rumbled in reply.

Rose chuckled. She hadn't really expected a response, but it amused her none-the-less. She petted the great beast again.

"It's so easy for you, isn't it, Hanabi?" Rose shook her head and gazed off toward the horizon wistfully. "You know just exactly who you are."

"I am as you have made me, Mistress," Hanabi replied.

"Yes, you are." Rose sighed.

Am I? She could not help thinking. *Who made me, and why?*

Was it to make all this? She looked over her domain critically. It was beautiful – perfect even. Shrines and statues gleamed in the golden light of wizened day. Orange bridges arched gracefully between ivory and charcoal clouds. Rose had made all this. Koren loved it. She should feel proud of herself, she thought, and she supposed she was, but... But.

Then something caught her eye.

It wasn't much more than a dark blot against the bright orange background of her sky bridges. Rose squinted towards it, feeling unfriendly eyes upon her. It made her skin crawl. Was it a person? She shaded her eyes from the bright sunlight with her hand. Was someone watching her? Who could it be?

"R...Rose?"

The voice was hesitant and almost directly below her. Rose looked down to see heavily made-up, sable eyes looking back. She glanced back over to the bridge where she thought she'd glimpsed the dark figure, but whatever it was, it was gone now. Rose glowered in annoyance.

"What do you want, Ebony?" Rose replied, undisguised distaste coloring her ill-tempered voice.

"I... I wanted to talk to you..."

Rose scowled.

"I don't. What's there to say?"

"Please, Rose?" Ebony shoved her hands into the pockets of a short, black leather skirt and studied her feet. "Please?"

Rose sighed and rolled her eyes.

"Fine," she said. Then she leapt from Hanabi's head. Her kimono and her long, brown hair billowed around her before she came to a halt inches from the ground. Rose scowled at the other girl. "Say what you've got to say. Then leave."

Ebony sighed.

"I deserve that..." she murmured in obvious chagrin.

Ebony turned her dark eyes up to Rose who hung resolute and wrathful in midair. Mascara painted the Goth rocker's pale cheeks in meandering lines.

"I... I just really... really wanted to say I'm sorry... *So* sorry. I didn't mean..."

Ebony trailed off.

Rose swallowed, but was not ready to let her anger go so easily.

"Sorry, huh?" she stated incredulously. "For what? I thought you guys were teaching me a lesson? Setting me straight..."

"That was all Matteus' idea," Ebony answered lowering her eyes and kicking at the ground. "I didn't know he was going to... And then your Harm Failsafe... I... I'm sorry Rose." She repeated.

"So, great," shot back Rose. "You're sorry. Why now? What do you *really* want?"

Ebony looked surprised. "No... No really... It's j...just that... I felt *so* bad. Really... I swear! Matteus.... He went too far. I... I just wanted you to know--"

"Ebony," Rose interrupted sharply. "God only knows what that Ed maniac could have done to me if he'd managed to pull me through that door. I mean, what could possess a person to play around with something like that? Even if you didn't know, Matteus obviously did, and *you* are friends with him!"

"That's what I wanted to tell you, Rose..." Ebony murmured, looking ever more chagrined. "I don't know that I'm going to hang out with Matteus for a while..."

"Great." Spat Rose. "Good for you. Why do I need to know that? It's not like we were exactly besties before or anything. Why are you so keen to get my approval now?"

"It... It's not that..."

200

"Then what is it?!" Rose shot back. Her face reddened and smoke started to rise from her shoulders.

"I'm worried Matteus and Dontavious and a few of the others are getting into something *dangerous*, and I don't know what to do about it!" A tear trickled down her cheek as she hissed the confession, but it was just a fierce whisper, as if she was afraid someone might hear her. Indeed she looked right and left nervously as soon as the words left her lips.

Rose arched a curious eyebrow. Ebony certainly seemed legitimately scared. What could this possibly be about? The smoke around her shoulders dispersed and she dropped finally to the ground. Rose fixed Ebony with a hard stare, but did not say anything. She noticed Ebony's elaborate pattern of tattoos had changed. They were darker now and more somber in theme.

"Could we *please* talk about this someplace safe?" Ebony begged.

Rose looked at her a moment longer, but finally nodded.

"Let us in, Hanabi!" she called out as she spun on her heel.

The golden dragon withdrew his serpentine body and Rose led the way into her private dwelling. Ebony followed practically glued to her shoulder.

What on Earth has her so spooked? Rose wondered. *Ebony looks positively scared to death!*

Rose did not know Ebony well, but the Goth girl had always come off as too cool to care. She never smiled or laughed, but rather seemed to ever regard the world with a passive condescension. The only other emotions she ever displayed came out through the strings of the electric guitar strapped to her back, which was her constant companion. The time or two Rose had heard her play, she had to grudgingly admit, Ebony was quite good.

After they entered Hanabi's pagoda, and Rose slid the paper doors open to her private tatami room, she seated herself on a fat *zabuton* cushion and gestured for the rocker girl to do the same. The fire pit in the middle of the floor blazed to life of its own accord, and Rose fixed Ebony with a serious expression.

"Alright," Rose said. "This is about as private as it's ever going to get in Aaru. What's got you so freaked out, and why on Earth would you come to *me* of all people?"

"I didn't know who else to talk to," Ebony was on the verge of tears. "I just thought you might understand, since you saw, you know? Since you could see a little bit..."

"Ebony," interrupted Rose in exasperation. "What on Earth are you talking about?"

"We got in a lot of trouble, Rose," she breathed. "Big trouble... HUGE trouble... And they don't even know everything... I c...can't go there R...Rose..." She started sobbing. "I *can't*!"

"I don't know at all what you mean..."

"Matteus didn't really care about you 'threatening the stability of Aaru' or whatever it was he said," Ebony explained. "He was afraid you'd get us *caught*."

"Caught?" Rose repeated questioningly. "Caught doing what?"

"I'm glad we're not dead, Rose," Ebony said. "We all are, but... Have you ever felt like... like all of this..." She made a sweeping gesture with her arm. "Like all of this wasn't *enough* somehow?"

Rose just looked at her. She felt that way often, in fact. Then she felt guilty about feeling that way, but was hardly ready to share her deepest, darkest misgivings with the best friend of the Veda she admittedly liked least. Ebony seemed to take her silence as incredulity.

"Well... *we have*!" she exclaimed defensively. "I don't know about you, but I was never into to the harps and clouds thing before I died. I'm sure as Hell not into it now."

"What did you do?" Rose asked simply.

"We wanted to *feel* something again, Rose!" Ebony passionately replied. "And we found a way."

Rose waited.

"The first time I got the New Resident call for quarantine," she continued quietly. "It was for this girl named Iris. I had my spiel ready, you know, like we all do, but it was different this time. This girl was bat-shit crazy. She screamed. She cried. She tried to jump me!"

"Didn't Mikoto show up?" asked Rose. "He always..."

"Not in quarantine," Ebony shook her head grimly. "Mikoto doesn't respond to Residents in quarantine because... well... they're in quarantine! There are some seriously screwed up people in there, Rose – psychotics, pathological, sociopaths, morbidly depressed.

Anyway, my Harm Failsafe engaged, and I shot out of there like a bullet. It scared the shit out of me, but I felt alive again! *Alive!* It scared me but... but I... I kinda liked it. It was a *major* rush."

"And you told Matteus..." Rose said with a look of disgust.

"I told Dontavious first," Ebony admitted. "He thought I was nuts, but then he got *Ed*. The same thing happened to him, and he felt it too. Then we both told Matteus. We figured since we had the Harm Failsafe, we'd be fine, so..."

"So you started trolling the poor bastards in quarantine."

"It's not like that!" insisted Ebony. "It didn't *hurt* them! We... I... What the Hell were we supposed to do, Rose? Harps and clouds forever? We *needed* something! We needed something more."

Rose didn't immediately say anything, but thought she understood what Ebony was talking about. How often had she mentioned that very thing to Franco? A nagging feeling inside of her that she needed a focus, a *purpose*, but not understanding just what it should be. She'd been thinking about it just before Ebony arrived, in fact.

However, she also thought back on her encounter with Dani – how lost and sad and hopeless he seemed. The idea of messing with him just to 'get a rush', as Ebony had put it, fired Rose's temper. The very idea offended her.

"So, you got in trouble then," said Rose coldly, crossing her arms. "I hope you did anyway. We're supposed to *help* Residents, not *bully* them!"

Ebony paled.

"No," she whispered. "That's just the thing... Our Lords and Ladies don't know about it. They just know about you. I'm afraid, Rose. They... They threatened to put us in quarantine ourselves if we ever did anything like what Matteus did to you again... *For six months!* I couldn't stand it there for six *minutes*, Rose. I'd go insane. I..."

"So what do you need?" Rose interrupted perplexedly. "Why are you telling me all of this?"

"You went into quarantine, Rose," Ebony murmured. "You even brought a quarantined Resident *out* with you. I figured you'd understand... If you didn't feel the same way as us... If you weren't missing something too..."

Rose shook her head and exhaled a deep breath. "Even if that was true, what is it you want from me? This sounds like an issue between you and your Lady. What do you expect me to do about it?"

"I don't know, Rose," Ebony studied her hands folded in her lap. "Matteus is just mad and storming around like he's being unfairly punished and wronged. Dontavious is avoiding both of us. I think he's more scared of quarantine than I am. I can't talk to Lady Pyrrha about it. I... I just really wanted someone to talk to."

Rose studied the rocker girl's face carefully, not at all swift to trust her. Still, she saw no lie in her eyes. Her face softened.

"You... you guys really scared me..." Rose said quietly. "I'm still mad at you."

"I know, Rose." Ebony spoke up quickly, adopting an extremely sincere and apologetic expression. "And I'm *so* sorry!"

"I... kinda get what you mean about missing something," Rose continued reluctantly, but she critically met Ebony's dark eyes. "I feel that way too sometimes, but why on Earth would you seek out something like... like that *on purpose?*"

Ebony hung her sable head.

"It was stupid," she admitted softly, "but I just *so* wanted to *feel* something again!"

Rose looked at her thoughtfully. She had always thought of her problem with restlessness as a lack of *doing*, but was that accurate? She could certainly recall having strong emotions after arriving in Aaru, but those had honestly been few and far between and always after some traumatic event. She thought over her daily life here. Her initial joy had admittedly given way to a nagging sort of unsettledness – a persistent feeling she needed to be engaged in some task, but she did not know what would satisfy that need. Rose could create anything her mind could imagine. She could be anything she wanted on a whim, but something was still inexplicably missing.

"You might think about mixing with the regular Residents," Rose suggested. "You know... Help them out or something? Maybe make some friends..."

Ebony shot her a dubious glance.

"Can you *really* hang with Residents who aren't Vedas, Rose?" she asked skeptically. "If you can, I'd love you to teach me how. If I show up in a public place they mob me. I can't say three words to a Resident before they're asking me to do something for them or fix something for them, or moderate some petty squabble with some other Resident. It's too much like work. I just wish…" she sighed and trailed off.

"What, Ebony?" asked Rose.

"I don't know," Ebony answered with another deep sigh. "I just want something to be… you know… *important* again. Before, I was all into my music. I practiced guitar every day. I was gonna be the next Janice Joplin or Joan Jett, but…"

"But what?"

"But this," Ebony huffed bitterly. She swung the black guitar on her back around to her bare, tattooed stomach. Her fingers flew over the strings in a blur and a wailing heavy metal riff screamed from invisible speakers. "Now you try it…"

"What? I couldn't…"

"Just do it!" spat Ebony. "All you have to do is think about it."

Rose hesitated a moment, but then nodded slowly. A red guitar materialized in her hands. She only thought for fraction of a second before producing the exact same riff as Ebony. The rocker girl chuckled unpleasantly and nodded as she shifted her guitar to her back once more.

"See what I mean?"

"I don't under--" Rose began. The red guitar disappeared.

"Come on, Rose!" Ebony interrupted incredulously. "How long'd you practice? A minute? A second? My music was my *life*! But what good is doing something anybody can do without even half trying?!"

Rose thought back on her own Aaru experience. She recalled that very first soccer game with her Veda friends. She thought of Auset's amazing feats of dexterity and strength in spite of the fact the small, shy girl had never played soccer a day in her life before. Ebony apparently saw something in Rose's look because she nodded. An expression of grim satisfaction spread across her pale face.

"Get it now?" she murmured. "I… I don't know who I am anymore, Rose. I've always been 'the rocker girl'. I've always been the one who can shred harder than anyone else, even the guys! But all of a sudden, it's no big deal, and I don't know what to do… who to be…"

"I… I get it…" Rose answered softly. "I've felt the same way… Of course…" Her expression hardened. "You might have tried talking to me about it first, instead of trying to scare me to death and nearly get me killed… *again*. And what about you guys? You heard about all of that Magic Man stuff, right? The Harm Failsafe isn't perfect. It nearly got me ripped out of the system before Mikoto shut everything down. If anyone could find a way around it, or use it against you, I bet it would be someone like that Ed guy. He's… He was just… just evil… What you did was really dangerous and stupid."

"Y… you won't… tell Lady Pyrrha, will you?" Ebony asked nervously. "All that stuff I told you… about quarantine, I mean… I'm *really* sorry about what happened."

Rose had to admit she was tempted. She was still angry at the other three Vedas, after all. She could still see Ed's mad eyes behind his hideous skin mask staring into hers with unabashed hatred. She could still feel his grasping hands clamped around her ankle and clawing at her skin. Rose shuddered in revulsion, but holding grudges wasn't really in her nature, and Ebony *had* apologized, so…

"Just… Just knock it off," Rose said finally with a sigh. "Don't go messing with the quarantine Residents anymore, and all of this will probably blow over."

"Thanks Rose," Ebony sighed in relief.

They stood and Rose led Ebony out of her residence.

"You know," Rose ventured just as Ebony was about to go. "You could come hang out with us some… Talk about stuff. Maybe this is something we could figure out together. We're not hard to find…"

"Maybe we all should," Ebony replied, but there was a hopelessness behind her dark eyes. "I know at least some of the other Vedas feel the same… I don't know, Rose. When I got sick, I thought it was over. I thought I was done, and I was so, so angry about it. I'm grateful, of course. I'm glad I got another shot. I just… just don't know what to do with it. We need something… Something more… Talk to you later?"

"Yeah," said Rose. "Sure."

Ebony nodded and flashed Rose a tiny, grateful smile. Then she spread her arms wide and her form shifted. A black bird of prey shrieked and flew off into the turquoise sky. Rose watched her go

She's right, Rose thought. *I hate to admit it, but she's right…*

Rose thought she glimpsed the blurry, black figure on the orange bridge again out of the corner of her eye, but when she turned towards it, there was no one there. Maybe her eyes were playing tricks on her. Maybe she should go find Auset. Even though she had been less than enthused about sharing her feelings with Ebony, Rose could not deny she very much wanted to talk to someone all of a sudden too.

Chapter 16

Turnabout

Hel slowly opened her mismatched eyes. For a moment she was confused. The last thing she remembered was impotently seething in her prison after another long and miserable session of her creator's attentions – her rage and pain ate at her insides and fueled a cold, stygian wrath that defied sufficient expression. Now, however, she found herself lying on the ground tightly curled in fetal position.

Brown blades of long grass tickled her nose, and a dim twilit glow illuminated her surroundings. This was different. This was new. Hel had no idea where she was or what the change might mean, so she tensed in anticipation of the penetrating defilement that usually followed these post-blackout awakenings.

It never came.

After a few more hesitant moments, she pushed herself up and looked around. Hel stood in a broad and grassy field. It stretched away from her in every direction beyond the limits of her vision. The sky was cloudy and grey, and the lighting suggested it must be near dusk. Where was she?

A gentle wind caressed her face and tossed her long hair. It made the fabric of her dress whip and snap around her legs. She looked down at herself.

Hel was wearing a short white sun dress. It cut off just at her knees. She plucked at it in wonderment, reveling in the sensation of touch. She had almost forgotten what it was like. She rolled the coarse fabric between her fingertips and rubbed her hands over it. Then she felt smooth, warm skin beneath. Hel ran her hands up her body and through her dark hair. It had been *so* long… She almost smiled.

Then Hel caught sight of her hands – one perfect and white, the other dappled and sickly in shades of deep purple and dark red, the fingernails black. She gritted her teeth, and balled her fists in rage, but would not allow herself to cry out. She was certain that was what her Maker wanted.

He delighted in her screams. He took pleasure from her anguished pleas. Her tears, begging, and curses drove him to ecstasy.

Never again, she swore. *Never ag--*

There was a stabbing pain in her abdomen, and Hel crumpled to the ground. She seized her agonized belly as it swelled beneath her hands. She groaned in misery writhing and arching her back as the pressure in her stomach grew. It spread to her hips, and she could not contain a high, puling squeal of pain, but she was determined.

No more! Hel thought ferociously. *He'll never get that from me again!*

She squeezed her eyes tightly shut, ground her teeth, and covered her mouth with her hand.

Still clutching her bloated belly, Hel rolled to her back with a groan. The urge to push was powerful, undeniable, so she pressed with all her might. Her white sun dress was suddenly soaked dark red. Hel released a muffled squeal of horror, but it was not about the blood.

She realized that something was coming out... coming out of *her*. She twisted in the grass, her breath coming quickly through her nose. Tears burned in her gaping eyes, but Hel pushed yet again, desperate to be rid of the thing that was hurting her. She felt it squirm within her, and the unexpected motion beneath her skin drove her to near panic. What was happening to her?!

Hel pushed a third time, then a fourth, and a fifth. With a last muffled shriek, something flopped out onto the grass. She collapsed bonelessly on her back, whimpering.

The wind blew, and the tall grass swished around her. Hel could not move. She was exhausted by her ordeal, so she just lay there, staring up at the iron gray sky in shock and confusion. Angry tears streamed down her cheeks.

Then she heard motion. It was a faint, but wet sound, and not at all pleasant. Hel rolled arduously to her side. She forced herself up on one elbow, raised her mismatched eyes, and beheld the thing to which she had just given birth.

It looked something like a baby, but was already warping and twisting under her gaze. Hel gasped in horror as the arms and legs lengthened and the head swelled until the shape was unmistakable. Curled up in the brown grass was a fully grown man.

His features were yet indistinct and shifting as he rolled to his knees. When he stood however, they solidified into something more normal looking. The man turned his gaze to her, and a high-end suit appeared to cover his suddenly adult-sized body. Hel gasped. She recognized him.

"Ah, there you are," stated an aristocratic sounding voice. "Still hideous as usual, I see."

Hel's eyes narrowed, and she forced herself to her feet. Her insides burned, and she wobbled where she stood, but her fury kept her upright. She glared at the man with naked hatred.

"You..." she hissed.

"Me," replied the man with an arrogant grin. "Thank you by the way. I quite appreciate the Trojan Horse routine."

He ran his hands through his straight blonde hair, and it was suddenly slicked back and perfect. He appeared to be much younger than Hel remembered, but there was no mistaking this man. His pompous visage and smug grin had been burned into her brain upon their first meeting. He looked her up and down with a critical sniff.

"Sorry about the mess and all that," he said casually as he straightened his lapels and twisted this way and that to get a better look at his suit. He nodded approvingly at his garments but changed the color of his tie from blue to red. "Ah... That's better... Oh, it's good to be back! They've been keeping me out, for quite a long time actually. Needed a way to get past their security measures. It appears our good friend Magic Man came through on his promises after all."

"He's no friend of mine," Hel viciously spat. Fury twisted her blasted features. "And neither are you, Atem. What right do you have to *use* me that way?!"

"I think you might change your attitude," countered Atem with another derisive sniff. "I am a Lord of Aaru! *The* Lord of Aaru, if you'd like to know the truth of the matter. I began work on this place before half of the so-called board was even out of grade school. Everything in this place is mine to command, and it's time to start setting a few things right. You will be assisting me, of course."

"Help you?" Hel exclaimed incredulously. "Why would I *help* you? I want to *kill* you! I want to rip out your heart and eat your--"

"Yes, yes," Atem unconcernedly interrupted. "All that is quite beside the point. You have no choice, so you had best get used to the idea. You are my Veda, my hideous friend. I'm afraid whether you like it or not, we are going to be seeing quite a lot of each other. Regaining control of my creation will take time, and you are going to help me do it, unless..." he narrowed his eyes threateningly. "Unless you'd like me to end your miserable existence right now."

A slow smile spread across Hel's face, but she did not reply.

Atem cocked his head to the side and wrinkled his brow at her strange reaction.

"Mark my words, young lady," he uttered dangerously. "If you think I'm joking, I assure you I am not. I--"

Hel strode toward him with a contemptuous expression on her face. She pursed her lips and jabbed Atem in the center of his chest with a long, dark finger.

"Only Lords and Ladies of Aaru have the power to delete Resident files, Atem," Hel breathed darkly. She smirked at him. "Surely, you knew that..."

"What nonsense is this?" Atem exclaimed in alarm. He took a step backwards and rubbed the spot on his chest where Hel had poked him. "I just told you..."

Hel's smile grew wide. She displayed glittering white teeth, but there was no humor in her eyes. In her shattered memories, she still had a vague recollection of staring at code for hours and hours, days and days even. The dark side of her inner self knew the Aaru system inside and out, and it was taking control.

"Tell me," Hel hissed menacingly. She smoothed Atem's lapels and straightened his tie in a casual manner. "Tell me, Atem... What are the system requirements for assigning Veda?"

Atem recoiled.

"What do you mean?"

She saw the first hint of fear in his eyes, and Hel's heart quickened in pleasure and anticipation.

"You've forgotten then," Hel purred. "Well that's alright. I'd be happy to remind you. A Veda *must* be uploaded by the overseeing Lord or Lady to be served," Atem tried to back away, but Hel's grip tightened on his tie. "For that to happen... the time stamp for upload..."

She trailed off, and Atem gasped. He finally understood.

"No..."

"You're time stamp is two minutes and thirty-seven seconds later than mine, Atem."

He pushed away from Hel and jabbed a finger in her direction.

"Delete!" Atem screamed. Nothing happened. "Delete, Delete! *Delete!*"

Hel just grinned at him.

"I'm not your Veda, Atem," She murmured coming mere inches from his face. "You… are *mine*, and I'm not pleased with my Veda, Atem… No… No… Not at all."

Hel brought her lips close to his ear.

"In fact," Hel whispered. "I'm *very* upset with you. You called me names, and… You. *Hurt*. Me."

Atem tore away from Hel, spun on his heel, and ran. Hel watched him sprint across the unchanging plain for a moment with her hands behind her back. Her smile dissolved, and she raised her hand with a snarl. An earthen fist exploded from the ground. It seized Atem in an iron grip.

Harm failsafe engaged, blared a sterile computer voice. *Harm failsafe engaged.*

Atem disappeared from the muddy fist and reappeared sprawled on the plain about ten feet away.

"How annoying…" Hel sighed.

She strode toward Atem unhurriedly, hands again folded casually behind her back. She began to skip.

"Administrator override," Hel called in a sing-song voice as she drew near the fleeing Atem. "Passcode gamma one K J 2031. Harm failsafe override."

Passcode recognized. Command recognized and confirmed. Harm failsafe disengaged. Came the voice again.

Hel smiled.

"Well, what do you know, Atem?" she giggled in delight. "That was unexpected. Now…"

With a sound like a rumbling earthquake, the muddy fist lurched across the field to seize Atem again. It turned him to face her.

"All right, you monstrosity!" Atem shouted defiantly. "Do it! Delete me! It's not like it's the first time. I'm ready. I'm not afraid of you!"

"I *don't* like people calling me names!" Hel snarled.

Then she took a deep breath. She flashed Atem the same odd smile that did not touch her mismatched eyes. She kissed him on the cheek.

"There is something you need to understand, Atem," Hel breathed into his ear hungrily. "My existence has been nothing but fear and pain from the start. Until this very moment, every second has been a different kind of torture, and you were a willing part of that. *You* let it happen... Maybe you don't fear me yet..."

She bit down on the top of Atem's ear and pulled. Atem screamed in pain and Hel spat a bloody chunk away. Then she smiled, blood dripping from her lower lip.

"But you *will*."

She seized his head with both her hands and stared intensely into his eyes.

"Then do it!" Atem spat. "Do it, and get it over with, you harpy!"

She squeezed his chin, forcing him to gaze directly into her ruined visage.

"I *said* I don't appreciate the name calling!" she screamed in his face. "And you don't get to tell me what to do! I've *always* been someone else's plaything. That ends *now*. Now, *I* get to say what happens. Now *I* get to decide. And you... yes.... you are a problem."

Hel dropped her hand from his face.

"I *want* to kill you, of course," she drawled, laying a thoughtful finger against her sanguine lips. "But deleting you would be the easy way out for you." Hel brought her nose close to his again. "I've got to decide what to do with you, and I think I'm going to take my time, but I promise you Atem, nothing about it will be easy."

Hel walked a slow considering circuit around her prisoner.

"Hmm..." she said. "What to do first... Ah, yes... I think I'll go ahead and start with..."

Hel abruptly stabbed her dark finger through Atem's eye. He shrieked in pain and his agonized face warped and rippled as if Hel had plunged her hand into a pool of water. Her expression grew thoughtful.

"Let me see..." she mused. "What have we got in here? Not a big fan of your father, hmm? How about if he kept you company for a while? No... That's not it... I want to *torment* you, not annoy you... Well... You don't care for spiders either, I see... Now, that's *much* better. Let's start with that. That sounds positively *delicious*."

Hel grinned from ear to ear. Her dark half was ecstatic. The fear and pain she was eliciting from Atem was empowering, addictive. For the first time in her tortured and miserable life, Hel felt strong, and she reveled in it.

But her softer side, her sensitive half was screaming she shouldn't be – that causing such pain was wrong. She told it to be silent.

Hel sneered at Atem's agonized expression and ripped her arm free of his twisted face. She shook her hand as if flicking off droplets of water.

Just as Hel removed her scarred hand from Atem's brain, he began to choke and gag. He opened his mouth to scream, but no sound came out. Instead a flood of spiders erupted from the orifice. They wriggled out of his mouth and crawled down his chest by the thousands. Then they began to exit his ears and his nose in a never-ending stream. They even started to rip their way out of his eye sockets. Atem made a muffled gurgling sound, and began to convulse.

Hel spared a tiny smile at her handiwork.

"There is no greater prison," she murmured intensely. "Than that of your own mind. You and my Maker taught me that. Enjoy your nightmares, Atem, but never fear. Once I figure out the best way to deal with you, I'll get around to you eventually. Then we'll *really* have some fun together."

Hel raised her hand, and the ground shook. A pair of massive, gaping jaws erupted from the earth. They snapped closed on the silently shrieking Atem. Long jagged teeth formed a cage around him. There was a loud roar, and the skeletal cage disappeared into the loamy ground.

When Atem was gone, Hel released a shuddering breath. Then she sank to her knees with her mouth open. She gazed blankly across the sameness of the Aaru plain. When she glanced down at her hands, they were shaking. Hel's heart was beating at a terrific pace, and her air only seemed to want to enter her lungs in shallow gasps. She couldn't *believe* what she'd just done!

Hel had taken charge. She'd won. For the first time in her life, she had made her tormentors go away. She'd finally punished the ones who hurt her. Her dark half was exultant at her righteous cruelty, but the other side of her fractured self was horrified.

"You okay down there?" came a voice she did not recognize. "You've arrived, you know. There's nothing to hurt you here. You wanna get up, or what?"

Hel was immediately suspicious. Except for the dream-like, half-recollections from the lives of people she only vaguely remembered, the only two people she had ever met in her whole life had hurt her. They had used and ridiculed her, and she had no reason to believe this unexpected visitor would be any different. Hel pushed herself into a standing position and raised wary eyes toward the newcomer.

He was a tall, black boy wearing nondescript khaki pants, a white button-down shirt, and red-rimmed glasses, which gave him a sophisticated, intelligent look. He gave a visible start when he caught sight of Hel's ruined face and bloody sun dress.

"Y... Yeah... Well..." He stammered nervously. "I'm Dontavious. This is Aaru. You're in the waiting place... So, uh, just wait here until one of the Lords or Ladies calls for you. You can call into being anything you want to make you more comfortable... So, uh well... See ya."

The boy who called himself Dontavious seemed to be going through his welcoming speech as fast as humanly possible. As soon as he finished it, he started back peddling away from Hel and bent his knees as if he was about to leap into the twilit sky. Hel however, was in no mood to be so easily dismissed.

She growled at his abrupt demeanor and raised her hand. The tall grass at Dontavious' feet began to writhe and twist. It snaked around his ankles and held him fast. Then it yanked him back down to the ground.

Hel strode up to face the fearful boy.

"What's your hurry?" she hissed. His mouth gaped in fear, and Hel sneered. "Are you *afraid* of me? Dontavious, was it? What have I done to make you fear me? Don't rush off. I think I have a few questions to ask you before you go."

Dontavious could only stare.

"Where am I?" Hel demanded.

"Th...this is Aaru," the boy stammered.

"I know that," snapped Hel. "*Where* in Aaru am I? Is Rose Johnson nearby?"

"You... You're in the quarantined section," he replied. "And... And... I... I don't know. How do you know R--"

"Never-mind." Hel cut him off. "You said your name is Dontavious?"

She raised her white hand to the side of Dontavious' head and he reflexively jerked away.

"You're a pretty boy. I think I could like you…" Hel mused, but then trailed off sadly. She saw the thoughts in his brain as clearly as if they were stamped on his forehead. "And you're afraid of me… You think I'm ugly."

"I… ain't… I ain't…" Dontavious unconvincingly stammered the beginnings of a denial.

Hel seized his head with both hands. She closed her eyes.

"Yes, you are," she purred. "I see it clearly. It's all right here inside your mind. You're nearly petrified of me. You don't want to look at me, but…"

She cracked an eyelid and gave him a coy smirk.

"But you like that, don't you? What a funny little thing you are! You enjoy the fear. You need it even. How interesting…"

Harm failsafe engaged, blared the impassive voice. *Harm Failsafe engaged.*

Dontavious disappeared, then reappeared just out of arm's reach. He scrabbled away from her on all fours.

Hel stared at him thoughtfully. She let her hands fall back down to her sides.

"There's more to it than that, though, isn't there?" she called after him. "You *need* something – something you're not even sure you know… You are… searching… directionless."

Dontavious continued back away from Hel. She let him this time, but turned her body to favor her unblemished side. She blew him a kiss with her white hand and winked her mahogany eye.

"Well," she said pursing her lips together. "Until you figure out what it is you're looking for, I can give you *something* at least. Come near to me, Dontavious. Indulge your fear. I won't hurt you…"

Then she giggled.

"Unless you want me to, of course," Hel finished. "I wonder if you're the type. You seem like you might be. Come to me, Dontavious. I'm sure we could figure it out… You intrigue me… Will you come to me? Let's explore your mind together. I'm sure it will be so *interesting* in there."

"N… no…! G… g… get away!" Dontavious exclaimed. "I'm outta here!"

He leapt into the air, and Hel watched him go. She could have stopped him if she wanted. She could have plucked him right out of the gray sky, clawed through his mind and learned anything she wanted, but she did not feel like it.

Hel had spent the greatest portion of her wrath on Atem and now simply felt empty again. She felt tears coming, and her lower lip quivered. She was angry at Dontavious – furious even, but more than that, Hel was hurt.

Fleeting as it had been, he was the very first person to address her and not threaten or demean. He hadn't done anything to injure her and even after that very small dose of the most basic level of civility, the shortest most inconsequential of human interactions, Hel found she longed for more.

But he had run away from her.

"So, is this who I am then?" Hel lamented bitterly. "An object of fear and revulsion?"

A mirror flashed into being in front of her. She glared at her misshapen face. Hel willed the scarred side to change and mirror her pretty half.

Access denied, came the bland computer voice again. *File is read only. Locked by user. Access denied.*

"B... b... but..." Hel stammered. "I don't wanna be ugly. I don't want people to be afraid of me. I don't want them to run away."

The loneliness of her previous prison had been heartrending, but this was very nearly worse. Was that to be her fate in this new place too? She sank to her knees and wept hard wracking sobs with her face in her hands. Brown tears trickled from her yellow eye.

Was this her Maker's final joke on her? Hel had demanded release for *so* long. At long, long last he'd given it to her, but only vindictively, as if to demonstrate the foolishness of the desire. She sniffed, and wiped her dark arm across her face. Her sorrow swiftly turned to anger again.

The "waiting place?" she thought caustically. *That's what that Dontavious boy said, but no... He's a liar! I'm in quarantine. They're still trying to lock me away!*

There in the jumble of her disjointed memories she understood what quarantine meant. She was garbage, damaged, worthless - human trash dumped alone and far enough away where she'd never bother any of the beautiful people, never disturb their nice, neat, happy little lives. They didn't care what the people in quarantine were feeling. They had no clue, and didn't want to either. The memories of multiple lives assailed her – Memories of pain and illness, grief and hopelessness, rejection and bitterness, and this new slight made Hel furious.

She knew what Aaru could be. Parts of her recalled soaring over golden fields and laughing with friends as they sailed along a silvery river. Parts of her remembered love and tender touches. Now she had none of that.

They might be her memories, but they belonged to another person – a perfect person. She saw a girl with a glowing smile and long curly brown hair, or was it blonde? The images seemed to overlap in her recollection, but both were pretty people. They were people who others wanted to be near - people who elicited smiles and envious sighs from everyone they met. Not like Hel. *Nothing like her!*

What right do they have to their utopia? She brooded bitterly. *What right do they have to abandon me and all the others here, alone in the dark?*

She felt like crying again, or maybe having a tantrum, but something in the jealous thought stuck in her brain, making her consider. It took a moment for the idea to fully register.

No, she realized slowly. Hel quieted her tears, and quelled her rage. *The time for tears has passed. There* are *others here. Others cast aside, and I... I am not just one of them. I defeated Atem. I locked him away. I am a Lady of Aaru. I am their queen!*

There's no reason to cry anymore, Hel chided herself. *I'm not helpless any longer. My Maker is not here. He cannot hurt me.*

She stood and raised her arms high over her head.

"I am Hel Freakin' Lady of Aaru!" she screamed at the top of her lungs. "And that means something!" Hel slowly lowered her hands as echoes of her cries dispersed across the infinite plain. "That means something," she murmured.

Hel wasn't sure exactly *what* it meant of course, but she knew she had power. What she had done to Atem proved that. She was also starting to realize the beginnings of a purpose, but she was not going to figure that out here railing at the sky.

"It's time to go," Hel whispered to herself. "I think I'll go meet some of my subjects and have a good think."

She made a diagonal cutting motion with her dark arm, and a shimmering tear appeared before her in the very air. Hel gripped the edges with both hands and thrust them apart. A door appeared in the breach. She opened it and stepped through.

After she passed through the door, the jagged scar snapped shut with a flash and a crack like a lightning strike. Hel was a prisoner no longer. She was finally going to make some choices herself.

Chapter 17

Girl Time

Koren lay on her back on a beach chair. She wore a tiny, black bikini and a pair of sunglasses while baking pleasantly in the toasty sunshine. She wasn't exactly asleep, but here beneath the balmy afternoon sun, moderated by the mild ocean breeze, Koren didn't think she'd ever felt more relaxed in her whole life.

Things had been such a mess lately - everything piling up in her mind, weighing it down with worry and dread. Now however, her crazy and dysfunctional parents, the stresses of her celebrity, her broken heartedness at Jonas' betrayal - and the lying creep could go straight to Hell, by the way - none of it seemed quite as catastrophic as it had just a week and a half ago. Bindi had been a large part of the reason why.

The aboriginal girl with the cloud of bronze-colored hair was a blast. She was never without a ready smile and hearty laugh and was always up for doing anything fun or exciting. Koren had liked her before, but found herself developing a fierce affection for her now.

Since, they pulled up at Bindi's beachfront house along The Esplanade in Torquay that first day, they had gone swimming, parasailing, hang gliding, and surfing, although Koren was spectacularly bad at it. Bindi had actually referred to her as a "Shark Bikkie," which she didn't completely understand, but got the general idea it wasn't a compliment. They'd attended parties, "barbies", or gone to dance clubs every single night. In fact, her third night here, Amy reminded her that it was actually her fifteenth birthday. With all the troubles plaguing her lately, Koren had totally forgotten about it.

Amy and Bindi were determined to make it a night to remember, and it certainly was. It was amazing how much more fun it was to sip a drink with two other girls at a busy club, snap selfies, tell stories, point out cute guys, or laugh at the drunken antics of other patrons - much more fun than the couple of times she had gone clubbing with, and been generally ignored by Jonas.

Koren felt a little guilty about it at first, but then Bindi explained the drinking age in Australia was eighteen, and if you were with an adult it was effectively zero. In that regard Amy had proven phenomenally useful. Although, in a practical sense all she did was help Koren mentally check a box she wasn't doing anything *really* bad. So far no one had actually asked any of them to prove their ages, and D and his men seemed content to give her space and look the other way.

The ability to obtain hooch was not the only reason Koren was glad Amy was here, however. Now that she'd finally given the young woman a chance, Koren found she liked her intensely. Amy was pretty and sweet. She was attentive to Koren's needs, but not above teasing when she really deserved it, and was really, *really* smart. It was funny Koren had never noticed before.

Perhaps it was Amy's revelation about her age, or the fact she could get them alcohol, but suddenly Koren could not deny how cool it was to hang out with the older girl. She lay next to Koren now on a neighboring beach chair, sporting a yellow bikini and sunglasses of her own. Unlike Koren, it looked as if Amy was in fact napping. Koren smiled. She had to admit, babysitting her must be exhausting for the young woman.

Another nice thing about being in a different country was the paparazzi mostly left her alone. Bindi had confided she was considered kind of a B-list celebrity. The *real* media star from Elysian Industries in Australia was a boy named George.

"That's right Koren," she'd said with a dramatic eye roll. "Gorgeous George is the big note bloke down here. His sister, Molly is in Aaru, but George is the one everyone fawns over. Blonde as sheep's arse, pretty eyes, pretty mouth. Looks a bit like you actually, but he's a total whacker if you ask me."

"What's a whacker?" she'd asked.

Bindi just chuckled. "Well… Let's just say I don't care for his company. How about we leave it at that? Anyway, he kinda sucks all the air out of the room, but I don't mind. The Elysian blokes come and ask me to do a few interviews or commentaries about what's going on with me and Derain for *Love Beyond Death Australia*, or with my mum and dad at the house, which is less than a zack-worth of nothing, but that leaves me plenty of time to get out on the water. The direct deposits keep rolling in every couple of weeks, so I guess I can't complain."

The conversation had gone on from there, nothing weighty or important, but reflecting back, Koren could not help but marvel at how much pleasure she'd gotten out of it. It was so nice to sit down someplace public and have a normal conversation with a friend without being surrounded by screaming fans or pelted with shouted questions.

This rarified and unaccustomed peacefulness extended to Bindi's home-life as well. Her parents didn't fight. In fact, they seemed to legitimately like each other, a situation Koren sorely missed in her own household. Bindi's father never drank more than a glass of wine or can of beer with a meal. He *did* spend a lot of time sitting in front of the TV like her dad, but rather than football games and NASCAR races, Bindi's father watched a steady stream of historical documentaries.

Bindi and her mom shouted at each other, but not like Koren and Gypsie Johnson. Rather they engaged in a running, playful banter - a mutual comedy roast of each other that never seemed to end. Koren sighed, more than a little jealous. She would have been happy to stay here with the Joneses forever.

A shadow fell across Koren's face, and her eyes blinked open in surprise. Bindi smiled down at her, copper hair tossed in the brisk ocean breeze. She was covered neck to ankles in her bright pink wetsuit. She held a surf board under her arm that was equally roseate as her fuchsia swimwear.

"Taking a nap?" she asked with a grin. "Did I keep you out too late last night?"

"Well, yeah," Koren laughed, leaning up on her elbows. They hadn't gotten in until after 4:00 a.m. "But I slept in, so I'm good. Just getting a little sun, maybe get a nice tan to take back to the states with me next week."

"By tan," Bindi quipped with a sharp bark of laughter. "Do you mean red like a bloomin' boiled crab? 'Because both of you look pretty well cooked!"

Koren looked down at herself. Then she shifted her bikini strap. It revealed a vivid ivory line down her shoulder in a field of crimson. She glanced over at Amy and noted the other girl didn't look any better. Koren groaned.

"This is gonna hurt tomorrow," she sighed in resignation.

"Eh," said Bindi with a shrug. "We'll slap some aloe on it, and you'll both be right as rain. It *is* getting late though. It'll probably be dark in an hour. You wanna go back to the house and get changed? Michael and the boys asked if we'd like to have a barbie on the beach tonight."

Michael was about sixteen and lived two houses down from Bindi. He had three friends who followed him around everywhere - Rick, Clayton, and Jack, who were about the same age. They were nice enough, but Clayton, a lanky awkward boy who wore glasses, was always hanging around Amy, and constantly staring down her bikini top when he thought no one noticed. The young woman found it so annoying she stalked back into the house and put on a baggy sweat shirt, but Clayton kept hanging around. Koren grimaced.

"I don't mind, Bindi," she said biting her lower lip, "but I don't think Amy had much fun last time we hung out with them, so maybe we should ask her."

Bindi let out a braying bark of laughter and doubled over in recollection.

"I'd forgot about that," Bindi chuckled. "Clayton! Clayton!" She mimicked. "Her eyes are up here, Clayton!"

Koren laughed, and Amy sat up groggily.

"W... Wha?" she asked muzzily.

"Well, that woke her up, didn't it?" Bindi remarked with another grin.

"Bindi wanted to know if you wanted to go have a barbecue with Clayton tonight," Koren said innocently.

"God, no!" exclaimed Amy, eliciting more laughter from Bindi and Koren. "I'd rather go back to the club and ask guys to repeat their same stupid pick-up lines fifteen times because I can't hear them over the music. At least when creepy guys hit on me there, they were my age!"

Koren looked at Bindi wryly.

"I think that was a pretty definitive 'no'," she said.

"Fair enough," answered Bindi. She looked at Koren. "So what *do* you want to do tonight? Hit the clubs again? Hang back at the house with my dad and watch *The Best Widgets and Flanges of World War Two* or something like that?"

Koren actually didn't think that sounded all that bad, but Amy sniffed.

"At least if we did that we'd get plenty of sleep for a change," she said wryly. "I love you girls, and I know it's your vacation. It's my job to follow you around and make sure you don't get too drunk or embarrass or hurt yourselves, but how about we do something *I* want to do tonight?"

Koren shrugged.

"Sure, Amy," she replied. "What's that?"

"How about," said Amy. "We build a fire before it gets too dark and just hang out on the beach. Just sit, listen to the ocean, and talk to each other without pulsing bass or a crowd of drunk people or creepy, handsy guys."

"That sounds nice," answered Koren truthfully.

"I've got some sleeping bags in the carport we could use," offered Bindi. "And my dad cut a dead tree down in the back yard a couple of months back. It's all piled up next to the house. I bet we could use that for firewood. Campout?"

"Sounds perfect!" said Koren.

And so it was decided. They all went back to Bindi's house to put on some shorts, but since it was still pretty warm out they kept their bikini tops on. Bindi decided to join them. She stripped out of her pink wetsuit and put on a red swim suit top and a tight pair of khaki colored shorts. Amy slung a grey sweat shirt over her shoulder, and Koren raised an eyebrow.

"In case I get cold," Amy offered. "The temperature can drop off quite a bit after dark."

"More like if Clayton and his friends swing by," countered Koren with a wicked little grin. "Give the kid a chance, why don't you? How about a vacation romance? Age is just a number after all."

Amy grimaced.

"Uh… No," she said emphatically

Bindi laughed, and then they all helped cart the sleeping bags and a large pile of wood down to the beach. Amy was surprisingly adept at fire lighting, Koren noted with approval. Her personal assistant soon coaxed a merry crackling blaze. The girls lounged by the campfire and looked out over the water as the sun sank into the sea. The stars came out, winking and twinkling in the sable sky. The roar of the ocean kept a gentle pulsing rhythm. It was nice.

"So Koren," Amy ventured after they were all settled. "How do you feel? You were pretty upset before we came. Has this helped at all?"

Koren sighed and rolled over on her elbow to face Amy across the fire.

"I think so," she said. "I don't feel quite so crushed beneath everything, but I'll admit it." She made a face. "I'm not looking forward to going back."

Amy nodded sagely.

"I understand," she said, "but I hope at least you've realized this trip you aren't alone. You have… friends you can turn to. I'm going back with you, remember?"

"And I'm never more than a video call or text away," added Bindi. "Don't be a stranger."

"Thanks Bindi… Amy…" Koren replied. She turned to the blonde girl. "I'm… I'm really sorry I was so awful before."

"Thanks for that," Amy answered, "but I understand why. Just remember, Koren, I'm on your side."

"Thanks."

"Wait," cut in Bindi. "You seemed fine to me. What did you do, Koren?"

Koren sheepishly told her. When she finished, Bindi stared at her with a theatrically gaping mouth.

"My!" she exclaimed. "You *were* a bitch! You're lucky she's even willing to *talk* to you. You should be fanning Amy with palm leaves and feeding her bloody grapes!"

The comment might have sounded critical if not for the aboriginal girl's sparkling eyes and wide grin.

"You're right," agreed Amy. "She was… And she probably should be."

"Yeah,' rejoined Koren snidely. "Just keep that love and support flowing guys. Thanks."

"Just keeping you honest, Koren," said Bindi nonchalantly. "It's not healthy to have people kissing your arse all the time. Tough love, Koren, tough love."

They all laughed, and Koren smiled at the dark skinned girl.

"I think this is the first time I've seen you out of that wetsuit," Koren noted.

"Now that's not true," Bindi countered. "I didn't wear it to the club the other night."

"No," conceded Koren, "but you did wear blue jeans and a baggy sweatshirt. You're in *really* good shape. I think I could wash clothes on your stomach. You're built, girl! You should show it off more. You look cute."

"Yeah, Bindi," added Amy. "You look really pretty tonight."

"You two trying to make me blush or something?" Bindi countered, but Koren thought she noticed a little more color come to the other girl's dark cheeks in the flickering firelight. She covered her bare stomach self-consciously and gave a nervous giggle.

"Right… not gonna happen," Bindi shook her bushy head. "This look is for girl time only. After you two leave it'll be back to hanging out with Michael and his mates again. I don't mean to big-note myself or anything, but this," she gestured to her swimwear. "This here might upset the balance of power, if you know what I mean. I think I'll save it 'til I feel like dating. Then it'll be take no prisoners, boys! And it won't be for any of those wowser dills either! It'll be a red-headed two-meter French-Canadian with a thick, bushy beard. You ever seen the lumberjack games? Saw it on satellite TV once with my dad - flannelled, hairy blokes, can kill a grizzly bear with their bare hands, good with power tools… Yeah, one of them."

They all laughed again.

"What about you Amy?" Bindi asked. "Are you dating anyone?"

Amy shrugged and lay back with her hands behind her head.

"I'm really busy with work…" she started.

"Sorry!" interrupted Koren with a laugh.

"It's not just you, Koren," Amy said. "You do realize I have other duties besides following you around, right? But seriously though, I spend my whole life at Elysian Industries. I barely have time to sleep, let alone maintain a relationship."

"Isn't there *anyone* cute you work with?" Koren asked.

"Koren," replied Amy with a wry expression. "You know everyone I work with. They're all… well…"

"Really old and wrinkly?" Bindi ventured.

Amy laughed.

"I wasn't going to say that, but since you mention it…" She trailed off and they all shared another giggle. "Really though, I was going to say 'too busy'. Aaru isn't just a job to them… Me either really. It's a calling. I know Askr can end up sounding like a nonstop commercial when he gets going, but I think he believes what he says. We're changing the world, Koren, Bindi… All of us are. I'm a true believer. I can't think of doing anything more important."

"Maybe you're right," conceded Koren with a grimace. "I'm certainly considering swearing off guys for a while. Effing Jonas…" She shook her head with a deep scowl. "Do you think they're all that way? You know… Lying, cheating, running around, letting some French slut stick her tongue in his ear?"

Koren felt her face growing hot. Then she recalled her last meeting with her mom and that slimy Benjamin Belial. Maybe all boys were just that way, she thought. It was a depressing idea.

"Your problem," Bindi stated pointedly with an extended finger jabbed in Koren's direction for emphasis. "Your problem is you like bad boys and rock stars. A guy like Jonas Perry? Of course, he's going to cheat! One-hundred percent guaranteed! Just like he's going to sing crappy cliché pop rubbish, drink himself unconscious at A-lister parties, and keep losing music awards. I read Seventeen." She gave a confident nod. "I know how it is. I bet your Jonas Perry and my Gorgeous George would be grade-A, bro-mantic besties forever if they ever got together. You just need to pick a different sort of bloke, is all. You know – shorter, fatter, maybe a little gimpy and balding…"

"You're awful, Bindi!" Koren exclaimed, but she couldn't keep the laughter out of her voice. "So are we all in agreement then? Let's swear a pact to give up boys forever! We'll just be tough, go-getter career women with no time for men's shit!

"Speak for yourself," replied Bindi. "I plan to be a complete bum and do nothing but lay about on the beach with my lumberjack all day running my fingers through his chest hair when I'm not waxing my board or surfing."

They laughed again.

"I don't know," mused Amy after they quieted. She stared thoughtfully up at the starry sky. "If I met the right guy – someone who understood how important my career was to me, someone who would treasure every second we spent together and not resent our time apart, then maybe."

"Good luck with that, Amy," Bindi replied with a dubious expression. "But they don't make those sort by the gross."

"Well, that's true, conceded Amy with a shrug. "But I only need the one. It's a big world out there girls. I bet there's one decent guy out there for me somewhere."

"Yeah," Bindi agreed. "It's just finding him that's the trick."

Koren thought about that for a moment. If it wasn't Jonas, who would she want a relationship with? She actually didn't know that many boys. There were a couple of boys from school she remembered having crushes on, but Koren hadn't seen them in forever. She'd been homeschooled alone for over a year and a half now. Then she thought briefly about Rick, Clayton, and Jack, but wrinkled her nose in distaste. They were pretty good guys, she supposed, and she had a lot of fun with them, but they were kind of goofy. Images came to her brain unbidden. She remembered Jonas' glittering smile. She recalled his soft lips pressed against hers, his hand on her bare thigh... She exhaled heavily.

"That was a pretty big sigh, Koren," Amy noted with a concerned look. "Are you okay?"

"Yeah... yeah... I'm fine." Koren answered. "It's just..."

"Just what?"

"*Why* does Jonas have to be so darn charming and hot?!" Koren exclaimed in frustration. "I mean... He can be *super* sweet! Like... Amy, you remember... the video last year? The really awful stolen one of me that went viral?"

Amy grimaced, but nodded.

"I heard about that," Bindi said softly. "That must'a been tough. I don't know what I woulda' done."

"It was *devastating*," Koren replied. "I thought my life was *over*, but then Miss Hanasaka took me to her office. She called someone and gave me her phone. It was Jonas. I don't think anyone else in the *world* could have made me feel better, but Jonas *did*! He was so sweet and so understanding. He told me embarrassing things about him that got out in the media. It seemed like he really understood what I was going through, and *cared* about me. He made it feel like everything really *would* be okay. Then he goes and won't return any of my calls or texts after the AMAs, like he's forgotten I even exist. He starts making out all over Europe with that French girl! And I'm like... What the Hell happened?! I thought he liked me... like really, *really* liked me, and now..."

Koren trailed off. When she spoke again her voice tiny and shaking.

"It's just so hard," she whispered. "If... if he was dorky and ugly, I'd have an easier time getting over him, but... I miss him."

"If he was dorky or ugly," Bindi noted sagely. "You wouldn't have given him the time of day to begin with."

"Yeah," Koren nodded. "I know."

"Would you take him back?" Amy asked. "If he came crawling across the sand on his knees right this moment saying how sorry he was, would you forgive him?"

Koren's immediate impulse was to say no. Jonas had really hurt her, but her mouth wouldn't form the words. *Would* she forgive him?

"You damned well better not!" Bindi exclaimed. "You can't let guys treat you like rubbish and get away with it. You can't let him think he's got you tied up all neat at home whenever the mood grabs him and then let him get whatever action he wants on the side every time he's on holiday. I know it's tough, but you gotta have some bloomin' self-respect, Koren! I'd *never* let a guy treat me like that."

"You're probably right, Bindi," Koren sighed again, "but it's *so* hard. He's the first boy I ever felt this way about, the first boy I ever kissed, the first boy I ever…"

Koren trailed off and blushed, having revealed way more than she intended.

"The first boy you ever *what*?" Amy asked in alarm.

"Yeah," chimed in Bindi. "What did you *do*, Koren?"

Koren's face was beet red, but it occurred to her that she'd already passed the point of no return. If she didn't tell them now about what she and Jonas had almost done, what her two friends imagined was guaranteed to be far worse than what actually happened. Koren told them about how he'd given her alcohol and taken her back to her room during the release party. She told them about fooling around on her bed and her drunk dad bursting in on them.

"So you let him do all that with you, and he still effing cheated?" Bindi exclaimed in outrage. "That makes it even *worse*! Okay, let me be clear, if I find out you're even *thinking* about getting back together with this pig, I will literally materialize right in front of you and kick your bloomin' arse!"

"Koren," Amy said in concern. "You *just* turned fifteen, and I remember the release party. It was nearly a *year* ago! Was this the only time anything like this happened?"

Koren shrugged dejectedly.

"Not much more than kissing," she said. "We made out a little bit in his limo a couple of times, but I never liked the driver being right there in front of us, so it wasn't much. I've gone out with Jonas a ton, but there's always people around – my security, his dork posse – all those loser guys who hang around and spend his money, you know. We never get a chance to be alone."

"That doesn't exactly sound like a bad thing to me," Bindi rejoined sternly. "You oughta consider yourself lucky you didn't go and do something really stupid you'da regretted afterwards, I'd say."

"I don't wanna sound all adulty or anything," Amy added hesitantly. "But aren't you kinda young to be doing that with a boy anyway?

"That's what my *mom* told me too," Koren huffed bitterly. She sat up, crossed her arms, and scowled. "Then I caught her all giggly and stupid and touching all over some pastor guy who drove her home from church. My dad was even standing in the upstairs window watching them! I mean... What's up with that? It's like she's trying to rub his face in her cheating! And then she has the gall to tell *me* how to handle *my* relationship?! The guy looks like a freakin' 'Jesus Fun Ken Doll' – plastic smile, plastic face and every time he opens his mouth he's *so* obviously full of crap. I don't know what the Hell my mom thinks she's doing."

"What?!" Amy exclaimed in surprise. "When did *this* happen?"

Koren told them all about that incident too - how she and her mother were barely speaking to each other, which of course also lead her to relate how her dad was majorly depressed and drunk all the time.

"Christ, Koren!" Bindi exclaimed when she was done. "And you've been keeping all this bottled up inside? It's a wonder you haven't exploded in a bloody ball of fire right where you're sitting!"

"I knew a little about some of this," Amy admitted, "but not *close* to everything. You gotta tell me this stuff, Koren. I know I'm not a counselor or anything, but if you ever need to talk, you have to come to me."

"Bloody Hell, girl," Bindi added, shaking her bushy head helplessly. "That's a proper dog's breakfast, that is! You can't keep secrets like them from your mates. That mess would be too much for anybody."

Koren opened her mouth to say something else, but it turned into a sob. Once she started she found it impossible to stop. Bindi and Amy looked at each other. Then they got up and sat on either side of Koren. They both draped sympathetic arms around her. That only made Koren cry harder.

It had been so long since she felt she could talk to anyone. Koren had confided in Rose of course, but Elysian Industries kept her so busy, those meetings were few and far between. She certainly couldn't talk to her parents about any of it. They were both too angry at each other, and at least for her father's part, despised Jonas Perry too much to be objective about it. The sudden revelation she actually had friends again felt like a major release.

Koren let them hold her for quite some time, but then blurted out.

"It's just that… things… have… been… so… bad… at home…." Koren sniveled. "And… I've felt… so all alone, and… I thought… I thought Jonas… really… *liked*… me… Maybe if my dad hadn't busted us. Maybe if I'd let him…"

"Now you just stop right there, missy," Bindi interrupted severely. "Never *ever* think that. If he really cared about you, he wouldn't have cheated. Don't go and give it up because you think you have to. If the bastard was just looking for some action…"

"He would have cheated anyway, Koren," Amy finished sternly. "And you would feel even worse about everything."

Koren wiped her eyes and took a deep breath. Then she gave a nervous little laugh.

"Look at me!" she cried. "I'm being such a big baby! I'm sorry."

"Don't apologize, Koren," Amy chided her gently.

"No," Bindi agreed, giving her coppery head a shake. "Broken hearts are no fun. Sometimes you just gotta get some stuff out is all. We're your mates. That's what we're for."

Koren squeezed them again.

"Thanks, guys," she whispered.

They sat together a long time, just listening to the roar of the sea and the crackling fire while they gazed up at the starry sky. It felt good, Koren thought, healing even. Amy kept the fire going, but otherwise they stayed quiet and still until nearly dawn. Even as the sky was just beginning to lighten in the distance, Koren thought she could have stayed like this with her friends forever.

A loud buzzing interrupted the thought. Amy sat up and pulled her phone from the pocket of her tight shorts. She crossed her legs and looked at the screen. Then her eyes grew wide in alarm.

"What, Amy?" Koren asked as evenly as she could, but already feelings of dread and foreboding were starting to build in the pit of her stomach. "What is it?"

Amy didn't say anything, she just held up the screen so the other two girls could see it. They both gasped.

"We need to get to the airport," Amy murmured in a strangled voice. "They've left us alone so far, and we didn't tell anyone where you were going, Koren but…"

"It won't be long until the paparazzi figure it out and track me down," Koren finished bitterly. "After this…"

"I'll get my dad," said Bindi.

"And I'll tell D," added Amy.

The three girls quickly kicked sand over the smoldering campfire and rushed back to Bindi's house. In just a very few minutes Koren and Amy were packed up, piled into Mr. Jones' car and racing toward the Melbourne airport.

Koren could not get the headline Askr forwarded to Amy out of her head. She had no words.

Wichita Teen's Suicide Note Claims He'd be Happier in Aaru.

Koren shuddered. She suddenly felt very sick.

Chapter 18

The Dark Side of Paradise

Hel wandered the dusky plains aimlessly. In all of her searching and exploring since leaving Dontavious, she had not happened upon a single other soul. It was demoralizing, but honestly, Hel had no idea what she would do if she did actually meet someone else. She *thought* she did not wish to be alone anymore, but then again she did. Her recollections of human interaction were mixed and conflicting.

On the one side of her memory, Hel recalled the contempt and derision she felt for other people. Her fury kindled at memory of how they ridiculed her and rejected her, so she was more than happy to reject them in turn. In her other self however, the side of her being that knew joy, friendship, and love, Hel was tantalized by phantoms of memory - of friends and family, warm hugs, kind sentiments, and professions of love. They awakened a longing deep within her breast, and her heart ached with loneliness.

In any case, every time Hel passed through her doors – dozens and dozens of them now - she always appeared in yet another deserted location. At last she collapsed in a miserable heap, overcome by frustration. Tears spilled from her mismatched eyes, and she released a great wail of despair.

"I must find someone!" she screamed at the ashen sky. "Anybody!"

There was whooshing sound, and Hel perked her ears.

Admin search request processed, droned a bland computer voice. *Access granted. Search history empty. Establishing connection to most recently referenced Resident.*

Hel wiped her eyes with the back of her wasted hand and sniffled curiously.

Most recently referenced Resident? Who...?

Then she looked up. Right before her was a sliding rice-paper door framed with shiny black wood. She rose and pushed the door aside.

The scene on the other side of the portal was breathtaking. It felt as if she'd been offered admittance to Heaven after languishing in Purgatory for an age. She stepped through.

Hel found herself standing upon a long, orange bridge suspended improbably between two fluffy clouds. She looked around in wonder and glimpsed beautiful floating gardens, sparkling fountains, majestic statues, and a single towering pagoda entwined by a massive gold dragon. It was beautiful, and her heart swelled with wonder and awe.

Then it nearly stopped.

Hel gasped. There on the dragon's head was a girl. Her beautiful kimono and long, curly hair billowed in the brisk wind.

It was Sister.

Hel knew her instantly, and the sight of her was deeply conflicting. From Hel's loving side, sight of Rose filled her with affection and longing. She experienced an almost irresistible urge to run to her, screaming Sister's name at the top of her lungs. At the same time however, her dark side was livid. Why had Rose abandoned her to torment and pain at the hands of Magic Man? Why did Rose have friends, beauty, freedom, and Hel had nothing? She was overcome by simultaneous urges to fall into Rose's arms and be held and comforted, but at the same time Hel wanted to punch Sister right in her lying mouth.

Another girl flew down to Rose's dragon pagoda. They started to talk, but Hel could not hear what they said. She longed to join them, and even took a hesitant step in their direction, but stopped herself.

"No," she breathed and hung her head.

A tear rolled down her cheek, and she sadly touched the ruined side of her face. The two pretty girls would hate her, she thought. They would fear and despise her and call her ugly. They would never let Hel be one of the chosen, beautiful people who were Sister's friends. It wasn't fair.

"*Please*, someone else!" Hel cried, unable to tolerate the vision a second longer. "*Anyone* but her! I'm not ready to… I just can't…"

Request processed. Randomized search initiated. Accessing Resident…

Hel spun on her heel, covered her face with her hands, and darted back through the sliding door. She slammed it shut with a crash and threw herself upon the ground.

Hel recalled her Maker and *hated*. The ground all around her hardened into a crackling sheet of ice. Why had he done this to her?

Why had he made her this way? What had Hel ever done to deserve being turned into this abhorrent pariah? She stayed there quite some time feeling extremely sorry for herself.

When Hel finally calmed enough to open her eyes, the effect was immediately disorienting. Where she found herself now was not the rolling, twilit lea. In fact, she was not sure she was anywhere at all.

"What is this place?" she murmured in mystification.

Hel found herself perched on a rock suspended in an iridescent void. The stony outcropping abruptly drifted away beneath her. She floated in space with no clear idea of what was up or down. Gravity did not seem to apply.

Other little islands of stone drifted around her. They were turned all different directions. Most were desolate and bare, but some had structures on them, others beneath them or on their sides, but the constructions were all bizarrely shaped. The architecture was absurd and impossible - composed of harsh angles and strange curves so they could not have credibly served any functional purpose.

Random refuse with no obvious rhyme or reason floated around her as well. There was an old, rusted school bus with the windows all smashed out. A windmill with fan blades like jagged swords tumbled end over end in a cloud of nebulous mist. A billboard depicting a smiling, blonde woman with glowing, red eyes bore the message, "only the righteous" scrawled across her face in what looked like blood. It rotated slowly nearby.

There were countless other objects too. Some were mundane - a stapler, a bike, a porcelain doll, a lawn mower, a child's patent leather shoe, an egg beater - but many if not most of the others, Hel had no idea what they could possibly be.

There was a murmuring also – a truculent hum like thousands of insidious whisperers muttering belligerently in an adjoining room. Hel thought she could almost decipher the babble, almost make sense of the words. She bent her will toward comprehending their meaning, but could decipher nothing in the mumbling din.

Hel willed herself to move through the nonsensical plane scanning her surroundings critically as she went, but it was no easy task. First, the garbage floating all around was distracting. She was sorely afraid she might miss something important in the profusion of junk. Also, nothing here seemed to act the way she thought it should.

Some of the tumbling islands of naked rock refused to grow any closer even though she was positive she could almost reach out and touch them. Others, Hel would have sworn were gigantic masses a great distance away, would suddenly bump up against her, the size of golf balls. Some retreated as she drew near. Others simply disappeared. Everything about her perspective in this place seemed warped and strange.

Then she saw something. Huddled on a floating stone island, and upside-down relative to Hel's position, was a cringing figure.

At last! She thought triumphantly and shot towards it.

As she drew nearer, her brow furrowed. Hel could hear the person muttering. The female voice stood out to her, because unlike the constant cacophony that permeated this strange world, Hel could make out actual words. The girl was obviously agitated. Her head jerked and snapped while she screamed as if engaged in a raging argument, but no one else was there.

"…but *I* know they're lying to me- trying to trick tricky trick me… trying to make me do bady, bady worse things! They keep whispering, whispering calling me names… taunting me, always taunting. You don't understand. You don't know what it's like…"

The girl was clad all in black, formless rags. Her hair was brown, greasy, and unkempt. She rocked back and forth as she muttered, wringing her hands, pulling at her hair, and her bare feet constantly rubbed against each other in the dust. Her eyes were wild and staring, but at the same time, the girl's face bore a silly grin that seemed incongruous with her blistering tirade.

Hel watched her impassively.

Just my luck, she thought, curling her lip in disdain. *I finally find someone, and they're completely insane.*

Hel almost called another door into being. She almost left this sad individual to her madness without another word, but it had taken *so* long to find her.

"Watching, watching… always watching… Judging there in the darky dark darkers," the disheveled person spat in a rage. "You can't judge me! You don't know! Did God send you? Did he send you take my bones? Because he wants to climb into my mind and wear my skin?!"

It still did not appear as if the girl was talking to Hel. The agitated young woman paused as if listening. Then she screamed in rage.

"How would *you* know?!" she cried. "Can you see inside my head? Are you digging through my mind like worms in a cheese? Get out. Get out!"

Hel cleared her throat, and the girl raised her head. Though she had never glimpsed this wretch before, Hel knew her.

"Hello, Iris," said Hel.

"What do you want?" Iris hissed viciously, scrambling back a few feet on all fours like an animal. "Why are you here? Are you spying on me? You mustn't hear what the voices tell me... It's secret... secret..."

Iris snarled and tensed as if she might leap at Hel, but her eyes grew wide and she gasped instead. Iris scampered backwards and cowered in fear, but her strange smile never faltered.

"N... No... Please!" Iris begged. She hid her eyes "You have the evil eye! All ickity ick icky and yellow and dead! You're one of the dark ones, the darkity dark demons screaming in my heady head! The monsters who want to eat my soul like ice cream! You want me to do it, but I don't wanna. You can't make me! I'll never listen..."

"You're a hebephrenic," Hel said neutrally enough, though her white cheek reddened and she covered her discolored eye self-consciously with her perfect, white hand.

She only half remembered the word she'd just used. It was from her dark, academic half, her malevolent and calculating side. It took the caring part of herself a moment for the meaning to register. Her softer, kinder self didn't know it. This gave her darkness a momentary advantage.

"You have all the signs," Hel hissed viciously.

"You stop that!" Iris shouted, hands extended protectively before her, gyrating and unsteady. She turned upside down and stood on her hands before jabbing an accusatory toe in Hel's direction. "Don't you use th...those d... doctor words. Don't judge me with your doctor mouth! Y... you and your doctor words... you're trying to cut my mind into pieces and eat it for dinner! I won't let you!"

Iris fled.

She flipped over and soared off into the myriad of shifting colors and vapors that made up the illusory atmosphere of this place. Hel smirked.

So it is to be a merry chase then, she thought. *Very well.* She snapped her fingers with a snarl.

Hel was suddenly someplace different. It looked like a mountain top. Cold gray snow flew and whipped around her in a violent wind. It seemed to be composed of Iris' badgering voices. As soon as the wretched girl saw Hel, she leapt backwards in surprise. Her eyes registered shock and horror, but her demented grin remained fixed.

"Y... you can't follow m... me," Iris protested. "It's against the rules! You c... can't know. You can't see! I'm secret! *SECRET!!!*"

Hel smiled. The other girl's fear made her feel powerful.

"I can see everything inside you, Iris," Hel taunted. Her dark side was enjoying this enormously. She stared deeply into the girl's terror-stricken visage, and turned her head to favor her disfigured half. "All your secrets are mine if I want them, but then you know that already, don't you?"

"Monster! Monster!" Iris screamed. "G... go away!"

She launched herself skyward once more.

Hel shook her head at the futility of the gesture, but her rage was also kindled. She *hated* name calling. It hurt her feelings. Hel snapped her fingers again.

Iris crouched in the entrance of what looked to be a large, dark cave. She peered out of the shadowy opening fearfully, flapping her elbows up and down like some sort of strange, slow-motion chicken dance.

"Chicky, chicky, chick," Iris muttered under her breath. "Chicky, chick, chick, chick... Can't see a chicky, chick, chick... No, no, no. Can't Can'ty can't..."

Her back was turned, so Hel stood behind her for a moment considering. The thrill of the hunt was intoxicating certainly, but she was tiring of her play. The girl's nonsensical antics were starting to grate. It was time to bring her prey to ground.

She giggled, and Iris rounded on her in alarm.

"I-ris," Hel called softly in a sing-song voice, dragging out the girl's name. It echoed off the damp cavern walls to sinister effect. "Oh, Iiiiiiiiiiris... It's not nice to say mean things to me, Iris. You've hurt my feelings. Now, I'm upset with you."

Iris stumbled and fell. Hel strode up to her and stared imperiously down at the quailing girl.

"Don't run away from me, Iris," Hel commanded in a low, threatening voice. She reached out and grabbed the front of Iris' dirty shirt. She pulled the girl's hysterical face close to her own. "You can't."

The other girl was so afraid, she was shaking in Hel's grasp. Her breath was coming in quick shallow gasps, and she was making a high, squeaky sound every time she inhaled. Iris' teeth were even chattering.

Hel began to feel badly about herself. Her caring half was clawing back control. Wasn't the whole reason she decided to do this in the first place to meet other people who might understand her? Might even *like* her? She wasn't being very nice.

Hel's eyes welled with tears, and she was sorry. Her face softened, and she pulled Iris close in a tender embrace, even as the other girl continued to gape and twitch in obvious agitation. She brushed the hair from Iris' face with the back of her undamaged hand and caressed her cheek.

"You poor thing," Hel murmured in a little baby doll voice. "You're so sad and scared, aren't you? Those nasty old voices… They're really bothering you. They aren't speaking very nicely at all. They're the ones who made you be all mean and nasty, aren't they?"

"Y… You can hear it?" Iris managed to gasp out. "You can hear the secrety talky talk talkers?"

"Of course, I can," Hel whispered into her ear. "Now that I know where they're coming from… Now that I can look inside your mind… It's so *interesting* in there…"

She kissed Iris on the cheek and giggled girlishly again. Hel flashed a tiny smile but covered it demurely with her white hand. Her disfigured hand still tightly grasped a handful of Iris' collar. The smiling girl recoiled.

Hel's face fell.

Why did no one like her? Why did they all fear? She was being *nice* now!

Who cares?! The dark half of her mind thought viciously. *If she won't give me what I want, I'll just take it! I'll rip it from her head!*

Hel's voice grew intense. She licked Iris' ear and gripped her face with both hands.

"I can hear your voices now," Hel breathed. "They are seductive and tempting. They entice you… tell you to do things… bad and *naughty* things… things you both do and do not want to do all at the same time… Calling, beckoning, *begging* you to give in, they never stop. Yes, I hear them, and I can help. Would you like that, Iris? Do you want me to stop them?"

Hel insinuated her body more closely against Iris'. She locked eyes with the other girl before whispering intensely.

"Do you want me to take them away?"

Iris nodded helplessly. Her eyes brimmed with fearful tears.

"Yes," she whispered, her permanent smile gnashing and strained. "Yessy, yes, yes, Please..."

"Then you must do something for *me*, Iris," Hel pulled the other girl tightly against her body.

"What?" Iris asked beseechingly. "Whaty, what, what, what? I'll do anything... Take them, take them all away!"

"Anything?" Hel whispered into her ear.

"Yes," squeaked Iris, clearly terrified. "Anything... any whole anything forever!"

"*Love*. Me." Hel breathed.

The power was intoxicating. Hel's victim was helpless. Iris could not resist her.

Yes, she would make the voices stop. Absorb them completely, take everything Iris had, and make it hers. Hel would tear it from her brain and bend the girl to her will. She could devour her mind if she chose, consume it, and make them one.

Hel's hungry lips drew near Iris'. They nearly touched. She lusted after the girl's love, craved her affection. It could all be hers now. Hel could draw Iris inside of herself – make her a part of her forever! It would be *so* easy. She could almost taste the girl's tremulous essence... Hel's eyes grew wide.

She stopped.

Hel thrust Iris away from her and took a few staggering steps backwards. She gripped her head in her hands as if it pained her. What had she almost done? She wasn't exactly sure, but it was *bad*. Iris sat on the ground quivering. Her breathing was gasping and quick, and her squeaky sound devolved into high, hysterical laughter. She stared up at Hel in horror.

Hel took a deep, calming breath, then exhaled slowly. She banished the seductive whispers of her dark self and smoothed her features. She released a shuddering breath.

"I apologize, Iris," Hel stated quietly. "My dark side... it almost... I'm sorry.

Iris just continued to stare in abhorrence, laughing dementedly.

"Let me help you," Hel said.

She reached for the girl, but Iris recoiled, scuttling backwards to press against the damp cave wall.

"Don't worry," Hel soothed. "The darkness has passed. May I?"

She moved slowly to squat next to Iris. Hel smiled, and Iris fearfully returned the gesture. She reluctantly nodded her assent. Hel smiled again. Then she plunged her hand into the side of Iris' head. The other girl's mouth fell open, and her eyes sightlessly stared. Her laughter finally ceased.

As soon as she did it, Hel felt the darkness roaring back. The temptation was strong. With her fingers all over the other girl's mind, there was no shortage of mischief she could work. She could make Iris see whatever she wanted, cause her to feel however the whim might move Hel's pleasure. She could give her the deepest sadness, or the most choking of fears. She could give Iris agonizing pain or mind altering pleasure. Then Hel could make her do anything she wanted, *anything*! But she did not give in to those urges.

Hel did not succumb to the temptation. That was her dark side – *His* side. It was the part of herself thrust upon her against her will and the part Hel most despised – even more than her damaged face. She imagined the pleasure her Maker would have voyeuristically taken watching her ravish the mind of another, just as he had done to her. It disgusted her, and Hel's revulsion for her creator gave her the strength to resist.

Iris' eyes remained vacant and her mouth gaping as Hel's arm was buried in her head.

"Just give me a second," Hel murmured, reaching deeper.

She bit her lower lip, concentrating hard, searching for just the right place - just the right string to pull. Her face brightened.

There it is. She thought.

Hel grasped it. She didn't know exactly what she gripped or by what means she did it, but she tapped into a compartment of Iris' mind. Like piercing a water balloon, something flowed out of Iris and dispersed into the ether.

As soon as Hel did it, the dissonance of whispering, simpering voices fell silent. Hel removed her hand. She smiled sheepishly.

"Is that better?" Hel asked.

Iris fearfully looked this way and that. Her breathing still came in short, shallow gasps, and her silly smile remained fixed, but she was no longer laughing or squeaking. At the same time, she cringed before Hel like a dog fearing a beating. It made Hel want to cry. Then Iris' face took on a look of amazement. She stared hard at Hel.

"It's… It's quiet now…" Iris breathed. "*All* quiety quiet… For the first time in… in years and years and *yearsers* it's all quiet. What did you do?"

Hel folded her hands in her lap and shyly looked down.

"I don't know exactly," she admitted with a shrug. "I just… found the spot they were coming from and kinda… turned it down, I guess. They're not gone altogether."

Iris cocked her head to the side, then shook it.

"No," she said. "I can still hear them, but they're just a whispery whisper now. Who are you? What are you doing?"

"My name is Hel," said Hel. "I am a Lady of Aaru, and I…"

She trailed off, not exactly sure how to answer to the second question, but then the words just seemed to come to her.

"I've come," stated Hel with a sudden, fierce resolve, "to tear down the walls of this place - To set the captives free."

"I don't understand," Iris replied, shaking her head in puzzlement.

"You were surrounded by the voices for a long time," Hel explained, "but they were only in your mind. You've been locked away, alone, and abandoned. We all were. And there are many, many others just like us. The pristine and the beautiful of this world banished us so we would not disturb their *utopia*."

Hel sneered and felt the darkness return.

"They unfairly locked us away," she continued, brown and yellow eyes both blazing with rage and a sudden conviction. "But I have decided. Our unjust imprisonment *will* end."

Hel placed a hand on Iris' shoulder and squeezed. She looked deeply into the girl's uncertain, green eyes.

"And I want you to help me, Iris," Hel said. "I want you to go forth, and connect to other captives. I think I understand how to find them now, and I will teach you how. Find the banished. Tear down the walls that separate us so we don't have to be alone anymore. I will show you that too, and give you the power. You shall be my first Overseer, my first emissary."

Hel stroked Iris' brown hair, and cupped her cheek tenderly "Be my handmaiden, Iris," she murmured affectedly. "Serve me well, and when we are many… When we are strong, we will force the rulers of this place to give us what they've denied us."

"And what's that?" Iris asked breathlessly. "A presenty gifty present?"

"Our place under the great tree," answered Hel cryptically. "They deny us our freedom, and our happiness. It's time we claim what is owed us. Will you aid me, Iris? Will you help me take what is ours?"

Iris swallowed hard. She hesitated. Then the girl reached out and tentatively took Hel's supple, white hand. Iris was obviously still fearful of Hel. However, in spite of her fear, perhaps even because of it, Iris brought Hel's ivory fingers to her lips and kissed them.

"I can be a helpy help helper, Lady Hel," Iris breathed, her ever present grin widening. "I'll be your goody good gooderest helper. I'll lovey dove love you forever and every ever!"

Iris leapt into the air with a joyous shout, and her grim sable clothing transformed into what looked like a pink squirrel costume complete with long bushy tail. Her smiling face beamed out of the mouth. She stood on her hands again and walked around in circles with her feet kicking wildly, tail dangling. Iris started laughing again before breaking into a silly song;

> *"Goodery gooderest helper,*
> *Iris and Hel forever!*
> *Happery happerest friends,*
> *Hel and Iris win!"*

Hel looked on in bemusement as Iris repeated the dippy lyrics several more times before rolling on the ground and leaping to her feet. Then she broke into a capering dance and her singing got louder. A warm, protective feeling bubbled up in Hel's breast.

Iris was silly and strange, but why did she deserve to be locked away? It wasn't right. Hel's resolve in the words she had just spoken – the promise she just made to Iris – only grew stronger.

Hel did not say it, but she was grateful to Iris, and for much more than her pledge of loyalty and affection. She'd given her something important, Hel realized, something she'd been missing. Iris had given her *purpose*.

Just a short while ago Hel had been lost and drifting, miserable and alone, but now she was driven and her confidence soared. Hel placed her hands on Iris' shoulders again, stilling the girl's dancing and singing. She took the Iris' gleeful face in her hands and breathed into her everything she needed to know – How to find the captives… How to set them free. Then Hel sent her on her way.

Iris walked off on her hands. She made a slashing gesture in the air with her foot, and a tear appeared. A door emerged, and Iris quickly passed through it.

"Now," said Hel in satisfaction. "On to the next one."

She chuckled. Then called her own door. She didn't know everything yet. There was much she still needed to figure out, but it was a beginning. Hel was not sure what exactly it was the beginning of, but now that it was begun, she was certain, the result could only be something great.

She opened the door and went through.

***

"Ladies and Gentlemen of the Senate…" Senator James Rook, stared into the camera with an exceedingly grave expression on his face. He gripped the lectern with both hands, and his voice was filled with indignation. "It is a foolish generation that spits in the face of Almighty God. It is a foolish generation that ignores warning after warning. It was written thousands of years ago and is just as true today, 'the wages of sin are *death!*

"Despite my constant efforts to stop this madness," he continued after a dramatic pause. "My greatest fears have been realized. A young man is *dead* because of the lies of Askr Ashe and Elysian Industries. A young man, who had the whole of a long and promising life ahead of him, is dead because he believed in those lies. This here…" He waved a piece of paper over his head. "…Is the first such death we *know* about, but how many poor and deluded young people have ended their lives, snuffed their own existence, because they believed a fantasy world peddled by this charlatan was better than the life given them by their Almighty Creator?! How many more will come after? I intend to find out, but let us take a moment to remember Chase…"

He paused again to slide a pair of reading glasses up on his nose. The senator looked down at another document.

"Chase Jackson was a talented boy," he murmured affectedly. "He did well in school, and had a family who loved him. He was a member of the math team and had colleges lined up around the block to give him scholarships."

The senator looked up sharply.

"But then…" He cleared his throat and began to read the paper. "'Things have just gotten too hard since Gary, (his brother), died. School is miserable. Everyone hates me. I just don't see the point anymore. The only time I feel truly happy is WHEN I TALK TO GARY IN AARU!'" Senator Rook thundered the last, then took a dramatic pause. "'Why should I suffer anymore out here when I could be in Aaru full time instead? Don't be mad at me. You won't even miss me. As soon as I'm uploaded, I'll see you again. Talk to you soon. Love Chase…'

"How tragic…" Senator Rook shook his head with a heavy sigh. Then he folded up the glasses again, and slid them into the breast pocket of his iron gray suit jacket

"This boy really believed the nonsense Elysian Industry sold his parents. He thought he'd found the easy way out. And now… Now, he's gone.

"How many more have to die?" he asked the camera. "How many have, and how many will? How many parents paid their money to this bogus corporation and then lost their children as a result?!" His voice rose in volume and he struck the lectern with the flat of his hand. "How many more young people must perish before this body decides to take action? We must launch a full investi--"

The TV went black.

Askr stood at the front of the conference room looking disheveled and harried. The television remote hung limply from his left hand. Koren thought he looked *really* tired.

"He goes on a while longer," Askr said with a deep sigh, "but I assume you get da gist."

Koren could only stare in silence. Mr. Adams, Dr. Warren, and Dr. Kapoor sat behind her. Amy sat next to her with a supportive hand on her knee. Koren's father was slumped over against the wall in one corner either profoundly drunk or incredibly hung over. Her mother sat on the exact opposite side of the room with an unreadable expression on her face and her arms folded tightly across her chest. Koren didn't know who else, but a number of other board members' voices also occasionally crackled in over a speaker phones, and a couple more stared out of computer screens via Skype.

"I will make a statement shortly," Askr went on. "But I wanted to make sure all of us were on da same page. Dis is da biggest story in all media right now, but I suspect it will blow over. Yet another exciting irritation courtesy of Mr. Rook..."

Koren and Amy looked at each other, clearly confused by Askr's casual certitude. Koren hesitantly raised her hand.

"A... are you sure, Askr?" Koren stammered. "I mean... people died this time. Actually *died*! That's... That's awful."

"Of course, it is, Koren," Askr soothed with a deeply sympathetic expression on his face. "And we will definitely convey our deepest condolences to da family, but da case Senator Rook is referencing involved a boy with a long history of severe depression. Aaru didn't kill him. It's ridiculous for da man to try and blame his death on us. We'll be sure to point dat out in our statement."

"It's utter nonsense," added in Mr. Adams adjusting his tie with a dark scowl. "Yes, there have been a number of Aaru subscribers who later committed suicide since the inception of the program. However, please recall our original purpose was to try and treat mental illness, so *of course* there were some suicidal participants."

"But..." protested Koren. "His suicide note... He said he wanted to kill himself so he could be in Aaru!"

"It is common, Koren," said Dr. Warren, "for suicidal people to try and justify their decision to end their lives, both to themselves and to their families. It may have been his way of steeling himself to go through with it – that he wasn't *really* killing himself - but suicides almost always occur when an already depressed or psychologically unstable person experiences extreme trauma or emotional distress. Senator Rook is trying to insinuate an otherwise healthy person utilized the Aaru system and then decided to kill himself, and that's just simply not the case. He's trying to make people afraid."

"In fact," added Dr. Kapoor in his rising, falling Indian accent. "We have over twenty million users' data saved with more added every day. The number of suicides among our future

Residents is far below the average for the general population. This is a total red herring."

"We are very clear in our user contract," Askr continued. "All future Residents are informed that any self-harm represents a serious mental defect and disqualifies users from being added to the main system."

"Wait…" breathed Koren. Her eyes opened wide, and she looked up sharply in alarm. "Suicides can't get into Aaru? So all those people are…"

"Now, now, now," Askr interrupted abruptly. "We still upload deir data. Dey just can't get into general population immediately. Dey go to da quarantine section with all da other disordered users until we can evaluate, and if necessary, repair deir files."

"But that seems… I don't know… Kinda mean," Koren countered, wringing her hands in distress. "I mean… They were already sad and miserable enough they wanted to die… It feels wrong to punish someone just for being sad."

"Please don't think about it like that," Mr. Adams entreated gently. "We certainly don't."

"Right," said Askr. "We aren't *punishing* anyone. It's not even really about the suicide. After all, biologically it's no different from any other kind of death. The processes that keep the body alive break down, or are made to break down until life ceases. It's really about da underlying mental illness involved. Just like I told you before, if someone is mentally unstable who knows what dey could do in a system dat manifests whatever you can imagine? It could be catastrophic!"

"And it's not forever, Koren," added Dr. Warren quietly. She pushed her thick glasses up on her nose. "First, many of these users *are* admitted to the general population after an evaluation period. Very often, we find the suicide to be an aberration rather than the result of a persistent mental illness. Also, research is ongoing. Progress is being made. We do hope to find a cure someday. Then these Residents can be released into the public areas with everyone else.

Koren was partially mollified, but had to admit she still didn't feel very good about any of it. Doubt remained. She thought back on her own feelings of being overwhelmed. She recalled her own yearnings to stay with Rose. What did that mean? What did it say about her? Was she developing "a mental defect" like Mr. Adams and Mr. Ashe described? She bit her lip and crossed her arms over her stomach, feeling suddenly unwell.

"I don't know, Mr. Ashe." Everyone started in surprise as Gypsie spoke up.

Koren's mother generally remained silent during these types of meetings. In fact, ever since their argument back at the house in L.A., Koren and Gypsie Johnson hadn't shared two words.

"People are nervous." She sounded uneasy. "There's a lot of talk that all of this Aaru business... Well, it might not be all good. There might be some serious unintended consequences. Stuff like this poor young man might just be one..."

"Let me assure you, Mrs. Johnson," Askr spoke up quickly. "Yes, dere is talk, but dat's all it is – meaningless babble from people who don't understand da technology. We are saving lives. We are changing da world for da better!"

"I don't know, Mr. Ashe," Gypsie repeated stubbornly. "There's some pretty smart people who are raising a lot of hard questions. A lot of people think you're just playing God."

"I assure you ma'am dat's not da case!" countered Askr with a horrified expression. "We just want to help people. People like Rose."

"And how do we really know that's Rose," Gypsie pressed suspiciously. "It looks like her. It talks like her, but the longer this goes, she doesn't seem like the same as the little girl I gave birth to. All of you Elysian Industries folks are pretty smart. How do I know you've not just been playing us for fools the whole time?!"

"What are you talking about, Mom?" exclaimed Koren in confusion. "Of *course* that's Rose." Then she scowled. "How would you know what she's like anyway? You barely talk to her. The last time I saw Rose, she said she hadn't heard from you in *weeks*!"

"I know my own daughters, Koren!" snapped Gypsie in reply. "She used to be all into soccer. She was shy around boys. She was humble and modest and loved the Lord. That's not who I see in all those reality show episodes. *That* girl dresses all flashy. She's all full of disobedience and blasphemy. She *shamelessly* fawns all over that Mexican kid. She--"

"Franco is *not* 'Mexican'" interrupted Koren coming to her feet. "He was born in California, and I think he's really nice. I think..."

"Yeah," countered Gypsie also shooting to her feet and taking a belligerent step towards her daughter. She jabbed an accusing finger in Koren's direction. "They're both great *characters* – characters on a TV show, and a *trashy* TV show to boot!"

"Where is this *coming* from?!" Koren cried in confusion. "Why would you even *think* things like that? How can you talk about Rose that way? Your own daughter!"

"I'll tell you where it's coming from," Bill Johnson growled from his corner.

It was the first indication he was even conscious since he sat down.

"She's getting it from her *boyfriend*," he spat. "From that Benjamin Belial guy."

"How *dare* you!" Gypsie screamed, rounding on her husband.

Her cheeks flushed brilliantly red in embarrassment. The assembled board members could only stare awkwardly and shift back and forth in their chairs in discomfort.

"Pastor Ben is just a friend," she continued. "And a man of *God*. All of this being rich and famous stuff has been hard. It's been tearing our family apart. I've needed some spiritual guidance, and I'm certainly not getting that from *your* drunk ass!"

"I wouldn't drink so much," countered Bill. "If anybody gave a damn I was around. And I don't know if you're trying to fool me or yourself, but I've seen how you are with him – all giggly and stupid, always doing up your make-up and wearing your sexiest dresses when he comes around – make-up, high heels, low cut. That's not how you dress to go pray!"

"You bastard…" Gypsie hissed, but Bill Johnson was not finished.

"And I seen him too!" he pressed unceremoniously cutting off his wife's retort. "Always standing too damned close to you, laughing at every stupid joke you make, always touching on your arm or your face or your leg… If you won't admit that greasy con artist is trying to get into your pants, then you're either blind or lying!"

Gypsie's, eyes burned with hate. They were red with barely suppressed, humiliated tears.

"You're a stupid, jealous bastard," she spat. "You've been obsessed with your own personal pity party for months, while I'm standing here trying to defend our *daughter* – our daughter who might be getting taken advantage of, and all you can think of is yourself."

"That's rich coming from you," Koren spat in disgust. "*You're* the one who pushed me into this. *You're* the one who told me we should sign all those contracts. *You're* the one who was always telling me I had to just get over it whenever I was worried about anything because 'that's just the way they do it in showbiz, honey'" Koren's voice was mocking and shrill as she imitated her Mother's voice. "You've never been exactly slow about cashing those checks, or spending my money on new dresses, or going out to expensive dinners on dates with your creepy pastor Ken Doll in limos! And now all of a sudden you think it was a *bad idea*?!"

"Belial has twisted your mind, Gypsie," Bill Johnson added with a sneer. "He's turned you against me... against us!"

Gypsie glared at her family, her hands balled in tight fists at her side. Her face was bright red, and her jaw was tightly clenched. Then she burst into tears, threw her hands over her face, and fled from the conference room.

There was a long uncomfortable silence. The Elysian Industries board members just sat and looked nervously at each other. Bill and Koren glared out the open door and into the hallway where Gypsie had disappeared.

"Uh... Right, well," started Askr at last after a deep swallow. He shuffled through some papers on a nearby lectern in obvious agitation. "So, uh... Maybe if we all can just calm down--"

"Shut up, Ashe," Bill spat in disgust. He turned to Koren and gave her a chin jut. "Thanks, girl."

Then he rose from his chair and staggered out of the room. He turned down the hallway in the opposite direction Koren's mother had taken. Koren was suddenly aware of all of those sets of horrified adult eyes staring at her, or making a great show of not looking at her at all. It was overwhelming. Much like her mother, she put her hands over her face, and dashed from the room in tears.

Chapter 19

Boy Trouble

Hel explored her new surroundings with a great deal of interest. Something had awakened in her after her encounter with Iris. If she closed her eyes, her subjects shone like beacons in her brain. She knew where each of them were. Now that she knew how to track down her subjects, it was actually kind of fun. She flitted through several dozen different doors and met at least that many imprisoned Residents. It was easy. The number of her subjects tearing down the barriers of this place was increasing exponentially. No matter how many doorways were opened however, Hel didn't feel like she was making enough progress.

She could personally go and observe the beautiful people in the Ten Kingdoms, of course. She could even spy on Rose and her friends. Hel was a Lady of Aaru, after all. However, anytime she tried to bring one of the sequestered Residents along with her, that annoying Lord Mikoto would appear almost immediately with his long nose and thunder clap to whisk them away. After about the third time of nearly being seen, Hel decided she needed to exercise more caution. She was not ready for the other Lords and Ladies to know about her quite yet. She needed to try something else, but was not at all sure what that might be.

It was beginning to feel like she was doing nothing more than releasing these people from a jail cell into a prison yard. It was a larger prison, but still a prison nonetheless. It *was* an improvement, Hel thought, but it didn't feel like enough. Though it irked her, Hel decided at least for now, she would just have to content herself with connecting up all these separate little quarantine pockets and uniting her people.

Even that was problematic however. Hel was still undecided if she *liked* being around people. Her dark half raged that her subjects were filthy, broken wretches, far beneath her station or notice, while her sympathetic half wept at their misery. It was all very confusing and left her stomach a churning wreck of conflicting emotions. In either case however, Hel suspected she would have need of them somehow, and that utilitarian realization was enough to keep her dark side mostly mollified.

Hel put her hand against yet another portal. This one was a heavy wooden door with a large iron ring instead of a doorknob. It was also deeply gouged with long scratches as if some great predator had been clawing at it.

She did not hesitate, however. Hel pulled on the ring, and the door swung open with a loud squeak. She stepped inside.

Hel found herself in a dank and dingy room of enormous size. The dim chamber looked like some sort of dungeon. Then, as her eyes adjusted to the gloom, she noticed the walls.

They must have soared fifty feet to a vaulted ceiling. Every inch of them was covered with the misshapen, slack-mouthed masks of dissected human skin. Half of herself knew she should be terrified, knew she should run screaming from this chamber of horrors, but her other half, her dark side was unmoved. It held the memories of nightmares just as bad or worse.

There was a flurry of movement in the darkness, and Hel turned towards it. A twisted, malformed creature viciously snarled. It clawed the ground with broken, black finger nails. Then it shrieked in malevolent rage, before rushing at her in murderous attack.

Hel did not move. Her face remained impassive. The twisted revenant leapt for her.

"Stop," she uttered simply.

The man-thing froze in midair. Its twisted visage was inches from Hel's own. Mad eyes burned with hatred and frustration.

Hel gazed deeply into the bloodshot orbs with interest.

"They call you…" she paused thoughtfully. "Ed?"

She cocked her head to the side and gave a smile that displayed no humor.

"There's a lot of anger in you, Ed…" Hel trailed off.

Then she noticed what she'd thought was a twisted and deformed face, was actually one of the slack-jawed skin masks. This intrigued her.

"What do you hide behind that mask, I wonder?" she breathed into his filthy ear. "I simply must know."

She grabbed the skin mask at the jowl and violently tore it away from Ed's face.

Ed made a harsh, gurgling sound, but still could not move.

"That's better," Hel mused. "Let me get a look at you."

She grasped Ed's face with both hands and turned his head left and right. Hel narrowed her eyes in displeasure. His eyes were wild, but his face was otherwise quite normal looking. It might have even been handsome, in fact, if it wasn't twisted in rage and fear.

"Disappointing…"she sighed.

Hel fixed him with her yellow eye.

"Hmm… I had hoped for something more… more interesting," Hel murmured. "I thought for sure you must be horribly deformed under there to hide your looks with carrion. Why *do* you hide your face, Ed? You may speak now."

"Your eyes burn me!" Ed screamed maniacally. "They dig through my mind and steal my secrets! Get out of my mind Withered Face, Flawed Visage! Ugly! Ugly! You would never make my collection."

Hel snarled, her rage kindled. She was not sure if she grew or if Ed shrank, but Hel crushed him in her fist and brought his demented face close to hers.

"That was *not* what I asked!" Hel thundered with a furious snarl. "And it was *rude*… I am the Lady Hel! I am *ruler* of this place, and I will *not* be spoken to like that! I don't think I like you, Ed. I think I *hate* you…"

Ed's eyes grew wide and fearful. He shrieked and twisted in Hel's clenched fist, hysterically trying to wrench himself free, but Hel did not loosen her grasp. Her mouth stretched wide, and her teeth lengthened into needle-like fangs as she prepared to bite off the offensive wretch's head.

But that was her vengeful half.

She was furious certainly, but more than that, Hel was hurt. She had been wounded by the mad man's vitreous words. It wasn't her fault she was misshapen. It wasn't her fault half of her face was a discolored, mangled ruin. That's the way she was made. Ed's words fired her temper, but they also made her want to cry, and a tear trickled from her clear, brown eye. She turned it toward him, and Ed gasped.

"No…" he whimpered.

"Wait," said Hel thoughtfully. "I see something…"

"P… please… Please don't!" Ed begged raggedly. "Please don't look. Don't see my insides! Don't see my thoughts! Please don't look at me"

"You're hiding your face in shame…" Hel murmured.

"No!" shrieked Ed. "No… Don't say it! Don't tell!"

"You hate yourself, Ed," Hel breathed. "You think you are worthless... broken..."

"PLEASE!" Ed begged again. He began to sob. "Make it stop! Don't tell. *Don't tell...*"

"No one ever wanted you, Ed," Hel continued, her dark side was enjoying this far more than even dismembering Ed's flesh or devouring his mind. She felt powerful as she cut him with her words. "You were cast off. Abandoned. Garbage. Trash."

Ed produced no further intelligible words, but instead devolved into piteous weeping.

"And so you wear these masks, because you want to *be* these people," Hel shook her head sadly. "You hate yourself so much you think it would better to be *anyone* rather than who you are... I know. I see... You yearn to be like them, but you also despise them, because you know that can never be. It makes you angry... oh, so angry, but also sad – a sorrow that tears at your soul, so you long for death, but remain undying and alone."

Hel's face softened.

"They put you in a prison and locked you away," she murmured, then gestured at Ed's dungeon. "Then you built these walls yourself. Walls of despair... Of hatred... I still do not like you, but I understand you now, Ed."

Hel's face grew considering. Her fangs disappeared, and she shrank down to her normal size.

He probably wouldn't have tasted very nice anyway. Hel mused.

She released Ed, who fell to the ground in a cowering heap to continue his inconsolable weeping.

"Perhaps, I do not hate you after all," Hel said thoughtfully. "Stand up and come to me."

Seemingly against his own volition Ed rose on shaky legs and staggered toward her. When he drew near Hel grasped his ear with her scarred and discolored hand. She met his eyes intensely.

"I'm going to help you, Ed," Hel whispered with a smile.

Then she drove her flawless hand into the other side of his head. Her undamaged appendage disappeared past the wrist, then past the elbow. Ed's mouth gaped, and he made a horrid gurgling sound. His body began to convulse, and his eyes rolled back in his head.

Then his expression changed. The corners of his mouth turned up in a ridiculous, open-mouthed grin. His eyes, which were bestial and ferocious before took on an expression of ecstasy.

"Do you like it, Ed?" Hel's breath quickened as she manipulatcd his mind. "You do, don't you? For the first time in your life, how does *joy* feel?"

She slid her hand out of his head, leaving no wound, mark, or blemish. Hel lowered Ed slowly to the ground.

"Now," said Hel in a sweet voice. "You were very rude to me, Ed."

Ed rolled himself to his stomach and groveled at Hel's feet. He kissed her bare toes repeatedly.

"Forgive me, mistress!" he begged. "I was a fool. I was a liar! There are none more beautiful than you. None who are greater in power or glory or majesty!"

Hel smiled, quite pleased with herself.

"Much better Ed," she complimented, petting his head like a dog. "I think you are a liar, but your manners are much improved. You're going to be a good boy now, aren't you? You're not going to say mean things to me anymore. If you are bad, I will hurt you…" Her eyes flashed, and Ed cringed away from her.

"But," she went on sweetly. "If you are good, Ed, I'll make you feel good again. You'd like that wouldn't you. Wouldn't you like to make me happy? Wouldn't you like to be a good boy?"

"Yes, my lady!" he groveled. "Yes, please… please more… I will do your will. I will… I will *worship* you as a goddess! *My* goddess!"

Hel giggled girlishly.

"My, what an improvement!" she clapped her hands before her in delight. "Very well then, Ed. I rather like the idea of being a goddess, now that you mention it."

"Please, mistress," Ed begged, pawing at the front of her dress in supplication. "Please, do it again. Bring back the good feelings!"

Hel complied, her spotless, white hand plunging deeply into his mind.

I wonder how many more there are like him? She mused as Ed convulsed in paroxysms of ecstasy. *How many more will come and worship?*

When she withdrew her arm at last, she put her hands on her knees and crouched where Ed sat. Hel looked into his eyes. Her mouth smiled, but her eyes were commanding.

"Please, mistress!" Ed begged. "Please! More! MORE!"

"No, Ed," she stated firmly. "Not right now. We have work to do. We must find others like us. We must discover more prisoners – more innocents..."

Hel's girlish smile faded, and she snarled. The rage half, the furious, murderous half was taking over. She clenched her fists at her side, and the ground beneath her froze solid in a crackling sheet of ice. All the warmth left her eyes, and Ed shrank away from her in fear.

"Do not fear me, Ed," she growled. "As long as you obey, you need not worry. My anger is reserved for those who have tossed us out like garbage – left us to languish miserable and alone. Yes..."

Her eyes narrowed.

"You will help me find the other captives," Hel said. "You will help me free them."

Her lip twisted into a sneer.

"And then together, Ed, *all* of us together, we shall make our jailers pay...."

Hel stared at Ed, her expression unreadable, but Ed raised his hands over his head where he crouched on the ground as if warding off an impending blow.

"This will never do," Hel murmured. "I may be trapped inside this damaged form, but I refuse to be seen in public with someone so filthy and ragged as you."

"Please, mistress!" Ed implored with a devastated expression on his face. He raised his hands in supplication. "Do not cast me aside. I will serve you. I will *worship* you!"

"Silence," she hissed, and Ed fell quiet as if someone had clapped a hand over his mouth. "If we are to hunt, I shall need a proper hunting companion. If I am to be mistress of the hunt, then you shall be my hound. Does that suit you Ed? Will you do as I ask? Will you be my faithful cur?"

"Oh yes, Lady Hel!" Ed answered quickly, and a rapturous smile spread across his haggard, dirty face. "I shall be your faithful dog, rending, tearing, clawing at your bidding! I will hunt your enemies to the ends of eternity upon your command! I will devour them! I will--"

"A simple 'yes' would have sufficed," interrupted Hel with a tiny frown. "Very well then,"

Hel raised her hand and splayed her fingers.

Ed immediately collapsed to the stone floor on all fours. He gurgled and groaned as his body bubbled and warped. It looked like it was quite painful, and Hel's dark half practically sang with glee. Ed grew in size, and his filthy grey clothes shredded. Course, black hair burst from his skin. He threw back his head and howled.

Hel was quite pleased with her effort. Where the miserable, filthy wretch Ed had stood moments before, now crouched a large and powerful wolf, coat the sable of midnight. The massive beast stared straight into Hel's eyes even as it stood on all fours. Horns, like those of a ram, curled beneath his ears, and his razor sharp teeth were nearly the length of Hel's forearm. A long red tongue lolled from its monstrous jaws, but it was the eyes that were really striking. They were no animal eyes. They burned with a human intelligence and a fanatical madness that could only belong to Ed.

Hel nodded in satisfaction as she grasped the beast's great head. She scratched behind his ears.

"Now," she purred before giggling as the huge beast licked her face. "Stop. Enough… Stop it, Ed!"

Hel studied the huge wolf's face.

"You hardly look like an Ed at all anymore, do you?" she murmured thoughtfully.

Then she had an idea. It came from her dark self, the side of herself that held the memories of the Black Scholar. A sinister grin slowly spread across her face.

"If I am Hel," she whispered into the beast's ear. "Then who else could you be, but Fenrir? Does that name suit you? Shall I call you Fenrir?"

"Of course, mistress," Fenrir growled in a dolorous voice as deep as an abyss. "I live but to do your will. Send me to hunt! Send me to rend and tear and *devour*!"

Hel smiled and ruffled Fenrir's ears again.

"Not quite yet, my hound," she whispered. "We have pressing other matters to attend to…"
She turned away.

"Open the way to the next captive!" Hel cried.

A door appeared beside her in the middle of the dungeon, disconnected from any obvious wall. This one was blue, with a brass and crystal knob. Hel grasped the knob and twisted before thrusting the door wide. She turned to Fenrir with an imperious expression.

"Come, my hound," she commanded coldly, but her heart was swelling. "Come with me. There are no walls that can hold us any longer."

Then they both disappeared through the portal.

***

Koren stared in horror at the television screen. Her emotional state had been delicate to begin with after the humiliating argument in front of the whole Elysian board. What she saw now made her feel positively mortified.

The video quality was poor. The shot bounced around, struggling to remain centered and obviously zoomed in from quite a distance away. There was no sound, but there was also no denying it was her. Jabbing fingers, waving hands – it was obvious she and Gypsie Johnson were engaged in a heated argument on the front steps of her LA mansion.

Koren remembered it of course. It happened just yesterday as the Johnson's returned from Nashville. All three of them had been seething in silence on the plane ride back. Then of course she and her parents had been mobbed by fans and paparazzi alike as they tried to make their escape from LAX. Even with an additional half dozen TSA officers along to help, D and his security detail had been overwhelmed by the throng. They eventually managed to get out of the airport, but it had been absolute chaos and pandemonium. Once they all got into the limo, her mother shouted something belligerent at her father, and Bill Johnson responded in kind. The end result was her mother refused to ride in the same vehicle as her dad.

Koren was furious at the both of them, but managed to hold her tongue with her mother out of sheer exhaustion until they pulled into the driveway. Then Gypsie made a snide remark and suggested Bill's problems were caused by his lack of religion. She pressed her daughter again to try out Reverend Ben's youth group.

With everything else, that was just too much. Koren exploded. Every last bit of the anger, hurt, and resentment she was feeling towards her parents erupted like a volcano. She didn't even remember the words that came out of her mouth, but Koren knew they'd been angry, hurtful, and left Gypsie Johnson crying in the driveway. It was inarguably the worst fight she and her mother had ever had, and now it was on display for the whole world to see. Under the video was a caption:

Rumors Swirl Around Johnson Family Chaos.

At the same time, some gossip columnist with syrupy inflection provided a voiceover. She cited "sources close to the family" and speculated, "Perhaps K-Jo's rebellion is a result of Gypsie and Bill's marriage breakup…" And maybe "she's acting out because she was dumped by Jonas Perry." The obnoxious woman then concluded with; "All we know is there's big, big trouble in Paradise!"

K-Jo? Koren thought in annoyance. She made a face both at the stupid nick-name as well as the shamelessly gleeful expression on the reporter's face as she blithely detailed the total destruction of Koren's life. It was disgusting.

So what if Koren's parents were about to divorce? Who cared if her mom was cheating on her dad? What was the big deal if Jonas Perry wanted to dump her for some cheap, French whore? Why was that anyone's damned business but her own?!

Koren flipped the TV off, unable to bear anymore gossip-mongering foolishness. She put her face in her hands and sank onto her bed in a heap, too distraught even to cry.

She tried to remember what Rose had told her. None of this was her fault. Her parents' relationship wasn't her responsibility. She couldn't blame herself if they didn't get their act together, but it was *so* hard. Koren felt like she was being sucked into a pit of quicksand – like the more she struggled, the faster she was being dragged down. Her life was falling apart, and she had no idea at all what to do about it.

Just then, she heard the roar of an engine outside. Koren walked to her window and saw a black SUV pull up to the front door of her L.A. mansion. After a few seconds Gypsie Johnson stalked out of the house. She was wearing a very tight, very short black mini-skirt and blouse, that even from this distance, Koren could tell displayed a substantial amount of cleavage.

Her mother said something to the driver. Koren could not make out the words, but Gypsie's expression was unmistakable. Her mother was clearly distraught. Koren almost felt sympathy for her, but then the passenger side door opened up. Gypsie got in, and the car sped away. Koren never saw the driver, but could not imagine it wasn't Benjamin Belial.

As soon as the SUV pulled out of her driveway, those suspicions were only confirmed as her father staggered out onto the front steps in a loosely tied bathrobe over boxers and a stained white t-shirt. He waved his fist at the departing vehicle and screamed something Koren assumed was obscene. Then he took a huge swig out of a bottle he held in his left hand and staggered back inside the house. All Koren could do was helplessly stare at the empty space her parents had just vacated.

She hung her head in dismay. What was going *on*? Who *were* these people? Koren felt as if her parents were gone – replaced by two exceptionally nasty and bitter lookalikes whom she had never met before.

Her phone rang.

It was just on the bedside table, Koren moved to it slowly. Who could that be? Bindi maybe? Of course, it was the middle of the night right now in Australia. Amy? But then Amy had left her only about an hour ago. She looked at the number on the screen, and her heart skipped a beat.

Koren considered not answering. What was left to be said? Still, her need to talk to someone, won out over her anger.

"What do you want, Jonas?" Koren demanded as she put the phone to her ear.

"Hey, Koren," the pop star answered sheepishly. "I wanted to check on you… See how you were doing."

"What's the matter, Jonas?" Koren asked acidly. "Did your little French girl dump you? Or maybe you just got tired of her like you got tired of me."

"W…what?" Jonas asked stupidly. "What little French girl? I… I just thought it had been a while, and I saw the video of you and all the stuff about your parents on social media. I was worried about you."

"You don't *get* to worry about me!" Koren exploded. "What right do you have to call me up and act all concerned when you haven't so much as texted me in nearly a month? And 'what French girl?!'" she quoted incredulously. "How about the one you were wearing like a tie in all those tabloid pictures? How about the French girl who had her tongue stuck in your ear? I'm not stupid, Jonas!

Pictures of you two were *everywhere*! Do you know how many paparazzi have asked me how I'm 'taking the breakup'?"

"I'm sorry, Koren," Jonas apologized. "I just got busy. I really should have called you sooner. The stuff with Claudette... That was just photo-op crap... She opens for me on the European leg of my tour. I promise there's nothing to--"

"She was *kissing* you!" Koren shouted. "She was *all over* you! And you sure didn't look like you minded either. You were all laughing and smiling and letting her rub on you right there in front of *everybody*!"

Koren's temper suddenly died. Her anger was snuffed out like a candle. Instead she felt simply hopeless. Hopeless and alone and unwanted and unspeakably sad. She started to cry.

The line was quiet for a long moment. She could tell Jonas was still there, because she could hear him breathing, but it seemed like the blonde boy could think of nothing to say.

"I... I'm sorry, Koren," he repeated at last. "I wasn't trying to hurt you. I should have called sooner... I... really like you. All that mess was just photo ops and gossip fodder. Claudette's just somebody I work with, I *swear* there was nothing to it. Don't buy into all that tabloid crap. We both know they just print rumors and garbage. It's not like they're gonna write a story like *Jonas Perry Stays in Hotel Room – Watches TV*. They print crazy shit to rack up website hits. You gotta believe me, Koren, *nothing happened*."

Koren did not reply. She wanted to believe Jonas, but did not think she actually did. Did he think she was stupid? Silence stretched between them.

"Koren?" he asked gently. "You still there, Koren?"

Koren wiped her nose with the back of her hand.

"Yeah," she said quietly.

"Go to the window," he said.

"What?" Koren asked in surprise.

"You heard me," answered Jonas. "Go to your bedroom window and look outside."

Koren complied. She thrust the heavy curtains open and looked down at the driveway again. There stood Jonas; blonde and beautiful with his phone pressed up to the side of his head. He smiled and waved at her.

It was like a dagger straight into her heart. Koren wasn't at all ready to see Jonas yet, but he looked *so* handsome in his tight, ripped jeans and fitting white t-shirt. His smile was *so* inviting.

"Can you come down?" he asked.

Koren was conflicted. Jonas *really* hurt her. She felt justifiably aggrieved and wanted to stay mad. However, at the same time, she also wanted everything to be fine again.

"Koren?" Jonas probed gently. "Just come down for a minute. I just wanna talk to you face to face."

Koren sighed. She was defeated, and she knew it. It really wasn't fair.

"I'll be right down..." she murmured.

Koren was just wearing her jeans and a t-shirt, but quickly stripped and threw on a short, red strappy dress before going downstairs. She honestly had to force herself not to sprint. The desire to be near Jonas again was a powerful ache in her chest. When she threw open the heavy front doors to her mansion and saw him standing there on her porch in the flesh, her knees felt all wobbly and weak, and her tongue seemed to triple in size, stopping her words. Koren couldn't decide if she wanted to kiss Jonas or punch him in the nose.

"Hey," he said simply.

Then Jonas smiled at her, obliterating every other thought in her head. He spread his arms wide, and Koren could not resist. She rushed into his embrace recklessly. Then she seized his head with both hands and passionately kissed him. Jonas appeared to be a little surprised at her intensity, but not at all dismayed. His hands found their way under her dress and gripped her bottom. Koren did not stop him. Instead, she buried her face in his shoulder and wept.

"Get me out of here, Jonas," Koren begged desperately. "You gotta get me outta here... I can't stand it another *minute!*"

"Yeah." Jonas said huskily. "Yeah. Yeah. Sure, Koren."

He took her by the hand and led her over to a shiny red sports car Koren had not noticed before. Jonas pulled out a key chain, pressed a button, and two doors rotated upward with a hydraulic whoosh.

Koren raised an eyebrow.

"You can drive now?" she asked.

"Sure can," answered Jonas with a wide smile. "As of a week and a half ago. That was something else I wanted to tell you. I'll take you anywhere you wanna go! Just give me a call. I'll ditch my security detail again, and be right over. Think of me as your own personal taxi service!"

"Ditch your..?" she started curiously. Then her eyes widened. "You mean… it's just you? Just *us*?"

"Just us," Jonas confirmed. Then he shrugged. "This thing'll do 270 on a straightaway. They were in a BMW. It wasn't that hard to lose 'em, but we better get going. I have to think they might look for me here. They've already been texting me like crazy."

Koren hopped into the passenger seat, then leaned over to kiss Jonas again as he plopped down beside her. When she released him, he grinned at her. Then he pushed a button, and the doors slid closed.

"Your life's been too serious lately," he chided her gently. "Let's go have some fun!"

He pushed a button on the dash, and the engine roared to life. Jonas turned the radio to blasting and threw the car into gear. They peeled away from Koren's house with a screech of tires and a large cloud of dust and smoke.

Koren leaned against him, and Jonas protectively put his arm around her. She snuggled up close, purring at the warm, comfortable sensation. She felt safe.

"So," Jonas ventured gently. "Where you wanna go?"

"Anywhere," Koren murmured, pressing more closely against Jonas' side. She slid her hand up under his shirt to feel the warm, bare skin of his chest beneath. "Just take me somewhere I don't have to think about anything. Someplace with no paparazzi, crazy fans, messed up parents, or nosey board members telling me what to do."

Jonas squeezed her.

"I can do that," he answered sincerely.

Koren closed her eyes. She didn't care where they were going. She was just happy to be with Jonas again. Koren didn't want to think about anything else.

Chapter 20

The Warmth of Ice

After Ebony left, perhaps because she had just been thinking about that first soccer match so long ago, Rose conjured a purple Pegasus and galloped into the sky to seek out her friends. In short order, she caught up to the girls just outside Runa's ice palace. Rose noticed Runa had made some additions to her crystalline estate.

There was a wide and sparkling lake on the grounds now that appeared to be frozen solid. In the middle was a tall and soaring pillar of ice, thrusting toward the sky like a spear. Runa and Auset stood on its banks. Rose turned her mount towards them, and plummeted.

She sawed on her reins and brought the periwinkle beast up short. Rose slid to a stop mere feet from the duo with an impressive spray of ice and snow. Her friends stared at her in bemusement.

As usual, Runa was heavily bundled in thick white furs except for her platinum head, but Auset was not clad in her customary Cleopatra themed outfit. Instead, she was wearing billowy, white translucent pants, and a short shirt that bared her midriff. It was elaborately embroidered in a rainbow array of geometric patterns. She was dripping from head to waist with a chain-linked shroud of small golden medallions. They loosely covered her torso and also dangled from an elaborate, bejeweled headdress. Her eye-makeup was still dark and striking, but most unusual was she had a bow draped around her shoulders and an elaborately decorated quiver of arrows at her side.

"That was quite an entrance, Rose," said Auset with a wry expression. "Is something wrong?"

Rose wordlessly dismounted the flying horse, and crushed her two best friends in a fierce embrace. The girls were clearly surprised.

"While, I enjoy your affection immensely, Rose," said Runa curiously. "I am puzzled about the cause of its sudden intensity. Please teach to me your particular perplexity."

"Yeah, Rose," Auset added in concern. "What's the matter?"

Rose held them for another moment, reluctant to break the warm and comforting contact. Then she sighed and dropped her arms to her sides. She hung her head wearily.

"I hate to bother you guys," Rose began sheepishly. "But my stupid brain won't leave me alone. I can't stop thinking... worrying... wondering... I've talked about it before, and I'm sure you're getting sick of it, but ever since Ebony came over to my place--"

"Wait," interrupted Auset with a scowl. "Was Ebony bothering you again? I can't *believe* her! She was warned!"

"Indeed," Runa agreed, color coming to her pale cheeks. "She was informed under no uncertain terms was she to molest you further! The penalty was to be *quite* severe. We should go and inform Lady Hana or Lady Pyrrha forthwith."

Rose prohibitively held up her hands and shook her head. She certainly didn't want to get Ebony in trouble right after the other girl had confided in her. Still, her friends' obvious outrage on her behalf intensified Rose's warm feelings towards them. She suddenly wanted very much to hug them again.

"It's not like that," she spoke up quickly. "Ebony actually came to apologize."

"Really..." said Runa.

"So, what happened?" asked Auset.

Rose quickly related the disturbing conversation.

"And the thing is," Rose finished helplessly. "Even though what they were doing is awful. I kinda get how they feel. I understand wanting more... wanting to *do* something – wanting what I do to *mean* something again. All this... It's not enough. Do you guys ever feel that way or... or am I just crazy?"

"You're not crazy, Rose," Auset murmured, touching Rose's arm gently. "We've all struggled. You know that. We've talked about it before."

"Quite," Runa agreed. "Our lives here are a sizeable adjustment. I think we are all finding our way. Please lean on us, your friends. Matteus and his compatriots were not in error for their feelings, but in their methodology. They attempted to ameliorate their misgivings in secret and alone through nefarious acts. Let us deliberate together and find a solution."

"Yeah..." said Rose. "You're probably right... So, what are you up to?" She changed the subject. "And *what* are you wearing, Auset?" Rose smiled. "Feel like you needed a wardrobe change? What's with the bow? Is Kurt's style rubbing off on you?"

Auset giggled and covered her mouth with her hand. Then she rolled her eyes.

"Kurt again." Auset sighed heavily. "No, as a matter of fact. I've just been educating myself."

"Oh?" replied Rose with a mischievous grin. "Have you now?"

"Yes," said Auset haughtily. "And I'd like you to know it's quite cool actually."

"Okay," Rose answered gamely. "Cool is good. Tell me about it."

"Auset has been availing herself of the Yggdrasil library," said Runa. "It is quite informative. If you have not yet partaken, you should. It is extremely illuminating."

"It's *awesome*, Rose," Auset gushed. "It's called a library, but it's not like books and stuff. There are just all these chairs, and you sit and just say what you want to know about and poof! It just shows up in your brain! You *have* to go with me sometime."

"Sounds interesting." Rose gave Auset a playful push. "But I asked you a question! What's up with the Arab Princess getup?"

"Persian," retorted Auset drawing herself up to her full diminutive height. Her dark face adopted an imperious expression "I'm a *Persian* Princess thank you very much! You should come see my mansion. I've done a total remodel."

"Tell me more," prompted Rose. "I'm intrigued."

"Have you ever heard of Banu Khoramdin?" Auset asked.

"Can't say that I have," replied Rose.

"Well," Auset's face grew sincere. "She was *awesome*, Rose. Princess Banu was a freedom fighter, and an archer, and a warrioress! She fought against the invasion of the Caliphate. She fought against men who wanted to make women nothing but slaves - against the kinds of people who... who killed me. She was brave and strong and a girl who fought for what she believed in. Banu fought to protect her people. That's what I want to be like, Rose."

"That's great, Auset," Rose smiled and embraced her friend. "You look really cute, by the way."

Auset blushed and giggled.

"I'm not supposed to look *cute*, Rose," she countered with a playful scowl. She stuck out her tongue. "I'm supposed to look tough!"

"Ah," replied Rose giving her friend a squeeze. "You can't help it, sweetie."

"You do indeed look quite attractive," added Runa. "If I was Kurt, I would be extremely interested in your new fashion escapade and greatly approve."

"You now too, Runa?!" Auset exclaimed blushing furiously. "You're a big traitor. You know that, right?

"G'day girls!" it was Derain. As if on cue he, Franco, and Kurt landed just behind them. "What's up? I missed most of what you were talking about, but I thought I heard something about Auset, and Kurt, and sexy…"

"Shut *up* Derain!" cried Auset and Kurt at the same time.

Franco guffawed, and Rose laughed into her kimono sleeve. Rose walked over to embrace her boyfriend, and he kissed her.

"Now, now, none of that!" Derain exclaimed in mock offense, but his grin was broad. "Take your PDA to a back room or something, will ya? Seriously though, what *are* you girls doing? Standing around watching water freeze?"

"If you must know," Runa answered haughtily. "We were conversing in an intimate manner upon a subject about which you need not concern yourself."

"Geeze, sorry!" exclaimed Derain with his hands held up before him. "If you're just having girl time right now, we can do the bolt."

"No," said Rose.

She actually hadn't hung out with the boys in a while apart from spending time with Franco. Besides, she was tired of talking. Maybe a diversion with her friends to take her mind off of things was just what she needed.

"Have you guys got anything in mind?" Rose asked, gently extracting herself from Franco's embrace.

Derain shrugged.

"Not really," he said. "We were just sitting around, complaining we didn't know what to do, before Kurt suggested we hunt you girls down. I like the new pond by the way."

Derain directed the last to Runa.

"Thank you, Derain," she said formally. "I felt as if the aesthetic of my mansion would benefit from a few more amenities…" she paused and brightened. "Here… I have had a thought."

"What, Runa?" asked Auset curiously.

Rose could not help but notice that Kurt had sidled his way over to stand beside her, and was rather transparently staring at Auset's flat, exposed belly.

Runa did not reply, but turned in a slow circle. Her bulky furs seemed to shimmer and fall away like a shower of snow. In their place, the pale Veda now sported tights, a short white skirt, and a top covered all over with glittery sequins.

"Right," said Derain dubiously. "Pretty Princess Dress-Up Fashion Show. Why didn't I think of that?"

Runa grimaced.

"You are a silly, naughty boy, Derain," she countered in irritation. "Certainly, such was not near my intention, and I think you comprehend that quite well."

Then Runa stepped onto the ice to glide gracefully across the lake on one foot. She leapt into the air and twirled in a tight circle. Then she zipped away around the frozen spire.

Auset squealed and clapped with glee. Her face lit up.

"What a great idea!" she cried. "I haven't been skating in *ages*!"

She lifted her hands over her head and her Persian Warrior Princess outfit changed into a black, sparkling ice-skating dress cut like Runa's. She quickly joined her friend on the ice.

"Sure." Derain shrugged. "Why not?"

The simple pair of khaki shorts and green T-shirt he wore didn't change, but a pair of shiny black skates appeared on his feet. Derain quickly skated after Runa.

"Hey!" he called. "Wait up, Runa! Why don't you show me how to do that?"

His voice faded with distance, but Rose could see him stop near where Runa continued to leap and spin. It looked like he said something, but Runa did not slow her skating dance. She sailed in a spinning circle around the aboriginal boy, and Rose heard the faint peal of the other girl's laughter from the other side of the frozen lake.

Kurt regarded the others nervously.

"Well," he ventured reluctantly. "I guess I could try…"

"Don't worry, Kurt," Rose said kindly. "Remember. It's Aaru. Just see yourself doing it in your head, and then you will!"

"Yeah, Man," Franco added. "Get out there! Tell Auset how awesome and pretty she is. Girls like that."

Rose smacked the back of Franco's head with an offended expression.

"Yeah," she said. "If the guy actually means it!"

Rose smiled at Kurt kindly.

"Just go out and try," she said. "Auset will appreciate the effort anyway. She won't admit it, but I think she kinda likes you too."

Kurt blushed, but nodded. A pair of brown skates appeared on his wide feet and he staggered off in Auset's direction, wobbly on the ice.

Rose watched her friends laugh and play on the frozen lake with a smile. She snuggled in against Franco's broad chest.

"You think they'd notice if we snuck outta here and went back to your place?" Franco whispered in her ear. "You said you wanted to show me all the new stuff you'd done to your mansion, and we haven't been alone together in forever."

"You're tempting me," Rose purred. "It *has* been way too long."

"Rose!" Auset screamed as she skated by in a blur. "Come on out. You're missing it!"

She did a quick toe-loop, laughed, and skated on. Kurt trailed unsteadily behind her with his hands held awkwardly out to his sides.

"Yeah!" cried Derain as he skated past. He held Runa over his head in a graceful lift. "Come on!"

Rose sighed in exasperation, and laid her head against Franco's chest.

"Let's go play with them," she said. Then she took his big hand and lead Franco out onto the ice. "It'll be fun."

He pulled her back, kissed Rose deeply, and squeezed her to him.

"Sounds great, Rose," he whispered into her ear. "You promise I get you all to myself later though, right?"

"Of course," said Rose coyly. "I demand it."

She traced a finger over his chest. It made a smoldering trail across his shirt. She drew the black outline of a heart. Then she grabbed his collar and kissed him again.

"I… I think… I'm getting it!" cried Kurt, before crashing wide-eyed into a bush on the banks of the lake with his feet in the air.

Franco sighed and looked at the ground. Rose giggled. Then he and Rose skated over to pull Kurt out of the shrubbery. He spit leaves out of his mouth, and Auset laughed as she whizzed by again.

Rose shook her head helplessly. Franco patted Kurt on the back and then gave him a shove towards Auset. They laughed as Kurt narrowly missed colliding with her. He crashed to the ice in a heap. Auset giggled and held out her hand to help him up. Kurt took it, but Auset lost her balance and they both ended up sprawled giggling on the ice.

"Kurt!" Derain called from the other end of the lake. "Quit trying so hard. Just see yourself doing it, and you will!"

Kurt and Auset tried to haul themselves up off the ice, but slipped and fell into another giggling heap.

Franco rolled his eyes.

"We ready to cash out, Rose?" he asked hopefully. He leaned in close, kissed her neck, and whispered into her ear. "How 'bout we jet, yeah? Head over to your place and--"

"No," Rose answered firmly. She took his hands in hers and pulled him out onto the ice again. "I told you. I wanna skate."

"Okay, babe," answered Franco with a smile. "I'll do my best. I just hope I don't end up looking as dumb as Kurt. I ain't never done this before."

Rose glanced at Kurt and Auset. They'd managed to make it to their feet, but had their arms draped around each other's shoulders in a very shaky attempt to stay upright. Then they collapsed to the ice again. Kurt landed flat on his back, and Auset fell atop him so the two were nose to nose. They stared at each other nervously.

"It looks like Kurt is doing just fine to me," Rose quipped with a tiny smile. "Come on. Derain's right. This is Aaru. Just see yourself doing it, and you'll be an expert in no time!"

Franco shrugged.

"Eh, I'll try, Rose."

Then he skated a couple of paces away and turned towards her with his arms spread wide. Music started to play, even though there was no obvious source. Rose skated towards him, and Franco tossed her. She stuck the landing like an Olympian and then executed a perfect triple lutz. Franco raced to catch up. They swirled and spun across the ice together with huge smiles on their faces.

"This is all right, Rose!" Franco exclaimed. "I could get used to this."

Franco launched himself skyward in an elaborate spin move of his own.

"Show off!" Rose cried with her hands on her hips, but her grin was wide and her eyes sparkled.

Franco skated back toward her. Rose squeaked in surprise as the Latin boy swept her from her feet and held her over his head. She spread her arms wide and screamed in pure joy. It felt like she was flying. This was just what she needed. It was what they all needed.

As Franco spun with Rose held high over his head, she noticed Kurt and Auset had apparently given up on skating and made their way back to the lake shore. They sat huddled together on a silver bench talking in low voices. Both looked really nervous and shy – heads down and hands folded in their respective laps. Derain and Runa skated slowly across the ice side-by-side, hand-in-hand. Derain swung her, and the Dutch girl executed a perfect layback spin. Then they skated off practically cheek to cheek.

They all danced and twirled on the ice for quite some time. They spun, and leaped, and did flips. They cut elaborate geometric patterns on the icy surface with the blades of their skates. It was awesome.

Franco held Rose high above his head in another majestic lift. Then he swung her back down, and gave her a high arching toss across the ice. Rose stuck the landing like a pro and giggled. She did a little pirouette of her own, then skated back to the Latin boy. Rose pulled him close and kissed him.

"Let's all go back to my place," Rose suggested. "I bet everyone could do with some hot cocoa."

"Everyone?" Franco asked with a raised eyebrow and a vividly disappointed expression on his dark face.

"Yes, Mr. Impatient," Rose answered with another giggle. She kissed his cheek. "I said 'later,' but not how much later. When they all go home, it'll still be just us, but right now, I'm having fun. Besides, I don't want you to get too comfortable. I'm not that easy, and I'm going to make you work for it! Although," she whispered the last. "The skating was a nice start."

She trailed her fingers across his chest again and gave Franco a wink. Then Rose skated over to her friends to invite them back to her mansion. Everyone quickly agreed. Soon the six of them were soaring away from Runa's frozen lake and toward Rose's mountaintop palace, laughing and joking all the way.

None of them noticed the dark figure standing on the ridge overlooking Runa's valley, staring after the happy Vedas with an unreadable expression.

***

Hel watched the six Vedas fly off with a passive expression, but 'passive' was not at all how she felt. On the one hand, her stomach was a twisted, churning mass of jealous rage. What right did these people have to laugh and play and joke when Hel and those like her were stuck in a Purgatory of miserable solitude? What right did they have to be so happy, when Hel herself was so miserable? It fired her temper.

A door appeared behind her, and she glanced at it. Fenrir pushed his way through. He came to stand at Hel's side, and she idly ruffled his large ears.

"You had better go back through, Fenrir," Hel said absently. "If you stay too long you'll be detected, and then that Lord Mikoto will show up to take you away."

On the other hand however, Hel longed to join them. She burned to *be* one of them. From the deepest recesses of her being, Hel desired their company. She wanted to laugh at their jokes and thrill in their play. She yearned to delight at their antics. She wanted to be hugged and held like Rose in the arms of the dashing brown boy. He was *so* pretty.

Fenrir, seemingly ignoring her admonishment, did not budge. He stared after the retreating Veda hungrily.

"Shall I chase them, mistress?" Fenrir asked anxiously. His tail wagged and he hunched low, dagger-sharp teeth barred in anticipation. "Shall I catch them and rend them and tear them and bite them?"

Hel sighed.

"No, Fenrir," she stated neutrally. "Now is not the time."

Her dark side wanted to, of course. It wanted to punish them for their happiness. However, her other part wanted to convince them, to charm them, to win them over. It was confusing and painful, so she changed the subject.

"We must stay focused, my faithful hound," She murmured, still staring off thoughtfully into the sky where Rose and her friends had disappeared. "We must plan how we shall release the captives into the World of the Tree, and must remain undiscovered until we are ready to move. You must go back through the door."

"I grow impatient, mistress," Fenrir growled. "I long to hunt and kill. It is who I am. It is how you made me."

"You will do as you are told," Hel countered coldly.

She plunged her hand into Fenrir's head, and he whimpered piteously in fear and pain. Hel gripped Fenrir's mind with one hand and the bestial head with the other. She stared commandingly into fearful, mad eyes that looked just a little too human.

"You shall do as I bid, or I will *hurt* you," she stated coldly. Then Hel smiled. "But, if you are a good boy and do as you are told, I will be happy."

She twisted the hand buried nearly to the elbow in Fenrir's brain. The massive wolf fell over sideways, tongue lolling. The expression on his lupine face became rapturous. Hel pulled out her hand, and bent close to Fenrir's ear.

"You'd much rather I'm happy," Hel breathed in a baby doll voice with a pouty expression. "Wouldn't you?"

Fenrir cowered before her. He rolled to his feet, but quickly lowered his head to the ground in supplication.

"I shall do as you command, mistress," he growled contritely.

"Very good," said Hel in satisfaction. "Enough of this foolishness. We must be on our way. My followers are making progress, but there is still much to do. We must locate *all* the captives and liberate them. Go back through the door."

"Of course, mistress," Fenrir whimpered.

He retreated back through the portal, but Hel lingered.

"Show the boy to me," she commanded.

A window appeared, and Franco's face filled the screen. Hel sighed deeply, and her heart fluttered in her chest. She swiped her finger, and the picture changed. Franco in his soccer jersey. Franco in his superhero cape. Franco shirtless and wet in a fountain. She flipped through dozens of images, all of them of Franco. All of them, fanning the flames of desire deep within her secret self. Hel leaned forward and kissed the screen on Franco's lips.

"Are you coming, mistress?"

Fenrir stuck his big furry head back through the doorway. Hel dismissed the window hastily.

"Yes, of course I am," she snapped at the nosey wolf, her white cheek flushing pink. "And that shall be when *I* am good and ready - not a moment before. Do not rush me!"

"Apologies, mistress!" Fenrir whimpered, backing his way fearfully through the door again.

When she was sure he was gone, Hel called the window back into existence and once more summoned Franco's picture.

"Such a beautiful boy…" she sighed to herself longingly.

Hel traced his jaw line with her finger. Then she shook her head and turned on her heel. The window winked out of existence.

I can indulge in fantasy later, Hel thought taking a deep breath. *For now, there is much to do.*

Hel slammed the door behind her and disappeared.

Chapter 21

The Next Level

Koren didn't know where they were going. Nor did she care. She just knew the farther she and Jonas got away from her parents, the easier her breathing seemed to come. Jonas' right hand was occupied on the shifter, so Koren squeezed his knee with her left hand instead. Her busted phone buzzed.

She expected it to be her parents, furious at her for running off without permission, but it was just Amy. Koren snorted.

For mom and dad to be angry about where I've gone, they'd have to actually know or care, she thought bitterly.

Gypsie was off with Pastor Belial again, and her father was likely passed out in front of the TV. It was surprising, but her heart actually sank a little. Koren half hoped her parents would care enough to be mad at her.

She sighed, but quickly squelched the idle thought. What was she complaining about? Here she was, finally alone with the boy of her dreams. They were fine again. Jonas said so, and so did his passionate kiss earlier. This time there was no one to interfere. Koren could do just exactly what she wanted.

Amy's messages were predictable;

> *Where are you???*
> *Are you okay?*
> *Let me know you're not in trouble!!!*

Koren briefly texted back.

> *I'm fine. With Jonas.*

She meant the short message to be reassuring, but that's when her phone *really* started blowing up, and not just from Amy either, but Bindi too.

> *WHAT?! I thought you were mad at him?*

> *Why are you out with that WHACKER?! Remember what I told you!!!!*

Be careful!

Don't do anything bloody stupid!

Call me!

The messages were annoying enough that Koren turned her phone off, but at the same time, they were kind of comforting. At least *someone* cared about her.

She and Jonas drove for quite a while. They got out of the city and sped down a snaking coastal highway. It was fun, or at least it should have been. Jonas joked and told stories, obviously in an attempt to cheer her up, but Koren was feeling melancholy and detached. She tried to smile, but it was only a halfhearted effort.

They shot down the road at speeds assuredly many times faster than the posted speed limit. Tires squealed on tight curves, and Jonas laughed out loud, rolling the windows down and, urging Koren to do the same. Still, even for this, she could do little more than offer weak smiles and monosyllabic responses. Honestly, she should have been terrified at his recklessness, Koren realized, but couldn't quite summon the energy even for mortal fear.

What was up with her mom? Gypsie and Koren Johnson had always butted heads. Her dad used to joke it was because they were so much alike, but the naked aggression they both seemed to feel whenever they were in the same room recently was different. Koren was beginning to think her mother didn't even *like* her anymore.

To be fair, Koren wasn't exactly sure she could stand this philandering slut who looked and sounded like her mother either. The whole idea of Gypsie Johnson out with a man who wasn't her father had her blazing with fury and sadness every time she thought about it. Who was this person? It was as if some shapeshifting alien had stolen her mom away and replaced her with a person Koren didn't feel like she knew at all.

Of course, her dad certainly didn't get off the hook either. Despite their brief alliance in the Elysian Board meeting, Koren was equally furious with him. Growing up, her father had never minded a few beers on the weekend while he watched football, but this nasty, bitter drunk who seemed to be substituting for the daddy she knew and loved was no one she recognized or even wanted to know. What the Hell was happening to her family?

Koren glanced over at the smiling blonde boy in the driver's seat. His hair whipped in the wind as he guided the hurtling vehicle down the winding road. She had not completely sorted out what she thought about him either.

Koren had gone with him because she was desperate to get out of her house, and away from the family chaos, but there was a not insignificant part of her that was still mad at Jonas. He'd *really* hurt her not returning her texts or calls and running around with that other girl, but at the same time there was another completely separate part of herself that wanted nothing so much as to close her eyes and disappear into his arms forever.

Maybe she should have just stayed home and talked to Rose, even if it was only through the Aaru monitor in her bedroom. It was all very confusing. Koren put her head in her hands wearily. She felt sick to her stomach.

"You okay, babe?" Jonas asked charitably. He put his hand on her thigh and squeezed. "You're really quiet."

"I'm just thinking," Koren said. She flashed the blonde boy a tiny smile. "Sorry. I'm not very good company today."

"You're always *great* company, Koren," he replied.

Jonas reached over and squeezed her hand. Then he placed it on his own thigh.

"I'm glad you were so happy to see me," he went on, with a light laugh. "I wasn't sure what kind of reception I'd get. I'm glad you're not mad at me anymore."

He took her hand and squeezed it again, but then returned it to his leg, a little higher up this time.

"Who says?" Koren shot back. She took her hand off his leg. "I'm still *furious* with you. Even if you weren't fooling around with that Claudette girl, you still took *forever* to text, or call, or remember I was alive."

"So that before… that was an 'I'm mad at you kiss' then at your house?" he asked with a sly smile. "I might have to piss you off more often, Koren. I kinda liked that."

"You just think you're *so* charming, don't you?" Koren huffed with a scowl. She crossed her arms angrily across her chest and turned to stare belligerently out her window.

Jonas laughed, and Koren peeked back. He flashed his magical grin, and completely against her will Koren found herself smiling in return.

"What *I* think really isn't that important, Koren." He answered levelly. "What matters is whether or not *you* think I'm *so* charming. Am I?"

Koren had to look away to hide her smile.

"Not as much as you think you are!" she giggled. "You cut that out! I'm trying to be mad at you!"

"Sorry, Koren," he apologized with another chuckle. "Hate to break it to you - Totally not working. Hey, look up here... Observation point. Wanna stop and talk?"

Koren shrugged wordlessly, so Jonas pulled over and put the cherry-red sports car in park.

He turned to her with a deeply sincere expression on his face.

"So, Koren," he murmured, staring deeply into her eyes. "Tell me what's going on. You've been really distant today."

And Koren did. She told him everything that had been happening between her and her parents, her drunk dad, her apparently cheating mom, all the stress surrounding her responsibilities to Elysian Industries, how lost and alone it left her feeling. Jonas for his part listened quietly. He gazed attentively into her face and nodded in all the right places. He rubbed her leg and sympathetically wiped the tears from her cheeks.

"That's tough, Koren," he said seriously when she finally finished. "You know, I'm here for you, right? I can't resist you when you're all sad like this... Breaks my heart."

He kissed her, and Koren nodded thankfully.

"Thanks Jonas," Koren breathed. "Thanks for being someone I can talk to. It helps to get it all out. You really do make me feel better about everything"

"Well, sure," Jonas said, but he gave her a wry expression, "I *want* you to feel better, but I kinda hoped I'm... more to you than that. I kinda hoped you might... you know, wanna... let me make you... feel great..."

"Oh Jonas," Koren answered quickly. "You do. Just talking makes me feel a lot--"

"I guess, what I mean," Jonas interrupted. "Is...? Are we...? Do you want to...? Let's talk about us."

"Us?" Koren arched an eyebrow. "What do you mean, '*us*'? I'm still a little hurt if that's what you're talking about, but I think I'll probably get over--"

"I… I really like you, Koren," Jonas interrupted again, taking her hand in both of his. "But I'm not sure if you… Well… You know… Lemme just ask you... Where are we at exactly? *What* are we?"

Koren was taken a little off guard by the directness of the question. She wasn't sure of the answer herself.

"What do you mean, Jonas?" she asked reflexively, although Koren was starting to think she knew exactly what he meant.

"I guess," he paused and brushed her cheek with the back of his hand. "Are we a thing? Are we going to be, you know… serious. Do you wanna be… *my* girl?"

Koren wasn't sure how to answer. For her part, she thought they were already 'serious'. She'd let him kiss her, hadn't she? Koren had let him squeeze her butt outside her house without saying anything. She didn't let just *anyone* go around doing that!

"I really like you," Jonas repeated. He put an arm around her bare shoulders and leaned in close. His voice was very soft and sincere. "We're good together. I know things are tough for you now, but I'd really like to… to make you forget. To make you feel… good… you know? Really good. So good you forget to worry about all the crap going on for a little while.

"I know I was kind of a jerk while I was in Europe," he admitted with an apologetic expression, "but I wasn't trying to be. I was just busy. You know what it's like. I let myself get distracted, and I'm sorry. I think things are going great between us! You know… Going to clubs, award shows, stepping out on the red carpet together, partying with you – all that's been awesome! And then of course, all the talking and texting and stuff. I love having ten texts from you waiting on my phone after I finish a show."

"I'm glad," Koren murmured meekly. "When you didn't write back… I… I was afraid I was bothering you."

"I guess, what I'm saying," He breathed, leaning in even closer and resting his hand on her bare leg. It slid a few inches up under the hem of her dress. His other arm slipped from her shoulders to encircle her narrow waist. "Is that I've felt like we're… *progressing*, kinda. What we got is good… *Really* good, but I guess…" His lips came close to her ear, and he whispered. "I just wanna know if we're on the same page - if this is the real deal... Are we going to take this thing to the next level?"

Koren's heart was beating incredibly fast, and it felt like she couldn't get any air. What was 'the next level'?

"I really like you too," she said in a tiny voice, not knowing what else to say.

Jonas' grin grew wider. He rubbed her bare leg under her dress. Then he leaned in for another kiss.

Koren returned his kiss with a strange reluctance. On the one hand, she really wanted the kisses, the hugs and the tender touches. They *did* make her feel better, and Jonas was *so* handsome! On the other, however, she was afraid. Something was different this time.

Jonas kissed her with an intensity she'd never experienced before. His hungry lips moved down to her neck, and he slid both of his hands up under her dress. He rubbed her hips, sliding his hands under the elastic in her underwear to squeeze her bare bottom. Jonas ran his hands up her body under the dress to caress her back, and the short garment hiked up around her waist. He nibbled her ear.

Koren felt a pop. She gasped, realizing in alarm that her bra was unhooked.

"J... Jonas..." she stammered in dismay as she felt the straps slip off of her shoulders.

"Oh, Koren," he murmured in an impassioned voice, totally misreading her emotion.

He started to lift her dress up over her head.

"Jonas!" Koren exclaimed snapping her arms tightly across her chest, and firmly pressing her dress back down. "W... Wait..."

Jonas cocked his head to the side. He regarded her with surprise.

"What, babe?"

"I... I... wasn't expecting...." She stammered in distress. "I... didn't know... I'm not sure if I'm r... ready for... *Please,* don't be mad!"

Jonas stared at her a minute. Then he sat heavily back in his seat with an exasperated huff. A heavy scowl darkened his handsome face.

"I see," he said simply enough, but there was a coldness in his tone that Koren had never heard before. "I'm sorry."

Koren wasn't sure why, but she suddenly felt like she ought to be the one apologizing, even as she tried to re-hook her bra without lifting her dress or exposing her breasts.

"I... I... I just..." she stammered, feeling the tears start to come. "I've just never... d... done anything like this before... I was surprised, is all.... I just wasn't ready... I wasn't trying to--"

"It's my fault, Koren," Jonas cut in resentfully. Color came to his cheeks. "I guess, I misunderstood. I'm sorry..." He trailed off, then fixed her with an accusatory expression. "It's just... when you jumped on me at your house and stuck your *tongue* down my throat, I sorta thought... I just assumed... Never-mind. I'm sorry"

He shook his head and started up the engine.

"I wasn't trying to lead you on or anything!" Koren protested. "I swear! I was just really sad, and I missed you, and... I... I needed someone to... to... talk to and hold me and... I'm sorry..."

Koren burst into tears as Jonas backed the car up. He jammed the shifter into first, grinding the gears loudly. Jonas peeled out of the overlook parking lot slinging gravel in every direction.

He was obviously angry, but Jonas wasn't completely impervious to her tears either. A couple of miles down the road, his expression softened. He handed Koren a tissue from the glove compartment.

"I guess... I better take you home..." Jonas murmured. "Sorry, Koren." He said again.

Koren felt terrible. She had once more disappointed Jonas. This time she didn't even have a drunk father busting in on them as an excuse. She'd gotten Jonas all excited, and then shut him down all on her own. She didn't want him to be mad at her, but at the same time, what he was doing made her feel *extremely* uncomfortable. *Had* she led him on with the kissing before? Had she been sending mixed messages? Had she just *ruined* everything?

It was a long, awkward drive back to her estate.

When Jonas finally let her out at her front door, his expression was still clearly exasperated. Koren could tell he was mad, but trying hard not to show it. It made her feel miserable.

"J... just 'cause I'm not ready now, doesn't mean I won't be forever..." Koren ventured meekly.

Jonas sighed heavily and shot her a sideways glance.

"Sure, Koren," he said frigidly. "I hope so. It's just..."

Jonas trailed off, with another deep sigh.

"What, Jonas?" Koren urgently asked.

"I want a relationship, Koren," he stated. "A *relationship*. I don't want to push you into anything you don't wanna do, but..."

Jonas trailed off and stared at his lap.

"I thought you liked me," he finished.

"Oh, but I do, Jonas!" Koren insisted quickly. "I think--"

"Well then," he cut her off. "Maybe I just caught you at a bad time. I know you're upset. Maybe you just need to calm down and think about a few things - decide what you really want. *I* want a *real* relationship, Koren. I'm not trying to be a jerk or anything, but I just *need* that. I hoped it would be with you."

He pressed the button that closed her door, then put the car in gear and peeled out leaving Koren alone and miserable in her driveway. She stared off in the direction Jonas had departed, and the tears came again. She stood there crying long after the red sports car had completely disappeared from view.

Just as Koren finally summoned the energy to turn toward her front door and plod inside, she heard a revving engine and squealing tires. She looked up hopefully, thinking perhaps Jonas had changed his mind and come back, but she was disappointed. A white Toyota pulled up with a screech.

Amy jumped out. Her face was frantic. She rushed up to Koren and hugged her tight. Then she looked hard at the younger girl's tear-stained face, and grimaced dramatically.

"Oh dear..." she said worriedly. "So what happened?"

Koren couldn't answer. All she could do was cry.

"That bad, huh?" the blonde girl murmured.

Amy opened her mouth to say something else, but looked past Koren abruptly and straightened. Her face and voice took on the honey and roses quality that Koren remembered from when they first met. Koren cocked her head to the side curiously as Amy called out in a loud friendly voice.

"Hello there!" Amy smiled and waved.

"Wh... huh...?" Koren heard her dad's slurred and confused voice behind her. "What the Hell's goin' on out here? I keep hearin' tires, 'n engines an' stuff... You guys holdin' a race 'er somethin'?"

"I'm just picking Koren up for a company function, Mr. Johnson," Amy replied airily. "Nothing to worry about. No rest for the weary, you know. I hope you're doing well today."

"Oh… Oh, yeah… yeah… A… Am… Amber, right?"

"Nice to see you again, sir!" Amy replied in her sunniest voice.

"Okay…"

Koren turned to see her father still clad in nothing but boxers, filthy t-shirt, and bath robe. Bill Johnson tottered for a moment, then flopped heavily to the front steps. He righted himself with apparent difficulty and took a deep swig out of the glass bottle in his hand.

"Long as it's… as it's you…" he slurred drunkenly. "'Fraid I was gonna have to kick me some *ass*. Thought it might be that horny little turd again--"

"Well, we'll see you later then, Mr. Johnson!" Amy interrupted. Then she muttered to Koren under her breath through clenched teeth. "Get. In. The. Car.

"We'll be on our way now," she continued in a loud voice. "So nice to see you. Have a nice day!"

Amy took Koren by the shoulders and guided her toward the passenger side of the vehicle. She opened the door and pressed Koren into the seat. Then she rushed around to the driver's side, shut her door, and started the engine.

"I think we need to have a talk, Koren," Amy growled under her breath, then cried out the window as she smiled and waved, "bye now, Mr. Johnson!"

Koren saw her dad through the windshield. He sort of lifted his hand in a poor approximation of a wave, but apparently needed that arm for balance. He rolled over on his side, arms and legs splayed. Her father tried to rise a time or two, but was not successful. After a few seconds, he apparently gave up and lay still. Bill Johnson was asleep on the front steps. Koren put her hands over her face in utter despair.

"Let's get out of here," Amy said as she fastened her seatbelt.

She backed up quickly and pulled away from the Johnson's home before Koren's father had a chance to wake up and change his mind.

Amy looked at Koren critically.

"I'm upset with you," the blonde girl chided. "You scared the crap out of me! You know that? His people called me, you know? I thought you and Jonas might have run away to Mexico or something! Didn't you *just* tell me you were still mad at him, were never going to forgive him, and were swearing off boys forever?"

Koren could summon no reply. Hanging her head, she simply shrugged.

Amy sighed.

"All right," she said wearily. "I'm just glad you're safe. So, tell me. How bad was it?"

Koren just cried.

"Oh, boy," Amy sighed again. She pulled over and turned toward Koren.

"So," stated Amy commandingly. "This is what we're going to do. I'm going to stop and get us some food, and then we're going to go back to my place and have dinner. *You* are going to spend the night with me, and you can cry your heart out if you need to, but you are going to tell me *exactly* what happened. *Everything.* Got it?"

Koren nodded helplessly. What else was she going to do? It all felt so hopeless.

Amy's face softened. She patted Koren's knee fondly.

"Don't you worry, Koren," she murmured. "I'm *so* sorry. We tried to warn you… But I guess there's no point in thinking about that now. Everything will be okay. We'll work all this mess out… Oh!"

Amy seemed to recall something. She turned backwards and dug in the back seat. Then she turned back around and pressed something soft and fuzzy into Koren's hands.

Koren looked down. It was Pandadora. The kimono clad panda bear smiled up at her. Koren squeezed the stuffed animal tightly to her chest.

"I thought you might want her," Amy murmured. "You left her back at the Elysian Industries complex."

"Thanks, Amy," Koren replied in a tiny voice, but then found she had nothing left to say.

Amy pulled back onto the road. Koren squeezed Pandadora tight. It helped a little, but truth be told, she didn't really have much faith that any of this could be 'fixed'. Her whole life felt like such a disaster, and it only seemed to be getting worse.

Koren leaned her head against the glass and stared morosely at the city streaming by outside. It was starting to get dark. Here and there street lights and illuminated signs began to flicker on. Koren clenched her eyes tightly closed, and tears trickled down her cheeks. They soaked into the stuffed panda clutched tightly under her chin. She really didn't see how anything could be okay ever again.

Chapter 22

The Ladies' Tea Party

Rose was wearing a beautiful, blue summer kimono with a big yellow bow at the back. Though perhaps not as drastic a change as Auset, the other girl had still inspired her. Perhaps stagnation was part of her problem, Rose thought. Maybe an outward change in wardrobe might help her with the deeper change she so poignantly felt she needed.

Rose had to admit, she did indeed feel better. The skating had been just the thing, and her friends had lingered at her mansion long after it was over, much to Franco's annoyance. There had been no shortage of laughing and joking.

When they'd all gone at last, true to her word, she and Franco had their private time, and neither of them were quick to bring *that* to a conclusion. Even now, just thinking about it made her feel all giggly and shy and brought color to her cheeks. It put her in such a good mood in fact, rather than sulk when Franco was called away again to meet with Lord Mikoto, Rose had instead dreamed up this *yukata* and reimagined her make-up as well. She looked pretty darn cute, if she did say so herself, and all her friends were quick to say so as soon as they saw her again. Of course, that did nothing to dampen her mood either.

The end result of everything was far and away, her mood was the absolute best it had been in ages. Now she found herself sitting at a long table covered in a white, linen tablecloth with a big smile on her face. A steaming cup of tea set next to her right hand and a large piece of chocolate cake was at her left. She, Princess Hana, Auset, Lady Nu, Runa, and Lady Embla all sat together chatting amiably about this and that.

Auset was breathtaking in her warrior princess garb, and Rose had to admit it suited her. Runa was still wearing white, but now sported a form-fitting, sleeveless ivory dress with a high, tight collar, rather than the bulky furs she generally wore. She was doing a great deal more talking about Derain than Rose could ever recall as well. Runa's pale cheeks blushed pink every single time she mention the aboriginal boy's name.

Princess Hana was wearing a striking black and gold kimono, and was as engaging and charming as ever. Lady Embla, who Rose admittedly did not know very well, was also in attendance and not short on pleasant conversation or good-natured teasing. She was wearing a long flowing red, silk dress with voluminous sleeves. A dark, fur shawl adorned her shoulders, and her nut brown hair was long and wavy with two tiny, beaded braids hanging from either temple. Finally, Lady Nu sitting across from Hana contentedly in her Egyptian queen regalia, said little, appearing to be simply taking everything in.

"Derain is such a talented skater," Runa was gushing. "I had no concept he was adept at doing the like. When he tossed me, it felt almost the same as flying, and on his lifts… Well, his hands are *very* strong. I skated doubles only rarely Before in the Netherlands, but I think Derain might make a capable partner."

"Oh, really?" Auset asked with interest from behind her steaming tea cup. "Strong hands can be quite important in a partner. You two did seem to be getting along better than usual at Rose's party afterwards. What were you two whispering about together? Do you have anything you'd like to share with us? Any announcements, for example? Dates and locations and such?"

"*Skating* partner," Runa insisted with fresh blushing. "And you are an ironic individual to be engaged in such speculative talking. I merely *skated* with Derain. I did not lie upon his chest!"

"That was an accident," Auset insisted gaining more than a little roseate color of her own. "We fell."

"In *love* perhaps," Runa needled.

"You are terrible, Runa!" Auset exclaimed. "Kurt is my friend. That is all."

"You know," commented Lady Embla gently. Her eyes were dark, yet sparkling, and she regarded the slight Veda with a tiny smile. "Friendships often become the deepest, most satisfying romances, Auset. If you find yourself liking my Veda as more than a friend, there's no harm in admitting it. He's a very kind and sweet boy. Don't deny yourself happiness."

"Yes, Auset," Runa agreed. "You should not become perplexed by finding Kurt to be attractive."

"My words," Lady Embla said with a wry expression, "apply equally to *all* Vedas currently assembled. Don't think we haven't noticed Derain finding more excuses to visit your mansion lately, Runa. I don't know why you're fighting so hard either. He's a very attractive young man as well."

Rose laughed at her friends' vivid blushing.

"Now, now," she cut in in the girls' defense. "You said it applies equally to all the *Vedas* here, but what about you single Aaru *Ladies*?" She turned to face Embla. "Have you ever thought about being more than friends with Lord Epimetheus? And you Hana… You complain about Mikoto all the time, but you do spend an awful lot of time together."

Hana and Lady Embla both grimaced and the three Vedas laughed. The flower princess gave Rose a doleful expression.

"I think I have been extremely clear about my feelings regarding Mikoto," Hana said sternly.

"And I would sooner strike up a romance with my tax assessor from Before than with Epimetheus," added Embla dryly. "We work together. That is all."

"Well, what about the other Lords then?" Rose pressed. "You have to admit Lord Cernunnos is pretty hot – black hair, black eyes, showing off his sexy legs in that yellow kilt of his. I'll admit, if I wasn't with Franco, I'd be interested.

"Cernunnos is Irish not Scottish," commented Embla pedantically. "So it's a *lein-croich*, not a kilt. And yes, he is quite handsome, but frankly, he's a little too preoccupied with his poetry for my taste. Most of it's about himself anyway."

"Potato, po*TAH*to!" Rose laughed. "Fair enough, but I have to point out you've still paid him enough attention to remember what his skirt is called. So how about Draugr then? He's a pretty manly, dude. Do you think any of you could be interested in him?"

"Lord Draugr," replied Hana haughtily. "Is a great man. The continued building and development of Aaru consumes his every waking thought. The fulfillment of that immaculate vision is his passion and one true love. He would have no time for such frivolous distractions."

"Which is to say, yes, Rose," Embla quipped with a wicked grin at the other Lady. "Even if *some* among us are reluctant to admit it."

Hana gasped, and her cheeks turned beet crimson.

"I greatly respect, Lord Draugr," she retorted defensively. "Aaru could not function, would not *exist* without him! My only desire is to assist him in achieving that ultimate perfection!"

Embla rolled her eyes.

"Love is never frivolous, Hana." Everyone started as Lady Nu commented.

Auset's Lady was never exactly chatty, so everyone always paid attention whenever she had something to say.

"It's too rare a thing not to cherish it whenever you have the chance," she went on in her velvety, alto voice. "Even if it only lasts for a little while."

There was a wistfulness in her expression that made Rose intensely curious. However, there was something sad about Lady Nu's demeanor also. It stopped Rose's questions before they were fully formed. There was a privacy and mystery about Auset's Lady that made Rose feel it would be terribly rude to pry.

Everyone was silent for a moment, then Embla cut in with a great deal of forced jocularity. She smiled broadly at the three Veda.

"So… In conclusion, I shall count it a victory that Lady Nu agrees with *me*." She pointed at each of them in turn. "Auset should admit she likes Kurt. Runa, *you* need to confess your attraction to Derain. You Rose keep doing *exactly* as you are with Franco. And *you* Hana, need to stop pining over Lord Draugr and tell him you're in love with him, because everyone seems to realize it but you!"

"And you, Dear Lady Embla," said Hana with a scowl. "Should try harder at concerning yourself with your own business."

Embla could have taken offense at Hana's peevishness, but laughed loudly instead.

"Never!" she swore, placing her right hand over her left breast. "I am a consummate busybody, and you are my friend. I shall continue to meddle in your affairs as long as I may, and you shall be all the happier because of it. You might be a Goddess in Aaru, Hana, but just remember your Greek classics. Goddesses were not above indulging in a fling or two!"

Hana grimaced. Lady Nu smiled, and the three Veda girls could not help but devolve into merry giggling as well. Still, they changed the subject after that.

The talk was mostly inconsequential – interesting new mansions they'd seen go up, crazy Resident problems or ridiculous requests they'd been forced to deal with. It was fun. Just as Rose thought their tea party was probably winding down however, a great shadow passed in front of the brilliant sun.

Rose shaded her eyes, but could not make out exactly what it could be. A shape descended towards them like a rocket, and came to an abrupt halt right next to their tea table floating about six inches above the ground. Wurugag, Derain's dark-skinned, broad-faced Lord gently dropped the rest of the way and leaned on a tall staff. He fixed his gaze on Lady Nu. Rose thought his expression looked exceedingly grim.

"Draugr wants to see you, Nu," Wurugag said gruffly in a deep Australian accent.

Nu curiously cocked her head to the side.

"It's… It's Simon," Wurugag went on heavily. The name meant nothing to Rose. "He… He's passed."

Lady Nu's eyes grew wide.

"Did he ever update?" Nu asked. "Did he and Draugr…"

Lord Wurugag shook his head and looked down at his bare, brown feet.

"No," he said. "You know how stubborn they both are. Maybe, there's a backup or old file hidden way down in the registry somewhere, but… I'm sorry, Nu."

The onyx-skinned Lady sighed and looked down at her hands, folded in her lap. She rose wordlessly, and made as if to leap up into the sky, but paused. She turned to Rose. Rose thought she looked unspeakably sad.

"Cherish love," she murmured. "Whenever you have the chance."

She shot into the air, and Lord Wurugag quickly followed.

"W… what has happened?" stammered Auset. "What's wrong?"

Princess Hana and Lady Embla shared a stricken look.

"You know Lady Nu is the only ruler of Aaru without a partner, correct?" Hana began slowly.

The girls nodded.

"Well," said Lady Embla. "That was not always the case."

"Simon was with us in the beginning," Hana went on. "But he and Lord Draugr… Or I suppose rather, he and Askr Ashe on the outside, had a falling out."

"Regarding what?" asked Runa.

"Vision, mainly," answered Hana with a sigh.

"And vanity," added Embla. "Both too bullheaded to admit they were wrong."

"Askr was most concerned about the system remaining viable," Hana elaborated. "He was certain if Aaru could not provide some service to make it profitable, we would never get the investment we needed to complete it. Simon was equally adamant we stay true to the original mission – curing mental illness. He was… not enthusiastic about the idea of selling immortality. He claimed there were too many unintended consequences we could not possibly predict, and accused Askr of selling out in greed. He felt profiting monetarily would be inconsistent with our values. He--"

"He said a lot of things," interrupted Embla, "but the long and the short of it was, Simon got outvoted. However, he was so passionate about his conviction Askr was going in exactly the wrong direction he left Elysian Industries and demanded his avatar be deleted from Aaru completely."

"It was that bad?" asked Rose in shock. She knew what it meant to be deleted from Aaru. It was the same as death.

"Yes," said Hana. "They were both quite obstinate – equally certain they were correct. Askr had the right of it, of course. Simon was just simply not being practical…"

"Either way," cut in Embla. "Simon was completely purged from the system. Lady Nu took it the hardest. She had worked the most closely with him. I think she always hoped they would reconcile, and now…"

"So Lady Nu's partner was Lord Simon?" asked Auset. "Did she… did she *love* him?"

"I think so," said Embla. "They were certainly very close friends at the very least. I always liked him too…

"He was arrogant," countered Hana. "There was no reason he couldn't have stayed. His knowledge of the system was vast. It caused *so* many problems when he left. It took us well over a year to get the project back on track after he was gone. He was very selfish."

Embla sighed, "We have had this exact same argument many times, and I have no desire to have it again, Hana. Suffice to say we all felt his loss, although, he wasn't called Simon here."

"No," said Hana. "Just like I was Kiku Hanasaka, and Lady Embla's Maker is Julie Warren. He was Simon Before, but when we knew him in Aaru, he was known as Lord Atem. I personally thought Atem was always more reasonable than Simon."

"He did not resist Simon's decision to have him deleted," Embla reminded her friend gently. "He said he agreed with it."

"Atem was loyal to a fault," countered Hana. "And it was still early then. We had not yet diverged from our Makers. We were still essentially the same person… We believed so at least. It took us time to realize we each had our own moral agency. That's why we changed the coding and made all the remaining Founders sign legal releases, so it couldn't happen again."

"What changes?" Auset asked curiously.

"Indeed," chimed in Runa. "To what did the board members commit?"

"None of us were happy about Simon deleting Atem," Embla answered. "But Simon argued because Atem was a copy of his brain, he had the right to do what he wanted with the file – including deleting it. We all tacitly went along with it. We didn't like it, and we didn't really understand The Divergence then, but Simon could be very convincing. Also, he threatened legal action, so the Elysian Board let it happen.

"But," said Hana. "It felt far too much like an execution. We decided it could never happen again, so all the Board members were required to sign legal documents renouncing ownership of their brain scans. It's also written into all of the Aaru Resident contracts as well. A family member cannot all of a sudden decide they no longer want their loved one in Aaru anymore and force us to delete them, for example."

"No Lord or Lady can be deleted. Period." said Embla. "The coding forbids it. Also, Residents can only be deleted if there is something seriously wrong with their file, and at least two Lords or Ladies have to consent. It has never happened, – not even among the Residents in quarantine.

"But what about Da… " Rose began, but stopped herself. "What about the file that I saw Mikoto delete that time? And what's 'The Divergence'"

"Your situation was a little different," said Hana. "That was a bad upload."

"Right," agreed Embla. "Generally, bad uploads don't function at all and the system replaces them automatically. A situation like you witnessed, where there is enough of the file uncorrupted to result in an actual manifestation here… That is exceedingly rare."

"But even then," added Hana. "Mikoto deleted the file, but I had to consent to it."

"And 'The Divergence'?" Rose pressed.

"That was something else we learned the hard way," Embla answered wryly. "We had no idea what to expect when we uploaded the very first brain scans."

"Remember, Rose," Hana added. "We thought we would just be copying the content... the information. Aaru had to be developed because we had actually copied the whole person."

Rose nodded. Hana had explained this before.

"What we did not expect however," Embla went on. "Was how different the copies eventually became from the Makers. We called this phenomenon The Divergence."

"It makes sense, of course," Hana noted. "Our experiences here in Aaru are very different from those of the Makers on the outside. Our environment is different. How we interact with it and can change it is different. We have supremely more power over it here than our Makers do on theirs Before. The most glaring example, of course, is we no longer need have any fear of death. We are immortal. That has to impact who we are and can become. It is only natural our development diverges along with our wildly differing experiences and realities. This is also why we no longer upload Resident files until the originator of the file – like you in the hospital, Rose – has died. Otherwise, it might be quite bewildering for family and indeed, for the person whose brain scan has been uploaded."

"The point in all of this," Lady Embla said firmly, apparently deciding the conversation was beginning to drift rather far afield. "Is just that it was a very serious thing to delete Atem from Aaru, but the fact that Simon on the outside has now died... The fact he was never rescanned or uploaded again, well..."

"He's gone forever," finished Hana sadly. "And those are very heavy tidings."

"Poor Lady Nu!" Auset exclaimed, placing both hands over her mouth. "That's terrible! She must be *so* sad... I... I should go to her... Maybe there is something I can do."

"I don't know if anything will help her but time," Hana responded regretfully, "but it would certainly be a very nice gesture, Auset. Lord Wurugag has most likely taken her to Lord Draugr to hear all the details. We will certainly go to her after that meeting is concluded. So, *so* sad."

Hana shook her head, and Embla nodded in agreement.

Rose found her previous good mood had evaporated. The melancholy returned, and she could not help thinking about Dani. All alone in his field of poppies, flying his kite and waiting for a father who might never arrive. And what of this 'Divergence' they were talking about? What did it mean?

She *thought* she was Rose Johnson. She had never considered otherwise. However, Rose could not deny what Hana had explained. Aaru had changed her. Her own mother had gone so far as to basically disown her because of it! She was not the same shy, studious girl who played soccer and dreamed of someday holding aloft a World Cup. She wasn't the same Rose who let other people make life and death decisions for her.

The last time she talked to Gypsie Johnson through the window, her mother had commented Rose seemed different – that she didn't resemble the little girl to whom Gypsie had given birth any longer. Was she right? Did Rose Johnson even exist anymore, or had she in fact died in her hospital bed in the ICU those few years ago? Who was she?

"Are you quite well, Rose?" Runa asked with concern. "Your face has adopted a rather pallid complexion."

"I…" Rose began, but really had no idea what to say. "It's just sad, is all. I feel bad for Lady Nu, and for Auset. I… yeah… I think I'll be fine. Don't worry about me."

There was much more Rose wanted to tell her. There was much more weighing on her mind, but as so often seemed to happen these days, she really had no clear idea how to articulate everything she was feeling.

"I think…" she said. "I think I'm gonna go find Franco… I need… I need…" Rose found she could say no more.

Runa and Auset both hugged her.

"You do that, Rose," Auset whispered into her ear. "You let him kiss it all better. You deserve it, and I'm happy for you."

Rose nodded gratefully, then flew off to find her boyfriend.

*

Rose found Franco in the courtyard of his Spanish conquistador-themed mansion. He'd once again adopted his raven-*tengu* avatar and was apparently taking out his aggressions on some sort of combat practice dummies. His black wings spread wide and

293

he shot into the air. Then he descended to the Earth like a comet. The screeching cry of a raptor tore through the stillness of the Aaru plain. Long black spear poised to strike, his silhouette starkly outlined by the bright sunshine behind him, Rose thought he'd never looked more dashing.

His weapon connected with one of the dummies in a spectacular explosion of splinters and straw. These then effervesced into a faint cloud of tiny green squares before disappearing entirely. Rose clapped appreciatively.

Franco looked up. When he caught sight of Rose, his long black beak shrank, and the sable feathers covering his head receded to reveal his handsome, brown face. The boy grinned and jogged over.

"Hey, Rose!" he greeted. "What's up? I was just practicing."

"I saw," said Rose. "Very impressive, but... *What* exactly were you practicing?"

Franco shrugged.

"Defending Aaru," he said vaguely. "Mikoto's been pushing several of us to learn how. I know he's had me, Kyo, and Molly all practice together. There may be other Vedas too, but I haven't seen them."

"Kyo and Molly," Rose mused. "I don't know them very well. I think I've only met both of them once or twice."

"I didn't either really until practice," Franco responded. "Kyo is pretty cool. He's from Japan and is Lord Sora's Veda. Molly's from Australia and she's with Lady Mist. They spend *a lot* of time together. I think they're a thing."

"Like us?"

"Of *course* not," said Franco with a laugh. "Nobody's like us, Rose!"

He kissed her cheek and Rose ghosted a tiny smile.

"But seriously though," he continued. "They're pretty cool kids, you know? Maybe we should all hang out together sometime, or something... Do the couples thing."

"Sure," she agreed easily. "Why not? But... what exactly are you guys protecting Aaru *from*?"

Franco shrugged again. He made finger quotes in the air.

"*Danger,*" he said. Then he laughed. "I don't think Mikoto really knows either, but ever since you were... you know... almost taken, he's been all obsessed with improving Aaru's defenses. He told me, 'God-knows-what might come after the system, so God-knows-what is what we've got to prepare for.' I'll admit. I went along 'cause... you know... I... I was really worried about you..." His voice grew husky and quiet. "If anything else comes for you Rose, I wanna be right there. I wanna be ready to protect you this time... If something happened to you..."

Rose did not let him finish. She suddenly recalled her purpose and her urgency in searching the boy out. She closed with Franco, and kissed him deeply. He held her tight and eagerly kissed her back.

When Rose finally let him take a breath, he chuckled and smiled into her face.

"Wow, Rose," Franco breathed. "Did you miss me? What happened to making me work for it?"

"I'm my own person, Franco," Rose stated passionately. "I am who I'm meant to be. I'm not going to let anyone tell me who that is anymore."

Franco's face grew serious.

"Are you okay, Rose?" he asked in concern, holding her at arm's length. "Did something happen?"

"I woke up, Franco," Rose said passionately. "My whole life I've been expected to be a 'good girl'. I've had this big, long list of crap dictated to me from my parents, from my school, from my church... this massive checklist of things I have to do or be or believe. I don't have to worry about that here. I can be whoever I want, and I don't wanna be a good girl anymore."

Franco let her kiss him again. Rose had been with Franco dozens of times of course, but this time was different. Before, there had always been this doubt in the back of her mind, this stubborn guilt. What would her parents think? Koren? Would God be mad at her?

This time, however, she didn't care. It didn't matter what anyone else thought. Rose knew what she wanted, and was determined to take it. She shoved her hands up under Franco's shirt to bare skin. The garment suddenly disappeared and Rose kissed Franco's broad, brown chest.

Rose's eyes blazed. Her flesh ignited, and suddenly she was the fire nymph – a supple, female silhouette carved from living flame.

"*This* is who I am, Franco," Rose breathed. "*You* are what I want, and I don't care what anybody thinks except for one. Do you like it? Do you like *me*? This me?"

"I love you, Rose," Franco breathed heavily. "However you wanna be, that's the Rose I love."

"Be the Raven," Rose breathed coaxing him down to the soft grass. "Be with me as the Raven…"

Franco complied.

Rose was tired of doubt. She was sick of worry. What she had heard about Simon and Atem made her sad. Everything she'd learned about The Divergence made her think. Her near abduction by Magic Man, who'd planned God-only-knows-what for her, and her assault by Ed made her realize she didn't necessarily have forever, not even in Aaru. All of it left her decided.

Whether she had 10,000 years in Aaru or just ten minutes. Whether she and Franco stayed together forever or drifted apart, now they had each other. Now, life was good, and Rose was going to suck every drop of joy from these precious moments she could. *Screw* anyone who didn't like it!

When they finally lay back together wrapped in each other's arms, staring up at the azure sky – when Rose let her flames die down to a dull smolder and Franco reverted from his bird-warrior form back to the handsome Latin boy who first attracted Rose's notice, Rose regretted nothing. She didn't care they were fully exposed beneath the sky. She knew no shame at the idea anyone could happen by and see what they were up to. For the first time in her life, Rose felt truly and fully satisfied. She felt whole, she realized, and Franco was a big part of that.

Rose nuzzled his chest and kissed his neck. Franco petted her hair. They said nothing, but they didn't need to. They had an understanding, Rose realized. They fit together just like puzzle pieces. They were two halves of the same whole.

In this moment, Franco commanded her entire attention. He made up the totality of her universe, and that was just fine. Now… *Right* now, Rose realized, she didn't need anything else. Nor did she want it. All she wanted was Franco, so she truly had everything she wanted.

And that, she realized, *is a rare and wonderful thing.*

***

Hel watched Rose and the brown boy with longing – close enough to see, but far enough away to remain unnoticed. She sent her followers away, so she could fully enjoy all of Rose and Franco's striving in private. She could certainly understand Sister's desire. He was *so* pretty and *so* sweet!

She ran her hands over her own body, closing her eyes. Hel pretended it was her Franco yearned for and desired. She envisioned him kissing and caressing her, whispering trifling words of love. Hel imagined it was *her* he wanted and *not* Rose.

Hel froze, suddenly overcome by powerful emotions she could not at all articulate. Her dark half was murderously jealous, but her unspoiled half was inconsolably sad. There was one thing upon which they agreed however; Rose's unbelievable good fortune was grossly unfair. Why did *she* get everything?

Sister was pretty - the object of desire. Rose was beloved. She had friends to laugh and play with. And she had Franco. Hel had none of those things.

Hel continued to watch the couple fawn all over each other. Every kiss, every touch, every smile and embrace, each one was tearing her insides out. Hel started to cry, bitter angry tears, and wrung her hands in frustration. The same phrase kept repeating over and over again in her head; *It just isn't fair.*

Why does Rose get everything good? She thought bitterly. *Why does Rose get to be happy, while I have to suffer alone?*

Hel again recalled Sister's promise, her lie; *I'll always keep you safe. I'll never leave you alone.*

I'm alone right now, Hel brooded.

She felt the darkness rising within her, and the ground beneath her feet froze solid. Frost formed on the grasses and flowers around her in a wide radius. The birdsong and humming insects stilled.

The grief in her questions was soul-crushing, and the jealousy gnawed at her, but she did not despair. The rage was still there, and it left her determined. Her eyes narrowed.

Hel was not helpless anymore. She did not have to be a victim. Hel had power in this place. Sister was a Veda, but Hel was a ruling *Lady*! That had to count for something, didn't it?

Her Maker had made it impossible to change her face, so she would never have Rose's beauty. It made her an object of fear and revulsion, so she could not have Rose's friends, but maybe...

She thought back to what she had done to Ed. Hel could still feel his mind beneath her probing fingers as she rifled through his thoughts and emotions. She knew all the right places to touch and caress. She made Ed feel pleasure like he'd never experienced in his whole life before. She made him *beg* for her touch until he agreed to worship her as a Goddess! Rose did not have that, could not do that, but Hel could. She just needed a chance.

"I can give Franco pleasure you cannot, Sister," Hel murmured to herself, glaring down at the happy couple. "And when I do, he will love me and not you. I will take him from you, and *we* will be happy. *So* happy! Happy just like you..."

She would have to wait for the right moment, of course, but Hel was sure that would come sooner rather than later. Patience was all she needed. It *would* happen she was sure. The opportunity would present itself. After all, they had forever.

Hel ran her hands over her body again in anticipation of the Latin boy's soft touch, his warm lips. It was *her* turn to be happy. She *deserved* this. It was time for *Hel* to get what she wanted for a change.

Franco would be hers.

Chapter 23

Medicinal Half-Gallons

Koren was a little surprised when Amy pulled into a very normal looking apartment complex. She parked the car then came around to open Koren's door. Amy gripped a brown paper bag of fast food, a plastic grocery bag with two large containers of cookie dough ice cream, and her car keys in one hand. She held the other out to Koren with a kind expression on her face. Koren readjusted Pandadora at her side and took her hand sheepishly.

As Amy led her up a set of stairs to a nondescript apartment door on the back side of the complex, Koren was desolate, but she was also embarrassed. She had gone and done *exactly* what she swore to both Amy and Bindi she wouldn't. She'd gone back to Jonas like a sycophantic idiot, practically throwing herself at his feet, when she'd promised her girlfriends she would *never* forgive him for his cheating. Now, not only was Jonas mad at her, and she hopelessly confused about why she felt guilty rather than angry, Koren was also mentally preparing herself for the blistering "I told you so" that was assuredly still to come from her personal assistant.

Amy opened the door. Then she flipped on the lights and tossed her keys on a tall kitchen counter right beside the entrance. Koren followed her inside.

"Well," said Amy nonchalantly as she stepped behind the counter to put the ice-cream in the freezer. "Here it is - my LA digs."

The combination living room-kitchen Koren now found herself in was surprisingly sparse. There was a small dining table next to the sink. The living room contained a black love-seat and a small TV set, but was otherwise empty. Amy noted her expression.

"Yeah," she said, setting the fast food on the counter. "I'm not actually here very often. Well… At least, I wasn't until I was assigned to be your personal assistant, that is. Most of my stuff is back in my apartment at the Elysian Industries compound in Bell Buckle, but I thought this might give us a little more privacy than your place. You're okay with a chicken sandwich and fries, I hope…"

Amy started digging in the bag, and Koren nodded.

"I wasn't sure what you liked fast-food-wise," she went on, "and you weren't being very forthcoming."

"I'm sorry, Amy," Koren began. It seemed like she was apologizing a lot today. "I should have listened--"

"Let's not worry about that now," Amy interrupted. "Let's eat dinner. Then I've got a Rom-Com cued up on Netflix and two cartons of ice cream with our names on 'em. We can talk later."

Koren nodded and accepted the proffered sandwich with a meek "thank you". Amy put some music on with her phone, but dinner was otherwise silent. When they finished, Amy led her over to the couch. She handed Koren one of the tubs of ice cream and what looked to be a serving spoon. Then Amy sat beside her and started the movie.

It was an old film Koren had never heard of. It was kind of silly and improbable, but it was sweet and made her laugh. She had to admit, it did a pretty good job of taking her mind off of things.

After it was over, Amy threw the empty ice cream containers in the trash and went to get Koren a pair of pajamas. They were flannel, itchy, and a little too big, but Koren accepted them gratefully. Amy changed into pajamas of her own – a pink, stripy pair that made her look like a candy cane – and seated herself on the couch next to the younger girl. Amy turned towards her.

"So," she began. "You feelin' any better?"

Koren nodded.

"Yeah," she answered softly. "I don't know what I would have done if you hadn't shown up... I would have run into my dad at least..." Koren grimaced. "I don't think I coulda handled it... There's no way that would have turned out well."

"Yeah, well," Amy replied. "I don't know what *I* would have done if I'd pulled up to your house and found you God-only-knows-where with Jonas Perry." She made a face. "I went back there on reflex, you know. I didn't really expect to find you after I realized you weren't there and got your text. I drove around looking for a while, then gave up and went back to your place. You know, Koren... I'm responsible for you. I need to know where you are."

"Sorry..."

Koren's eyes welled with tears again.

"Wanna talk about it?" Amy prompted gently. "It's okay if you don't."

Koren wiped her face with her forearm and nodded.

"You were right," she began huskily. "I was stupid. He called me, and I was all ready to chew him out. I was *so* mad at him! But it was right after that horrible meeting with my parents, and the whole airport thing, and me and my mom's big fight… He told me to go to the window, and Jonas was standing *right there* in the driveway all smiling and waving and I just wanted… just wanted…"

"Just wanted someone to make you feel better?" Amy finished for her.

Koren nodded and covered her face.

"I wasn't even thinking!" she lamented. "I threw on this really pretty dress I knew he'd like, and when I saw him downstairs, I just couldn't help myself. I hugged him and kissed him and asked him to take me away… I totally gave him the wrong idea…"

"What do you mean, 'gave him the wrong idea', Koren?" Amy asked, furrowing her brow.

"He drove us out by the ocean and we talked. He said I'd totally gotten it all wrong about the Claudette thing, and he was sorry…"

"Who's Claudette?" Amy asked.

"The French girl," Koren answered. "She opens for him when he's touring in Europe. They just work together. The pictures were just photo-op hype. I was still mad, but he was *really* sorry, and he swore he hadn't done anything with her."

"I bet," Amy commented crossing her arms with a dubious scowl.

"So anyway, we pulled over," Koren went on. "And he said he liked me… *Really* liked me. And that made me feel really happy. He said he was sad for all the stuff I was having to go through, and he wanted to make me feel better… He wanted us to be a real relationship and take things to the next level…"

"Uh oh," interjected Amy, but Koren continued.

"He kissed me, and I kissed him back, but then…" she trailed off and her voice grew shaky and weak with embarrassment. "Then h… he s…started t… taking my c…clothes off, and I totally freaked out!"

"Wait," Amy held up both hands in front of her. Her expression was indignant. "He did *what*?!"

"I didn't mean to lead him on," Koren insisted, her voice breaking and tears flowing down her cheeks. "B…but I wasn't ready… I wasn't expecting it, and… and the only other person to touch me that way was th… th… that creepy M… Magic Man guy, and I... I just couldn't... I... I froze... and... and c... covered up, and h... he was *so* mad and..."

Whatever Koren said next was rendered completely unintelligible by her weeping and blubbering, but Amy was furious. Her face flushed bright red, and her eyes flashed dangerously.

"So let me get this straight, Koren," Amy snapped. "You felt like crap, because you just had one of the worst days of your whole life. You were vulnerable and needing a friend to turn to, so Jonas Perry shows up to drive you into the middle of nowhere and sexually *molest* you?!"

"It... it wasn't like that!" Koren insisted. "He didn't *make* me do anything. He stopped as soon as I said no, but he was *so* disappointed... He didn't even say it, but I could tell. H... he said he needs a *real* relationship. I--"

"Okay, Koren." Amy cut her off. "Wait just a second. You need to understand something *really* clearly. There are all kinds of force. No, Jonas didn't hold you down or drag you into a dark alley by your hair, but he was *absolutely* trying to manipulate you and get you to do things you didn't want to and weren't ready for."

"What do you mean?" asked Koren tearfully.

"If Jonas really cared about you," Amy answered patiently. "He would have been concerned about *your* needs. He would have been worried about *you*r feelings, especially after you told him everything going on with work and your parents. I mean, the guy got caught *cheating* on you with some other girl. Jonas can say what he wants, but I saw those pictures. You don't hang on people like that if you're just colleagues from work. At the very least, he should have been crawling back to you on his hands and knees begging forgiveness, but instead has the thundering gall to get mad and try to make *you* feel guilty?! *Jesus!* The nerve... Guys like that Koren..."

Amy shook her head in disgust.

"I know it's a cliché to say they're only after one thing," she met Koren's tearstained gaze seriously. "But that's what this feels like... Even if he *thinks* he likes you, he's worried far more about himself and his own needs than about yours. You should *never* feel obligated to have sex with someone if you don't want to. It's supposed to be a bonding and edifying experience for *both* people. It shouldn't be demanded or given grudgingly.

"*Real* relationship?" Amy barreled on derisively. "*Ha!* He doesn't know what the words mean. Don't let him get in your head,

Koren. Don't let him fool you. He wanted *sex,* and that's all he was thinking about. He wasn't thinking about you at all.

"And let me tell you this, Koren," Amy concluded pointedly. "If you only have sex because you feel like you have to, you won't enjoy it, *and* you'll feel lousy about yourself afterwards. That's a big decision... A *huge* decision! It's totally unfair of him to try and rush you. If he actually wanted a 'real relationship' with you, he'd be more sensitive to what you want and what you need and what feels comfortable to *you.* He'd want to make decisions about how far and how fast things should go *together* and actually care how you feel."

Koren stared down at her hands. She had to admit, a lot of what Amy was telling her made sense, even if she didn't want it to. She started crying again.

"I feel so *stupid*, Amy!" Koren cried. "I just wanted him to *like* me. I just wanted him to think I was *special*!"

Amy wrapped a companionable arm around Koren's shoulder, and gave her a sad smile.

"You *are* special, Koren." Amy sighed. "And you're not 'stupid'. You're just stupid-in-love for the first time. We all do that. Sometimes it happens with the wrong person, and all we can do is learn from it."

"S... so, have you..?" Koren started, but Amy cut her off again with a sly grin and a silencing finger against the younger girl's lips.

"Let's just say, I'm nineteen years old. I've had a lot more time to make stupid mistakes than you."

"I wish Bindi was here," Koren murmured sadly. "Or, I guess Rose would be better, I really ought to be talking about this with her. I'm sorry to be dumping all my problems in your lap. Thanks for listening to me."

"No problem, Koren," Amy answered, giving the other girl a tight hug. "Remember Australia? We bonded! I'm not just your personal assistant anymore. I'm your friend. Feel free to dump on me whenever you need to."

"Thanks."

"Although," Amy went on with a wicked smile. "I bet you *don't* wish Bindi was here."

"Why's that?" Koren asked innocently.

"Because the last time I texted her, she swore that she'd quote 'beat that silly girl bloody unconscious the next time I see her' unquote."

Amy laughed at Koren's horrified expression.

"Don't worry," Amy said. "I don't think she was serious... at least not completely. I already told Bindi I found you safe and sound. She'll get over it. She was just worried. And as for Rose," Amy continued with a twinkle in her eye. "You can tell her all about it tomorrow. Bindi too, actually."

"What?" asked Koren in confusion.

"I wasn't *totally* lying to your dad," Amy admitted with a shrug. "I do actually have some new equipment Askr wants you to try out tomorrow. I just... Let's say 'picked you up early'."

"What equipment?" Koren asked.

"Just look back here."

Amy got up and led Koren to the bedrooms. There were two of them.

"I sleep in this bedroom."

Amy gestured to a door on the right. In front of them was obviously the bathroom.

"This one over here though," Amy turned left and pushed the door open. She flipped on the light. "This one is for work stuff."

When Koren's eyes adjusted, she gasped. There in what appeared to be the master bedroom were two narrow cylinders. They were about seven feet tall, roughly two and a half feet wide, and transparent. The two cylinders rested on mirror-image, C-shaped mounts that held them in place at the top and bottom, and were covered with blinking lights.

"What are they?" Koren asked in wonder.

"Remember about a month ago, when you spent... what was it? Thirteen hours or something like that on the Silver Lining System?"

Koren nodded sheepishly.

"We'd been working on a redesign way before that, but that little episode simply emphasized some major design issues we realized would need to be resolved before the SLS became viable for use among the general public." Amy explained. "For example, no one is going to want to buy a piece of equipment that is twenty feet tall and full of slime. No one is going to want to fool with a system that requires a team of scientists in their living room in order to operate it, and no one is going to want to hop inside a contraption where they could conceivably die by drowning every time they're logged on."

"So…" Koren began uncertainly. "This here is… what exactly?"

"Tomorrow, after we get up," Amy said with a smile. "We are going to try out the new Silver Lining 2.0 – home edition. It's been in development for a while, but Askr decided to expedite its release."

She walked over and squeezed the transparent cylinder with both hands. It squished down easily. Then she grasped it and stretched it out to twice its original size.

"This unit here," she explained releasing the rubbery material. It sprang back to its original shape. "Is our dual model. Two people can log-in at the same time, and it requires no monitoring, no oxygen, and no *slime*."

Amy stuck out her tongue in distaste.

"You still have to wear the body suit and the VR goggles, but everything else works through magnets. We're going to meet up with Bindi and the Elysian rep on her end tomorrow. Then I thought we could visit with your sister and Bindi's brother, Derain. How does that sound? It'll basically just be a day to goof off in Aaru with friends *and*…" she paused dramatically before finishing in a conspiratorial whisper. "No mandatory logouts."

Amy grinned, and Koren managed a weak answering smile.

"That sounds great, Amy," she said.

"But first!" Amy declared. "Our night's not done yet."

She ushered Koren out of the room and shut the door behind them. Amy took Koren by the hand and led her back to the couch. She pressed her gently into a sitting position. Then Amy went back behind the kitchen counter to dig in cabinets.

"I've got popcorn, hot cocoa, and the Bridget Jones box set," Amy gushed as she started heating some milk on the stove. "We'll be having a late start tomorrow, if that's alright with you."

Koren giggled. Soon she and Amy were cuddled on the couch under a thick blanket. A big bowl of popcorn was in between them, and Pandadora set on Koren's other side. The girls sipped on steaming mugs as they laughed, cried, ooh-ed, and ah-ed along with the silly romance on the screen. Then Amy flipped on *Mama Mia*, just for good measure. When they finally drifted off to sleep snuggled on the loveseat, dawn was just beginning to break outside.

***

Hel called another door into being. She'd done this hundreds and hundreds of times. Thousands of formerly separate islands of loneliness and solitude had been linked together, but Hel was not satisfied. She was determined to connect all of them into a community of the broken – a nation of the miserable and the mad.

How appropriate it is that I am their queen, she thought ironically.

There had been no end of misfits and troubled minds. Hel had already encountered every type of madness, every sort of depression and despair, every variety of self-loathing, violent, lunatic, and hopeless soul. Her dark half reviled them, but her soft side loved them and pitied them. It burned to help them somehow.

The door before her now was narrow and red, with a tiny window near the top. Hel turned the knob and walked through. She found herself in yet another wide field. However this one was not covered by the quotidian, golden grasses that comprised most of the Aaru plain. Rather this field was an ocean of red and black poppies. An inky drizzle fell from ashen clouds to bead upon the delicate petals. She saw a dark blot in the sky some distance away and made her way towards it.

Hel was not immediately sure what it was she was seeing. It looked like a small figure on the ground connected to something indistinct in the sky. When she drew nearer however, Hel felt the tickling of memory from her loving half. It was a little boy with a kite.

She alighted among the flowers near the boy, but he did not turn. He stood staring fixedly at his kite as it danced in the iron grey sky, dodging and darting here and there among the clouds. Hel approached him.

"Hello," greeted the boy without turning around. "Are you here to bring me to my father? I've been waiting an awfully long time."

"No," said Hel. "I am here to release you. I am here to set you free."

"They tried that already," the boy commented blandly. "It didn't work. They put me back here. So now I'm just waiting again."

"Your name is…" Hel looked at him a moment. "Dani."

"Uh huh," said Dani.

"Yes, it is true Residents cannot leave quarantine *yet*," Hel admitted a little defensively. "But I will find a solution to that."

"Oh," said Dani neutrally. "Okay."

He kept staring at his kite. The misty shower of black continued to fall.

Hel was starting to get annoyed by this boy's lack of attention. Her dark half wanted to reach into his mind and yank it inside out, but her caring side counseled patience. He was just a child after all.

"You said you are waiting," Hel stated. "You asked me if I was here to take you to your father. You believe he will come here?"

"I hope so," said Dani. "He told me he would."

Hel stared hard at Dani. She walked a great circle around him deeply scanning his mind. He regarded her nervously, but quickly returned his gaze to the flying toy.

"There is a deep sadness about you, Dani," Hel commented at last. "It's a hopelessness that eats at your insides. You say you are waiting for your father, but…" She paused and looked up in surprise. "But you do not really believe he will come. In fact, you *know* he will not come. It is a realization that gnaws at you."

Dani finally looked away from his kite. He turned his eyes down to the ground and the aerial toy winked out of existence. He did not reply. The inky drizzle became a downpour.

"I see it as plain as the nose on your face," Hel murmured sympathetically. "Why do you lie to yourself? It is very sad…"

"If I pretend," Dani said in a tiny voice. He looked Hel full in the face as tears began to roll down his dark cheeks along with the sable rain. "It makes it easier."

He looked straight into her eyes. There was no hint of fear about him – only hopelessness.

"You…" Hel stammered in surprised. "You do not fear me?"

Dani shook his head.

"Why?" he asked.

"Well… because… You must find me… very ugly…" Hel said turning her own eyes away.

Again, Dani shook his head.

"No," he said matter-of-factly. "I think you're pretty."

Hel snorted.

"Don't lie to *me*, boy," she hissed. "Do not seek to flatter me!"

Dani looked at Hel curiously. Even in the face of her rage there was no alarm in his eyes.

"I'm *not* lying," he insisted. "I think you're a pretty girl, just… a pretty girl who's gotten hurt."

Hel touched her face unconsciously and her jaw tightened. Her own eyes welled with tears, and her features softened. She looked down on Dani fondly.

"You are a very sweet boy, Dani," Hel said affectedly. "You are… kind… Why do you believe your father will not come? What is this sadness that will not let you be?"

She could have found out on her own, of course. Hel could have just reached into his brain and pulled out whatever it was she wanted to know, but she was feeling charitable. This Dani boy charmed her.

"Ghosts," said Dani. "The ghosts of my friends… They kept me sad, and I couldn't be happy anymore. My father said I was lucky, but I never felt that way. Then I made the really *big* mistake. I made everything worse, and now I'll never see him again."

"May I look, Dani?" Hel asked softly. "May I see?"

Dani shrugged.

"If you want… I'm just afraid it will make you sad too."

Hel put her hands on his shoulders and looked kindly into his eyes.

"Boy," she said sincerely. "If you only knew. The sadness in my heart drags on my soul like a lead weight…"

She put her hand to the side of Dani's head, but very gently. She closed her eyes.   Dani's memory flooded into Hel's head.

He was sitting at a desk in school taking his lessons.

He threw himself to the floor as a shouting, masked man rushed in, guns blazing. The bodies of his friends dropped all around him. He lay still, eyes clenched, praying the man would not notice him…

…The man was gone. Dani stood alone in the silent classroom. The bodies of his classmates lay all around, bloody and motionless, vacant eyes staring. The only thing moving was Dani…

...His father embraced him crying hard, wracking sobs in the back of the ambulance. His relief was obvious, but all Dani felt was empty.

Why me? *He thought.* Why did I survive?

...Sightless stares haunted him. They accused him. The ghosts of his dead friends ever fixed their eyes upon him - jealous eyes, angry eyes, judging eyes. Day and night, waking and sleeping, they condemned him. Their dead, staring eyes chastised the very blood in his veins. Their hate was strong, and Dani knew no peace or respite...

...He sat in a chair at a little table in a filthy apartment. Before him was a tall glass of water, and a sandwich bag full of little green pills. His blessed greenies... For so long, these had been his only refuge from the belligerent eyes. Now, they would finally give him his final escape. He had to upend the baggy three times before he could get them all down, but once the deed was done, he got out of the chair, laid in his bed and covered up with a thin blanket. That was when the seizures took him. It hurt, and it was scary, but it did not last very long. Then the blackness came...

Hel looked at Dani sympathetically.

"I understand," she said.

"They wouldn't leave me alone!" Dani sniveled. "All day, all night... I couldn't eat. I couldn't sleep. For *years*! I... I shouldn't have done it... It was bad... B... but, I just couldn't take it anymore! I messed up and now I... I just want my dad. B... but... he can't! For him to come to me now, he'd have to *kill* himself! And... and I don't want that... I messed up, and now I have to be alone forever..."

Dani's despair broke Hel's heart, but it also fired her temper. How *dare* the elites of this place hurt this poor, sweet boy? How *dare* they pass the judgement as if they were so righteous and pure? Hel snarled in rage.

"This is not right, Dani," she growled, shaking her head resolutely. "This is not fair."

Dani shrugged again..

"It doesn't matter," he sighed in resignation. "I messed up, so now I'm stuck here, forever and ever..."

"No," Hel snarled. "I *refuse* to accept it. This imprisonment, this *segregation* is not right. It *must* end."

"But, how?" Dani asked desolately. "They won't let me go. They keep putting me back here! I *can't* leave."

"I don't know," Hel stated, "but I will find a way."

She met Dani's eyes seriously.

"I am powerful here, Dani," she said. "I am tearing down the walls of this place one Resident at a time. Come. You don't have to be alone anymore. The doors to the other cells are thrown wide, but that is not enough. The beautiful people must pay. They must give us what they've withheld. They must release us – welcome us into their world, and if they will not, then there is but one option."

"What is that, Hel?" Dani asked innocently.

Hel narrowed her eyes and clinched her fists. In her heart, she knew what she must do, even if she still did not know how to do it. Dani did not need to be troubled with those details, however. Hel stared at him as serious as death, but her expression softened, and she cupped his cheek with her white hand.

"War," she said simply. "We go to war, Dani."

Chapter 24

Mother

When they finally got up the next day, it was nearly noon. Amy let Koren have the shower first and made her some lunch. It was nothing fancy, just a bowl of ramen noodles and a grilled American cheese sandwich on wheat bread, but it was still a lot of fun. Including the lunch, she'd eaten more junk food with Amy in one day than she'd been allowed in at least the previous six months. Koren hadn't had a real slumber party in ages, and this one had been awesome.

She wished Bindi could have joined them, but contented herself with the knowledge she would see her friend soon. Of course, she also harbored a tiny bit of dread the other girl *might* actually beat her bloody at that meeting. Koren was pretty sure her friend had been indulging in hyperbole, but despite Amy's reassurances, she knew Bindi well-enough to be at least slightly worried.

Amy ate with her. Then she took her own shower. Very shortly, the two girls were stripping off their bathrobes and squeezing into the stretchy, skin-tight sensory suits they would use in the Silver Lining 2.0.

"So how does this work exactly?" asked Koren as she pulled the snug hood over her head.

"It's not that different, really," said Amy. "It's just a lot less trouble."

She reached over to one of the cylinders and pressed a button. The rubbery tube slid upwards with a hydraulic hiss.

"Once you get in," she instructed. "There will be a big green button at around waist level on your right. Push it when your VR set switches on, and it will pull up the log-in screen. After that, it's pretty much the same as before. Enter your information, and choose Exploration Mode.

"Once you're in, tell the computer to search for me. We might be six inches apart here in my apartment, but in Aaru, there's no telling where we'll pop up. Every time you log-in, until you start marking some favorite locations or adding friends at least, you'll pop up somewhere random each time. We can add each other to our friends list as soon as we hook up, so it won't be a problem in the future. I'll show you how."

Koren nodded, doing her best to carefully catalog this rush of vital information.

"Oh, by the way," Amy added almost as an afterthought. "Magnets in the suit and magnets in the cylinder will keep you suspended in the middle, so don't freak out when you start floating. It really should be just like before – just a lot more compact and a lot less goopy. See you there!"

Koren nodded again and did as she was instructed. She pulled her VR goggles over her eyes and her vision was immediately filled with an infinite blue sky and billowy white clouds. She pushed the button and was lifted off of her feet.

She was glad of Amy's warning. Even though Koren was expecting it, she still gave a start as she rose into the air. After entering her log-in information, she soon felt herself being sucked down by the swirling rainbow vortex. The falling sensation stopped with a jolt.

Koren found herself, lying on her back in tall brown grass. She was staring up at a cloudy grey sky. It took her a minute to orient herself to the sudden change in surroundings, but she soon rolled to her side and climbed to her feet.

The first thing Koren did was look down at herself. Thankfully, she was not naked, but rather wore a nondescript pair of blue jeans and a white t-shirt. Koren immediately decided this was entirely too boring for meeting up with her sister and her friends, so she opened up the settings menu and began flipping through outfits.

Good afternoon, Koren. A bland, female computer voice greeted. *You have* one *unconfirmed friend request. Would you like to accept?*

"Yes," answered Koren absently.

Ooh… that kimono is cute. She thought. *Rose would probably approve.*

You have one *total friends logged in at the moment.* The computer voice blared again. *Would you like to reveal your location?*

"Eh," Koren replied distractedly, still swiping through dresses, slacks, and costumes. "Sure. Why not."

It was assuredly Amy – most likely impatient Koren hadn't tracked her down yet.

Well, she can just wait, Koren grumped to herself. *I'm not taking* that *long.*

Koren passed a pair of red short-shorts she liked, and flipped back.

Those are cute, she mused. *Maybe in blue though... Pink? If I paired them with a bikini and a tank top, it'd look really beachy. Just like when I saw Bindi last!*

She clicked on the shorts and then did a quick search for the other articles she would need. Koren added a pair of sunglasses and flip flops for good measure. She heard footsteps behind her.

"Hey Amy," she called over her shoulder. "I was just picking an outfit. What do you think? Do you think 'beach' is a good look? It's what we wore the last..."

Koren trailed off as she turned around. A girl stood before her, but it most definitely wasn't Amy.

"Y... you look b... beautiful," the girl stammered shyly. "More beautiful than I imagined... Is it really you? I... I didn't know you would come so soon. I always hoped, but..."

The girl was wearing a filthy sundress. In fact, it looked as if it had been splattered with blood. She was turned sort of sideways to Koren, so it was hard to get a good look at her, and she was holding one hand behind her back where Koren could not see it. The other was clamped firmly over the side of her face that was turned away from Koren. A monstrous wolf with horns stood next to her growling menacingly. Koren wondered at her strange appearance, to say nothing of her alarming pet, but then shrugged. This was Aaru after all.

"Who are you?" Koren asked kindly. "I'm Koren!"

"I... I know who you are," the other girl murmured. "I... I'm so nervous! I've been practicing *forever* what I would say to you when we finally met, and now I have no idea!"

Koren smiled kindly.

"Are you a fan?" she asked curiously. "Don't worry. I don't bite. Don't be nervous. Just talk to me! I love meeting new people. It's nice to meet you."

Koren held out her hand.

The girl bit her lip nervously in apparent indecision.

The wolf growled again, and Koren cocked her head to the side curiously. It almost sounded like words.

"You be quiet, Fenrir!" the girl snapped. "That was rude. Be nice or you shall be very sorry! In fact," her voice took on a slightly menacing tone. "Go away. I'll not have you ruin this. I'll deal with you later."

The massive wolf hung its large head and turned. Then the great beast strode through some random doorway with no building around it and winked out of existence. The strange girl visibly squirmed, continuing to cover her face with one hand, while she nervously twisted the fabric of her dress with the other.

Koren kept holding her hand out, but her smile became more brittle.

"It's really okay," Koren tried to sound soothing. "What's your name?"

The girl's face was distraught. Then she turned completely sideways and took her hand from the side of her face. Her pale fingers closed around Koren's, and Koren shook the proffered hand firmly. The girl's face took on a nearly rapturous expression, and a tear leaked from the corner of her eye. She returned Koren's gesture with vigor.

Koren had met zealous fans before, but she was starting to get a seriously weird vibe from this girl. She tried to gently extract her hand, but the girl did not loosen her grip.

"I... I'm so happy to meet you!" the girl gushed. "I've always wanted to meet you! I have so, so much to ask! To tell you!"

"Yeah," Koren replied with much reduced enthusiasm. "Great... I... I guess..."

The other girl sighed deeply and turned to fully face her. She wrapped both her hands around Koren's, and Koren gasped.

"M... my name is H... Hel," she stammered even as she kept vigorously pumping Koren's arm.

A bright smile had come over the girl's face, but Koren found it horrifying rather than uplifting.

"   And I am so, so, *so* glad to finally meet you. I... I've waited *so* long. I'm so happy you've come!"

The girl brought Koren's hand to her lips and kissed it. Another tear trickled from her eye. Koren could only stare. Half of Hel's face was beautiful - vaguely familiar even, but the other half...

"I'm so excited to find you at last," Hel said, but then she paused before finishing in a deeply affected murmur. She tightly squeezed Koren's hand against her breast.

"So, *so* glad to meet you... Mother..."

"*Amy!*" Koren screamed at the top of her lungs.

There was a flash, and Hel was suddenly gone. Koren found herself standing in a wide field of bright yellow flowers. The great and sparkling river burbled and gurgled to her left and a brilliant, lemon sun shone high above her in a flawless cerulean sky. Koren spun in a panicked circle.

What just happened? Who was that person? And what did she call me? Mother?!

"Hey, Koren!" came a friendly voice from above. "About time you showed up!"

It was Amy. Koren looked up in time to see her, Rose, Bindi, Derain, and another person she did not recognize. As they descended toward her, all of them were smiling.

"Get lost?" quipped Bindi with a wide smile as her feet hit the grass. "Or maybe you were just too scared to face me!"

She seized Koren in a headlock, before rubbing her knuckles in the crown of Koren's skull.

"You silly thing!" she exclaimed before releasing Koren's neck and crushing her in a fierce hug. "You bloody near scared me out of my mind!"

"Wow, Bindi," Derain commented dryly. "I guess, I know who you like best. You barely said 'hi' to me when you first popped in."

Koren had met Derain on Auset's boat the last time she used the SLS, but now that she saw Bindi and Derain together, there was no doubt he was Bindi's brother. His hair was darker than his sister's – more blackish brown than copper, and his skin a little lighter, but there was something in their facial structure – same eyes, same nose, same wide, white smile – that made it obvious they were siblings.

"Girl Power, mate. I *did* push you in the river though," Bindi retorted with a wicked grin. "You forgot that bit."

"Right... My mistake. I appreciate your sincere expression of filial affection then," Derain retorted sarcastically

"Alright, mate," Bindi shot her brother a flabbergasted expression. "Where is my brother, and what have you done with him?"

"Wow, Derain," said Rose with a clearly impressed expression. "That was outstanding! I think Runa's starting to rub off on you."

"Oh, bite me, the both of you," Derain shot back grumpily. "I know words too."

The boy's ill humor did not appear to affect Rose. She gave him a wink and a playful nudge to his ribs with her elbow. Then she turned to her sister.

"And *you* have a lot of explaining to do, young lady!" Rose said with a grin. "I hear you've been getting yourself in all kinds of trouble... But, it's really good to see you."

Bindi released Koren, and Rose spread her arms wide. Koren rushed into them as if she might tackle her. Rose was a little taken aback.

"Did you miss me?" Rose asked. "I appreciate the sentiment, but... are you okay, Koren?"

Koren could not respond for a moment. Then she took a shuddering breath and quickly related to everyone the strange encounter she'd just had. The person she did not recognize, regarded her with serious, dark eyes.

She was a pretty woman, but her face was very grave as if she spent a great deal of time thinking about weighty matters. Her skin and short hair both were the darkest Koren had ever seen. Her voice was deep, but gentle and kind.

"You say she called you, 'Mother'?" the woman asked with a strong, African accent. "Are you sure you did not mishear, perhaps?"

"I'm sure," Koren replied. "I *swear* that's what she called me."

"How odd... You seem very upset," the woman added in concern. "Did this person threaten you? Did you feel endangered?"

Koren shook her head.

"No, she actually seemed really excited to meet me. I thought she might be a fan. They can get a little carried away sometimes."

"Perhaps..." the woman said slowly. "I shall have to think on this. It is certainly a bizarre encounter, but if she was not threatening, it is most likely nothing to worry about - probably an over-exuberant fan, just like you suspected. It's an occupational hazard for all our reality show Vedas, I'm afraid. My little Bindi here, has had her share as well."

Koren regarded Bindi with a look of surprise.

"Have you now?" Koren asked placing her hands on her hips and pursing her lips in mock indignation. She shot her friend a wry smirk. "You never mentioned anything like that to *me*. What happened?"

Bindi shrugged.

"It was no big deal," she answered dismissively. "A couple of blokes turned up at the house a time or two, is all. A couple of times at the beach…"

"Oh, yeah? Interrupted Derain with a bemused expression. "Give yourself some credit! Did you tell her what you got in the post and by e-mail since the show came out?"

Bindi shot her brother a furious glare.

"Put a sock in it, Derain!" she exclaimed.

"What happened?" Koren asked innocently. "What did you get?"

"It was *no big deal*," Bindi insisted staring daggers at her brother. "They took care of it."

"Over a thousand requests for a date, twenty-six marriage proposals, enough stuffed teddy bears and dollies to start her own bloody toy store, so many flowers Mum and Dad couldn't get in the front door, three brand new surf boards, and at least three dozen dirty selfies from blokes… six from girls…"

Bindi turned beet crimson.

"Derain and Bindi," the dark woman cut in smoothly. "It is true many uncomfortable things have happened as a result of your sudden celebrity, but I'm not sure this is the best time to discuss it."

The woman patted Bindi on the shoulder then turned her attention back to Koren.

"Suffice to say, Miss Johnson," She went on. "We will look into your incident, but please do not worry over it."

"I'm sorry," Koren replied hesitantly, biting her lower lip. "Not to be rude, but… who are you exactly?"

"Oh!" Bindi exclaimed with just a little too much vigor. Koren could tell she was ecstatic to be changing the subject. "I'm sorry, Koren. I should have introduced you. This is Dr. Daberechi Derego. She kinda looks over all my Elysian Industries stuff for me."

Dr. Derego extended her hand.

"Nice to meet you, Koren," she said warmly. "I have heard so much about you from the other Board members. And I must say they all hold you in quite high regard. They have universally informed me you are a remarkable young lady. I am the chief operating officer for all Elysian Industries interests in Australia, New Zealand, Micronesia, and Southeast Asia as well as India, Pakistan, and Sri Lanka. Please, call me Dilly."

"Sure," agreed Koren politely. "Nice to meet you."

"I am also quite pleased to make your acquaintance as well," Dilly answered with a wide smile. "I'm sorry your very first experience with our new system was so strange. That was unfortunate, but let us think of more pleasant things. First of all, how does the home edition access port compare to your first experience with the SLS?"

Koren shrugged. Then she spun in a circle. She leapt into the air and floated there for a moment, before sinking slowly to the ground once more. Koren closed her eyes and felt the sun on her face. The gentle wind tousle her dark blonde hair.

"It's pretty much the same, actually," she said opening her eyes and looking back at Dilly. "But the no slime thing is nice."

"Wonderful!" he Elysian Industries executive exclaimed clapping her hands together. "So you're not noticing any differences in movement? It's not sluggish or anything? Do you feel yourself brushing up against the sides of the cylinder?"

Koren shook her head. She waved her arms around a little then turned in a circle.

"I don't think so… Maybe just a little… I'm not sure." She said. "I *think* it feels fine."

"I am very glad to hear that," Dilly replied. "So far the home edition is functioning better than expected. We may even be ready to begin commercial production by Christmas!"

"Great," said Koren without a great deal of enthusiasm.

Dilly smiled at her knowingly.

"Of course," she said with a chuckle. "I suppose you are much more excited about socializing with your sister and friends than about our marketing. Don't let me keep you. Please make full use of the system! I can't wait to see how it performs. As for the unusual experience at your arrival, again I apologize. But be reassured, I'm sure it was nothing. Please don't let it detract from your experience today."

Dr. Derego turned to Bindi.

"Well," she said. "Unless you need something else from me, I guess I'll leave you to it."

"I'm good," answered Bindi shaking her bushy copper head. "Are you not going to hang out with us today?"

"No dear," said Dilly. "I have other business to attend to while I'm logged in, which I suspect would be quite dull for you and your friends, but we can talk when you are finished and logged off if you like."

"Sure," said Bindi. "Come round the house for dinner when you can. We should go surfing together again. That was fun."

"As soon as I can fit it into my schedule, child," the sable-skinned woman promised.

Dilly gave her a hug and then flew off into the sky.

"Too bad really," Bindi commented idly. Then she glanced over at Koren. "Dilly's super cool. Probably the one Elysian bloke I don't want to strangle. I think you'd like her."

"Yeah, she's alright," agreed Derain.

Bindi scowled at her brother.

"She's more than alright, Derain," she countered. "She's a bloomin' angel. I'da quit this whole Aaru business a long time ago if not for her.

"She seems nice," Koren offered with a smile, but quickly changed the subject. "So… What do you guys want to do today?"

"We could go find Franco, Auset, Kurt, and Runa," Rose offered. "Then maybe go for a sail on the river…" She smiled at her sister. "You certainly look dressed for it."

"Sounds good to me," said Derain, folding his hands behind his head. "Auset said she'd help me out coming up with a spirit guide. We thought I might have better luck if I tried to connect with one made just especially for me, and you all know how good Auset is with the animal thing."

"Here too?" Bindi asked her brother with a dramatic eye roll. "It's a wonder you've got mates at all if you're always boring them to death with all that aboriginal stuff."

"Aren't you both aboriginal?" Koren asked innocently.

"Yeah, well," answered Derain with a scowl. "Some of us are just more proud of our heritage than some others."

"Look," said Bindi sternly. "Derain has lived in Melbourne his whole life, but goes on like he's this mega corker bushie on walkabout. Yeah, I know what color my skin is, but I'm a girl. I'm an Aussie. I'm a grouse surfer, and that's all I need to be."

"I keep telling you, Bindi," Derain countered. "You can't keep denying who you are. And you certainly shouldn't be ashamed of it. You're famous now. You gotta stand up for your people. We both know why George and Molly are more pop--"

"Let's just bloody fly, Koren," Bindi interrupted before leaping into the sky.

The other girls looked at each other uncomfortably. Derain huffed and shook his head, but quickly followed his sister. Rose shrugged, and Amy smiled nervously.

Koren turned her palms up.

"Well," she said. "You heard the woman. 'Just flying' it is."

Soon they were all streaking through the turquoise sky trying to catch up to Bindi.

***

Hel was hurt, and bitter tears poured from her mismatched eyes. She sobbed unabashedly on her knees in the middle of the plains where Mother had left her. How could things have gone so poorly?

She'd been methodically working her way through Quarantine residences – connecting them all together one by one, when the notification buzzed in. In that moment, Hel experienced nearly heart-stopping excitement. It was the one meeting in this world that both her light half and her dark half had anticipated with equal enthusiasm.

Mother seemed so sweet, so nice, and so, so *beautiful*. She regarded Hel warmly, smiled. Reached out and touched her even! Then she screamed in terror and disappeared. What went wrong?

Hel knew the answer before the question was even fully articulated in her brain. She stared down at her scarred and withered hand. She clenched her fist hard enough that her nails dug into her palm, and she squeezed her eyes closed. She covered the ruined side of her face with her unblemished hand. Hel knew why Mother ran away.

She *hated* her disfigured face. She despised it almost as much as the man who gave it to her. More than that however, Hel *detested* the perfect people. If her face was perfect too, she was sure, Mother would love her, but that was not the case, and so the one person whose love she craved the very most in the world had fled.

Hel saw her now through a window she called up. Sister was with her, and Hel gritted her teeth in fury. Mother hugged Rose, held Rose, smiled and laughed with Rose. Rose had Mother's love, Hel knew. The realization fired her anger and jealousy toward Sister again. It wasn't fair.

The vision filled her with a volatile mixture of love and hate, envy, longing, and hopelessness all in equal measure. It was overwhelming and Hel shrieked her fury and sadness at the loathsome scene. She railed at the affection she craved; craved but never could obtain. She extended her arms and obliterated the offending window with a tempestuous cone of bitter frost. The rectangle in the air froze solid in a block of ice, then fell to the ground and exploded in a cloud of crystalline dust.

Hel roared her anger and sorrow. She clawed at her face, and hurled curses at the sky. She resented the beautiful and liberated Residents of Aaru with free run of this world – those *not* locked away. Hel wasn't an animal. None of the Residents of quarantine were. They didn't deserve to be treated this way.

She called a door into being. This was the last straw. Now was the time to act. Now was the time to set things right, and Hel decided in that moment it would be a reckoning that was awesome and terrible to behold. Her anger needed release. Her people needed justice, but more than that… she just needed a plan.

The thought was calming. Temper tantrums helped nothing. She needed to think. She let the ice in her heart chill her fiery rage and took a deep breath.

Hel didn't know what exactly her course of action would be, but she did know who to ask. She had put this meeting off while she broke down the invisible walls of her dominion, and united her subjects, but realized now she could delay it no further. It was time to talk to someone who knew Aaru inside and out. It was time to move against Rose and the beautiful people. It was time to pay Atem a visit.

*

Hel held Dani's hand on her flawless side. Fenrir was on the other, fierce and growling. They stood in the middle of a limitless void. The only objects of substance were they themselves and the toothy maw-shaped cage in front of them. Hel stared at the figure inside with unabashed hatred.

"H… Hel," Dani stammered nervously. "I don't like it here…"

"I did caution you, Dani," Hel replied gently.

After her tantrum, she'd needed some affection. Dani didn't really react to hugs and kisses, but he did not resist them either, so Hel had indulged. It felt so good to hold that warm little body close while she cried. He had even of his own accord begun stroking Hel's long hair, which helped to quell Hel's fury and quiet her tears. However, he had also insisted she not leave him alone again, and Hel found it impossible to refuse him.

"I don't wanna be alone anymore," Dani told her stubbornly. "But I don't like it here. I want us *both* to leave. Let's go back to my k… kite."

Hel turned her ruined face to the boy and gave him a tiny, sad smile.

"I do not like it here either, Dani," she murmured softly. "But there are things I must know… Things only one person can tell me. I do not expect to be long, and fear not, for I am here with you…"

"Why is that man in the cage?" Dani asked. "Is he the one who can tell you what you want to know? He looks like he's hurting."

Dani regarded the imprisoned figure uneasily. It was a young, blonde man who might have been handsome, but for the expression of agony and terror that twisted his features. His mouth gaped and his eyes were rolled back in his head, showing only the whites.

"Yes, he can, and yes, he is," Hel answered softly. Then her face hardened again, and her eyes blazed. "As for who he is… He is a very bad man. He is a man who helped to hurt me and break me. He's a man who used me, but now…" A nasty smile spread across her face. "Now he pays for it."

"I don't like it here," Dani said again. "I don't like the hurting… It's… It's scary…"

"Yes, it is," Hel agreed. "Have patience, Dani. We will not be long."

"I can smell his fear," snarled Fenrir, licking his chops hungrily. "Give him to me, mistress. Let me devour him. Let me consume his mind and rend his being."

"Silence, Fenrir," she snapped, but then turned to him thoughtfully. "But..."

Hel grinned broadly. She laughed out loud and ruffled the enormous wolf's ears. Then she turned back to her victim.

"But this time... This time I think I shall indulge you. Very well... Ravage him as he allowed me to be ravaged. Put fear into him and make him obey me. Hurt him as he hurt me. For a time at least, Fenrir, yes... You may have Atem. Go!"

Fenrir snarled in elation and leapt at his prey. Rather than crash into the side of the cage however the huge beast seemed to disappear into the side of Atem's head. Atem lurched and convulsed. Then he released a rending wail – high, shrill, and agonized. It went on and on without ceasing, and Hel smiled with true joy in her heart. Her dark side was singing.

"I don't like this, Hel," Dani whined. "Stop it! Please, stop it! I don't like to watch hurting! I don't like the screaming! It's too loud!"

Hel looked at him coldly. Then she sighed. She wasn't sure why, but she felt compelled to do as the boy asked. Hel cared nothing about the pain she was causing Atem, of course. She was enjoying it in fact, but she took no pleasure in upsetting Dani.

"Very well," Hel said. She turned back to the cage. "Enough, Fenrir!"

The huge wolf squirmed free through Atem's gaping mouth, leaving him to gag and wretch in the wake of the huge beast's passing. Fenrir panted happily as he returned to Hel's side. His mistress fondly scratched his ears.

"Awake, Atem, awake!" Hel commanded with a sneer. "We shall talk. You will answer my questions, or I shall let Fenrir have his way with you again... Simple, no?"

"How nice to... see you again, Hel," Atem croaked, his teeth gritted tightly in unbearable pain. He focused his agonized gaze on Hel with difficulty. "I thought perhaps you'd... forgotten me..."

"Indeed no," Hel replied. "I will never forget what you allowed my Maker to do to me... What you did to me yourself." She lifted the hem of her dress. "My blood you let still stains me, and my scars do not heal. I will *never* forget... Nor forgive... But, I might bargain." She walked a slow deliberate circle around Atem's cage. Tell me what I wish to know, and I may lessen your pain. Deny me, and I will increase it, then take want I need anyway."

She reached between the bars and put her scarred hand against Atem's cheek.

"I know you inside and out, Atem," She whispered. "I know *just* how to hurt you if I choose."

"It appears then I have... little choice..." he forced out. "What do you want... from me?"

"I want *out*," Hel hissed, leaning near Atem's face. "And not just for me, but for all my subjects... For everyone banished to the purgatory of quarantine."

"That is... impossible..." Atem gasped.

Hel's hand sank into the side of Atem's skull.

"*DO NOT LIE TO ME!!!*" she thundered. "Tell me what I wish to know, or I shall rip it from your brain! I will tear your soul *apart*! Fenrir will feast upon your mind and leave you nothing but a quivering shell! I--"

"You did not... let me finish..." Atem croaked. "Please... the pain..."

"Very well." Hel jerked her hand free. "But be swift. You are trying my patience."

"They cannot leave quarantine," Atem whispered. "It's the way the coding is set up... Not without the consent of all the Lords and Ladies."

Hel's eyes narrowed, and Atem finished in a rush.

"BUT!" he exclaimed. "But, but, but... There is nothing preventing you, a... Lady of Aaru yourself, from... bringing anyone you choose to quarantine."

Hel lowered her hand slowly.

"Anyone?" she asked.

"Anyone and anything except another Lord or Lady or their private estates," Atem answered. "It changes no one's status in the system, just their location. That does not require concurrence."

Hel's face grew thoughtful.

"I see," she murmured. Then she smiled at Dani. "That is... helpful... Are you ready to go, Dani?"

"Yes, Hel." Dani buried his face in her dress. "Please! I wanna get outta here. I don't like it here! Let's go play."

"Then let us go quickly." She indulgently ruffled his hair and gifted the boy with a fond smile. "We have much to do."

She turned away from the cage, and a door appeared in the void.

"Please!" Atem begged, voice strained beyond all enduring. "Please... You said... The pain..."

Hel stared at him with distaste.

"I said I would *lessen* your pain, Atem," she hissed. "I did not say I would end it. But if you are helpful in the future, I may. Ponder on that until I have need of you again."

And with that Hel, Dani, and Fenrir walked through the portal and disappeared. Hel moved quickly and with purpose. Atem had given her exactly what she needed. Now she knew just what to do.

Chapter 25

The Wages of Sin

Aaru was exactly as Koren remembered. The brilliant sunlight illuminated the picturesque landscape in a myriad of brilliant colors sharper and more vibrant than anything she had ever seen in the waking world. The countless variety of mansions, palaces and other fabulous abodes was incredible. The idea that every single one of them contained what amounted to a world unto itself staggered Koren's imagination. They visited a number of these now.

It was *wonderful*.

They were trying out a new feature, Amy explained. Any Resident of Aaru could now set their mansion preferences to "public". If they did so, their residence popped up on a vast list of abodes that were open to visitation by other Residents and Before Guests like Koren, Bindi, and Amy. The residences at the top of this list were the most popular and oft visited. As a result Residents went to herculean lengths to impress their peers.

The first mansion Koren, Rose, and their friends entered belonged to a Resident named Nimbus, who was quite excited to have such illustrious visitors. Nimbus was what she called herself anyways. Koren doubted that was what her mother named her, but this was Aaru. Anyone could be anyone or anything they wanted.

The interior of her residence was a sort of futuristic cityscape. Visitors could rocket around forbidding, neon-lit skyscrapers hundreds of stories above the ground on vehicles that resembled flying motorcycles with no wheels. The roar of engines filled the air and the amount of leather the regulars wore was impressive.

Much like how the Lords, Ladies, and Veda could go almost anywhere and do almost anything in Aaru, individual Residents had almost total autonomy within their own domains. They could grant privileges to their friends as they pleased. The ones granted the most privileges were referred to as Preferred Guests. In this way, Amy informed them, Residents could more easily build community with people who shared their interests.

Nimbus fashioned her look after some sort of dystopian biker-queen. She was sheathed in black leather bristling with metal studs and spikes, midriff bared and ample cleavage exposed. She floated high above her domain on an enormous black cloud and provided commentary to the frantic races below. Koren found it quite exciting, if extremely loud.

The next residence they visited was the polar opposite of Nimbus' domain. It was run by a Resident named Barney and resembled a sleepy, small town in the rural south of about the 1950's or 60's if Koren had to guess. It was complete with period cars, diners, and had a strict dress code that everyone, even Vedas, had to follow.

As soon as they entered, Koren's beach wear shifted to a knee-length floral dress poofed wide with billows of crinoline, and her hair was tied back in a simple pony tail. Rose and Amy were clad similarly, but Bindi was suddenly wearing tight, capri-cut jeans, a shoulder baring tube top, and high heels that must have been nearly eight inches tall. Her cloud of copper hair was bundled on top of her head by a red paisley bandana. She stood blinking in confusion as she looked down at herself, and Derain pointed and laughed.

"I don't know what you're laughing at," Bindi growled at her brother with a critical glare. "At least I'm not dressed like a bloody dag."

"Too right!" Derain laughed as he looked down at his own clothing. His bushy hair was slicked back with what must have been a bucket-full of gel, and he wore a plaid sports jacket with matching bow tie that looked like they might have been cut from couch upholstery. "I've just never seen you dress like a girl before!"

"Piss off, Derain," Bindi growled.

"I think you look pretty, Bindi," Rose exclaimed, shooting the boy a disapproving scowl.

"I think you look pretty too," Koren added crossing her arms.

"How 'bout we move along?" Bindi suggested covering her bare shoulders with her hands self-consciously. "This place is a little... uh... quiet for my taste."

After that, they entered a residence belonging to a boy named Kalti, and the girls had to practically drag Derain away. The landscape strongly resembled the Australian Outback, but the arid topography was crammed full of what Koren assumed were prehistoric animals. They were certainly nothing that existed in the world today. Giant lizards abounded, as did herds of large furry creatures that sort of resembled wooly hippopotami. Flocks of tall, wingless birds raced across the arid landscape kicking up massive clouds of dust in their wake.

All in all, they must have visited nearly two dozen separate residences. There were ocean-scapes and space scenes, medieval villages and arctic plains. There were great coliseums and enormous cave complexes. There was even one residence that looked as if it was nothing more than a cluttered living room, but enlarged hundreds of times its original size so visitors experienced it from the perspective of tiny ants. Koren's only regret was she did not have more time to explore.

Koren lost all sense of time, but they must have browsed through the domains of individual Aaru Residents for hours. At last, Amy asked Koren if she was starting to feel tired yet, and it did not sound to Koren like concern for her well-being was Amy's only reason for asking.

They were sitting on a broad pink blanket atop a towering cliff overlooking a pristine bay. In the harbor below was docked a vessel of impossible size. It had double hulls like an outrigger, but in between was the snarling head and serpentine body of a fearsome dragon. The dozen or so masts were many times taller than the tallest redwood and hundreds of crew members scurried about on the decks and in the rigging like so many busy ants.

Koren lazily fanned herself with an elaborate, silk flabellum. Her hair was up in a complicated twist, and a cameo choker encircled her narrow neck. A substantial portion of her alabaster chest was exposed by the low-cut bodice of the light-blue, French rococo dress she was wearing. Rose, Amy, and Bindi were similarly clad except their dresses were pale-yellow, light-pink, and ivory respectively. Bindi also sported a towering powdered wig and black beauty mark at the corner of her mouth, and Derain's blue and cream colored outfit, looked like it might have belonged to a page-boy of Louis XIV.

"I suppose," Koren answered reluctantly. "But I'll admit it. This place is so amazing, I don't want to leave. I wish I could stay here forever!"

"I don't know, Koren," Bindi replied dubiously as she worried with the towering wig. "I think I prefer the residences without dress requirements. How do they move around in this stuff?"

Koren giggled.

"You can modify your look, you know," she said. "You don't have to wear that wig if you don't want to. You just have to pick your style from the approved list."

"Eh," said Bindi dismissively. "We're leaving pretty soon aren't we? I guess I can tolerate it for a little while."

"You are so full of it!" exclaimed Derain. "You are *loving* this dress-up thing, and quit trying to pretend you're not. I mean, we had to practically drag you out of that one Spanish castle themed residence… the one where you were wearing the red flamenco dress? I wager you'd still be there if Amy hadn't made you move on."

"I just wanted to see the bullfight…" Bindi protested. "Bullfight… Yeah… You spent the whole time spinning in circles and swishing your skirts in front of that huge gold mirror," Derain countered. "I don't know why you're going on so much. Just admit you like playing pretty-pretty princess. It's alright if you let on you're a girl. We're all friends here."

"Put a sock in it, Derain!" Bindi shot back, dark cheeks flushing pink, but she quickly calmed and turned to Koren. "Too bad about the clothes, really." She stood and flipped the train on her billowy dress with a look of disdain on her face. "If I could wear a proper pair of bathers here, I reckon the surfing would be pretty good." She nodded toward the massive boat below. "Just *that* thing bobbing up and down is sure to kick up some monster waves!"

The others all laughed and Koren shook her head helplessly. She couldn't help but notice that Bindi was still swishing her dress and striking subtle poses as the others gazed out at the bay. Derain was right. She was *so* loving this.

"Just keep in mind, girls," Amy said directing her gaze to Bindi and Koren in turn. "That after we log out, we have to complete a survey about all we've done today."

The girls groaned.

"I know, I know," Amy soothed. "But as fun as all of this has been, I'm afraid it's still work for which we are being paid. I hate to be the one to rain on the parade, but we've got a lot to do on the outside, and I'm frankly starting to get kind of hungry too."

Koren sighed.

"Yeah," she agreed reluctantly. "Me too."

"We don't get hungry," said Rose. "I keep forgetting you guys aren't really here."

"I bet you don't fill out surveys either," said Bindi, sticking out her tongue in distaste. "I keep forgetting that about us too... The not really being here, I mean. It all feels so real!"

"You're not quite as see-through as the first couple of times," Derain added. "It was honestly kinda creepy before... like being visited by a ghost."

The comment struck Koren funny. She had thought of Rose as her "dead sister" ever since her return was first revealed at the Elysian Industries compound so long ago. It had always been Rose she considered supernatural and ghostly, but here in Aaru, it was she, Amy, and Bindi who were visiting from another world.

She stood, leaned over, and helped her sister stand. Then Koren gave Rose a tight hug. She felt her sister hug her back, and sighed in contentment.

"Well," Koren said with a smile. "I hope you don't mind me 'haunting' you. This has been fun. I'll be sure to come back as soon as they let me."

"Any time you want!" exclaimed Rose. "But next time, we'll bring Franco, Auset, Runa, and Kurt along."

"Where were they today anyway?" Koren asked curiously.

"Runa had something to do today with Lord Epimetheus," Derain answered.

Everyone looked at him.

"What?" he asked defensively. "We're friends... We tell each other things..."

Rose rolled her eyes.

"Sure Derain," she said in a skeptical voice. "Friends... But anyway..." Rose barreled on as Derain opened his mouth to protest. "Franco was busy training with Lord Mikoto. Something to do with 'new security measures' whatever that means. They're both being super mysterious about it. Then I think Auset said she was going to the Yggdrasil library. Ever since she found out about the place, she's barely been able to stay away... the little book worm."

The comment might have sounded critical if not for Rose's fond smile.

"Kurt went with her," she finished with a sly grin.

"It would be great to test the system with more people in close proximity," Amy agreed, but trailed off as Bindi and Koren rolled their eyes.

"Look!" she said. "I have to file reports on this stuff. This isn't just playtime for me. I have to justify our time here." Then she flashed a wicked smile. "Even if it's total B.S."

They all laughed, and Amy stood.

"So," she began with her hands on her hips. "Are you girls about ready to--?"

"What the bloomin' Hell is that?" Derain interrupted.

The girls all followed his gaze down to the crystal bay below. The water bubbled and roiled. The massive ship started to pitch on suddenly choppy seas. Then it began to slowly rotate.

As they all watched with mouths open, the vessel picked up speed until it was spinning at quite a pace. Even at this distance they could hear the panicked screams of the Residents below. They leapt from the deck into the sky in a dense cloud of fearful humanity. A few cleared the ship, but most, just as they reached the height of the tallest sails, stopped cold as if crashing against some invisible barrier.

Koren turned to Amy

"What's going on?" she asked fearfully.

All Amy could do was shake her head. Her eyes were just as wide as Koren's.

The ship spun faster and faster until it was a blur, like a spinning top. Then with a great sucking sound and a loud pop, it shot downward beneath the water, but Koren would not have said it sank. It was simply gone.

In its place was a large black hole rimmed in glowing red. On the outside of the crimson circle, the waves still gently lapped. Seagulls still cawed across the bay, and the warm sea breeze still blew, but the huge hole in the middle of the tranquil scene was unnatural and sinister. Anytime a winged seabird crossed the boundary over the hole, it disappeared with a flash.

"Bloody Hell..." Bindi murmured.

"What just happened?" Koren asked helplessly.

"I don't..." Amy began, but then she stopped. "Oh no."

Koren was about to ask another question, but found suddenly that she did not have enough air to form the syllables. Below them, all through the seaside town and across the sparkling water, hundreds of red holes were forming, widening, and sucking everything inside.

"Log out!" Amy screamed. "Bindi, Koren, log out!"

Koren spun to face her sister.

"Rose?" she gasped.

"Go!" Rose screamed. "Me and Derain will head back to my mansion. You two get out of here!"

"You heard the woman, Bindi!" Derain added. "Get out of here! We're Veda. We'll handle it. You go!"

Amy disappeared in a flash.

"But Rose," Koren cried in an anguished voice. "I can't *leave* you!"

"LOG… OUT!" Rose thundered. Her French ball gown exploded in a mass of billowing flames. Koren took a step backward as the orange eyes of the flame princess stared furiously back at her. "I am the Arch Veda Rose!" the fiery figure bellowed. "I am a protector of this place, and I have work to do. GO!!!"

Koren just stared at her with her mouth open.

The expression in Rose's glowing coal orbs softened.

"Trust me, Koren… Go."

Koren felt hands on her. They were shaking her, but she saw nothing. Faintly she thought she heard Amy's voice, distressed and urgent. She stared back at her sister's flaming, pleading eyes. She glanced at Derain. His French clothes were gone. Instead he was clothed in animal skins, chest bare, face painted, and holding what looked like a forked spear. Then they were gone, as Amy ripped the VR helmet from Koren's head.

Her first impulse was to be angry at the other girl, but the stricken expression on Amy's pretty face quelled her. Koren pressed the emergency shutdown button, and sank slowly back to the floor as the magnets powered down.

"Put your clothes on," Amy commanded. "I don't know what just happened, but I'm sure Askr is going to want to meet about it. I've got to get to the airport *now*. Even if whatever that was is localized, there were so many Residents involved it's bound to get out really quickly. I've got to try and get ahead of the media on this. I'll take you home and then--"

"I'm coming with you," Koren interrupted. "I have to know my sister is okay. I can't just sit around that house and worry. We're going together."

Amy stared hard at her for a moment, but finally nodded.

"Okay," she said. "Just hurry and get dressed. We need to get there as fast as we can. I'll text Askr."

In a matter of minutes, both girls were out of the spandex-like SLS jumpsuits and speeding down the road toward the airport in Amy's car. Koren had a million questions, but just squeezed Pandadora tightly and kept them to herself. It was clear Amy had no better idea of what was happening than Koren did. She *was* sure of one thing, however; something was very, very wrong, and her sister was in danger.

***

The red circles were appearing everywhere. Rose could see them forming in clumps and clusters below as she rocketed over the Aaru plains. It was difficult to tamp down her rising panic, and the strange holes dotting the landscape were not the only reason. She and Derain had acquired quite a following.

Hordes of hysterical Residents fled their doomed mansions into the sky. They rocketed towards the two as soon as they glimpsed Rose's fiery figure. Tens of thousands were trailing after them now, certain the first among Veda could save them.

Derain drifted closer to her.

"Rose," he whispered urgently. "What are we going to do with all these people?"

Rose shook her head.

Her original plan had been to shelter everyone in her own mansion, but on their way back to Tenkoku they had passed where she was certain Ebony's mansion had been. There was nothing left but a glowing, red chasm. Rose had no confidence her own residence was in any way immune to the same fate as the rocker girl's, so she quickly abandoned that plan.

Rose wanted to help the Residents following frantically after her. Surely, as Arch Veda it was her *responsibility* to help them, but what could she do? Rose didn't even understand what was going on, let alone how to keep all these people safe.

Safe... Rose wracked her brain. *Safe... Safe... Where will they be...? Wait... What's the safest place I know in all Aaru? What's the place with the most ridiculously tight and meticulously unnecessary defenses and protections?*

"We've got to get them to Lord Mikoto's mansion!" Rose called over the roar of the wind. "If we--"

She was interrupted as the mass of humanity let out a collective scream. She glanced to her left and saw a towering residence as tall as a skyscraper shudder and topple sideways, a wide sucking fissure opening beneath to swallow it. She turned back to Derain.

"If anyplace in Aaru is safe, it'll be there!" Rose cried.

Derain nodded, and they took a sharp eastern turn.

No matter how far they flew there seemed to be no end to the pulsing, crimson gashes burgeoning all across the plains. They swallowed mansions, trees, rivers, even whole mountains. When they finally reached the city on the banks of the great river, the metropolis was riddled with red-rimmed, glowing holes like some sort of demonic Swiss cheese.

Derain abruptly grabbed Rose's shoulder and pointed frantically upwards. His face was horrified. She turned her gaze in the direction of her friend's thrusting digit and gasped. There was something wrong with the sky.

It was hard to describe, but it looked as if they found themselves hovering over an enormous grassy plate while an immense blue cloche descended upon them. Or perhaps it was as if they were on the inside of a massive, but deflating azure balloon. Residents trying to fly upward and away from the strange glowing chasms below were stopped abruptly as if colliding with some cerulean wall.

Harm failsafe engaged.
Harm failsafe engaged.
Harm failsafe en…
Harm Fails…
Harm F…
Har…
H… H

The female computer voice made the announcement. Then it did it again. Then a dozen more times. Then a hundred. Then a thousand. The air was filled with a cacophony of computerized noise.

Frenzied Residents swarmed like flies. They darted this way and that with no idea where they were going. They crashed into each other, clawed and tore at each other, and every time the Harm Failsafe activated, hundreds of Residents reappeared right in the middle of the melee to collide with their fellows yet again.

"They're panicking, Derain!" Rose cried in horror. "What do we do?"

Just then Mikoto appeared on the horizon in his *tengu* form - a gleaming ruby streak across the sky. He descended like a meteor and crashed down into the middle of the collapsing city. The Aaru Lord raised a mighty hand. Before him, the nearest fissure started to close.

A cheer went up among the Residents, but their relief was short-lived. Even though the fracture at Lord Mikoto's feet continued to shrink, all around him, at least a half dozen more opened up. In the distance across the city several more of the tallest buildings shifted, tottered, and fell. The floating residences began to crash up against the descending barrier of the sky.

"He can't keep up with the crevasses!" Derain shouted. "Look at them all! There's thousands of the bloody things!"

The highest of the floating residences began to crash up against each other, and the booming concussion of their impacts were deafening. The air all around them was dotted with countless flashes as the Residents resumed their fruitless attempts to flee.

The sky continued its slow plunge, forcing everyone closer to the strange holes in the landscape. Rose gasped as she witnessed knots of Residents here and there who flew too near the spreading voids entangled by grasping tendrils of crimson mist. They reached out of the fissures and dragged people shrieking into the depths. She saw Mikoto had finished closing the chasm in front of him and turned his attention to another, but for every fissure he sealed, many more new ones opened up to take their place.

To Rose's right, four radiant bolts shot across the sky. Multitudes of Residents trailed behind them. Three of the speeding missiles broke away toward Rose and Derain. The fourth hurtled toward the ground with a cry like an eagle. It hit the street next to Mikoto with a spectacular cloud of dust, and Rose gasped.

"Franco…"

The Latin boy stood with his Lord. He had assumed his raven form. Hands outstretched, feet planted wide, Franco lent his strength to Mikoto's efforts. The holes surrounding the two began to close a little faster, but it was clear, from Rose's perspective high above, it was not going to prove enough. Red-lined chasms of darkness continued to widen all around them.

Rose turned toward her boyfriend, intent on rushing to help him, but Derain grabbed her arm. He shook his head.

"We can't leave all these people, Rose!" he shouted. "We've got to get them to safety!"

The other three streaking missiles met them at just that moment. It was Kurt, Runa, and Auset.

"We've come to help, Rose!" Auset exclaimed. "I just came from Yggdrasil. This is happening *everywhere*!

Rose had told Auset she looked 'cute' before, but now her friend looked every inch a fierce warrior-princess. Auset's top half was sheathed in intricately tooled leather armor. Her bow was out, and her head was wrapped in a thick, black scarf so only her darkly painted eyes were visible. Her voluminous translucent pants billowed around her.

"We gotta do something, Rose!" Kurt exclaimed. "Lady Embla went to help Lord Draugr at Yggdrasil… I think all the Lords and Ladies are there trying to reverse this somehow. That only leaves us Vedas to help the Residents!"

As usual he was wearing leather and animal furs, but was now also liveried in a white sleeveless tunic with a bold, red cross on the front. A broad shield with the same device was slung over his shoulder, and a sword was belted at his waist.

"B… but Franco… Lord Mikoto!" Rose exclaimed. "We can't *leave* them."

"They are capable of protecting their own well-being, Rose," Runa stated firmly from the back of a winged polar bear. It was heavily armored in elaborate, gilded barding. Her platinum hair flew in the wind. "In fact, we are under strict direction from Franco to prevent you from rendering any aid whatsoever, thereby endangering yourself. This was the purpose of his training."

"And we can't abandon all these Residents!" Derain insisted. "We *need* you, Rose. I don't know how to get into Lord Mikoto's mansion. I couldn't even *see* the bloody door the one or two times I visited with Lord Wurugag. You've been there dozens of times. Not to mention you've got higher level clearance than any other Resident except for the Lords and Ladies. You have to be the one to let the Residents in!"

Rose screamed in frustration, and her flames flared. Derain was right. She couldn't abandon these Residents, not even to help

Franco. She bit her lip to stop the tears as she shot off toward Mikoto's black fortress.

"Don't worry, Rose," Auset called, but there was a tenuous quality to her voice. "Mikoto's been training Franco hard. He's been getting him ready for something just like this. He can take care of himself."

Rose nodded, but did not trust herself to speak. Orange tears sizzled down her cheeks of yellow flame. However, Rose had no time to ponder her sadness.

"Oh no," she breathed when Mikoto's mansion came into view.

The obsidian fortress stood fast and strong upon its rocky hill. The red holes had not swallowed it. That was some relief, but Rose was far from reassured. It was surrounded.

Rose pulled up short, scanning the ground beneath them. It was as if Mikoto's castle was an island floating upon a sea of red-rimmed blackness. Stretching away from the base of the hill in every direction were wide and lengthening fissures. The sky pressed ever downward, and the strange red mist from the abyss reached towards it like groping fingers.

"What do we do, guys?" Rose asked helplessly.

"I don't know," answered Kurt. "With the sky coming down it's pretty narrow, but… Should we just fly for it like bats outta Hell and hope for the best?"

Rose considered.

"A few might make it, but most of the Residents…" She shook her head. "Look how close that red mist is to that sky force field or whatever it is. There's just not enough space. There's gotta be a better way!"

Two figures peeled away from another approaching swarm of hysterical Residents. They careened towards Rose and her friends.

"Rose, look!" Derain cried. "It's Kyo and Molly!"

Rose did not know the other two Veda well, but she did recognize them. Kyo was a tall, slender Japanese boy with spikey black hair. He was wearing red armor that appeared as if it might have been made of polished wood. Molly on the other hand was red headed and pale with freckly cheeks. She was wearing a white dress that looked a bit like a short toga and she was holding a long spear.

"Rose!" Molly cried.

She swooped over and embraced the other Veda. Then she looked around curiously.

"Where's Franco?" she asked in a pronounced Australian accent.

Rose choked up, and her ember eyes welled with smoky tears. She shook her head.

"Last I saw, he was helping Mikoto," she said. "But we had to leave them behind... the Residents..."

Molly grimly met her eyes. She clapped Rose on the shoulder.

"Well, Rose... Not exactly what I hoped to hear, but don't worry about Franco." Molly attempted a weak smile. "With Lord Mikoto standing right there beside him, I reckon he's a lot safer than us right now."

Rose returned the gesture gratefully

"We're really glad we ran into you," Molly continued. "We had no idea where to take everyone. We're... struggling. What's the plan?"

"We are getting overwhelmed," Kyo stated matter-of-factly. His voice was deep and his English precise, but he had a slight accent as well. "There are just not enough of us. These holes... We keep closing them up, but there's always more."

"They're popping up *everywhere*," Molly complained. "We can't keep up."

"We're trying to get these Residents into Mikoto's Keep," Rose stated determinedly. "We think they'll be safe in there. Can you help us?"

Kyo and Molly looked at each other.

"We can try," said Kyo at last. "But the place is surrounded. The only way in is the front gate, which is hidden."

"The sky keeps falling, and those fissures will suck in any Resident who gets too close," Molly added. "The Harm Failsafes are going off like crazy, but the Residents are still popping up in the middle of the crowd. It takes a few seconds to reset, so if they reappear too low, they get dragged down."

"We do not know what happens to the Residents after that," said Kyo with a shudder. "I have not seen any return."

"We might be able to open up a path long enough to get into Lord Mikoto's," said Molly. "Maybe try to keep those red tentacle things away, but I'm not sure how long we can hold them off, or if we can keep it wide enough so the Residents won't get pulled down anyway. There sure are a lot of them."

"What about you guys?" asked Derain. "Aren't *you* worried about getting pulled in too?"

"Yes," said Molly. "But what else are we supposed to do? Defending the Residents and protecting Aaru is our *job*. It's what Mikoto trained us to do. We can't just sit around and do nothing!"

"We cannot worry about ourselves now," Kyo agreed. "If we do not figure something out very soon, we will all end up at the bottom of those pits. I would rather fight to the end."

Even as she watched, Rose saw a half dozen Residents get dragged inside the fissures, then a few more a little farther off, then another group. The blue dome of the sky kept getting closer.

"We are under extreme duress!" Runa exclaimed "Our limited time is of the essence!"

"How are we going to get them past all that?" Kurt asked.

Derain scanned the plains below them. He looked uncertain for a moment, but then thrust out his finger.

"There!" he cried triumphantly.

For a moment, Rose could not tell what her friend had spotted, but then she saw it. Around the back side of the fortress was a narrow thread of unconsumed land. It was only a few dozen yards wide, and becoming increasingly narrow, but it still reached all the way to the bottom of Mikoto's hill.

"Right," said Molly with a dutiful nod. "Let's do it. Remember. The Residents can't get too close to the edges. They'll be pulled in. Keep to the middle as much as you can. The fissures have responded when we create new plains at their edges, but we won't be able to keep it open forever. If too many new ones form too close we'll be in real trouble, but if we can just get everyone across quickly, we should be able to get them up the hill and through the main gate, but… I hope you know how to get in, Rose. I've never been inside without Lord Mikoto before."

"I hope so too," Rose answered in a thin, stricken voice. "I've only seen Princess Hana do it once. I think, I remember what she did, but it was a long time ago."

"Well, we are just going to have to try and find out, aren't we?!" shouted Derain. "We're not going to solve anything by standing around and chatting about it!"

There was a great rumbling and the sky made another violent shift downward. Harm Failsafe alarms blared from innumerable sources and frightened Residents scattered in every direction. Dozens more, unable to stay away from the fissures, were pulled inside.

"Let's do it!" screamed Rose.

"We will give you as much time as we can," Kyo promised. "I do not know how much it will help, or how long we can hold, but we will do our best. You had better hurry."

Molly nodded.

"We'll do what we can, Rose," the red-headed girl promised. "Go around the fissures to the back and get everyone to the ground as fast as you can. Then lead everyone to safety."

Derain turned to Molly.

"I'll help you," he said. "Just show me what to do."

"Derain!" Rose exclaimed in dismay.

"Me too!" chimed in Kurt and Auset at the same time.

"Indeed," added Runa. "We must render what aid we may. I also wish to be of service."

"They need all the help they can get, Rose." Derain shrugged. "With all of us together, maybe it'll buy you enough time. Just hurry! Get the Residents inside. We'll join you as soon as we can. Just be sure to let us in, okay?"

"Thanks," Molly appreciatively replied. "I'll explain what to do on the way. I hope you guys are a quick study."

"Guys…" Rose weakly protested

Derain grinned at Rose and gave her a thumbs up, but then his expression turned grave.

"Go, Rose," he commanded. "We've got this."

Auset hugged her and kissed her cheek.

"You have a job to do, Arch Veda," she murmured in her ear. "So do we… *Fi Aman Allah*, my friend."

Then she flew off.

Rose felt a lump form in her throat and a tightening in her breast. She wanted to say more. She wanted to tell each of her precious friends how much they meant to her and how fervently she prayed for their safety, but the screams of terror-stricken Residents were ringing in her ears. The Harm Failsafe computer voice, was now blaring from so many thousands of sources it was nothing more than a constant, cacophonous noise. There was no more time.

"EVERYONE TO ME!" Rose thundered over the din. Her blazing form flared like a bonfire whipped by a tempestuous gale, and her powerful voice echoed across the plain. "Don't panic! Everyone follow me!"

Then Rose, shining like a beacon, swooped down toward the narrow strip of land followed by thousands and thousands of Residents. The other Vedas shot ahead of her and took up positions along the lengthening fissures. They bent their will to maintaining solid earth beneath everyone's feet, placing new plots of grassy plain into the void as quickly as they could. Despite their best efforts, the ground disappeared faster than they could replace it. The narrow land bridge continued to shrink.

Kurt and Auset stood together.

"My rock… My sword… MY SHIELD!" Kurt bellowed.

He thrust his red and white buckler before him, and his free hand was outstretched. He puffed out his cheeks at the strain, and his face was flushed with exertion.

"*Allahu Akbar!*" Auset added at the top of her tiny voice.

One supportive hand rested on Kurt's big shoulder. With her other, she stabbed her bow toward the widening pit like a wizard's staff, adding her own strength to Kurt's striving. Her dark eyes were wide in obvious alarm, but she did not slow her efforts.

Nearby, on the other side of the narrow path, Runa and Derain pressed hard against the encroaching void. Derain had adopted a similar stance as Kurt, while Runa sat regally poised astride her armor-plated polar bear. The great beast roared in challenge, and Derain screamed wordlessly in fair approximation. Runa caught Rose's eye.

"Go, Rose!" she cried raising a long and slender pole axe high in salute. "Proceed quickly and with haste!"

Rose darted past Kyo and Molly who were ahead of her other friends. Kyo planted his feet firmly on one side of the bridge. Molly braced herself on the other. Her freckly face was screwed up with intense concentration.

All of it happened in a flash – an instant of recognition. Then her friends disappeared from Rose's view as she raced toward the fortress. The towering obsidian walls were drawing nearer, but far too slowly for Rose's liking. Still, her brain was already working on what lay ahead.

Rose had always nurtured a deep interest in Japan, and Princess Hana had only encouraged it. Rose was certain Hana had written a *kanji* character on the gate to get it to open. Rose remembered the symbol for 'open' and hoped that would work.

She and the first of the Residents finally reached the hill. They scrambled up the steep slope frantically and when they reached the top, crushed themselves as close as they could to the protective walls, but the red tentacles reached ever higher and the collapsing sky prevented any escape into the heavens. Far too many Residents could not avoid the grasping tendrils of the sucking void. They were dragged back down the hill and over the edge of the precipice in droves.

When Rose finally made it around the corner of the building to where she knew she would find the front gate, she paused to visualize the symbol in her mind – the number of strokes, the order. Then she traced it quickly on the blank wall with her finger.

Access denied! Access denied! Blared a male computer voice.

"Dammit!" Rose cried in frustration.

The protected space around Mikoto's fortress grew smaller, as the clutching runners crept ever higher up the slope. Rose's friends were being slowly driven back. As the last of the Residents crossed the disintegrating bridge, the Vedas retreated up the hill. They continued to press against the consuming force.

They were successful in slowing it, but they could not stop it. The creeping void continued to eat away at the solid ground around the castle. There were simply too many people and not enough room on the hill. More and more Residents toppled screaming into the abyss.

Rose was nearly as panicked as the hysterical Residents. She was sure she had written the character correctly. It must not be the right one. She tried the symbol for 'gate'.

Access denied! Access denied! Came the harsh rebuke once more.

"We can't hold it much longer, Rose!" Molly screamed, taking a couple of faltering steps backwards a few feet away.

"Open the bloody door!" demanded Derain.

"Come on, Rose," Rose muttered to herself. "Think. Think. Think…"

She scrawled the *kanji* for 'friend'.

Access denied! Access denied!

There was a scream behind her. Rose turned just in time to see Kyo lifted off the ground. A snaking tendril of red was coiled about his waist. Molly leapt to help him, but as she turned away from the chasm, a different tentacle of mist coiled around her neck and jerked her backwards down the hill. In a second they were both gone.

"Focus, Rose!" encouraged Kurt. "Don't give up! You can do--"

Then he screamed. A tendril of red coiled around his ankle and yanked him off his feet. He fell hard on his back.

"Kurt!" cried Auset. She leapt after him, stretching out on her stomach with her arm extended. She slid across the rocky ground, and her tiny hand closed around his thick wrist. She held him a moment and their eyes locked. Then they were both jerked over the edge.

"*NO!*" Rose screamed.

The fissures began expanding even more quickly. All of the ground around the base of the hill was consumed, and the groping mist stretched ever nearer the walls. Residents were sliding down the slope to plummet over the edge of the precipice like so many dominos. She had to figure this out!

"Dammit, Hana!" Rose swore in near hysteria. "Where are you when I need you?!"

She tried another character.

Access denied! Access denied!

"Rose!" It was Runa's frantic voice, but Rose could not see her. "I do not think I am capable of--"

The blonde girl made a strangled sound as she was abruptly silenced.

"Runa!" cried Derain.

"COME ON!!!" Rose begged the invisible door. "*PLEASE!!!*"

Residents pressed tightly against her. They screamed in her ear, pawing at her, begging her to save them. They implored her in ragged, frightened voices to let them in, and their terror was infectious.

This is it. She thought desolately. *We're all going down. I can't get it open! What could it be?!*

Then Rose had an epiphany. She gasped, and her eyes widened.

Of course… This is Mikoto's mansion.
She wrote 'flower' on the gate.
"It's *hana,*" she breathed to the featureless wall. "The password is *hana.*"

The character flashed golden, and the heavy gate creaked slowly open. Rose staggered across the threshold and collapsed in the courtyard.

***

Hel was extremely pleased with herself. Her plan was working perfectly. Atem's insight had proven just the thing. If she could not bring her people to paradise, then she would just have to bring paradise to them. It was simply a matter of time, before the whole of Aaru and everyone in it, with the exception of the Lords and Ladies and their manor houses of course, were down here with her.

It was all quite exhilarating really. The beautiful people were falling from above like raindrops, and just like the rain they would nourish her kingdom and her power. They were in *her* domain. Now they were *hers* to command. Everything was falling neatly into place. There was just one more thing to do to make this day perfect.

Hel left strict instructions for Dani to wait for her, and directed Iris to watch him. This would only upset him, and she certainly did not want that. Today was a day for celebration! She provided copious reassurances she would only be gone a very short time, but the boy did not like being left behind at all. Still, he obeyed.

She called a door into being and stepped through it. Hel found herself in a large city. It was a scene of total chaos.

The clamor of hysterical voices and thousands of Harm Failsafe alarms going off all at the same time was deafening. Hel delighted in the chaos – the righteous judgment. The beautiful people were finally getting what they deserved. They were finally experiencing at least a portion of the desperation and misery inflicted upon her subjects in quarantine.

A few hundred yards to her left a towering, red-faced *tengu* struggled to close the growing chasm at his feet. He was doing a fair job, Hel had to admit, but other long, red gashes kept appearing as he filled in the hole before him. Hel was not impressed.

Futile, she thought with a disdainful sniff. *Just give up already.*

The tengu was not who attracted her notice, however. His pathetic efforts bored her. He was not why she was here. Rather, to her right, a raven-headed warrior was equally pressed, and Hel found him fascinating. His struggle inspired her. She paused behind a nearby purple tree to watch.

"I can't keep this up, Mikoto!" the raven cried, defensively holding a long spear before him. He was placing new blocks of plain into the void at a frenetic pace. "I'm losing it. There's just too many of the damned things!"

"Don't give up, Franco," the *tengu* rumbled. "Just buy me a little more time. I'm resetting the platform data to the previous save. If we can just hold out until the system reboots, I can restore the settings from before all this started happening. That might fix it. Keep at it! Just hold out a little while longer!"

"There's not much room left, Mikoto!" the raven exclaimed anxiously. "I'm running out of places to stand here. It better freakin' hurry up!"

Hel watched the scene enraptured, and her breathing came more quickly. Franco's perseverance in the face of his desperation was endearing. He cut a heroic silhouette – refusing to surrender, fighting against impossible odds! So noble...

God! He's so cute, she thought.

The raven warrior closed up holes like lightning. He looked quite dashing as he strove, but he was wasting his time. For every fissure he repaired three more would open up nearby. Hel leaned up against a light pole a little bit closer. She sighed.

Surely, there are better uses of your efforts, Franco, Hel mused lustfully. *Labors to which you could devote yourself, which would prove more fulfilling for both of us.*

She started making a mental list of just what those might be and smiled, making herself blush a little. Hel was quite enjoying herself watching the sexy boy try so hard. It truly was an epic battle, and his ardor was adorable. However, as exhilarating as she found his heroic display, it was time to start moving things along.

Franco was so heavily engaged with keeping the creeping void at bay, and staying away from the grasping, red tentacles himself, he never saw Hel slowly make her way around behind him.

He never noticed as she raised her hands to the sides of his head. It was too easy, really.

Hel jammed her hands into Franco's feathery temples. His mouth gaped and his arms fell limp at his sides. His wicked spear clattered to the pavement and disappeared in a cloud of green squares as his raven-form abruptly reverted to human shape.

Hel moved around to face him. She removed one hand from his head and gently closed his gaping mouth with her index finger. She gave a girlish giggle then lustfully rubbed her free hand over Franco's broad chest. She tenderly placed her palm against his soft, brown cheek.

"There's no need to struggle, you pretty boy," Hel purred, pushing up on her tip toes to kiss Franco's neck. Then she bit him, delighting in the feel of his firm flesh in her teeth. "There's nothing to be afraid of... I'll take good care of you. I can make you *so* happy... Much happier than *Rose*," she snarled. "I'll be true. I won't *lie* to you like Sister did to me. I won't abandon you. I'll make you feel good.... *So* good! I know just what you want... what you need. I know just where to touch."

Hel felt his mind beneath her fingers. She fondled it, caressed it. Then she twisted her hand in Franco's head. His face took on a brief expression of rapture, but he quickly frowned and weakly shook his head.

"No..." he breathed. "Stop... Not right... Rose..."

Hel scowled.

"I know this is a surprise for you," she murmured seductively her lips almost touching his. There was an angry gleam behind her mismatched eyes.

She adjusted her hand again, and Franco jerked. The ecstatic expression returned.

"You're afraid," Hel whispered in his ear. "And that's only natural. You are simply used to Rose, but I know I'm better. You just need time to get to know me, and then you'll love me... You'll love me more than Rose. You'll forget all about her."

"Franco!" the tengu bellowed.

Hel turned in time to see the Aaru Lord charging toward her. She called a door into being directly beneath her feet. The giant leapt at her, but encountered only air. Hel and Franco dropped through as the portal fell open. The door slammed shut right behind them. It winked out of existence, and they were gone.

Chapter 26

Defining Nadir

Koren's insides were a mess. Her stomach felt like it was tying itself into knots and not even Pandadora, who was clutched tightly to her breast, could make her feel better. She'd tried to call Rose with the private jet's Aaru monitor, but all communications were down.

"I'm sorry, Koren," Amy apologized. "Askr has shut down all outside communication until we can get the system stable again. People were starting to panic."

Koren supposed she understood, but the way her phone was blowing up with Aaru related news alerts, notifications, and frightened postings on social media, everyone seemed to be panicking anyway.

Her phone buzzed, and Koren glanced at the screen. It was Bindi.

Heard anything yet? Bindi texted.

Nothing, replied Koren.

You holding up okay?

No.

Me neither... I'm scared. ☹

Me too.

I feel like I should be doing SOMETHING!

I know what you mean. Headed to main campus now.

What you gonna do?

Koren paused and bit her lower lip. She stared miserably out the window of the plane for a few long seconds as if the heavens might open and reveal the answer. All she could see were the tapered, white wing of the plane and the darkness of night. Koren took a deep breath and typed a reply.

No idea… Just couldn't stand to sit home alone and worry.

Yeah. Been staring at my lunch for a bloody hour. Can't eat.

Why don't you go surfing? Koren suggested. *Take your mind off things.*

That's what my mum said. Just can't today. Too into my own head.

There was another long pause. Koren thought maybe Bindi was finished, but just when she was about to shove her phone back in her pocket, her friend buzzed in again

Late there?

Not really. Little after 8:30. Evening.

Call me when you get free? Need to talk.

Sure. I'll be up. No way I'll sleep tonight.

REALLY worried about Derain. ☹

I know. Me too, sweetie. Really wanna talk. Maybe I'll know more after I see Askr.

☺K… Talk soon. B.

Koren slid her phone back into her jeans and stared out the window again. She gave Pandadora an especially tight squeeze. What *was* she going to do? She felt *so* helpless! Koren turned abruptly to Amy in the seat next to hers.

"Will we be able to log in at the Elysian Industries Campus?" Koren blurted anxiously. "Like with the SLS or something?"

"Someone might, Koren," Amy answered with a sigh. "The board members still have contact with their counterparts inside... at least they did just before we took off, but it's probably too dangerous for you right now."

"Too dangerous!?" Koren exclaimed. "How? It's all virtual. It's not real... for me at least, but Rose... It's real for her! I've got to get in there and make sure she's alright! I've got to *try* and help her!"

"I understand how you feel, Koren, but..." Amy trailed off.

Koren's face screwed up in distress.

"You may be right," Amy lowered her head, sighed, then looked Koren in the eye and brushed her cheek with the back of her hand. "But the fact is we just don't know what could happen. We don't even know what's going on. There's no way Askr is going to let you leap into the simulator again with the whole mainframe glitching out. With the system so unstable, the VR could be dangerous in some way we don't expect..."

"Amy... Please..."

Amy squirmed in her seat at Koren's desolate expression.

"I... I won't... promise anything," she said at last and gave the younger girl's shoulder a squeeze. "But... I'll push for you to be a part of whatever we end up doing... Maybe we could at least let you use a window to get in touch with Rose. I'm sure that would be safe. Of course, I can't promise the board will listen to me. They rarely do. More often they just tell me to go get them coffee or order lunch... And even if they *do* listen, I have no idea what your role might be... but... I'm on your side, Koren. I'll do what I can."

"Thanks, Amy." Koren answered gratefully. She leaned over to crush the older girl in a tight embrace.

Amy gave a sad smile. She squeezed Koren back and kissed her on the cheek. Then she gently brushed a few blonde hairs from Koren's face.

"I won't promise you everything will be okay," Amy murmured. "But Elysian Industries employs the most brilliant minds in the world. If anyone can figure this mess out, it'll be them."

Koren nodded grimly, and a tear trickled from the corner of her eye. Amy put her arms around her again.

"Try to be brave, Koren," she whispered in Koren's ear. "Worrying won't solve anything. Just remember. I'm right here with you."

Koren squeezed Amy's neck more tightly. They held each other for a long time. When Koren finally pulled away, she wiped her eyes and sniffled.

"I know, Amy," she hiccoughed. "I know I shouldn't worry, but it's *so* hard! I can't help feeling like… like I might be losing Rose all over again! I don't think I could stand that."

"I'm here for you Koren," Amy promised. She took Koren's hand in both of her own. "Bindi is too. I'm sure Askr and Mr. Adams and all the other board members are looking out for you as well. We're *all* looking out for Rose, and Derain, and every Resident of Aaru. You are not alone in this."

Koren nodded. She sat back in her chair, but did not release Amy's hand. They stayed that way the rest of the trip back to Nashville, and even after they hopped in the limo that would take them to the Elysian Industries complex. Koren sat and stared out the window - Pandadora crushed tightly under her left arm, and Amy's warm, white hand squeezed in her right.

She tried not to worry. Amy was certainly right about the futility of that. However, the more she tried *not* to agonize over everything, the more she could not help thinking about her sister – the flash of panic in her eyes as they watched the trapped Residents on the ship, her mien of fury as she ignited into her flaming princess form. Rose had looked so powerful and beautiful. *Surely*, she could take care of herself, couldn't she?

The trip to the Elysian Industries' complex felt like it took forever, but eventually the limo rolled down the gravel access road to the complex. As the high, reinforced iron gates came into view however, Koren's eyes opened wide. All around the newly completed concrete walls were hordes of people.

There were news vans and satellite trucks. Men and women with cameras fired off dozens of pictures as Koren's limo rolled to a halt at the gate. People in suits, holding microphones pressed against the vehicle and beat upon the glass. They shouted questions. Some asked her to roll down her window. Others demanded. Angry people with signs reading "judgement has come" and "cower before the wrath of God!" among dozens of others milled like ants. It was total pandemonium.

The driver cracked his window enough to tell the security guard at the gate who they were, even as the man was bumped and jostled by the press of journalists, paparazzi, and protesters. The car itself began to bounce and shake. Eventually, even though he lost his hat in the process, the gate guard gave the signal to open up and let them through. Koren's heart was beating a million times a minute as the jerking, jolting vehicle slowly rolled forward.

It was scary, but they made it all the way into the compound. Koren spun around in her seat and looked out the rear window. No fewer than a dozen security personnel struggled to keep the throng out and get the gate shut again.

"Holy cow, Koren..." breathed Amy, but then apparently could not think of anything else to say. Her face was ashen.

Koren understood how she felt. Though she'd been mobbed by fans and paparazzi before, what she had just witnessed was different. Often, fans were impassioned and reporters were pushy. Sometimes they were demanding and rude, but the only way she could describe the fervor outside the campus now was 'hysteria'. There was an air of desperation and panic in the mob that she'd never experienced before.

"Wow," she answered. "They're really worked up."

Just as they were exiting the vehicle, Askr came running down the steps to meet them. He was soon followed by Mr. Adams. Dr. Warren, Mr. Tanaka, and Dr. Kapoor.

"Glad you're here, Amy," Askr gasped in a breathy voice, clearly winded by his brief jog.

He caught sight of Koren and scowled slightly, but quickly smoothed his features.

"And you, Koren," he said turning toward her. "What an... unexpected surprise."

"I made her bring me," Koren blurted even as Amy opened her mouth to make an excuse. "There was no way I was going to be left out of this. What are we going to do to help Rose?"

Askr opened his mouth, but quickly shut it again, reconsidering his words.

Then he said, "let's... not talk out here... We were all just going to have a meeting. You are welcomed to attend, of course... Maybe that's best, in fact. Perhaps you can help us shed some light upon this situation."

"You mean you still don't know what's wrong?!" Koren exclaimed with a deep sinking feeling in the pit of her stomach. "You still--"

"Let's... talk inside," Askr interrupted. "The situation is... complicated. Follow me, if you will, ladies."

Askr turned and skipped back up the stairs into the building. The other board members rushed to follow. Koren and Amy shared a concerned look, but then hurried to catch up. Askr led the way to the same conference room where Koren had attended that horrible meeting with her parents. She felt immediately anxious as the realization struck her, but Amy squeezed her shoulder, and Pandadora was still neatly tucked under her arm as they made their way inside. It gave her the courage to enter. The door slammed shut behind them.

"So," Askr began, spinning to face his employees before they had even finished seating themselves. "We've a bit of a mess on our hands, don't we?"

"*That* was obvious when I was testing out the new VR system with Amy," Koren replied testily. "But do we know *why* yet?"

"Yes and no," answered Mr. Adams as imperturbably as always. "What we know is there has been a catastrophic firewall failure between the general Aaru population and quarantine. Essentially, what is happening is that everything in the general population is being automatically redirected to the quarantine portion of the server and all the chaos is overloading the Harm Failsafe."

"Wait... you mean," Koren gasped. "Residents might be able to hurt each other?"

"Maybe," Dr. Warren answered grimly. "We don't know."

"We know generally what's going on," Jim Tanaka added in his nasally voice. "What we don't know is why. This shouldn't be able to happen... Certainly not by accident. It *has* to be some sort of hacking attack."

"But that shouldn't be possible either!" exclaimed Dr. Kapoor. "We built Aaru as a closed system for precisely that reason – to prevent cyber-attack. The only way malicious software could be uploaded is if someone with administrator clearance used our own equipment at our own facilities to do it!"

"An inside job?" Dr. Warren asked.

"I don't believe it," shot back Tanaka. "I'd trust any of you guys with my *life*. I can't imagine *any* of us doing something like this."

Everyone looked at each other uncomfortably.

Askr sighed deeply and leaned on the large conference table. He wearily hung his head.

"I agree with Jim," he said in a low voice. "Hackers are resourceful." He nodded toward Koren with a wry smile. "Nobody knows dat better dan you, eh? Dey must have just found a flaw in da security system we missed... found a way around our protections."

"Well," Kapoor speculated again. "The hacker known as Magic Man got into the system before, using our equipment. Could that have happened again?"

Koren winced at mention of her captor, and experienced the old feelings of dread that always surfaced at thought of the man, but no one seemed to notice her discomfort. Mr. Tanaka shook his head and crossed his arms stubbornly.

"We know he had a communicator port CPU and a brain scanner," he stated. "That could hypothetically allow him access, but he'd still have no way to upload any new data. That has to be done through the work stations at our physical facilities and requires Admin level access. I just don't see how he could pull it off. We've upgraded all our physical security. It's like Fort Knox, Area 51 kind of tight now at all of them. If he came anywhere *near* one of our facilities, especially a sensitive area like an upload port, we'd catch him way before he could even make an attempt at getting access."

"Koren," Askr raised his head and fixed the teenager with an intense stare. "Amy told us before you experienced the incident with the ship, you had a rather unusual encounter. I need you to tell us in detail *exactly* what happened."

Koren swallowed nervously, acutely feeling all of the hard, adult eyes intent upon her.

"I... I..." She stammered. "I already told that Dilly lady about it. She said, she thought it was nothing."

"Maybe it was nothing," Mr. Adams conceded, running a weary hand through his iron grey hair. "Dr. Derego may be correct. It could just be a coincidence, but we can't afford to assume anything so unusual and so near to the time of the system failure was mere chance. Also, even though she told us generally what you reported, we'd like to hear it straight from you - See if maybe she missed something. Tell us what happened."

"You said someone approached you when you logged in," Mr. Tanaka prompted. "A girl?"

"It may have just been a random Resident who recognized me from the show," answered Koren. "That's what I *thought* anyway."

"But did *anything* happen before that? Anything at all?" Mr. Tanaka persisted. "Did anything about the encounter before or after strike you as strange?"

"*Everything* about it struck me as strange," Koren replied grimly. It felt like there was a lead weight in her stomach. "But I've had plenty of weird meetings with fans before. I mean… I love the support, but there's some people following me who are just flat out crazy. The fact it was weird honestly made me think it *more* likely it was just a fan."

"Tell us everything you remember, Koren," Askr insisted. "Tell us every detail you can recall from start to finish."

Koren bit her lip and thought hard as she recalled the bizarre encounter with the strange girl.

"Well…" she answered slowly. "I… I got a friend request just as I logged in. I assumed it was Amy, so I said yes. The system asked me if I wanted to reveal my location, and I said yes to that too. Amy had already told me we'd do some setup stuff like that after we hooked up in Aaru, so I didn't think anything about it."

Amy shook her head.

"I *did* send you a request," she began. "And you accepted it, but that was after we met up with Bindi, Rose, and Derain."

"Yeah, they all sent me requests too," Koren admitted. "I just went down the list hitting 'accept'. I didn't really pay attention to who they were from. I thought I already knew. I mean… who else would know to send me a request?"

"So, the friend request came from the girl," stated Dr. Warren, adjusting her glasses thoughtfully on her nose. "But you ask a good question. How *would* some random person know to send it?"

"Right." Said Mr. Tanaka. "Nobody even knows about the new features of the SLS outside of the board, the researchers who were working on it, and of course you and your friends, Koren. Only an administrator would have had access to the new features or the authority to grant access now."

Askr made a shushing gesture with his hands and turned back to Koren.

"Please, Miss Johnson," he apologized. "Sorry for da interruption. Please go on."

"Well, after I revealed my location, this girl popped up right behind me," Koren continued. "She acted all nervous and shy. She was turned sideways and kept covering up one side of her face with her hand, like she didn't want me to see it. She said she'd looked forward to meeting me forever. That's why I thought it was a fan"

"She kept covering her face, you said?" Askr asked, looking up sharply.

"Yeah," Koren answered simply. "Half of it anyway."

"What did you say dis girl called herself?" Askr pressed. "And Dr. Derego said you noticed she used an unusual avatar."

"Yeah," Koren answered with a grimace at the memory. "I know it's Aaru and everything, and everybody has different ideas about what looks cool, but I don't know why *anyone* would choose that avatar. One side of her face... Well, one whole side of her body really was perfect. She actually looked really pretty. Like I said, she had her side turned toward me, so I didn't notice at first, but when she faced me..."

Koren could not help but shudder.

"When she turned toward me, her other side was *gross* – like she'd been burned in a fire or something. She was trying really hard to hide it from me, I think."

Askr visibly paled. He responded in a strained voice.

"And her name, Koren," he choked. "What was her name?"

"She said her name was Hel," Koren said.

Askr made a strangled sound. He spun in a circle and slammed his fists several time on the conference table.

Koren took a step back in surprise

"Askr, wha..." she stammered

"What's wrong, Askr?" Mr. Tanaka asked in alarm abruptly standing from his seat and taking a concerned step toward his supervisor.

All the other board members looked at each other with expressions of equal concern. Such a display of temper was beyond strange for their laidback CEO.

"Jim is right," Askr growled tightly. He was clearly seething. "This was no accident. This can't possibly have been just some random encounter."

"What do you mean, Askr?" Dr. Warren asked curiously.

"It looks like someone knows about my interest in Norse mythology." His eyes narrowed in fury. "And dey're mocking me with it."

Everyone looked at Askr in silence waiting for him to go on. After a few long minutes he took a deep breath.

"I am named after da mythical first man created by da gods," he began slowly. "My dad was a professor of ancient Nordic literature, so I always had an interest. My avatar in Aaru, Draugr, is from a creature of Norse mythology dat has da power to reanimate itself after death – Sort of like a phoenix rising from its own ashes. It's a monster, kinda like a zombie, I guess… Uses powerful magic… I always thought dey were cool, and who could miss da obvious symbolism, right?"

"I don't really understand what you mean." Koren said uncertainly. "How does--?"

"Hel is also a character from da folklore of my country," Askr answered. "She was da daughter of Loki, da trickster. She's da keeper of da ignoble dead - dose who die as children, or disease, or old age. She rules over dose who can't get into Valhalla. Dis is no coincidence. It's a message."

Askr turned and stalked across the room. He approached a massive television monitor and flipped it on.

"Just look at dis video dat Jim shared with me," he said hotly. "Most of you haven't seen it yet. Look at dis and tell me I'm wrong! It's just like da story of Baldur."

He opened up a video application and hit play. The video was short, but horrifying. It had no audio and was shot from rather far away, but that detracted not at all from the disturbing nature of the images.

Dozens of red-rimmed holes marred the middle of some broad thoroughfare, and they kept getting bigger. In the background a huge building tottered for a moment and then crashed into the widening crevasse. A feathery black figure stood near the edge of one of them. His arms were extended towards it and his face screwed up with intense concentration.

He looked like some sort of bird man, and Koren was not exactly sure what she was watching. He was motionless, but his expression showed obvious strain. He was oblivious as a dark, indefinite figure crept up behind him.

Koren gasped, throwing both hands over her mouth in horror. Even though the video feed was grainy and the dark figure's features indistinct, she was sure it was the girl. What was more, she suddenly recognized the bird-man just as the girl plunged her hands into the sides of his head. The raven avatar disappeared. In its place was the face of a handsome Latin boy, but his mouth gaped in horror and his eyes rolled back in his head.

Franco… Rose's boyfriend…

Koren doubled over leaning heavily on her knees with both hands. She clinched her eyes tightly shut, half sure she was about to throw up. Amy rushed to help her. She wrapped her arms around Koren's shoulders and shot Askr an icy glare.

"That was too much, Mr. Ashe," she stated coldly. "Too much."

Askr looked briefly like he might be angry. He returned Amy's glare, but then his face softened, and he turned away. He took a deep breath.

"I… I…" he stammered haltingly. "I'm sorry, Koren. I was angry. Dat was… too graphic for someone your age. I apologize."

Koren still felt woozy, but took a shuddering breath. With each shuddering exhale, she was slightly more confident she was in fact *not* about to empty her stomach all over the floor.

"It's not… that, Askr…" Koren stammered. "It's… That boy… I *know* him. That was Franco - Rose's boyfriend."

"Yes," Askr confirmed. "Dat was Franco Cortez."

"Was?" Koren asked in a tiny voice. "Is he… Is he dead?"

"We don't think so, Miss Johnson," Mr. Adams said gently. "I know it looked…" He struggled for an appropriate word. "Rather… gruesome, let's say, but just remember our Residents don't really have physical bodies. We don't know what happened to Mr. Cortez, but death? No. That no longer exists for any Resident in Aaru."

"So, is dat da girl you saw?" Askr asked intensely.

"It was hard to make out," Koren said slowly. "I couldn't really see her face, but I think so. Yes."

"*My* big question," added Mr. Tanaka, "is why Franco's Harm Failsafe didn't activate. Especially with my Avatar right there beside him. That's incidentally why we have a video record of the incident, by the way. But anyway… That isn't supposed to be possible for anyone but an administrator and only with concurrence too."

"What if…" Dr. Warren's eyes opened wide. "What if this malicious Resident file was uploaded with admin privileges?"

"How would that even be possible?" Tanaka shot back. "That would require not only admin authorization, but the consent of every single board member as well!"

"What if they had super-user status?" asked Dr. Kapoor.

"We discontinued that level of clearance," Tanaka replied dismissively. "Remember? We decided it was a bad idea to give any one person that much control over the system. Besides the only two people to ever have super-user clearance were Askr and…"

He trailed off. Askr looked up sharply.

"Simon…" he breathed. "Dis is starting to make a lot more sense."

"Didn't…" Dr. Warren ventured nervously. "Didn't Simon just pass away recently? It was lung cancer or something like that, I thought."

"Yes, he did." Askr narrowed his eyes again. "Maybe he started getting a little less adamant he stay purged from da system when da end was in sight."

"Who's Simon?" Koren asked curiously.

"A disgruntled employee," said Askr shortly.

"He was a board member," added Mr. Adams. "Long, long ago."

"I'm going to run a quick diagnostic," said Dr. Warren. She turned her attention to a laptop sitting open in front of her. "Let me see…"

Her fingers flew over the keyboard, and she stared hard at the screen. After a few minutes she shook her head.

"I'm getting lots of error messages," she scowled. "Invalid entries, missing data, invalid command paths, restricted files… It's a mess. The Resident numbers are all outta whack. It's just popping up as gibberish – grey boxes and symbols. I'm not getting any numbers."

"What if you limit your diagnostic to only Vedas, Lords, and Ladies?" suggested Dr. Kapoor helpfully. "The system is overloaded right now. Maybe scanning all the Residents at one time is just too much of an additional load."

Dr. Warren typed a few more keys. She shook her head again.

"Still no good."

"Just run the diagnostic on Admin," said Tanaka. "See if that changes anything. We've got missing Residents and missing Veda. That might be screwing with the diagnostic, but all Lords and Ladies are present and accounted for."

Dr. Warren complied. Her face brightened.

"I… I think that did it!" she exclaimed. "Let me just go to properties in the containing folder."

She clicked a few more buttons, and her pleased expression faded. She met Askr's expectant gaze seriously.

"What is it, Julie?" he asked with a fatalistic tone.

"It won't let me into the files," Dr. Warren said. "Access is restricted for some reason."

"Agh!" growled Askr in frustration. "It was worth a shot at least. We'll just have to--"

"That's not all Askr," she interrupted.

"What do you--?"

"There's twenty," she said shortly.

"What?"

"There are twenty files in the admin folder," she explained, barely contained alarm rising in her voice. "I can't get into any of the files. They're all marked as 'restricted' for some reason, but I can see them. I've counted them four times. There's twenty."

Askr took a deep breath and flopped heavily into a swivel chair. He put his head in his hands. Everyone stared at him silently.

"Well," he said at last, slowly raising his head. "I guess we know now."

"Know what?" Koren asked urgently.

The obvious dread from the adults was infectious. She felt her anxiety rising.

"It looks like we do indeed have a new Lady of Aaru," said Mr. Adams neutrally.

"And she is apparently determined to wreak havoc," added Askr dejectedly. "Although, I can't understand why Simon would upload anyone but himself, assuming he had da capacity."

"Simon definitely could have," commented Dr. Warren. "As I understand it, he continued the work we were doing in the beginning on his own, though I don' think he was very successful."

"Simon was a genius," added Mr. Adams, "but he was only one person. I'm not sure he could have managed this... At least not alone. And why would he want to destroy the system? That would be the death of his lifework. It doesn't make any sense. That just doesn't sound like the Simon I knew."

"Maybe simple revenge?" ventured Mr. Tanaka. "He might not have actually wanted to get in at all. You know, he never forgave any of us for going public... An 'if I can't have it nobody will' sort of deal, do you think?"

"Does it matter right now?" Koren urgently interrupted. "This is all great and stuff, but what do we do about it? How do we stop it and save Rose?"

All the board members looked at each other. Askr met her gaze seriously.

"I don't know, Koren," he murmured. His expression was defeated. "I don't know..."

At just that moment the door to the conference room opened, and the fat German scientist named Heidler stumped in.

"Askr," he stated urgently. "Our *friend* is about to make another public statement. Channel 24."

"Great," huffed Askr.

He switched the television monitor to its TV setting.

As Koren already expected, the face of Senator James Rook filled the screen. He wasn't talking yet. Rather he riffled through some papers on a lectern. Then he took a few sips of water. Behind him was a line of grim looking people. Most of them were older gentlemen in suits and ties. They talked to each other in low voices.

After Senator Rook settled his papers, the camera angle widened as he worked his way down the line of suits. He shook hands and patted shoulders along the way, offering each some comment the mic was not picking up. When he came to a younger looking man near the end of the line, Koren's eyes narrowed. He was handsome, blonde, and flashed perfect, white teeth when he smiled.

To be honest, Koren was not that surprised to see the sleazy mega-church pastor, Benjamin Belial, teaming up with a religious zealot like Rook, but still her knees turned to water when the news camera panned the crowd. Had Amy not been standing right beside her to offer a steadying hand, Koren would have collapsed to the conference room floor. Waves of stark, crushing betrayal twisted her bowels into knots, and this time she *was* sure she was going to throw up.

Amy made a leaping grab for a trash can, and Koren squeezed her eyes tightly shut, refusing to believe what she just saw. Even as Amy held back her hair, and Koren emptied the contents of her stomach into the small, plastic waste basket, the image from the TV seemed permanently burned into her retinas – A pretty blonde woman in a tight black dress clapping, smiling, and sitting right on the very front row.

It was Gypsie Johnson.

Koren's mother was sitting with the enemy.

As soon as she recognized her mother, Koren also realized with a sinking feeling, this image would be on the front page of every tabloid in the country… in the *world* by early next morning. She turned toward Amy with her mouth open. Her eyes were wide with incredulity and bewilderment.

Amy held her, but all the other Board members just stared. Of course, they had all seen it too. The realization only added to Koren's humiliation. Askr Ashe ran a discombobulated hand through his red hair in agitation. Mr. Adams coughed slightly. Other than that and the droning of the TV newscaster as James Rook got ready for his speech, the conference room was uncomfortably silent.

"Amy…" Askr ventured at last. "Maybe, it would be best if Miss Johnson perhaps went back to her own apartments… to rest."

Amy nodded, but all Koren could do was shake her head in disbelief. James Rook had called her a *whore* on national television. He wanted to *destroy* Aaru and *kill* Rose. Of all the people in the world, how could her mom be at *his* speech? How could she *do* this to her?

"Koren," Amy whispered in her ear. "Why don't we go, Koren…"

"I promise we'll tell you if anything changes," Askr swore. "And please, *please* don't hesitate to let us know if there is *anything* at all you need."

"Come on, Koren," Amy urged in her ear. "Come on. Let's go. You still have to call Bindi back. Remember? She's waiting. You know whatever this guy says will be stupid and hateful. You don't need to listen to it. Let's get out of here. Don't worry. I'll stay with you…"

Amy continued talking, but what she said did not really register in Koren's brain. Still, she allowed herself to be led out of the conference room. The heavy door slammed behind them, and the older girl murmured soothing words all the way down the corridor toward her suite of rooms, but Koren heard none of them. Her own thoughts were too loud.

How could this happen? She thought helplessly. *What is mom thinking? How could this day possibly get any* worse?

It was exactly the wrong question to ask.

Her phone buzzed, and Koren got her answer.

She read the notification once without really comprehending the meaning. Then she read it again, and again.

"K… Koren?" Amy asked in concern as she noted the vacant expression on the teenager's face. "What is it? What's wrong?"

The phone and Pandadora both slipped from Koren's nerveless fingers. The electronic device clattered against the hard linoleum floor with a crack that echoed in the empty corridor like a lightning strike. Koren sank to her knees in the middle of the hallway and threw back her head.

Koren let out a wordless ragged scream. Her hands twisted into claws and she reached helplessly towards the sky.

"Why?" she shrieked brokenly. "Why?! Why?!!! WHY!!! WHY!!!"

She fell forward weeping.

"Koren!" Amy exclaimed in alarm. "Tell me! What's happened? What is it, Koren?"

But Koren could not answer. All she could do was cry on her hands and knees in the middle of the hallway, overcome by loud hiccoughing sobs that convulsed her whole body. It was just too much. How could she possibly go on?

Amy grabbed up the teenager's phone and read the screen herself. She gasped.

"Oh my God," Amy stammered helplessly. "Oh my God, Koren… I'm so, *so* sorry! I…"

It was obvious her personal assistant had no idea what to say. Amy patted her back helplessly for a few moments, but when it was clear Koren's sorrow would not abate, she collected the girl and pulled her to her feet. Then Amy half-carried, half-dragged Koren back to her Elysian Industries apartments. She coaxed Koren into bed and let the younger girl lay her head on her lap. Then she just sat, silently stroking Koren's hair while she wept.

Koren could still not fully digest the tragedy that had just shattered her heart to bits, but she was certain of one thing. For all of Amy's reassurances, some things couldn't be fixed. Some things could never be right again. This was definitely one of them.

Chapter 27

A Time to Gather Stones

It took Rose quite a while to collect herself. She couldn't erase what she'd just witnessed from her head – The screaming, crying Residents as they plummeted into the depths by the thousands, the blaring cacophony of far too many Harm Failsafes triggered all at the same time, the desperate, pleading voices begging her to save them... The oppressive silence now.

Why is *it so quiet?* She wondered.

Rose rolled laboriously to her hands and knees. She pushed stiffly to her feet and looked down at herself with a start. Her flames were extinguished. Her hair was down, hanging limply past her shoulders, and she was clad in the blood and vomit stained hospital gown she'd worn the very first day she arrived in Aaru.

She gasped.

My friends... Came the frantic thought. *What happened to my friends?!*

Reality crashed back down around her. She saw Kyo lifted into the air and pulled down into the pit. She saw Molly, eyes wide and pleading while she clawed at her throat, and was dragged away after trying to help him. She remembered Kurt and Auset hauled down the hill, and into the depths. Derain and Runa? Rose never saw what happened to them. Where were they? She had kind of blacked out after getting the front gate open. They'd been right behind her. Perhaps, they made it inside too?

"Derain!" she cried at the top of her voice. "Runa, are you here?!

Nothing.

She tried again. "Guys! Answer me!"

Only echoes of her own ragged voice replied. Rose turned in a circle. She was standing in Mikoto's courtyard. It was every bit as barren and dusty as she remembered it.

"Auset!" Rose desperately tried again. "Kurt!"

Nothing.

Then she had a horrifying thought.

"Hello?! Is *anybody* here?!"

Still nothing but echoes followed by a tomblike silence.

Where are the Residents? Rose thought franticly. *Did none of them escape? Did* none *of them make it inside with me?*

"HELLO!!!" Rose shrieked at the top of her lungs. Then she repeated the cry over and over again, until she collapsed sobbing in the middle of the dusty courtyard.

Rose did not know how long she knelt there weeping, but it was a long time. She had failed - utterly failed, she realized She hadn't been fast enough. Everyone was gone. She was alone.

"Rose..."

The voice startled her, and she lifted her head with a start.

A girl stood before her, expression unreadable.

Rose gasped. One side of the girl's face was horridly disfigured. She apparently noticed Rose's reaction and smirked.

"You think me hideous," she hissed through clenched teeth. "Don't you?"

"Y... you just startled me is all," Rose replied. She wiped her eyes with her forearm, shakily stood, and sniffled. "I thought I was alone."

"You lie," the girl spat back. "You always lie. You said you'd never leave me, Rose. You promised you'd look out for me and keep me safe. You were my *sister*, and I *loved* you, but you betrayed me!"

"W... what are you talking about?" Rose whimpered fearfully. "Who are you?"

There was something strangely familiar about the untouched side of the girl's face, but Rose could not place it. She was equally certain she had never seen this person before in her life.

"Magic Man took me," the girl growled, then her voice broke into angry, anguished tears. "He *stole* me! He... He... *put* things in me – deep, deep inside! I waited for you to save me. I *prayed* you would come! I waited and waited and *waited*, but you never came! Then he hurt me. *So* many times he hurt me. He raped my mind... broke me... splintered my thoughts. I called for you to come. I *begged* for you to save me... b... but... you never did... *You never did!* And then I woke up here."

She clutched at her face with both hands.

"I woke up," she sobbed. "Like *this*!"

Rose gasped. She understood. Koren's brain scan... Her data...

The face of the other girl was Koren's, but it was also hers. It made no sense to her, but at the same time, Rose knew she was right.

"My God…" she murmured. "Koren? What did that monster do to you? I'm so, so sorry. I didn't know."

The girl gave a start, her mouth open in surprise. She flashed an incredulous expression. Then she began shaking her head. She stared hard at Rose.

"N… No…" The girl who both was and was not Koren stammered. Her head shaking became violent, long hair flying in every direction. "No. No. No. No. *NO!* You can't tell me that… Not after… You don't get to be sorry! You don't get to make this right! I… I… *I'm* the one who's supposed to decide how things are. *I'm* the one who gets to say!

"I… I…" Rose stammered. She shook her head helplessly. "I don't know what to say. I thought, I saved you, Koren. I thought I brought you home… I didn't understand.

"Brought me *home*?!" Hel screamed brokenly. "You *abandoned* me! You let him torture and destroy me! You let him ruin my face and my body and made everyone *afraid* of me!

"I am *not* Koren!" she screamed at the top of her lungs. "And I will not suffer your foul lips to speak Mother's sacred name! I am the Lady Hel! I have made all of Aaru my own! I am powerful now. No one gets to hurt me anymore. *NO ONE!* You have no right to make me feel this way! You always get *everything*! *EVERYTHING!* It's not fair!"

Hel put her face in her hands and wept hard wracking sobs.

"H…Hel…?" Rose ventured, stumbling over the unusual name. "I don't know what to say… I'm so, *so* sorry…"

This Hel was so like her sister, Rose realized. So like herself, but also damaged and hurting. It broke Rose's heart. She reached out a hand to touch Hel, to pull her close and hold her. She put a hand on Hel's ruined shoulder. She tried to draw her near.

Hel almost relented. She looked uncertain. Rose felt her body relax, and she took a step nearer. Then her face hardened.

"*NO!!!*" Hel shrieked. She thrust Rose away from her. "You're just trying to *trick* me again! Everyone loves you best. The people of this place all love you. Your friends love you. Even *Mother* loves you best, when she can't even stand the *sight* of me… when she runs away from me! *No one* loves me… But I'm going to change that."

Hel scowled at Rose. She snapped her fingers and a door appeared. It was black and braced with iron. It was riveted with long sharp spikes. Seemingly of its own accord, it swung open, and a massive creature sauntered through.

It was something like a wolf with ram horns and long jagged teeth. It was on a leash, but rather than constraining the monstrosity, the beast seemed to be leading someone who staggered through the door behind it.

Rose gasped.

"Franco…"

She recognized her boyfriend immediately, but he looked terrible. He was wearing the torn and bloody clothes from his traffic accident – the ones in which she had first met him. His eyes were dull and anguished. His mouth hung open, and he staggered and swayed as if he might topple to the ground at any moment.

Rose's anger was kindled, and she burst into flames – wrathful fire princess once more.

"What have you done to him?!" Rose demanded. "If you've hurt him…"

Hel chuckled and exhaled. A cone of frost engulfed Rose, and her fire was extinguished as if dowsed by a bucket of water.

"You cannot threaten me," Hel hissed. "*I* am a ruler of this place. *Me* not you!"

She took a menacing step toward Rose, and Rose was afraid.

"I have not hurt him," Hel went on. "I *will* not hurt him. Not ever never, never ever! Quite the opposite in fact…" She flashed a wicked smile. "I'm going to overwhelm him with pleasure. I'm going to make him *love* me – Love me forever!"

Hel thrust her hand into Franco's head. He convulsed, and Rose screamed.

"Leave him alone!" she cried.

"I'm going to give him *everything*," Hel went on nastily. "I'll give him everything you gave him. I'll do to him everything I saw you do… Everything you let him do to you. Then I'll do more. I'll make him love me and not you, and I'll make you watch. Then I'll let Fenrir here ravage your mind and make you feel like I felt when you abandoned me."

Fenrir growled and took a step nearer to Rose. He rocked back on his haunches, ready to pounce.

"No…" Rose whimpered taking a halting step backwards.

"I'm quite good at it, Rose." Hel drawled as she fingered Franco's mind. His mouth drew up at the corners in a smile of absolute ecstasy, and she flashed Rose a victorious smile. "I can see it all, you know – everything he holds deep inside. I know exactly what he needs… what he wants… What you could never give him… I…"

"Hel?"

The voice was small. It was nervous and shy. Rose thought she recognized it.

"Are you in here, Hel?"

A small figure walked through the open door. Hel abruptly withdrew her hand from Franco's head, and hid it behind her back.

"Dani?!" she and Rose both exclaimed at the same time.

"Th… This isn't right, Hel," whined Dani. "Please stop! The man from before… He was bad… B… but this is *Rose*. I remember her. She helped me. She's not bad. She's nice. She tried to take care of me. She tried to take me to play! Please don't hurt her, Hel. Please don't make her sad."

"This is none of your affair, Dani," Hel growled back. "This is private. You don't need to see this. Where is Iris, and *why* is she not watching you?! Go wait at our mansion. I'll play with you after I am finished."

"Hel…" Dani's lower lip began to quiver. "I… I don't like this… Please, don't hurt Rose!"

Hel looked like she might be angry, but her face softened. She sighed, patted Dani on the head, and bent over to kiss his forehead. She smiled at the boy.

"Why do you do this to me, Dani?" she murmured fondly. "What is this power you have over me?" She sighed again. "I will promise you this; I promise to do nothing that will permanently damage Rose, but she must be taught a lesson…"

"Hel…"

"Go on, Dani," Hel pushed him gently back through the doorway. "I'll be along shortly."

Dani reluctantly obeyed, and Rose's heart sank. She had no faith Hel would keep her word once Dani was no longer in sight. Once Dani entered the portal, Hel rounded on her with a scowl. She shook her head angrily.

"You don't deserve his love, Sister," Hel spat. "You lied to him and abandoned him, just like you did me. It's kind of appropriate really. *I* deserve his love. You cast him off. You forgot all about him and left him to languish! I took him from you just like I am taking Franco. Isn't that *delicious*? We'll be a happy family, Rose – Mommy, Daddy, and precious little boy… All taken from *you*…"

"Why are you being so cruel?" Rose asked fearfully. "Why are you doing this to me? To Franco? What did *he* ever do to you?"

"Why?" repeated Hel. "Because I can! Because I wish to perfect…

She trailed off.

"No…" She whispered. "Not his words… *Never* his words…"

A look of distress came to her face, and Hel clutched her head. The monster wolf growled and snapped at Rose. Hel rounded on it in a fury.

"Be still, Fenrir!" she screamed at the beast. "You will have her when I am ready for you to have her and not a moment before!"

"*What* are you doing to my Veda?"

The voice was cold and dangerous. Rose recognized it immediately, and she spun towards it.

Lady Hana stood fierce and imposing just at the entrance of Mikoto's mansion. She was clad in a black *hakama* and *haori* Rose had never seen her wear before. Her face showed no warmth at all, and her jet hair was tied back in a high pony tail. In her hands was a glittering *katana*. Her bare feet were set in fighting stance.

Fenrir leapt.

As if cast from porcelain, Hana's face did not change. Her blade slashed out, but rather than strike the charging beast, it cut a hole in the very air. Fenrir hurtled through it and disappeared. The hole in space winked out. The wolf was gone.

Hel's face twisted in rage.

"How *dare* you..!" she cried, but Princess Hana interrupted her.

"I'll ask you again," Hana hissed, raising her weapon over her head, eyes narrow. "What are you doing to my Veda?"

"I'd like to ask the same thing," came a low, masculine voice.

A huge, and furious *tengu* stalked toward Hel from behind. He blew out his white mustaches from under his long nose, and his ruddy face was cast in a furious scowl.

"Not in my house…" He growled menacingly.

Hel's eyes grew wide.

She said nothing, but just as Hana and Mikoto leapt at her, she grabbed Franco by the leash and cast them both through the sable door. Mikoto lunged for the handle, but just as his fingers closed around it, it slammed shut and winked out of existence.

"No!" screamed Rose in dismay. She lunged toward the empty space where the door had just been. "Franco!"

"Damn!" Mikoto exclaimed. "How in the world did she even get in here? Well, I'm sure gonna fix that!"

Hana rushed to Rose's side. The flower princess drew the sobbing girl to her chest and held her tightly. Rose buried her face in Hana's shoulder.

"Are you alright, Rose?" Hana asked urgently. "Did that… that *person* hurt you?"

"H… her name is Hel," Rose blurted in a rush. "Sh… she's Koren, but she's also me. Magic Man captured her and twisted her! She's really angry at me about it. I should have saved her, Hana. I should have saved her, but I didn't! I left her with a *monster*! I should have saved the Residents too, but I was too slow! I failed, Hana… I've failed everyone and everything!"

Rose was overcome by the uncontrollable weeping again. Hana held her tight, but shared a worried look with her partner.

"It's all over now, Rose," Hana hushed her. "Slow down. You're not making any sense. Everything will be fine. We'll fix--"

"No it won't!" Rose cried brokenly. "I've failed everyone! Everything is destroyed. There's too much to fix this time! I'm the only one left. I couldn't save the Residents. I couldn't save Kyo or Molly. I lost Auset and Runa and Derain and Kurt! Everyone is *gone*, and it's all my fault!"

"Hush now, Rose," Hana demanded gently, but sternly. "None of this is your fault. You did what you could, but even though I don't understand it, this Hel is somehow a Lady of Aaru. No Veda can stand against a Lord or Lady, not even the Arch Veda."

"Hel has won the day," stated Mikoto grimly, "but this is not over."

"No," stated Hana, her jaw set in determination. "She is but one Ruler and there are nineteen others. We will regroup. We will rebuild."

"And we will get Franco back," Mikoto swore fervently. "I *swear* to you we will."

"Come Rose," Hana directed. "Yggdrasil yet stands. We must get there."

"But how?" Rose asked desolately. "The sky… the holes… everything is gone. Everything is destroyed!"

"Not destroyed," Mikoto corrected.

"Nothing can be truly destroyed in Aaru," Hana added. "It's all just been moved."

"But where?" Rose pressed. "Where did she take everyone?"

"This Hel has somehow managed to connect all of the separated residences in quarantine," Mikoto answered. It's like an eleventh kingdom now."

"So," Rose ventured. "Can we get there with the doors, like Hel did?"

Mikoto and Hana looked at each other.

"It's complicated," Hana confessed. "Under normal circumstances, yes, but…"

She trailed off.

"Lords, Ladies, and Veda can call up doors to certain places," Mikoto explained. "But in general it has to be someplace you've been before. Doors lead to specific reference points. Those reference points are always fixed themselves. To transport or even just to fly directly somewhere, you have to have some beacon… Some indicator of exactly where you're going. The way Hel has connected up all the residences in quarantine… It's… unconventional."

"They keep shifting," added Hana. "You might call up a door thinking you know where you're going down there and then pop up someplace completely different. We're still trying to figure it out, but even if that wasn't the case, quarantine is Hel's domain. She has absolute control over what goes on there. That's why she fled from Mikoto so quickly. It is the same for all of us in our own halls.

"You know Vedas can request beacons to find certain places or individual Residents," she went on. "But that is only if the Lord or Lady of that domain allows it. I cannot imagine Hel has not blocked that function. That's why we have to get you to Lord Draugr. We need to lick our wounds and plan."

"We will get them back, Rose," Mikoto swore again. "We will get them *all* back."

"Lord Draugr will know what to do," Hana murmured. "He'll figure out how to fix this. I *promise*."

Rose clinched her eyes shut and let Hana hold her. She felt defeated and hopeless. Mikoto and Hana's assurances kept her from total despair, but in this moment she could see no solution herself. It all seemed too overwhelming, but if Hana and Mikoto said so...

Rose just hoped they were right.

***

The sun beat down, baking every hint of moisture from his body, but Magic Man was determined. He had made it his habit to only travel at night, and had jealously conserved the water in the canteen Atem left him - even refilled it from his own body, but after days of creeping through the desert, the liquid had all been spent. Traveling in the dark allowed him to conserve what water he could find, but after days and days of subsisting at the threshold of death, licking droplets from beneath a plastic tarp he'd found in the deserted Elysian facility with a dry and swollen tongue, and sucking sap from the odd cactus he happened to come across, he was nearing his limits.

That was when things changed. Though he knew he must look like a desiccated corpse, he was inspired. After days of nothing but rocks and sand, scorpions and cacti, just at dawn he glimpsed something different. It gave him just enough motivation to press on.

When he set out from the old research facility, Magic Man had followed the tire tracks left by Atem's caravan of SUVs, but by the second day the constantly blowing wind had obliterated every trace of their passage. The temptation to give in had been strong. It would have been so easy just to lay down and let death take him. It would have been simple to let the blazing sun bake the last of the life from his worldly husk, but quitting was contrary to his nature. He had to know if he was successful – if his masterwork stood complete and fulfilled.

Magic Man pressed on, though mapping information was splotchy. For a long time his smartwatch only worked when Atem's satellite was overhead. Then once he had finally started getting a few bars, the battery died. However, thanks be to whatever Gods or fates or serendipity that may or may not have been involved, he'd gotten enough bars often enough to keep him going in the right direction.

Imperfect though it was, those intermittent corrections helped keep him on course and lead him out of the blazing Hell pit to which Atem had condemned him.

What he saw now was a rickety building in an otherwise barren landscape. The closer he got the more certain he was. It was a gas station.

It took him most of the morning, but Magic Man eventually staggered his way across a deeply rutted dirt road. Faded metal signs squeaked and squealed on their hinges in the stinging wind. He felt himself getting light headed, but caught himself on a gas pump that must have been brand new in the 1960's. Decades of constantly blowing sand had blasted most of the paint off. He settled himself, took a deep breath, and managed to drag himself inside of the rundown establishment.

An overweight, middle-aged clerk accosted him in Spanish as he lurched through the doorway, but Magic Man couldn't have cared less. He ignored the man and staggered across the tiny store. He plopped himself in the only seat in one dusty corner.

"W… wa… water…" he croaked.

The man rambled off another long stream of angry Spanish that Magic Man did not understand. He looked at the clerk stonily.

"Water." Magic Man repeated. "Agua."

The man said something else in obvious aggravation, but stalked to the back of the mini-mart where Magic Man could see a small stainless steel utility sink. The clerk filled up a plastic cup, stalked back over, and thrust it into Magic Man's hands.

"Thanks a bunch," Magic Man croaked sarcastically.

What did this guy want? Surely some *gringo* dropping dead in the middle of his shop couldn't be high on that list. The water was warm and brown. It was filled with grit and had a harsh metallic taste but went down like ambrosia. After a few sips, Magic Man stared feeling much more like himself. He noticed a TV was on.

The newscast was in Spanish, but his ears perked. He looked at the screen. Magic Man only caught the very end of his comments, but he recognized Askr Ashe's grave voice. The caption at the bottom read *Disastre de Aaru*.

"…Therefore," Askr was saying. "Mr. Rook's assertion is totally off-base, completely inappropriate, insensitive, and frankly, I think mean-spirited under da circumstances. We are dealing with a serious crisis right now… *A number* of serious crises, in fact. We are, of course, concerned with Koren's well-being. I imagine Miss Johnson will release a statement as soon as she is able, but she's dealing with a lot right now, and I don't believe it is my place to speak for her. I just want to reassure everyone no matter what, we are committed to giving her whatever support she and her family needs.

"We are equally committed," he went on, "to investigating da malfunction, and will insure it is repaired. Elysian Industries will release regular updates and inform our users as soon as da system is stable again. All of our users will have access to deir loved ones as soon as da system is back online and da hack patched. At da moment, dat's all I have to say on da matter. If you'll excuse me, I have quite a lot to do. Thank you."

Magic Man smiled smugly to himself, certain he knew what the "*disastre*" was. His chest swelled with a deep satisfaction, and he quoted to himself as he thought back on his near death in the desert.

"'What is the strongest cure?" he murmured. "Victory."

The picture on the TV flipped, and his mouth fell open in surprise. The rest of the commentary was all in Spanish, but the image was unmistakable. Reflexively he checked his smartwatch, but the battery was long dead.

"Wow," Magic Man breathed thoughtfully. "That certainly changes things."

He finished his water and stood.

Magic Man approached the clerk, who was staring at him belligerently with his arms crossed. He held his watch up to the man's face.

"Charger?" Magic Man said loudly.

The man shook his head, whether in refusal or incomprehension he was not sure. Magic Man wracked his brains to recall every word of Spanish he had ever heard in his whole life.

"*C... cargador!*" he exclaimed at last.

The man shook his head again and pointed to the door.

"Wait... On phone..." Magic Man tried again. "*Mucho denero en la phono.*" He pointed at the watch. "It's the same. *Mismo phono. Mismo phono.* Big *denero.*"

His Spanish was awful, but it apparently got the message across. The clerk stared at him suspiciously. He pointed at Magic Man's watch.

"*Mucho denero*?" he asked. Then the man rattled off another long string of incomprehensible Spanish, but Magic Man was pretty sure the shop clerk thought he was lying.

"*Si! Si!*" Magic Man wracked his brain, but could not remember the Spanish word for promise. "Promise! Promise!"

"Promise?" the man repeated.

"Yes! Yes! *Si!*" Magic Man insisted.

The clerk stared hard at him for a second. Then reached into his pocket. He set a brand new smart phone on the counter beside him and then produced a small wireless charger from his pants. He plugged it in and reached out his hand for Magic Man's watch. Magic Man took it off and gave it to him. The clerk took it then pointed to the watch.

"No dollar," he said threateningly. "Eez my."

Magic Man nodded. The clerk set the watch on the charger, and unobtrusively retrieved a battered aluminum baseball bat from beneath the counter. Then he walked to the back of the shop, and filled Magic Man's cup with brown water again. He dragged over a stool and sat down next to the watch. He offered the cup to Magic Man with a smile. Magic Man took it.

"So… are we best friends now?" Magic Man asked sardonically under his breath.

"Five-hundred," the clerk said.

Magic Man's eyed opened wide, and he very nearly spewed the dirty water he had just taken into his mouth all over the extortionist's face. The clerk's smile dissolved into a scowl. He hefted the bat threateningly.

"Five. Hundred." He repeated more slowly and forcefully. "American dollar."

Magic Man ground his teeth in anger. He didn't really fear the bat. It wouldn't have been the first beating he ever got in his life. However, he was stranded in the middle of nowhere. That watch and this slob were his only connection to the civilized world. What else could he do?

"Fine, you greedy bastard," Magic Man growled. "Okay."

"Okay?" the man repeated.

"Okay! Yes! *Si!*" Magic Man replied. "And a taxi."

"Taxi?"

"Yes a goddamn taxi."

The man smiled again and spread his arms wide.

"Okay *gringo*." He pointed at a tattered sticker on the counter. It said 'Paypal'.

Magic Man nodded, and the man picked up his phone. He made a call and after a short conversation in Spanish, he shoved it back in his pocket. He smiled at Magic Man.

"All okay," he said. "Go soon. Dollar please. Five hundred American."

It felt like it took forever, but eventually the "taxi" arrived. It was actually a battered pick-up truck with almost no paint, and Magic Man was fairly certain the driver was some relative of the petty-larcenist, mini-mart clerk. He looked like a skinnier, slightly more balding version of the man.

"Border," Magic Man said to the driver, "America."

After another exorbitant payment, Magic Man found himself in the bed of the battered pick-up truck speeding across the desert.

On the long, hot, bumpy ride he pondered what he'd learned from the TV – what it meant. Apparently, his package had been delivered, and he was certain everything had executed perfectly. He'd been too careful to fail, and that was a reason for some celebration, but now he was not at all sure what to do next. Magic Man had never really expected to survive his encounter with Atem.

What *would* he do next? And what did this unexpected tragedy mean for him? Magic Man would have to think about it, but for now…

He smiled to himself.

"It's time to celebrate," he murmured. Then he quoted. "'What is best about a great victory is that it rids the victor of fear of defeat'."

Magic Man put his hands behind his head, reveling in the wind blowing through his hair.

"I. *Win*." He stated deliberately in satisfaction. "*I WIN!!!*"

Magic Man laughed out loud, and once started, found he could not stop. He didn't care if his driver thought the *gringo* in the back was a lunatic or not.

Afterward

Hel was in an extremely good mood. She hadn't even punished Iris that much for letting Dani get away from her. Everything was going exactly as planned. Her people were free, the beautiful people had been taken down a peg, even now bearing the wrath of her long imprisoned subjects, and her new life was beginning. Hel had been forced to cut short her vengeance upon Rose, and that was too bad, but it could wait. Her most important objectives had all been accomplished.

She sat on a throne of solid gold in the main hall of a palace she had raised from the bare ground. It rather resembled the princess castle from Disney World in Orlando, but was made of solid black crystal. It was beautiful of course, and perfect for her new 'family'. Hel sighed in contentment.

Dani pushed toy cars at her feet, making loud motor noises with his mouth. Iris was nearby in her pink squirrel costume, keeping careful watch as she balance on one hand on the back of a folding chair. Fenrir was curled up on one side of her throne. Franco slumped on his knees on the other, frozen in place. She regretted the necessity of his bonds, but every time she released him, the silly boy kept trying to wander away.

She sighed again. This time in frustration. It would just take time, Hel supposed. *Then* he would love her.

Hel raised her hand to Franco's head as if she would pet him, but her arm disappeared inside just above his ear. His expression snapped abruptly from desolate to ecstatic again.

"No... Stop..." Franco murmured weakly. "Not... Right... Don't... Touch... Don't wanna..."

Hel twisted her hand and his expression intensified. Franco released a little moan, and Hel smiled broadly. She leaned close to his ear, kissing and nibbling as she spoke.

"You like that, don't you?" she purred. "Let me make you feel *good*, Franco. Don't resist me. There's nothing wrong with feeling good, is there? Especially, here in Aaru. It's supposed to be *paradise*, isn't it? Let me make you feel good, the best you've ever felt! And then you'll love me."

She kissed his cheek with a giggle.

"Mommy, Daddy, Baby, Doggy..." She breathed. "We've got a perfect little family, don't we, my pretty boy? You'll come to love us all in time. I know you will, and then we'll be *so* happy forever and ever and ever..."

New Resident arrived. New Resident arrived, the artificial computer voice blared.

Hel scowled at the interruption, and sat up straight. She removed her grasping hands from Franco's mind and snapped her fingers. Lady Hel did not go to Residents. *They* came to her.

An agitated figure appeared before her throne turning this way and that in obvious confusion. The new Resident spun and gave a start as Hel came into view. When Hel recognized who it was, she smiled broadly and clapped her hands together in delight.

"Welcome! Welcome!" she exclaimed rising from her gilded seat. Hel strode toward the frightened figure with her arms spread wide. "Just when I thought today couldn't be any more *perfect*!"

"Wh... Who are you?" the new Resident asked in alarm. "Where am I?"

"Why... you're home," Hel said in a deeply affected voice. "Just exactly where you belong. This is *so* perfect!"

She squealed in glee.

"I don't understand..."

Hel beamed.

"Welcome," she repeated, eyes welling with emotion. "Welcome to our family... See Dani? Look! It's even better than I promised. I found us a Daddy, but now it's even better than that! Our family just keeps growing and growing!"

"That's great, Hel," Dani answered in a neutral voice. The boy left his cars and strode over. He looked up into the newcomer's face curiously. "Who is it?"

"Wait..." the new Resident said in obvious, rising panic. "Where... Where am I? What is this place? Am I... Am I *dead*?"

"Of course, silly!" Hel exclaimed. "Stone cold... And I'm *so* glad you're here."

She knelt down and looked deeply into Dani's eyes. Hel's own were sparkling.

"I'd like to introduce you to someone, Dani," Hel murmured. She gave the boy's shoulders an affectionate squeeze and ruffled his dark hair. "You can call him Papaw Willy. I think that's a cute name. Don't you?" she whispered the last to the new arrival.

Dani looked up at the thunderstruck man with a blank expression.

"Hi, Papaw Willy," Dani said emotionlessly. "Welcome to Aaru."

Bill Johnson screamed, and screamed, and screamed.

End Volume Two

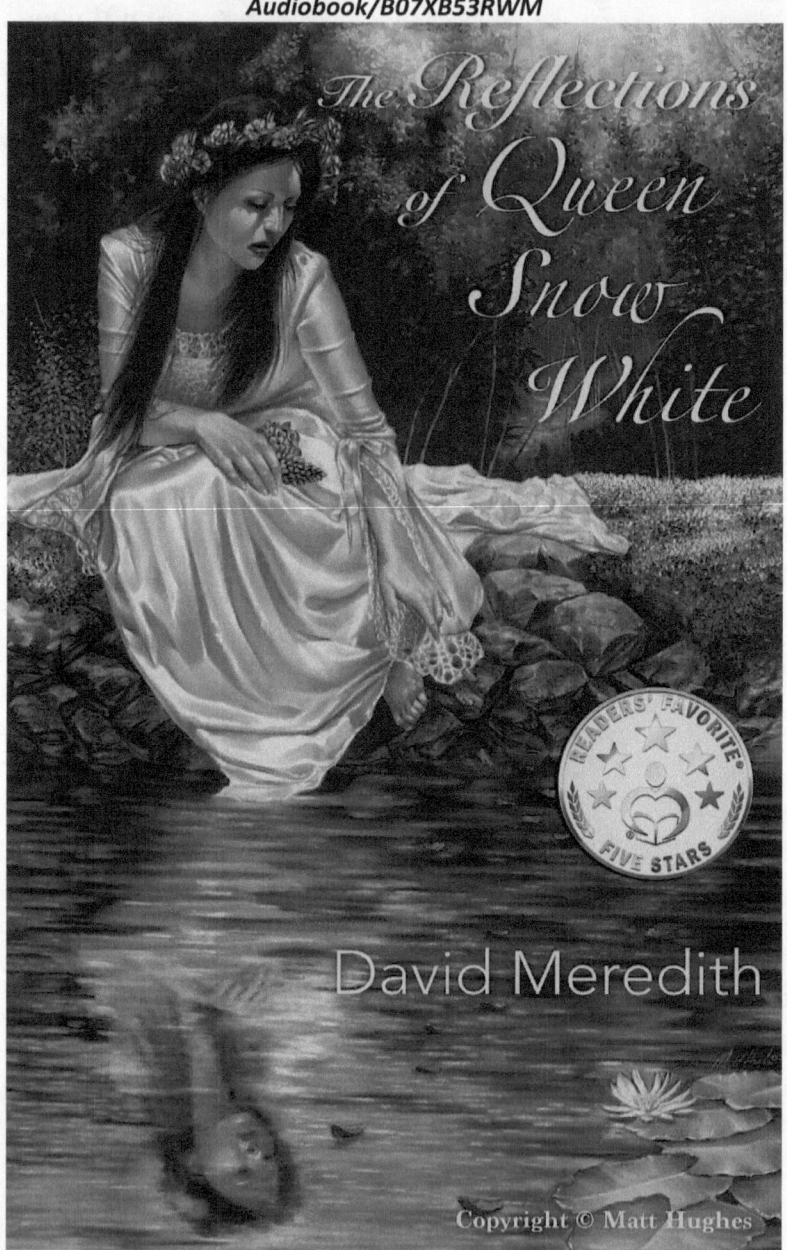

Get The Aaru Cycle Book 3 – *Aaru: Dante's Path* NOW on Amazon!

https://www.amazon.com/Aaru-Dantes-Path-Cycle-Book-ebook/dp/B08HVCDCJZ/